Blood of Like Souls

A Julie Madigan Thriller #1

Val Conrad

Black Rose Writing | Texas

Second printing

ISBN: 978-1-935605-22-5
PUBLISHED BY BLACK ROSE WRITING
www.blackrosewriting.com

Printed in the United States of America
Suggested Retail Price (SRP) $21.95

Blood of Like Souls is printed in Times New Roman

*As a planet-friendly publisher, Black Rose Writing does its best to eliminate unnecessary waste to reduce paper usage and energy costs, while never compromising the reading experience. As a result, the final word count vs. page count may not meet common expectations.

ACKNOWLEDGEMENTS:

Writing this story took so much research into topics the reader never sees, but threading fiction through real history is not a simple task. Any mistakes in events or procedures are solely mine.

Thanks go to many people who prodded me to keep writing. My first thanks goes to those who read the early versions and kindly told me to delete a scene or two. To Caron and Scott and Harry, for helping turn a manuscript into something much greater.

Thanks to a couple of DEA agents who bought my lunch and provided details of their lives with the promise I would not use their names or location. To a lab manager who showed me where I'd find *Naegleria fowleri* and smiled while I peered into a microscope in disbelief.

To my parents – my mother always told me I should go into nursing, and I'm sure she's laughing about that now.

There are so many more I can't name them all, but I hope they know who they are.

Last, my thanks and love to my husband Bill, for reading and rereading, and never rolling his eyes where I could see.

CHAPTER 1

September 1995.

Blood everywhere. In a panic, I punched 9-1-1.

"The number you dialed is not in service."

I dialed again. Same message.

"How many times in a row can I screw up 9-1-1?" I shrieked, fingers fumbling again on the phone keys.

It was only a dream.

The first Sunday morning in September was a hangover of a restless night. I'd finally reached sleep, only to be stuck in nightmares, like this one – needing to call for help but never getting the numbers right. And the phone kept ringing.

Ringing. Ringing.

Not part of the dream.

I reached out to find the spot next to me empty before I stumbled off the bed to answer the phone, only to be blinded by a white flash of pain as my toes smashed the bed frame beneath a heap of comforter kicked off during the night. Cursing in my groggy, waking-up voice, I picked up the handset from my dresser and crumpled into the chair.

"Madigan," I said through gritted teeth, trying to catch my breath.

"Sorry to wake you, Julie."

"Yeah, right," I said, disappointed the voice wasn't my missing bedmate.

I flipped on the light and propped the receiver on my shoulder so I could examine my foot when my eyes quit watering. My third toe was already turning red and swelling, clearly broken. The fourth throbbed. A dying-animal groan escaped when I straightened them.

"You okay?" Deputy Matthew Shannaker asked.

"Stubbed my toe. I'm not on call this weekend, Matt." I hoped in the three years he'd known me, he knew not to expect pleasantries at 5 a.m. and not to take it personally.

"Body. EMS thought it looked like a suicide. Dr. Katz wants you to bring the ALS and that infrared photography stuff you like so much."

"For a suicide?" I asked. The logic escaped me. Alternate light sources can be used to locate evidence invisible to the naked eye. When the scene has been cleaned up.

People who commit suicide don't clean up after themselves.

Okay, most people. I'd seen one exception in my career – a man who had used a bucket of soapy water to mop up the bloody mess in his kitchen after the first bullet from his revolver only grazed his skull instead of penetrating it. He'd actually bandaged his head and then fixed himself lunch before having another try at putting a .38 caliber chunk of lead and brass into his brain.

The scenario always baffled me. Desperation, yeah, I understand that. But a tuna sandwich?

I didn't ponder the similarity to this case, other than the fleeting thought that completed suicides don't clean up *after* they're dead, and someone was dead because the medical examiner was on the scene.

So much for my weekend off, I thought.

I guess it didn't matter. My bed was empty anyway.

I microwaved a cup of yesterday's coffee while getting dressed and braiding my hair. Then I needed to stop at the office for the requested equipment.

Approaching the turnoff to the address Matthew Shannaker had given me, I saw three Grand Traverse County Sheriff Department patrol cars, including Matt's K-9 unit, and the ambulance and an engine from the Whitewater Township Fire Department. A deputy blocked the road but waved me by when he recognized my gray Chevy Suburban, and I pulled in close to the patrol cars.

Still an hour yet till sunrise, scene lights illuminated an aging two-story farmhouse set back a hundred yards on the gravel drive, barely visible from the road through the heavy trees. Beyond the house and slightly uphill stood a barn that was probably a century old, maybe older. A few of the boards were cracked and missing, but the structure looked sound.

A group of men huddled near the open door, talking. My boss, Medical Examiner Gerald Katz stood out not only by his lack of uniform, but because of his height and posture. He reminded me of a mad scientist stooped to mix potions in a cobwebbed laboratory in some macabre science fiction movie from the fifties. Gene Wilder in "Young Frankenstein," maybe.

He left them and came to meet me halfway. "Sorry to drag you out, Julie. This is unusual. The 911 call came from someone who said he was driving by and had stopped to relieve himself. How quaint. He told the dispatcher he heard a man yelling for help, but he didn't feel it was safe to get involved. He gave directions to this location, left no name. Called from a pay phone at the gas station on the highway, but did not stay to make contact with the deputy as requested. I'm sure everyone was expecting a hoax at four in the morning," he explained. "The ambulance arrived in the area and spent ten minutes driving the road, looking for matching landmarks. They drove in and saw the only lights on were in the barn. No one answered the door at the house, so they came down here and found the patient barely conscious, with an obvious airway problem."

"Why didn't they transport?" Although I'm a medical examiner investigator now, sometimes the paramedic in me can't stay quiet.

He smiled. "They said they wanted to scoop and run, I think was the phrase, except this patient's legs were manacled to the stone wall with a heavy chain. Still are. He died. Or melted down, more specifically. Appears he ingested nitric acid, based on the bottle next to him. Very old, by the look of the label, maybe twenty years or more. The acid may be more concentrated than original, or it could be something else altogether. He vomited on the shackles, and the acid ate away at the metal. We may have to put him in a hazmat container to do the autopsy." Katz looked over his shoulder. "Dehydrated, emaciated, various non-fatal injuries. Might be suicide, but a very painful choice."

Again, in the history of suicides I've seen, this still wasn't the most bizarre, but it moved up in my top-ten list another notch or two.

Dr. Katz picked up one of the equipment cases, and we continued toward the barn.

"Matthew was trying to cut the chain when he saw a note scratched into the wooden floor beneath him," Katz said, checking his note pad with his free hand. "Reads, *Sorry they're dead. I didn't* with no end punctuation. On the rock wall behind him are the letters *BOI* written in blood, most likely from a fresh arm wound on the deceased. I found blood on his fingers."

They. Who or what were they?

"After the medics stopped the resuscitation attempt," he continued, "Matt discovered a trap door in the wooden flooring. No sounds from below. He didn't go any further. Just called for me and a crime scene team."

Although Gerald Katz hated that his job sometimes involved people who died before full and happy lives, no one enjoyed more deciphering the clues about the circumstances of death.

Outside the barn, beneath the scene lights, we sat down the cases so I could set up what he wanted.

"Rescue and deputies already trampled through here, including an ugly dispute amongst the EMS crews. I wanted to get the laser in the barn while it was still as dark as possible," Katz said, checking his watch. "Fifty minutes to sunrise. I'm not sure what we will find below the floor, but I have a suspicion." One he didn't share with me.

I set up the laser for Dr. Katz; then I took the digital camera and video unit to follow him around as we searched the barn.

Urine, semen, saliva, and many illegal drugs all contain chemicals that fluoresce in various wavelengths of laser illumination. Bone and teeth fragments are brightly luminescent. Blood does not fluoresce under a laser without a chemical reagent such as Luminol; however, because it absorbs light at 514 nanometers, blood instead shows up as a black stain.

Dr. Katz moved first to where the dead man had been shackled to the wall. Non-specific spatter patterns glowed and blacked out around the floor and wall nearby. Shiny, heavy-duty hooks and hasps, eye screws and such protruded from the aged wood and rock wall.

The floor of the barn was almost all packed dirt except for a corner area about 20 feet by 10 feet near the stones of the wall. This deck lumber looked much newer than the rest of the barn.

Dr. Katz nodded to a trapdoor, a square measuring about four feet a side.

Aiming the camera down, I understood where we were ultimately going. My nose twitched at a faint odor, or maybe it was a memory of other scenes where my sense of smell had diagnosed trouble long before my eyes could see it.

Considering the horrible way this man died, I didn't want to imagine how he might torture someone else.

CHAPTER 2

Them.

People.

I looked over at Matt, wondering if he recalled our discussion last fall about a mother who reported her teenage daughter missing. Witnesses said the girl left a party with her boyfriend. He said he let her out at the end of her block so her mother wouldn't see him. The girl never arrived home. Obviously, despite the facts, some piece of truth was missing, just as Kathy Horn.

I'd joined orange-clad volunteers one drizzly weekend, searching the woods, hoping not to be mistaken for a deer in hunting season. Finally thawed enough to climb out of the tub and into comfortable sweats, I'd just snuggled up in a blanket on the sofa when Matthew and his shaggy K-9 partner Laser dropped by my house, offering a pizza and a six-pack of beer.

With a grin, Matt explained, "Laser said it was your night to cook."

Matt told people he and I were obligate buddies because his K-9 partner likes me. I told them the dog's name was Laser because Matt couldn't spell *Kalashnikov.* The three of us were pretty good friends.

We settled down to pepperoni pizza and beer, and I began grumbling about how I thought the organizer of these volunteers was way off in his strategy to find the girl.

"We're past a rescue now," I said, opening a bottle of beer and taking the first few swallows that were so cold my temples throbbed.

"Why do you say that?" Matt asked, leading me further into a conversation I wished I hadn't started.

"She could get water from the rain, but after twelve days without food or shelter, without making any sort of contact, my bet is that we won't find her alive."

"Some optimist. The boyfriend?"

I shrugged. "If the boyfriend killed her, he wouldn't risk getting his sports car stuck off the highway. He'd choose an area he was familiar with but one not associated with him. If a stranger picked her up, it's someone who hadn't planned *this* crime but still might be better prepared. In either case, neither would carry a body two miles through the woods in the middle of the night and risk getting hurt himself, and that's where we've been looking. I had trouble walking in daylight. If she's alive, we're looking in the wrong places."

Matt threw Laser a pizza bone – the crust. "Okay, what would you do with a body in the middle of the night?"

"If I were hiding one, I'd look for an abandoned house or an old barn. . ."

* * *

Barns.

Matt's eyes met mine, and he looked a little green. Did he remember that conversation?

An abrupt smell fired synapses in my brain. Something besides the strong odors of blood, vomit, feces and urine, and other dank smells from the barn itself. Maybe it wasn't even an odor, just memory, but my nose said it smelled something bad, and my imagination agreed that whatever was in the space under the barn was somewhere between dead and dust.

Them.

The word echoed in my mind until it sounded more like a chant. *Them them them them theeeeem. . .*

I turned my head, hoping for one last breath of somewhat fresher air as we investigated how to open the trap door, which sat flush and tight with the other boards of the flooring. Only the perfect square outline had given it away. One of the firemen went to go get a Halligan, a forcible entry tool that combines a claw, an adz-type blade, and a pick into one of the most versatile hand tools in fire service.

I nodded and added we could probably use a wood block for leverage, too.

"Wait," the township fire chief said. "We should send down a fire crew with air packs first. No sense exposing yourselves to God-knows-what down there."

Gerald Katz shook his head, but the chief insisted.

"That man melted alive, so there's no telling what other chemicals he has."

Katz looked at me for diplomatic options.

"He is in charge of safety here," I conceded to Katz. I took out my wallet and showed the chief my New Mexico State University Fire Academy identification. "But if it's okay, maybe I could gear up and take the first look? Since this may be a crime scene, we'd really like to preserve the chain of evidence for admission to court, if possible."

No one disputes the chain of evidence reason, mostly because it can lead to a courtroom.

The chief squinted at the card, then at me with a you-gotta-be-kidding look and shrugged.

"Go get my gear from the truck," he told another one of the firefighters standing nearby. "At least mine is clean."

The young man headed off to the squad truck parked in front of the house.

The chief spoke into his portable radio and asked for an ETA of a unit to the scene. The response was ten minutes.

"Something else, too, while you're suiting up. We sent to Traverse City Fire for a sniffing device. It'll tell us what gases are present. I don't know if that would be helpful to you as evidence or just plain peace of mind, but it can't hurt knowing beforehand."

I appreciated the insight, although I suspected whatever gases were below the floor probably were present above it.

"This whole thing gives me the woollies," the chief continued talking to Dr. Katz as I looked around the barn, only half-listening. "See, back when I was a kid, my granddad farmed the orchards north of here, and we lived with him after our house burned. I was nine or ten, I guess. The Tuckers have lived on this property for a century or more."

I wandered to the barn door, leaving Dr. Katz to the chief's tale as it carried on.

"I always thought J.P. Tucker was cruel. He was a year behind me in grade school, and more than once I saw him out beatin' the daylights out of a dog or cat or another kid. He bragged about using firecrackers to blow up small animals, squirrels and stuff."

Two volunteer firefighters in turnouts and helmets returned, one carrying the chief's turnout bag, the other with his helmet and a self-contained breathing apparatus for me.

I stepped outside to put on the gear.

"What are you doing, Julie?" Matt whispered from behind me, as if I were out of my mind.

"Putting on someone else's turnouts," I said. I hoped I could get the fireproof pants and coat on without having to adjust everything. I figured I was four inches taller and a hundred pounds lighter than the chief.

"I *see* that. Why?" he said in exasperation.

"The first person in the hole can't contaminate the evidence, Matt." I pulled a Nomex hood over my head, then tucked my long braid under it in the back.

Fighting fire is noble, but you either love it or you don't. I don't. It had been a part of my previous job in New Mexico, but Matt didn't know that, which explained his bewilderment. Now was not a good time to explain why I was qualified to do this.

I'd been in Michigan three years. The previous thirty-two years of my life were more or less a mystery to everyone here, including Matthew, who was probably my best friend.

He shrugged and stomped toward his patrol car.

Snippets of the conversations around me still passed, not so much processing them as much as letting the words pass through my brain as I added some forty pounds of equipment I'd hoped never to put on again.

"Once I found a goat all cut up, and I told my granddad," the chief continued. "Later, I heard him talking to my dad and one the fruit pickers, telling them to watch out for those kids, meaning those Tucker kids. Not long after, we moved back to town."

While the other two firefighters set up the sniffer, one helped me get the SCBA fitted. The self-contained breathing apparatus is a dry-land version of a scuba tank but uses a mask to cover the entire face in a fire and provide air. When we were done, I'd walked less than five feet into the barn when I needed to scratch my nose. Yet another of the many reasons I didn't like firefighting. You can't scratch. Anything.

As I approached the trap door, one firefighter eased it up a few inches with the Halligan and propped it open with the block of wood. The other dropped in the sensor by its cord, but it didn't fall very far. He edged it toward the hinge, and it dropped another foot or so.

I leaned close enough to read the display through the facemask of the air pack, but I was breathing so hard, it had begun to fog, which pissed me off even more than my nose itching.

Relax!

My anxiety snickered at the command, ratcheting up my heart rate.

Nodding the sample was complete, the firefighter pulled out the sensor and began rolling up cord. "Little methane, ammonia is a bit high. Not toxic, and not unusual, given that it is a barn. No hydrogen sulfide or carbon monoxide," he told me.

His partner reached down to lift the trapdoor.

The scene lights barely illuminated the first few steps. The trapdoor was perpendicular to the outside entry where we'd been standing.

I pointed a four-cell Maglite down onto more wooden risers and took a deep breath.

When I took a step forward, one of the firefighters said he'd go first.

"No, I'm looking for evidence. Could you just hold the door and watch? I'll let you know if I need assistance." My voice bellowed inside the mask, probably not sounding as polite as I meant.

I descended into the dark hole, hoping the stairway was as sturdy and new as it looked. I counted eight steep risers. I stayed as close to the dirt wall as I could without brushing against it because there was no railing on the open side.

Halfway down, I looked around at the sides of the room.

The chamber was approximately ten feet by twelve feet, counting the area taken up by the narrow stairs on the longer wall, and about eight feet deep from the framing. On the wall opposite the steps were five orange plastic barrels, smaller than a standard metal 55-gallon drum, with no markings. I nudged each, finding only that the barrel closest to the stairs seemed empty.

"Sorry they're dead," the cryptic note had read. *Them.*

Surely not, I thought, fighting a wave of nausea.

After a couple of deep breaths, I made a thorough walk around the walls, looking for something else besides the barrels to think about. I couldn't carry one upstairs, but hopefully there was other evidence. Anything but what I feared was in those barrels.

Them.

The word echoed in my head again like lyrics to a bad commercial and finally set itself to the ominous first four notes of Beethoven's Fifth. *Themthemthem – them.*

The chief would not appreciate me puking into his SCBA mask.

No footprints on the floor. In fact, it seemed the dirt had intentionally been packed smooth and then swept to erase just such evidence. I walked around the room twice before I saw what I decided were broom marks near the barrels. Not a scrap of paper. Not a single cigarette butt. Nothing but the barrels and hard-packed dirt on the floor.

I'd need more equipment to look for blood or other trace evidence.

Both firefighters stood where I'd left them.

With one more slow turn around the chamber, I declared the scene safe enough to bring down the laser and video camera. I pulled off the gloves and started toward the stairs, hoping to get out of the SCBA as soon as I got to the top.

I was considering the other potential dangers of a place where a man's life ended by drinking acid. A man who died chained to the wall of a barn with barrels in a hidden cellar. A man who left notes scratched in wood and in blood.

Not "them," I thought. What? Something else nagged me.

Notes. Unfinished notes.

Three letters. B - O - I

The fire chief's words about the creepy neighborhood kid were just starting to formulate a feeling of dread in my guts.

B - O -

I looked up and saw it – a neat bundle strapped to the floor joist beside the trap door. Away from the stairs, so I could not have seen it coming down. Hidden by the single vertical beam so I didn't see it from the center of the chamber or near the barrels.

Panic surged through my body. I bolted up the steps two at a time but stumbled on the second riser from the top. One firefighter shoved the door open to grab at me, to keep me from falling. I may have tried to yell a warning. Muffled through the mask, I don't think anyone heard me.

B-O-M-B.

CHAPTER 3

The first blast splintered the wooden flooring up underneath us like a volcano, pitching me upward and throwing me against the stone wall. A second explosion followed within seconds, blowing a good portion of the roof away, scattering boards and shingles and sheet metal over everything for over a hundred-yard radius.

Or so I learned later.

Instead of helping to dig through the debris and evidence, I was in ICU.

I detest hospitals. I have enough experience to say that unequivocally as an expert.

Consciousness came in individual senses, slowly. Beeps and chirps of electronic equipment. Strong odors such as alcohol, iodine, bleach. Blood, dirt, sweat. Words I recognized but not always meanings or voices.

At some point, I noticed my feet were hot, cramped under the covers. I wanted to kick them free, but somehow, I couldn't. My right shoulder was cold and my hand was numb. I tried to reach up and pull the blanket, only to discover my left hand was tied to the railing with a soft tie-down.

I tried to bend my right arm and discovered it similarly restrained. I tried to cross my legs at the ankles, and sure enough. All four extremities. And my neck in a cervical collar.

Oh shit. . . not my neck again.

I closed my eyes and went back to piecing together the memories.

What did I last remember?

I came home from duty and . . . No, that was in New Mexico.

I'm in Michigan now.

I'd gone to a call.

I'd had cameras, at a barn. . . in a barn. . . under a barn. . .

And then it slipped away again.

Over the next few hours, as I was able to stay awake long enough to remember the basics of how I'd come to be here, I set about making an assessment of myself.

A rigid cervical collar was fitted under my chin and around my neck, which alarmed me. I tried turning my head, hoping I wasn't back in permanent traction. I wasn't. I couldn't move my neck very far because of the collar, but that meant it wasn't broken again.

The left side of my chest hurt with deep breaths, but I didn't feel rib ends grating together, another unpleasant medical familiarity.

My head throbbed like the worst Sunday morning tequila hangover I could imagine, and I've had a bit of experience in that arena as well.

When I lifted my head, I could barely see a cut that had been sutured on the little finger side of my left hand near the wrist, as well as a small burn, and several superficial cuts and scrapes on both hands.

I suppose I should have left the gloves on a few minutes longer.

I wiggled my toes, comforted I hadn't been there long enough for my fractured toe to heal.

Two IVs dripped, but I couldn't read their contents. Most annoying was the nasogastric tube. *I must have been really unconscious for them to get a tube up my nose.*

Hospitals force you to endure such irritating things as bleached, scratchy sheets on a narrow bed that has long surrendered its effort to be comfortable. This one felt stuffed with broken bricks and covered in wool rejected by the Confederate Army prisons as cruel and inhumane. And always, nurses who chilled their hands in the freezer next to their stethoscopes before touching me.

I was struggling to make my toes more comfortable when a nurse entered the room. "Well, hello," she said, seeing me awake. "Welcome back."

Matt, who'd been snoozing in the corner in a chair, woke

suddenly, thinking she was speaking to him.

"We've all been so worried about you," he said, taking my hand when she finally yielded bedside space to him. "I've got to call Dr. Katz. I promised him I would let him know as soon as you woke up."

"How long was I unconscious?" I asked, my voice dry and squeaky.

The nurse explained as she untied my hands. "About four hours, they say. Then you were sedated for twenty more to let your brain rest. Nothing serious other than the concussion." She let me take a sip of water that, in combination with all the other odors, reminded me of a chlorinated swimming pool. "We let the drugs wear off slowly."

I tried to nod.

Matt held the phone to my ear.

"It's hell the things I do to get a weekend off," I said to Katz, my voice scratchy. I assured him I was going to be fine and needed nothing at the moment.

The nurse enforced the no-visitors rule once she finally got Matthew out of my cubicle. He didn't want to leave, and I wanted answers. The staff had to do their jobs and insisted I needed more rest. I considered arguing, but really didn't have the energy.

Of all my injuries, my head hurt the worst, then my ribs. The miscellaneous cuts and bruises hardly registered.

The neurologist treating me, Dr. Donald Harper, made rounds later that afternoon and explained he had been concerned about possible brain swelling noted on the CAT scan, especially since I was still unconscious long after they brought me in. However, he said, the swelling had resolved with diuretics and steroids while I was sedated. As he tested my reflexes and sensory functions, he mentioned my ears would probably continue to ring for a few days.

"Thanks," I grumbled, "I hadn't noticed that till you mentioned it."

"I see by the x-rays and scars that you've had a little surgery before," he said in amused understatement. "Very nicely healed, it appears. Did you have any deficits with the original injuries?" he asked, tapping my patellar tendon with his reflex hammer, and my quadriceps muscle jerked appropriately.

"Nothing from the cervical fracture," I said, feeling panic. "Is there something wrong?"

"Oh, not at all. It seems quite stable," he said, reaching to take off the stiff neck brace I'd probably had on since the paramedics had transported me, as dirty as it was. "Tell me about your previous injuries." He continued his examination.

"Initially, I had pain radiating to my legs due to the lower back injury. I have a little residual numbness in my right hand, but it was most likely from the shoulder fracture and dislocation, even after the surgery," I answered, wiggling my fingers. "Resolved except my ring and pinky fingertips sometimes get tingly."

"Well, the films and CT of your neck are fine, but I thought it best to leave the collar on until you could tell us what might be residual versus acute, since we had no comparison films. I don't think there's anything to worry about, but I want to know if you develop any numbness or weakness now. You'll know what to watch for, I gather."

He ordered my nasogastric tube removed and clear liquids to start with. One of the two intravenous lines could be disconnected. I insisted on bathroom privileges, hence removal of the catheter. He conceded.

"I bet you've been told before you aren't much of a patient, haven't you," he said with a wink. "Anything else you want?"

"Something to cover up my neck," I said, touching the four-year-old scar that ran from under my left ear across my throat.

He gave me a serious look of doubt, and then nodded. "I think one of the nurses wears turtleneck shirts under her scrubs, I'll see if you can borrow one."

Within the hour, someone brought me a dark blue turtleneck and helped me get into it. I was most grateful I could hide the scar.

CHAPTER 4

Despite my pleading that evening when he returned during his shift, Matthew refused to tell me anything and only stayed a few minutes.

"As if I haven't had a long nap?" I asked testily. But I felt like I could sleep another couple of days.

He promised to drop by the next day after I was moved out of ICU.

Dr. Katz and his wife came for a few minutes, too. Dr. Katz assured me my keys and truck were safely in his possession, and he would see about feeding my fish.

I wanted answers, but MaryAnne refused to let him talk business with me either.

"Is there anything I can bring you? Errands you need done? They didn't leave much of the clothes you had on." She said this in a hushed whisper, as if I might have been surprised my clothes had been cut away.

The ME's office probably owed the fire chief for a new set of turnouts, too.

I asked her if she could bring me a couple of my silk turtlenecks from the house, a robe, and clean clothes to go home in.

"Absolutely. I'm so glad you and Gerald were wearing your vests," she said with genuine gratitude.

I looked at Dr. Katz, who nodded sheepishly. "Me, too. I don't know why, I just put it on before I left the house. I took a piece of debris in the chest, but it hardly bruised. Looking at you, I'd say it was a great investment for us both."

That was as close to work as MaryAnne was going to let us discuss, and she dragged her husband out the door. After they left, I took both pain pills the nurse offered, drifting off to nightmares.

I can't exactly remember what made them bad dreams, but I woke several times during the night feeling an unfocused fear. Once I sat up and turned on the light to make sure I was alone.

The night nurse assured me it was not unusual for patients in intensive care to suffer panic attacks, nightmares and such. ICU neurosis, she called it. I'd been in ICU before, and that name didn't make me feel any better.

The next morning, I was moved to a private room on the med-surg floor, and I begged to get a shower after breakfast. I could feel the dirt and grime in my hair, and despite the nurses' attempts to clean me up, the smell of sweat was enough to make my eyes water. Even the sheets showed the dirt from the barn explosion yet to be washed away.

I had been fully dressed and covered in turnouts, so where all the dirt had come from was a mystery. Like patients I'd seen in serious auto collisions – they end up with glass fragments in places you could not imagine, such as their underwear and shoes.

Must be the opposite effect of those missing socks in my dryer - amazing reappearing debris.

I felt almost human to be clean again, but the showering process was slow and painful. I hadn't realized how weak I would be, and I had to use the shower chair, but the water felt wonderful even if I had to sit down.

I returned to my room to find MaryAnne had dropped off a bag with the shirts and robe I'd asked her to pick up for me. I slipped into a clean turtleneck, soothed by the cool touch of silk against my skin instead of the starchy cotton gown and sheets.

By noon, I was exhausted and weak, but I definitely felt better. And along came my next dose of pain medications before lunch.

All patients in a hospital complain about the food. Maybe I'm pickier, but I scraped slices of unidentified meat off the bread and ate the remaining cheese sandwich and sipped the bland chicken broth. I left untouched the green beans – a despicable institutional food not a single teacher ever coaxed past my lips in school, ranking right down there with canned spinach and black-eyed peas in my book. Then I covered the Jell-O with a napkin because I also refuse to eat anything that wiggles or comes in iridescent toxic waste colors, with or without stuff suspended in it. There were days in my first couple of years in school where the bread was all I would eat off my plate.

Matt knocked and came in, toting a waxed paper bag. "Thought you might be hungry."

"Whatever it is, I'll take it." I scooted over to give him room to sit on the foot of the bed. The bag contained an apple bran muffin and a banana. I opted for the muffin first. "Now talk. No one will tell me what happened."

"That's not true," he protested. "I told you everything in ICU. You just kept snoring."

I nudged him with my leg. "Come on. Please?"

"Okay, just the basics. We identified the dead man as James Patrick Tucker, 43, the owner of the property. Unmarried, inherited the family farm from his parents about ten years ago. He was self-employed in some sort of video or graphic arts business at the house."

I munched on the muffin. A question along that line of thought drifted on pain medications just out of reach in my brain.

"We know the cause of death was the acid ingestion. Very nasty way to die. However, Dr. Katz determined Tucker was also probably in handcuffs for at least five to seven days prior, and had been severely malnourished. There was something in his intestines, but Katz says he'd be guessing for now. There's no indication so far as to why Tucker was chained in the barn. There were also other findings on the autopsy, but Katz should probably fill you in on those."

He paused when the dietary person came to remove my lunch tray, leaving a card to make choices for the next day's meals.

I took a pen from his shirt and wrote, "Broiled lobster, fettuccine Alfredo, and a nice German white wine. Would settle for pepperoni pizza and beer. No chicken or guessmeat, please!" I knew that was guaranteed to get me turkey-something-or-other and more of my least favorite vegetables, probably lima beans or spinach. Maybe Brussels sprouts.

And the staple of hospitals and schools across the country – Jell-

O.

"What about the explosives," I asked.

"The state police bomb guys are still trying to determine that there are no others. That's slowing down the scene investigation. Nothing so far."

"Was anyone else injured?" I asked, hoping it wouldn't be bad news.

"One fireman was hurt by falling debris; the other who was nearest you is in critical condition with burns. He was flown to Grand Rapids. There were several others who were treated for injuries from flying debris, including several deputies and Dr. Katz. Nothing serious. Laser and I weren't even close." He paused. "God, I'm so glad you're okay," he said, squeezing the foot with the broken toes through the sheet and blanket. "Laser helped find you."

I put my arm around him and hugged him. "Tell your dog I owe him a steak dinner."

When he stood up, his eyes were watery, but I pretended not to notice.

He explained that the bomb expert figured I was heaved away from the trap door toward the stone wall during the first explosion, which probably saved my life.

Experts agreed that I would not have survived under the wood flooring.

Something Matt said clicked as I took the last bite of the muffin and held up my hand to interrupt him. Finally, I got it chewed up enough to speak. "Wait, you said in the first explosion – there were more?"

He nodded. "Two bombs. Katz's best guess is there are four bodies down there, but we weren't sure what you'd seen. How many barrels, I mean. It's pretty obvious the explosion was meant to destroy the evidence. He said he thinks the most recent death was within the last few months."

"Five. I counted five barrels, but one seemed empty," I said.

"Deliveries, dear," said a white-haired lady knocking at the door, admiring a large wildflower arrangement almost bigger than she could carry. "And aren't these beautiful?" she said. She plucked the card from the holder and tucked it in with the mail I'd received, including a small box from a local candy shop. "Be sure to ask the nurses before you sample those," she said in a grandmotherly manner.

I opened a couple of the get-well cards. One was from the sheriff's department, saying they hoped I was back at work soon. Another from Connie Thompson, our department secretary. The flowers were from the Katzes.

I peeked into the candy box. "Ooh, my favorite."

I sat the box down to look at the attached card, which had no signature, but the message was handwritten.

So sorry you were injured. You must be a very strong woman to have survived so much. My thoughts are with you.

"Secret admirer?" Matthew asked as I read the card.

"They aren't from you?" I asked, turning the card to him.

"Um, no. I never took you for a flowers-and-candy kind of girl. Diamonds and Harley's, but not roses and chocolates."

Though entirely true, I wasn't sure if he meant that as a compliment.

He eyed the box. "I may have to revise my thinking by the way you're drooling."

"Can you pour me some water?" I asked, holding up my cup. While he poured, I backed up the conversation. "What else has the investigation turned up?"

"Detectives think the room was like a monument or shrine of a serial killer." Matt pulled up a chair.

"No, not a monument. It wasn't personal. Just cold storage."

He shook his head. "How do you know that?"

"I saw it. The conclusion doesn't take a genius." I knew I'd stepped outside my envelope yet again with Matt.

"Not what you saw. It's how you interpret any evidence. More like you. . ." he paused, struggling for a phrase I hoped wasn't supposed to be "*thinking like a criminal.*"

I interrupted him. "I have a degree in psychology, Matt. I've studied criminal behavior. Doesn't mean I'm right. Monument infers an emotional attachment or a connection to the victims or the crime. I didn't sense that at all. If they meant something, why destroy them?"

Matt stood. "Don't change the subject. You don't have to be

right, but you process through pieces and find a way to eliminate illogical wrongs. You sift it down to the right questions."

"It's nothing more than psychology, Matt. And logic doesn't always apply to the criminal mind. I love to solve the mystery before I finish the book," I said.

Working on mysteries without any clues...

Trying to make Bob Seger go away, I reached up and rubbed the dull ache in my temple.

"No mysteries. You are going to take a nap." He reached for my hand and squeezed it. "This will still be a case when you wake up. I promise not to let anyone solve it while you're asleep."

After Matthew left, I wanted something to do, something else besides thinking about this case. No sense trying to work a jigsaw puzzle when you can't see the pieces.

I leaned my head back into the flat used-to-be-fluff someone had stuffed into a plastic pillow and shoved into a pillowcase bleached and pressed to the consistency of sandpaper.

I'd done it again, I thought. Protecting my past isn't going to succeed if I kept revealing my police investigation and criminology background. Eventually I might have to face up to this, but I hated the idea of people knowing what happened to me before I came to Michigan.

CHAPTER 5

The nurse brought my afternoon medications, two Darvocet and a muscle relaxant. I decided I didn't want to be asleep when MaryAnne came. The nurse wasn't paying attention when I took them, so I palmed the Flexeril.

No pillow fluffing, as if that would have possibly helped the lump under my head.

I flipped through the channels of the television. Soap operas and talk shows. So much electricity wasted on nonsense and stupidity, I thought. Today Oprah Winfrey was having one of her more sedate conversations with Dr. So-and-So – the guru du jour preaching that depression and anxiety are caused by unresolved issues from our pasts and sells promises that, by using a self-examination with his six-question analysis explained in his book for only $39.95 in two easy payments, we can all be happy and well-adjusted.

Though I doubted it, he *might* be right, but I could see this line of thinking waddling right toward my own closet full of skeletons and secrets. Somewhere else I didn't want to go, even with two easy payments.

I shut off the television.

Find something else to think about.

Picking up the phone, I dialed my calling card numbers from memory, I called my mom in Albuquerque. I didn't think she'd heard about the explosion, but I wanted to tell her I was okay.

The machine picked up.

"Can't get to the phone right now, leave a message!" the ever-changing recording said in her cheerful, slight German accent.

"Hey, Mom. Just called to see what's up. I'll get back to you soon. Love you, bye." One doesn't leave a parent messages about bombs and hospitals on a machine.

I dialed another number. No-nonsense voice mail said, "Leave a message."

"I was hoping to talk to you. Give me a call in a couple of days, okay?"

Diversion, all of about sixty seconds, had ended. No one else to call.

The flowers caught my eye. I picked up the cards again. As informal as the message with the candy was, I did not recognize the writing, but it could have been written by a delivery person, more feminine with a round, open cursive.

I turned my attention to the smell of chocolate wafting from the box.

Knowing that since I'd been served lunch, eating these was probably only a sin because I hadn't asked the nurse, so I opened the box. What could they do, take away my pain pills?

Someone had to know how much I love these – white-chocolate-covered caramel cream. I had a box stashed in my desk at work, one beside my favorite chair at home. But they weren't a luxury you could pick up on a whim. This little piece of wickedness was a bite-sized self-indulgence I'd stumbled on years ago in Albuquerque and brought with me to Michigan.

Traverse City has always been known for cherries and fudge. And though I like fudge, especially maple pecan, I finally bribed a local candy maker into getting the recipe and making me a batch now and then. This box came from the same store, a little shop on Union Street.

I bit off a corner to reveal the creamy center and licked the caramel out of the white chocolate shell until it was nearly empty, then popped it into my mouth to finish melting.

Fabulous. I decided to sin in moderation, so I had one more, then put the box on the table beside the bed.

I was thinking maybe I should call MaryAnne to bring me a book. Then I figured there was nothing stopping me from going to the gift shop downstairs.

Nothing except those aching muscles and painful ribs or the designer back-less gown and IV pole. Or being able to find my wallet. I assumed it was in my belongings, but I hadn't checked.

The phone rang while I was making a decision about getting up. MaryAnne, who must be psychic.

"How're you doing? I wanted to see if you needed anything. I was on my way to run some errands."

"Now that you mention it," I said, "I was hoping to get something to read." I named a couple of recent bestseller titles and repeatedly declined her offers of snacks, lotions, make up, comfy cotton gowns, and a Walkman with her collection of jazz.

I've nothing against it, but jazz is as much ambiance as music. Really good jazz is kinda like really good sex – it's live, hot, sweaty and loud. Neither is suitable for a hospital.

Content that I didn't have to make it to the gift shop for a book, I was left with the question of whether my wallet was with my other belongings.

When I ignored it, another idea formed about my clothes. Both dissolved in Darvocet when I closed my eyes.

I hadn't meant to doze off, but a full-body muscle twitch jerked me painfully back to consciousness. When I tried to relax again, that dreamy in-between place I kept fading into had bad images or twitches.

Before long, I couldn't stand either and had to find out about my wallet.

Swinging my legs off the bed, I sat for a moment, a little surprised at the wavy black spots before my eyes. When I thought the light-headedness had passed, I stood up and took three or four steps toward the closet next to the bathroom, using the IV pole for support.

I remember reaching out for the stainless steel handle, thinking how it seemed to melt and run down the bulging door.

Then the wall began to avalanche toward me.

CHAPTER 6

Images flooded back in flashes of pain – memories twisted inside bizarre unrealities.

"Julie, go change shirts," my husband said as if I were a toddler wearing my clothes inside out.

"That's ridiculous, David," I responded. "This shirt is fine."

We were going to El Paso to meet some of his buddies and go dancing. I was wearing a black tank top and jeans.

"Fine so every guy in my outfit can see how hard your nipples are?" He punctuated the question with a backhanded slap across my face, and then dragged me by the arm to the bedroom to change. "And you weren't here last night when I called. Where'd you go? Who're you screwing? You know I'll kill you both if I ever find out."

"David, I told you --"

He left another stinging imprint on my cheek. "You jumped into bed with every man you met before we were married. Now I can't get you to kiss me goodnight. Someone else must be getting it." He bulldozed me to the floor. The knuckles of two fingers smashed against my right temple. "Prove you aren't fucking someone else. Prove it!"

The pain began to unravel my thoughts as David kept driving his knuckles into my skull, crushing my head against the carpet. With a deafening crack, my skull seemed to explode in lightning bolts of blinding white-hot agony.

Certain I was dying.

I heard voices all around me. People pinning me down just like David had.

". . . we found her on the floor. . ."

". . . Valium yet?"

". . . She's not having a seizure, she's fighting. . ."

". . . responsive to pain. . . "

Too much pain. Stop hurting me, David!

". . . blood pressure is 180/100, pulse 148 . . ."

". . . called Dr. Harper . . ."

I struggled against men shooting bullets of ice and fire into my head, cutting me into pieces, suffocating me.

". . . CAT scan is ready whenever we get her sedated. . ."

". . . opened her eyes."

"Julia? Can you hear me? Julia?"

Don't call me Julia!

". . . can you hear me?"

Damn it, David, I shot you! Why don't you just DIE?

I tried to focus on the faces swarming around me.

Too bright, too loud.

Sounds and colors were inseparable, bursting like balloons filled with paint before my eyes. Everything caused electric, searing pain.

Too much pain.

I couldn't tell what was real from what was not, but I knew it couldn't all be happening.

Too much.

I tried to cover my face, but hands pinned my arms to the floor. My chest seemed to be collapsing under the pressure – I could hardly breathe.

When I opened my mouth to speak, a wave of nausea caused me to jerk away from the hands that had been apparently holding my head, and I threw up violently.

". . . 100 milligrams IV push . . ."

". . . see if she's got a bleed. . ."

Bleeding?

Dying. If I died, maybe the pain would stop.

". . . she's down. Let's go . . ."

And then the world faded to black again.

Dead? Couldn't I just be dead now?

Please?

Voices coming from a distance it seemed.

". . . no bleeding . . . swelling. . ."

Not so much pain.

". . . vitals have stabilized . . ."

Not dead.

". . . back to ICU . . ."

". . . give her some dr. . ."

Some dreams?

Dreams. . . .

I dreamed someone chased me into a barn and shackled me to the floor to wait until it exploded, when my body was vaporized into thousands of conscious molecules still communicating the shared agony.

I dreamed of waking up inside a morgue drawer. My fingers clawed in panic against the seamless polished steel surface, except for a small placard I knew ironically read, "You are not locked in." But there was no release latch, lock or not.

I dreamed that after I shot him, David sat up from the pool of blood and laughed because he wasn't dead. I was forever his victim, his toy.

I dreamed there was a man holding my hand, softly telling me I was going to be okay when I woke up.

Eventually I slept.

Or maybe I dreamed I was finally dead.

CHAPTER 7

"Julie?" a voice said softly. "Can you hear me?"

Squinting my eyes before opening them, I feared blinding lights and pain, but the room was dim. I licked my dry lips and tried to think of something to say while I struggled to put a name to the man standing beside the bed.

"Julie, everything is okay now. Would you like a sip of water?"

I blinked.

Matt, I remembered, but my brain was running so slow.

He held a glass with a straw for me while I took a couple of cautious sips. My tongue was sour and sticky.

I felt hung over and a little nauseated. I nodded I was done. Pain shot down my neck between my shoulder blades. I could not silence the groan as I moved my head back to neutral on the pillow.

Turning only my eyes, I saw that Dr. Katz stood on the other side of my bed.

"The doctor said you might be in a lot of pain," he said softly. "You've been through quite an ordeal."

I didn't answer. I didn't know what to say. So far my only communication, a mere nod, had been excruciating. My head throbbed, drumming up waves of nausea. The back of my neck burned like a blowtorch. My entire body seemed too weak to move.

Great. Back in ICU.

Already the beeping of all the ICU monitors and pumps was torture. Even the sounds from the hallway and other patient rooms boomed in my head.

Matt's and Dr. Katz's silence was even more bothersome.

"What happened?" I asked, the sound of my voice reverberating in my head. Everything was way too loud. "Shhh."

"I guess we were waiting for you to tell us," Matt said in a whisper I felt certain would have echoed through a stadium. "When I stopped back before my shift, I ran into Mrs. Katz in the lobby and walked with her up to your room. When we got there, you were on the floor with half a dozen people trying to hold you down."

I wrinkled my eyebrows in confusion. "I remember bits and pieces. Some of it couldn't have been real."

"Looked real enough. It was frightening, watching you fighting, yelling," Matthew said. "At first, they thought it had something to do with your injuries from the explosion, the concussion. The doctor told us the CAT scan was okay, but they were a little baffled. I mentioned that you looked like someone on angel dust. He tested you – you were positive for PCP."

"I've never—" I started to object, my voice cracking. The unconscious attempt to sit up ended in several agonizing minutes of retching over the side of the bed.

When I'd finally finished, Dr. Katz helped me get comfortable again, wiping my face with a cool washcloth. A nurse mopped up the floor.

"No one said you took it intentionally," Dr. Katz explained.

"The drugs were in the chocolates you received, remember? Four other pieces tested positive for PCP, two for LSD. It looked like you'd had two of them, maybe three," Matt continued.

I closed my eyes, thinking about what had been drug-induced hallucinations. "Why would someone. . ." I asked, my own mind finding too many possible answers.

The nurse gave me an IV injection for the nausea, and I gave in to its effects.

The next morning, I woke to find Dr. Katz and Dr. Harper standing next to the door, talking about me. No doubt they had quite a conversation already.

"That was a bizarre wrestling match on the floor yesterday," the neurologist summarized with a raised eyebrow. "You're pretty strong, they tell me. Other than the drugs, I see nothing new in your tests, which is good news. I've got a rather lengthy surgical case scheduled for this afternoon, so my physician assistant is making rounds for me later and will check on you. I'd think you could go home the day after tomorrow, providing there are no residual effects to the drugs – any hallucinations or nightmares, let us know."

He was casual, almost too unhurried to be a neurosurgeon. Usually I feel like I'm the last patient standing between the office visit and an afternoon golf game.

"I always wondered how someone would know whether something was a hallucination. It was all too very real," I said. "Shall I remember to tell you if I become confused or forgetful, too?"

He smiled a mouthful of perfect white teeth. "I keep hearing you're everyone's favorite patient, despite that projectile vomiting episode straight out of *The Exorcist* yesterday."

"Then they shouldn't serve pea soup. I'll try to behave the rest of the day if you'll let me out of ICU now," I bargained. "The bells and whistles are making me crazy."

"See what I mean about hallucinations?" he said over his shoulder to Dr. Katz. "Beeps, blips, buzzes, bongs. Not a single bell here." He turned back. "I'll have Evonne see to it this afternoon, but you have to promise to stay out. I can't do everything for you."

A neurosurgeon with a sense of humor. "Twisted, but funny."

The difference between a neurosurgeon and God? God doesn't play doctor.

He left me with Gerald Katz.

"How are you feeling?" He looked thoughtful. "I've noticed doctors seldom ask their patients that these days."

"Never heard you ask yours, either," I quipped. "Better than last night, I guess. Hungry."

"You're sure? I'll call Matthew. He can bring you something palatable. Something we can count on being safe." He placed a call on my bedside phone. "She's awake and hungry."

When he hung up, I asked him to tell me more about the barn. "I could use a diversion while we wait."

He hesitated, weighing the options, then nodded, expression all the more serious. "This Tucker case is getting more complicated. First, it was a possible suicide, then more likely murder. Add to that the basement level where you found the barrels with the bodies.

We're sure there were four bodies floating in an acid. Then it became a bombing that killed a man." He answered my question before I could interrupt, "Yes, the one firefighter died last night."

"Damn, I should've seen that bomb sooner!"

"Julie, you weren't meant to see it until it was too late, if at all. State bomb expert thinks they were rigged to go off separately, not simultaneously. It's not clear yet how they were armed, possibly the trapdoor. Maybe the idea was for the bomb to interrupt the process of opening a barrel, but certainly to rupture and destroy the contents."

While I was mulling this all over in guilt and self-criticism, Matt entered the room and presented me with a bag from a nearby shop. Sesame bagel with bacon and a side of cheddar cream cheese. And a bottle of tea. Matt knew this was one of my favorite lunches.

"Thanks," I said, getting ready to take a bite. "Go on."

"The barn thing, that will wait. Right now, the priority is finding out who drugged your candy." Katz looked over at Matt. "After Matt made the connection with the drugs, he took the liberty of checking your house last night."

"I found a note that read, 'Welcome home, hope you enjoyed your *trip*. Will be seeing you soon,'" Matt said.

"In my house?" I exclaimed with a mouthful of bagel, clamping my hand over my lips to keep from spitting crumbs onto the sheets. More pain shot through my head, and my ribs ached.

"Please don't throw up again. I don't have any more clean shoes," Matt said, moving back a step, only half in jest. "The note was on your pillow."

"How did he get in? Did he take anything? What about prints?" The panic boiling in my throat tried to speed up the professional part of my brain slogged in residual sedatives.

Matt motioned like he was stopping a runaway train. "I've been through the house, Julie. There's nothing gone as far as I can tell. We've removed any of the food that could have been tampered with, which only consisted of a box of cereal, a week-old gallon of milk, and two pints of ice cream," Matt kidded. "We also took anything else that could be contaminated, so you're going to have to go shopping. We'll test anything suspicious for other drugs or poisons."

"He could have killed me with the candy, if that were the goal,"

I said crossly. “Why would he drug me?”

“We’re working on that. But there is something else. While you were hallucinating yesterday, you were . . . um, saying things. I don’t want to jump to any conclusions, Julie,” Matt paused, obviously uncomfortable, “but who is David, and did you really kill him?”

CHAPTER 8

Well crap. So much for keeping that secret.

There was no way to explain just part of what had happened.

"David Wesley was my husband," I said, then hesitated. "Yes, I shot and killed him."

Something wild flashed in Matthew's brown eyes, and he wheeled to stomp out the door before I could explain.

"Please stop him," I begged Dr. Katz. "I only wanted to leave my past behind. I explained to you I didn't want people to know why I left the state police and came here."

Dr. Katz went out in the hall and was gone for a while. They finally returned, but Matthew looked pissed off.

"The truth is, I was married to David Wesley, but I guess you could say it ended in divorce by Smith & Wesson," I said. My sarcasm was so bitter I tried to laugh, but it resolved into tears, relieved to confess the whole hateful, sordid story. It took a few minutes to regain my composure and continue. "First, I'm sorry if you think I lied to you, Matt. I needed to leave all this behind me. I hope when you know what happened you'll understand why." I took a deep breath. "I met David Wesley while I was taking a course in computer programming at the community college, about two years after I'd been transferred to New Mexico State Police District 3 in Alamogordo."

With that revelation, Matt rolled his eyes, but he still didn't look amused.

"David asked me out after the third class. We started dating on a casual basis. We were both busy, and for a while, things were sporadic at best.

"David was stationed at Holloman Air Force Base in Alamogordo," I said. "He'd been a B-52 bomber pilot in the 410th Air Wing in Marquette until he injured his back during a pickup basketball game when someone knocked him to the ground. Two weeks later, David failed to turn over command of the aircraft to the copilot when he realized he was having trouble. A bad landing caused structural damage to the aircraft, grounding the entire flight crew during an investigation."

There had been rumors of court martial for the incident. Despite winning that battle, David refused a medical discharge. This resulted in flight status revocation, followed by a transfer to Holloman Air Force Base to the 46th Test Group, to work on navigation and guidance systems, and radar signatures especially with regard to the testing of the F117A Stealth fighter.

David had been in New Mexico less than a year when we began dating in 1988. We got married a year later.

During my story, Matt had retreated to the corner of the hospital room, as far away from me as he could get. Nothing he'd heard had been worthy of secrecy, I supposed, so I continued.

"The Gulf War was just becoming a possibility, so the advanced cruise missile exercises and test flights became more frequent," I said. "David deployed to the Persian Gulf region, but I never asked details, and he never offered specifics. He seemed to be unhappy about going overseas for these exercises, but I believed his anger was centered on loss of his flight status. He felt he was a better pilot than those who were flying the tests he was monitoring. He'd been forced out of his chosen career, but he did what the air force paid him to do and went where it sent him, determined not to lose his retirement."

Shortly after his deployment and return, David started to act like a different person. He yelled about what I fixed for supper. He threw his books on the floor and stomped out when he couldn't calculate an answer. He screamed at me if I went to bed before he came in from work, but he stayed later at the base each night. The unfocused anger seemed to escalate, but then it would vanish for days. Then he began pushing me harder about things we'd never disagreed on before.

He wanted to know why I wasn't being a good Air Force wife,

someone who participated in the politics and ceremony. Why didn't I support his career? I refused to be involved early in our relationship, declaring I was doing my part to protect the home neighborhood and had better things to do than bake sales and potluck dinners with the other wives when the men were gone. I had friends of my own, but none were Air Force wives. "His leap of logic?" I said. "Accusing me of having an affair."

"This didn't strike you as inappropriate or threatening behavior?" Dr. Katz asked.

"It did, but it was so intermittent at first, I didn't know what to do about it," I said, feeling like I was making excuses for David. "Then he began to have storms of anger at me over nothing. More physically aggressive and irrational – breaking things, hitting walls. As these episodes intensified, he became obsessed with controlling me. He started telling me how to dress off-duty, especially about how tight my shirts or jeans were. If I didn't provide a detailed summary of work or if I was late getting home, he was out of control, demanding I check in with him during my shift. He followed me while I was on patrol until Captain Rader pulled him over and threatened to throw him in jail for obstruction of justice. This only riled David more, and he specifically accused me of sleeping with Eric Rader." I looked at Matthew. "It never happened."

Then David was sent on a three-week assignment off base in February. As always, he wasn't supposed to tell me where they went or what they did – and I never asked – but this time he told me anyway. It was like he was testing me or playing a game, knowing I would feel obligated to keep his secrets. Most of it was useless information to me. I didn't care where they went to fire guided missiles from bombers and didn't care if the accuracy was within ten miles or ten inches. I didn't know what kind of radar imaging they could or could not get on the rumored new secret "stealth" jet everyone was whispering about and anyone could see flying around over Alamogordo. We all knew it didn't look like anything else we'd seen before. So what?

But David came home with a new twist. He not only told me what a lousy cheating wife I was, but he began insinuating that he knew I was a spy, so he identified me to his commanding officers as an East German sympathizer and a traitor.

"East Germany?" Dr. Katz asked.

"The Wall had fallen, which had been a significant event to me," I explained. "I went to see the new Berlin because I'd been born in Germany just months before the Wall was erected. I was moved that a symbol so powerful had been torn down, something I thought I'd never see in my lifetime. Yet he taunted me with this as evidence that I was a spy."

David told me the condo was bugged. He promised that if I ever left him, they would track me down and convict me of stealing secret military information from him. Only if I stayed with him, he told me, could he assure them I was being a good little wife.

"David told me the only reason I was still around was that the Colonel told him to keep an eye on me.

"One moment he seemed fine, and others, he lost touch with logic and reality. I began to see that his rage had a psychotic undertone, something beyond depression. I tried to get him to go see a doctor, any kind of doctor, but the suggestion only infuriated him more. I have a degree in psychology. He was edging closer to a breakdown, but I never imagined it would shatter so fast. I had considered going to his commanding officer, but I wasn't sure what to say, especially if what he said about this spy business was true."

Three weeks after he'd returned home from that last deployment, I came home from a day shift to a firestorm.

CHAPTER 9

"By blind-siding me, David gained the advantage of size and fury over my training in physical combat. Once I was down, he pummeled my face repeatedly, broke my nose, split my lower lip against my teeth. When I tried to roll away, he yanked my right arm up behind by back so far my right shoulder was both fractured and dislocated."

Telling the story, I could feel my heart rate climbing.

"He pulled my braided hair loose from the bun and jerked my head around by it to show me he had the duty pistol from my belt, a Smith & Wesson Model 5904, a 9 mm semi-automatic with fifteen in the magazine and one in the chamber. He pressed the muzzle against my temple, whispering words I couldn't understand, laughing."

I refused to beg him for my life. At that moment, I surrendered to the idea he'd blow my brains out, and I only hoped that when he pulled the trigger, I'd die without flinching. I remember relaxing completely, calmly waiting.

"That must have really enraged him. Last thing I remember him saying was that I didn't deserve a bullet," I said, trying to control my breathing, to keep my voice from becoming a shriek. From my hospital bed, I had no way to get up and burn off the adrenaline rush.

"David must have done something that caused me an extraordinary amount of pain, and I blacked out. Maybe that's when he cut my throat. When I woke up at the bottom of the stairs, around the corner from the kitchen, I was on my right side in a large pool of blood, which I wasn't surprised was mine. Woozy and weak, I had difficulty taking a breath. The pains were nauseating – my neck, chest, shoulder – it was all I could do to keep my eyes open and concentrate."

My hands were bound together palm to palm in front of me with one of my Flex-Cuffs.

I reached for my throat, which felt like it was on fire, but the movement caused grating pain in my right upper arm and shoulder. I'm sure I made some sort of noise, because I heard him in the kitchen, talking about me, but he stopped.

About watching me die.

My hands were cold and almost numb, maybe from the blood loss or being bound, but I couldn't feel my legs, couldn't tell if they were moving.

My duty shirt was gone, as was my Kevlar vest, leaving a blood-soaked t-shirt. He'd taken my duty weapon from my belt, but I hoped I still had the Smith & Wesson .38 Special Centennial Airweight in my ankle holster. Five shots.

Through pain that dimmed my vision, I managed to pull my left leg up far enough I could reach under my pantleg just above my boot. Seemed to take minutes before I could wrap my left fingers around the compact revolver and free it from the holster. I remember the sticky feel of my bloody hands on the grip. I pulled the hammer back slowly with my left thumb when I heard David coming. I couldn't do more than roll to my back to aim the gun over my head using both hands, my left arm supporting all the weight of the weapon and my shattered right arm.

"Oh, look what we have here," David said as looked down to see the barrel pointed at him. If he was surprised, he didn't show it. He grinned and started taunting me again, telling me I wouldn't shoot him. Chanting that he'd take that tiny gun away from me and put a bullet in my brain. That he'd get a medal for catching a spy.

The muscles in my dislocated and broken right shoulder were locked in a burning spasm. My eyes blurred from the pain and my vision began fading to black. The coppery taste of blood from my split lip and broken nose nauseated me.

My arms wavered, and the gun trembled in my hand. But I was no longer afraid.

He took another step toward me. "Julia," he whispered singsong, making fun of my name, knowing that it infuriated me. "Ju-lie-uh, you can't do it, can you, Ju-lie-uh?" He kept talking, saying other weird things that didn't make sense.

Then he leaned forward and reached for the gun in my hands.

Had he taken a step to either side, he would have moved outside my aim, and I wouldn't have been able to hit him.

"Just as his fingers wrapped around the barrel, I pulled the trigger."

I opened my eyes to see the two men standing in the hospital room with me, almost four years and nearly two thousand miles away from dying.

My heart thumped wildly, reliving the fear.

Dr. Katz nodded to me, understanding now how my career had ended with the New Mexico State Police. He'd asked me during my interview why I was willing to take a job in his office as a department manager, given my background. I told him I was injured in an assault and unable to return to duty.

In the corner, Matthew stood like a statue. His face was pale. Lips tight like he was willing himself not to speak.

I closed my eyes as the rest of the evening played out in my memory – I couldn't help myself. My brain had to run the whole scenario every time.

The first round I fired went through David's hand into the center of his chest, and I saw genuine surprise in his brown eyes. The gun slipped from his fingers. With all my remaining strength, I pulled the trigger again, and he took one staggering step backward and fell to the floor with a heavy thud.

My arms collapsed over my face. I lost consciousness again.

Someone called the police. The first responding officer arrived eight minutes later. I don't remember who it was, but I vaguely remember hearing panic in his voice as he radioed to dispatch for the ambulance to hurry, pressing on my neck to stop the bleeding.

I remember screaming in agony when they cut the nylon strip that held my wrists together and lowered my arms to my sides. Then nothing again.

My fellow officers and the emergency room staff went way beyond the call of duty to save my life that day. Looking at me, Eric

Rader said, no one was interested in what had happened to David. Apparently, I was more a mess than I could have realized.

Captain Rader stormed into the emergency room in Alamogordo and demanded to see me after I'd been given two units of blood and begun to make sense. He argued briefly with the doctor before coming to stand beside me.

I felt calm when Rader took my left hand.

His skin seemed hot against my cold fingers.

"Julie?"

I tried to open my eyes. One almost was swollen shut, and it was a huge effort to focus as they seemed to barely be under my control. I whispered his name and squeezed his hand.

"You're going to be okay, Julie."

If that was meant to be comforting, it wasn't.

"Can you tell me what happened?" he asked.

I was drugged with Demerol or morphine or something that wasn't quite doing its job, strapped snugly into a head immobilization device to keep me from moving my broken neck.

Honestly, I'd been hoping he would tell me.

Then the room had spun lazily, and my eyes closed again into blissful blackness I'd hoped was death.

"So what happened?" Matthew asked, interrupting my thoughts. His voice sounded irritated, impatient. "What had your husband done to you?"

"David had cut my throat, from below my left ear about two-thirds of the way around the front of my neck, leaving a laceration seven inches long, low and shallow," I said. "It barely missed the carotid arteries on both sides but nicked the left jugular vein, superficially cut the trachea half an inch below my larynx. I suffered multiple facial lacerations and fractures from the beating. My right shoulder had extensive ligament and cartilage damage as well as fractures of the collarbone and the upper arm itself. I had broken ribs, a broken sternum. Both knees and shins were bruised up. I had one broken vertebra in my neck and one in my lower back, most likely suffered when I got thrown down the stairs."

The adrenaline in my system subsided, and my heart began to slow.

"After that night, I spent a total of four months as a patient in either the hospital or in residential rehab, recovering from the injuries he inflicted before I shot him," I said. "It took another seven months and five more surgeries for doctors to put my body together. I'm lucky to be alive. But so much of my life ended that day, and I was still putting it together when I left New Mexico."

Honestly I was waiting for a day I would feel alive again. Occasionally, I still faced moments when I really didn't care whether I died, but not so many now.

"I took a lot of little steps along the way, forward and backward. Moving to Michigan was a big step to walking away from a past I tried very hard to forget. I didn't want it to follow me here," I concluded.

That secret had been revealed, but could I hide the rest?

CHAPTER 10

"I didn't leave because being a cop is something I can physically never do again. I left because I couldn't stand that look from people who knew I'd killed him. I didn't want to have to keep explaining how or why. Killing someone is not an easy thing to live with."

Dr. Katz nodded.

I turned to Matthew. "I shot David to survive, but it was still devastating. I felt little guilt that I shot him. And then I felt worse that maybe I didn't feel guilty enough, because I was glad he was dead after what he did to me."

My last memory of David was the impact of the bullets in his chest and that look on his face. At first, I celebrated in the blackest corners of my heart that he knew I'd won. Later, I realized all I had left were the nightmares and pain.

"So I came here, still putting pieces of me back together, learning how to live again. I only wanted it to be history. I'm sorry."

Matthew Shannaker shook his head and walked out of the room.

"He needs time to absorb this, Julie," Gerald Katz said me in a fatherly voice. "He's very fond of you, but that was a bit more than either of us expected."

"I'm really sorry."

"Most everyone has history that should stay in the past. Even me. No apology is necessary on my account, Julie." He stood to go.

An apology to Matt was still in order, but it wasn't like I could chase him down the hall.

"Um, for the record, Dr. Katz. There is more to the story that maybe you should know. Apparently David really had convinced someone at the base I was a spy."

Dr. Katz sat down to listen.

"I don't know exactly when it started, but for several months before the shooting, especially while David was gone, I'd noticed I was under a loose surveillance. He *told me* the house was bugged, but I didn't believe him, and besides, I had nothing to hide. They didn't try to keep me from knowing I was being tailed, but I wasn't sure who it was or exactly why. David told me that since I was born in Germany and my grandfather had been part of the Nazi movement, I must have connections there. He even suggested my grandfather might still be alive, making it easy for me to move sensitive information and money back and forth through Germany or other countries.

"Before I left New Mexico, I finally talked Captain Rader into looking up who had called 911 for me. The call originated from the airbase. Rader told me he found out that someone listening to the bug called the police after the gunshots. I would have died if they hadn't been listening, but they didn't call until I shot David. Whoever *they* were."

"I see. Was there ever any explanation for this?" he asked.

"Not to Captain Rader."

"Did you ask the Air Force?"

I shook my head. "I figured if they wouldn't tell a state police captain during an investigation of the death of a military officer, they wouldn't tell me, either."

Without any authority, there was no way I'd find any answers on my own. I had no desire to go back to Alamogordo for anything after I was released from the hospital. I'd even asked my mother to empty the townhouse and sell everything she didn't recognize as mine, then put the property on the market, too.

She brought back my Jeep, my motorcycle, and four boxes of belongings and clothes.

"We'll see if we can get to the bottom of all that later," he said. "You need to rest now. Telling us your story had to be very tiring."

Although Dr. Katz left, MaryAnne came after lunch.

I figured since my secret was out, I should tell her, too.

She listened to a more condensed version with the same nonjudgmental and sympathetic expression her husband had. She didn't ask many questions, but she had cried with me at the end.

We finally got past the tissues and tears.

"I don't understand what could possibly be left to cry about." I said.

Counseling was offered frequently during my physical recovery, but I refused, unwilling to reveal the anger and grief.

"I wouldn't have gone to David's funeral. I had nothing to do with the arrangements. His parents never visited me. They never sent a get-well card. I didn't tell them I was sorry. I don't know if anyone ever told them what really happened or if they think this is my fault."

David was dead. Bitter as it sounds, I still hoped he'd spend eternity in hell paying for my scars. "I'm not proud to say I'm happy he's dead, but I am. I survived. I walked away from all the memories I could. I live somewhere beautiful, and I work with terrific people doing something I really enjoy. I have wonderful friends like you around me. Why can't I let it go?"

MaryAnne looked at me with all her motherly wisdom and said, "You've done everything but forgive yourself."

And as usual, she was correct.

But forgiveness was something I still couldn't find, even for myself.

* * *

Matthew peeked around the door at midnight to see if I was awake.

"I hoped you'd come by," I said, waving him into the room.

He nodded and took a few steps inside my room, looked at the floor, then out the window into darkness. Wordless still, he finally sat down, but he didn't move the chair any closer.

This was exactly why I didn't want to tell people about my past. The silence.

"You can imagine how hard it's been to try to hide this in the back corner of the closet of skeletons I live with. It's painful to have people know about it. That's why I couldn't stay in New Mexico with the state police, even at a desk job. I didn't mean it to be a lie,

Matt, but I wanted to pretend it never happened."

He stared at me, struggling for something to say. Finally, he stood up and came to the side of the bed. "Show me," he said. He lifted my long hair away from my neck, and I pulled down the collar of the turtleneck so he could see the scar. "It never occurred to me you always wear shirts with turtlenecks or high collars."

"And long sleeves and scarves," I offered.

His voice wavered between accusation and understanding. "Is this why we never slept together? You didn't want me to see the scars and ask?"

"We've been friends, and I wasn't looking for anything more. I didn't think you were, either. Hiding the scars might be part of the reason I didn't want a different relationship, but I have scars on the inside, too. It's hard, knowing I'd loved a man who could do this to me. I'm still afraid."

"Afraid of what? That I would ever hurt you like that?" he asked, his feelings twisted on his face.

"Afraid you couldn't accept me, knowing I'd killed him. That I don't regret it."

"If he had been anyone else, would you feel so bad about shooting him in self-defense?"

"I don't feel bad that I shot him," I said. "I feel like I'm supposed to feel bad and I don't, so that's why I hide it."

"He assaulted you with deadly force. He was killing you, and you shot him. Screw the idea you should feel any differently about that because his name was on your marriage license." He sat down on the bed beside me. "I can't imagine how much that's changed your life, Julie. I'm sorry I was such a jerk."

We sat for a long time in silence. What else could I say?

"I understand why you wanted to protect your privacy. Everyone has secrets to keep." He smiled. "I really should have known you were a cop. It's so clear now, some of the things you've said and done."

I shrugged and smiled back.

"I know it's really late, Julie, but I need your help on the case," he said.

"Okay," I said, unsure what he meant.

He went to the door and motioned in two men. One was in a Grand Traverse Sheriff's Department uniform; the other wore an expensive well-tailored suit. He introduced them as Detective Sergeant Brandan Callaghan and FBI Special Agent Nolan Forrester, who was consulting on the case.

"This really couldn't wait any longer," Matt explained. "Your knack for details and theories will be a huge step forward in the Tucker case. I took a chance that if you were awake, this might be okay."

I didn't argue, but I felt a little tag-teamed.

Forrester spoke up with typical FBI authority. "I understand you've been through quite an ordeal, Ms. Madigan, but I believe that the brain tends to fill in details, given time to process them. You were the only one who saw the sublevel of the barn intact. Can you tell us about it? Anything you can recall."

"Look, I've been unconscious and drugged –" I began, but Matt cut me off.

"Julie, just tell us what you saw. Close your eyes and talk. Start with when I called you Sunday morning."

"Right. I got out of bed to answer the phone and broke my toes against the bedpost," I said and rolled my eyes. "No guarantees on any of this."

I started with Matthew calling me at home, trying to fall into a stream of memory of the day. I hoped that by telling it in a long sequence of events, maybe my memory would not stumble on any big holes.

"What surprised me about the barn was the wooden floor," I explained. "The part of the barn where Tucker was found used to be plain dirt floor, like the rest of the barn, but a wooden flooring had been built in that corner, over the chamber. Expensive deck wood. Newer than anything else in the barn, though it did show a little wear, so I'm guessing it was a couple of years old. The trap door was cut to exactly fit the boards in the floor. The grain matched. We should have video if the cameras survived. The door didn't have a handle, but it didn't look like it had been pried open using a bar like we did. There must have been another way to get it up.

"There was a single bulb hanging at the bottom of the stairs. I had to stand on the last step to reach the string, so I'd guess from that he is over six feet tall if he could reach it from the floor. The risers were all clean going down, no mud or oil that I saw. No denting or scrapes in the wood like moving heavy objects could cause, no wheel marks from a dolly. You need to figure out how he lowered the barrels."

I opened my eyes and took a sip of water.

They were watching me carefully.

"There were no visible shoe prints on either the stairs or the floor, no stains or tracks in the dirt. It was packed hard. I saw brush marks, so he swept the floor to remove tracks. I saw nothing remarkable on the one dirt wall by the stairs. The other two walls were shored up with inexpensive lumber, secure but not perfect. The fourth was mostly stone from the wall above. He's a decent carpenter, considering the construction of the flooring, but he didn't waste time on unnecessary perfection below. There was a lot of time invested in this hole, but not for show."

"Go on," Forrester said, nodding. "This is excellent."

"I wanted to take samples of the lumber, look for markings, see if we could get a local distributor. Same with the flooring."

"What about the barrels?" Callaghan asked.

I opened my mouth to speak, but other than a blur of safety orange, there was nothing in my memory to describe. "I'm sorry, I know there were five. One was empty. I . . . "

"We'll need measurements, if you can," Callaghan said, scribbling in his little notebook.

I was searching for some other description, but there was nothing. A blank in my memory. "I'd have to stand up for perspective in size." I felt stuck on that detail. "I don't remember any markings on them."

Matthew took advantage of the silence and asked, "What did you feel down there, Julie? What did it mean?"

That got Forrester's attention, but he didn't speak.

"It was very clean. Deliberately clean." I paused, focusing on my gut feelings. "Why would a killer maintain a storage room so carefully for his kills when he destroys the bodies in acid? The storage of a victim might be a part of the ritual or of the kill itself, but

I didn't feel this was a monument. It was a collection site or hiding place, not a memorial." I looked at Matthew. "I don't know what else Dr. Katz found with the male victim, but I'd guess there is evidence indicating another man was involved in this, right?"

Forrester shot Matt a look that would have shattered glass.

"I swear I didn't say a thing. She's very good at this," Matt shrugged. "So tell her."

With obvious reluctance, Forrester told me Katz and the FBI forensic anthropologist had agreed there was evidence of repeated sodomy of Tucker, including semen that was being sent for DNA profile. The acid he'd drunk was extremely corrosive, and they estimate it had been consumed within half an hour of the time Tucker was found. They had not immediately identified the grainy meat-type substance in the small intestines, poorly digested but well past the stomach.

I sniffed air that smelled like hospital. "Dog food," I said, earning looks of surprise. "Something cheap."

Matt began to nod. "Yeah, I remember that smell."

Forrester explained the forensic teams hadn't made much progress with identification of the bodies in the barrels. "The barrels did rupture, but the bodies were not significantly damaged by the blast. They started with what appears to be the most recent, and there is a strong possibility her throat was cut. No clothing. They were all nude, apparently."

I tugged at the collar of my silk turtleneck.

I saw Matthew watching a motion he'd probably seen hundreds of times and now understood the significance.

"Young adult, between 18 and 25," Callaghan said. "Average height and build."

"Were they dismembered?" I asked.

"No, it didn't appear so."

"Surely they are not all from this area. I guess this was the 'they' Tucker's note referred to on the wood? 'Sorry they're dead. I didn't' – but he didn't *what*? Kill them?" I stopped and took another sip of water. "My opinion is Tucker was killed by whoever killed these victims."

"His fingerprints are on the bottle," Callaghan argued. "No

others."

"Yeah, even if he bought it brand new, there'd be someone else's prints on it," I contended. "The call was made knowing Tucker had consumed the acid, but while he was alive. In his condition, he couldn't have made that call from the gas station and gone back. So who called 911?"

Three men nodded.

"I think his death was a stage show, even if he chose to drink the acid, but for whom?" I asked. "Matt, from where Tucker was shackled, could he have reached the door to open it?"

Matt shook his head. "No, nor would he have any leverage or tools."

"So he must be another victim," I concluded.

"You don't think Tucker killed those people in the barrels?" Callaghan tried again.

"Tucker is either the killer or a victim, but it doesn't make sense he was both. If he was the killer, why leave a warning about the bomb in his own blood?"

"He could simply be a coincidental victim, perhaps he stumbled onto the killer's hideout," Forrester argued.

"You're back to who called 911, and it can't have been Tucker. There is evidence of another male, and the caller was male," Matthew stated. "DNA evidence will be key. But why didn't Tucker identify the killer?"

"Maybe he tried. There is the possibility the letters B-O meant something else," I said. "That third character could also have been an L or any incomplete letter with a left downward stroke, such as B, D, E, F, etc. After the detonation, we guessed it was BOMB, but why not a name? I should have known it wasn't an 'I.' Few English words start with those three letters except names."

"You provided good information, Ms. Madigan. Callaghan tells me you were with the state police in New Mexico?" Forrester concluded.

Wow, word gets around fast if a detective is telling the FBI now.

"I was in a public safety department in the White Sands area. We did everything – police, fire and EMS. Not your typical state police unit," I said.

I thought about the duties the state police public safety unit handled in the three-county region around Alamogordo. Despite the lack of dense population, auto crashes, often with alcohol and high speeds as contributing factors, were routine. Other death investigations were less frequent, such as the gang-related shootings and stabbings, drug dealing, and domestic violence.

And then we had our really nasty calls.

Like the drug-addicted teenage mother who was so angry with her screaming infant, she shoved the three-month-old into the oven. Then she went to the K-Mart where she was busted for shoplifting and possession. It was only when she called her parents to come bail her out that anyone brought up the infant.

No, we were not in time.

Or the guys who drove around the neighborhoods in the middle of the night, setting fire after fire, apparently knowing responders would never be able to get to them all. Once every emergency unit in the area was tied up on residential fires, the criminals broke the windows out of fourteen downtown stores. Their timing coincided with a full moon and the Sunday of a Thanksgiving weekend when the businesses had a good deal of cash on hand.

As I recall, the spree netted them over $54,000 in cash and electronic merchandise. It cost the lives of two elderly people in their home, six more families their houses and all their belongings, and cost the county more than $40,000 in Workers' Comp claims for two injured officers.

These two guys aren't worthy of rotting in jail, but will probably be out before I turn 40, despite a solid conviction on multiple counts.

So along the way, my career provided a sliver of insight into what criminals do, and the methods they choose on the paths of least resistance.

"Who taught you to profile criminals?" Forrester asked, bringing my attention back to the hospital room.

"I'm not profiling the perpetrator," I explained. "Profiling looks at the crime and guesses demographics. I look at a situation and look for behavior patterns under stress. By looking at evidence and circumstances, I guess what sort of probable human behavior might result in the future, given certain motives." I shook my head. "Either way, you don't get a name."

CHAPTER 11

If the nurses bothered me the rest of the night, I was unaware of it. I woke to the soft knock I'd come to recognize as MaryAnne's.

"I brought bagels and cream cheese," she said, setting the bag down. She scurried into the bathroom and returned with a warm wet washcloth for me to wash my face and hands. "They're fresh," she continued, arranging paper plates and napkins on the table, pulling out food like a magician pulls rabbits from a hat. "Oh, and strawberries. You're not allergic, are you?"

"Not at all," I said, smearing a glob of cream cheese on a toasted bagel that was still warm. "You amaze me. How could any human be so cheerful and organized in the morning?"

She actually blushed. "Yes, but it's lights out at ten these days. Keeping up with a doctor's schedule and two teenage girls is not easy."

"Isn't that the truth? I don't mean to intrude," Dr. Harper said from the doorway, "I won't interrupt such a lovely breakfast, but I thought I'd offer you a chance to have lunch in the privacy of your own home today."

"Oh, and I was just getting used to the sandpaper linens here," I quipped. "Sign on the dotted line and I'm outta here?"

"First, the rules. You have to promise you will go home. You are to be on limited activities for a week. It's simple," he directed me. "If you think it might hurt, don't do it. If it hurts, don't do it again. If it hurts and two Darvocet don't make it stop, call me."

Comfortable I understood his medicalese, he continued with details that my head injury could still manifest symptoms at any time. I was to return to the emergency department for fever, headache not relieved by Tylenol or the Darvocet, nausea and vomiting, confusion, numbness or tingling in my hands or feet, and so on.

I nodded solemnly as he went through his conditions for discharge.

"And you promise to cooperate with the police?" he concluded.

"Sure, I had a lengthy chat with three of them last night," I said. "I told them everything I remembered."

His eyebrows scrunched and he shook his head. "No, the ones assigned to protect you."

I opened my mouth to argue I didn't know I was supposed to be protected, that I didn't need to be protected. But I was smart enough to understand such a line of rebuttal would earn me another day in the hospital to reconsider the idea. "Oh, yes, of course," I said instead. "Full cooperation."

I'm not sure he bought that as a promise, but he let me go.

Bless MaryAnne. She had already brought street clothes when she dropped by my house for silk turtleneck shirts the first day. She even remembered to bring my sunglasses.

While I was changing, she packed up everything from my closet in drawstring plastic bags from the hospital. I signed a hundred forms and escaped before someone had a change of plans.

MaryAnne drove me home, and then she insisted on going shopping to replace what the evidence teams had considered possibly contaminated and removed. Cereal, bread, sugar, salt and pepper, flour, butter. Everything not sealed in a can, jar or bottle, basically. Hadn't been much food for them to remove, but they did leave me a grocery list of sorts - a copy of the evidence record.

How thoughtful.

Other items I was surprised to see on the list – shampoo and conditioner, soap, detergent, lotions, anything I might apply to my skin. My makeup was gone, not that there was much. All my non-prescription drugs – aspirin, Tylenol, cold remedies, vitamins. A couple of bottles of prescription drugs, too. All would have to be replaced.

"They can't throw out all that!" MaryAnne exclaimed on my behalf.

Well, yes, they could.

At least they didn't take the nine remaining bottles from a case of wine I'd bought a few months ago at a local vineyard, probably because they had metal caps instead of cork. Someone had removed the seal around the neck of one bottle to determine this before taking them away.

I don't drink anything expensive, but it's the principle. I'd only drunk three bottles of the dozen, and knowing the alcohol had been poured down the drain would have pissed me off.

Like the rest of this hasn't?

From the evidence list, I copied items that I might need over the next few days – milk, bread, butter, sandwich makings. It seemed silly to buy things I didn't use. I couldn't remember the last time I needed flour or oregano. No reason to get sunscreen in September. I could do without ice cream for a few days.

I called the pharmacy with a list of refills, explaining to the pharmacist my unusual circumstances.

I gave MaryAnne the lists.

"This can't be all you need, Julie," she said, browsing my kitchen and bath for ideas of her own before she finally left me in the quiet of my home.

Thinking of her maternal instincts reminded me I still hadn't talked to my mother since the explosion.

In her mid-fifties now, my mother is that busy-all-the-time social creature some widowed women simply become, on top of being a nurse at University of New Mexico Hospital in Albuquerque. Of all things, in the last few years, she took up both horseback riding and photography. Last time we talked, she was planning a ride with a few of her friends into the Pecos Mountains. She left me e-mail saying she would return around September 5 or 6.

Without knowing what sort of national coverage the explosion received, I was glad she wouldn't have seen any of it. I didn't want to tell her everything that had happened, but apparently mothers have to know.

I dialed her number.

"Hello?" a man's voice answered.

The surprise caught in my throat.

"Hello?" he repeated.

I cleared my throat and tried again. "May I speak to Dagmar?" I asked, pronouncing it as she did, with soft vowels.

There was a slight pause. "Sure, one moment."

There was background conversation and then an exchange of the receiver.

"Hello?" Musically, those two syllables used about four notes.

"Hey, Mom. How are you?"

"I'm splendid, Julie! I got your message. How are you doing? Snow yet?" she jibed.

"Not yet. How was your trip to the mountains? Did you have a good time?"

"Marvelous. You should have come. I've tons of photos to send you." She chatted on about the ride, pulling a four-horse trailer up to the trailhead, twenty miles of bad road that took nearly two hours. "The horses could have pulled the truck and trailer faster," she laughed. "I wasn't sure they wouldn't have preferred that. Probably was worse coming back down."

"Who answered the phone?" I hoped it didn't sound like an accusation, but I could hear her smiling as she spoke.

"That was Everett. He didn't get to make the trip with us either, so I invited him over to see the photos. He's busy in the kitchen." Then she whispered as if in conspiracy, "I tried your idea of finding a man who can cook. Really very clever, dear."

"It can certainly have its advantages."

She told me she met Everett in March waiting for the tram, heading up for a day of spring skiing at Sandia Peak. He saw her camera and started a conversation. He was a professional freelance photographer and traveled, but they'd gone out on occasion when he was in town.

"He has a cabin down near Ruidoso and has asked me to spend a weekend there with him this fall."

I guess I was a little surprised to hear my widowed mother had been going out with a man long enough for an overnight trip. But it was apparently news she didn't wish to continue discussing.

"I've found a fine six-year-old gelding I'm thinking of buying," she said changing the subject. "I'll send you pictures."

"Shall I give you the same lecture you gave me when I bought the motorcycle, Mom?" I teased.

"Well, I'm hardly going to be hit by a drunk driver in the middle of the mountains, Julie."

"Yeah, and my Harley has never stepped on my foot, kicked me, or bucked me off and left me to walk home. It doesn't bite. It stops when I brake and doesn't bolt from loud noises. Oh, and I don't have to feed it when I don't ride or muck the garage all winter."

"Point taken, but it won't stop and feed itself when it gets low on gas, either." She laughed. "So have you been out riding lately?"

Since she hadn't mentioned it, I was sure she hadn't heard about the barn incident.

"Not for several weeks. It's almost time to tuck it away for winter," I paused. "I suppose you didn't hear about this on the news. There was an explosion at the scene of an investigation where I was, Mom, but I'm okay."

So I told a lie. I'm not exactly sure what size the lie was, but not very big.

I explained how I ended up in the hospital, skipping the tainted candy. Traumatic injuries she could handle. Street drugs scared the shit out of her.

The conversation consisted of her motherly nursing inquisition regarding my state of health. She was especially concerned about the possibility of re-injuring my neck.

"Everything seems fine," I lied again, splinting my sore ribs with my arm. "A bonk on the head and a few scratches."

Okay, so I left out the part about being unconscious. She didn't ask specifically. *That really wasn't a lie, was it?*

I stretched out on my bed as we talked, but I found I couldn't be horizontal, so I got up and wandered around my house with my cordless phone, half listening to her voice, half looking for missing objects.

"I wish you'd come down for Thanksgiving. Will you try?" she asked in that motherly guilt-inducing tone. "It would be good to see you. I'm worried about you now."

What she meant was that she was even *more* worried. She was a professional when it came to me, especially after what David had done.

"I'll check on a flight, or maybe I'll drive down. But right now, this case is pretty deep. I'll check with Dr. Katz and call you soon, okay? I love you."

"I love you, too, darling. Take care," she said and hung up.

I sank down onto the couch, taking full measure of how it felt to know someone had not only drugged me but had broken into my house to find out how to do it. Violated twice. Someone had pilfered my things, looking for something in particular. The crime scene techs removed practically everything else. It seemed a fruitless chore, replacing everything that might have been drugged or poisoned. And even if the evidence team did remove all the possible substances that could have been contaminated, I couldn't stay here forever to guard them after I replaced them.

He gained entry once, why not a second time? How much effort had it taken him to send me drugged candy or leave me a note on my pillow?

My stomach churned. There were no antacids in the cabinet.

I strolled over to my fish tank, happy to see none were floating dead or missing, so I figured Dr. Katz had fed them. The tang floated to the glass, blowing me little kisses. The red anemone waved in the current. The clown fish darted lazily through the bubbles nearby. A seahorse swayed in the current from a piece of rock. The candy stripe shrimp danced across the bottom.

The bubbling was normally very soothing to me, but not today. The noise seemed to rumble through my skull like a jet engine.

How would I ever feel safe?

I remembered feeling that way in Trauma ICU when David nearly killed me, but this was worse. At least then, I knew David wasn't coming after me again, no matter how real the dreams seemed.

What if the techs missed something in the house? Should I risk eating anything?

What if it's the guy who delivers my pizza?

Should I even be here? Where would I be safe?

"Stop it," I told myself out loud. "It's a power trip, a game of terror."

I walked through the house again to see what else was missing besides the food and other possibly contaminated stuff. But I realized it wasn't just food or personal substances that could be contaminated. LSD could be saturated into my clothing or linens and then absorbed through my skin.

I decided to launder my sheets as a starting point – when MaryAnne returned with detergent.

The anxiety ratcheted up another notch.

I started into my office where anything of real value in my house would likely be. Nothing seemed to be missing, but there were things that weren't sitting the way I'd left them. My chair was pulled away from the desk, for example.

Of course, the crime scene crew moved things around.

Then I saw what was wrong. On the far corner of my desk was a bright yellow 3-1/2 inch floppy with a coffee cup sitting square on top of it.

Instinctively, my right hand went to my hip, reaching for the security of a gun that wasn't there.

CHAPTER 12

Geez, how outdated was that habit?

My gun.

It hadn't been returned to me at the hospital when I was discharged. Wasn't in the bags MaryAnne packed for me.

How the hell could I have forgotten that?

I went to the kitchen and picked up the cordless phone again. *Call who?* The anxiety doubled to panic. I went to my bedroom and yanked open the nightstand on my side of the bed.

The Glock 17x9 I usually carried stayed in the holster with my vest, but I kept the Smith & Wesson 5904 in my bedside table.

It wasn't there.

Great. Two guns missing.

The phone chirped in my hand. I almost dropped it.

This is entirely out of hand.

"Madigan," I answered.

"I'm curious, do you ever just say 'hello'?" Matt asked. "On vacation, maybe?"

Cutting past the warm-fuzzy small talk about how I was feeling, I blurted, "Where are my guns?"

"I called to – what gun?"

"Guns. Plural. Did the evidence team take any weapons from the house? And where is the Glock I was carrying the day of the explosion? MaryAnne said they had cut off my clothes, but neither the gun nor the holster were in what I brought home from the hospital this morning." I sounded near hysteria. "The 9 mm I keep in the drawer next to the bed is missing."

"Slow down, Julie. I took your Glock at the hospital. It's here at the station in my locker," he said. "I know that Smith 9 mm was in your bedside table when I found the note, but I don't know about when they inventoried. I also saw the J-frame revolver in your dresser."

I tried to be rational. I got up and looked – the Smith & Wesson Centennial .38 was still where he said.

"I'll check with Glenn Corbitt," Matt said, meaning the crime scene director. "Maybe the techs took it to lockup. Hang on. I'll call him right now."

Whatever I meant to say didn't come out as words.

"What's wrong, Julie?"

"Did the evidence team print anything, maybe take photographs?"

"I don't know exactly what they did. Let me get Glenn. We'll get everything and be right over," he said, waiting for my approval.

"Yeah, okay."

I pushed the disconnect button on the phone, slumping as I had Sunday morning when I broke my toes.

It seemed like so long ago.

The phone rang again. Too quickly to be Matt, I thought.

"Madi— Hello," I said, changing my mind about my phone manners.

A male voice I did not recognize chuckled softly. "It's good you've made it home, Julia. I left you a couple of gifts. Did you find them?"

"Who is this?" I demanded, jumping to my feet. Pain shot through my ribs but the woozy feeling washed away with adrenaline.

"All in good time. I bet you've located my inanimate present, haven't you? But you haven't opened it yet. Waiting for your deputy friend, I suppose." His voice was very authoritative, a smooth baritone. "Don't forget to look for the other gift. And even though you haven't thanked me for all my presents, Julia, welcome home, anyway. I'll be in touch soon."

"Wait! Tell me —" but I was talking to a dead connection.

I sat down on the bed. Hundreds of things ran through my head, needing to be sorted out, but I couldn't grasp any of them. I leaned back and pulled the unmade bedclothes up under my head as a pillow. I closed my eyes.

Two gifts.

One inanimate.

I'd found the disk, which was certainly not alive. The only living things in my house were the very few plants that survived of their own tenacity, and my fish.

I got up and made my way to the saltwater tank that takes up a good portion of one wall of the den. The tang, two clowns, a pair of candy-cane shrimp, a small sea horse now anchored to a swaying plant. There was nothing else, I thought, and was about to turn away when I saw the slightest movement at the back of the tank, near the rocks.

I leaned closer and saw a tiny puffer fish, hiding shyly.

CHAPTER 13

Checking his notes and Polaroid shots, Glenn Corbitt was able to verify neither the coffee cup nor the disk were on my desk when the team was there collecting evidence.

"So he's been in here twice, at least. He called me just to chat," I yelled at no one in particular. "Deadbolts haven't stopped him. What am I supposed to do?"

Laser offered his suggestion as a low growl from his corner of my living room, then went back to his state of pre-nap relaxation.

"Let's look at his disk," Matt offered. "We could take it to the office?"

"No, he wants me to read it – might as well be here where he left it."

Glenn finished with the coffee cup. "Nothing on here as far as prints. Maybe saliva on the rim, but the cup appears unused," he apologized. "I doubt there's any prints on the disk or the drawer, but I'll work on them."

Instead, I diverted him to my fish tank, specifically those parts one would have to touch to add a fish, then I went back and sat down in my chair, powered up the computer and waited for it to boot up and flash the screen for a password.

"Any chance he could have bypassed this?" Matt asked.

"My guess is that if he could have, he wouldn't have left the disk," I answered, putting on a glove to handle the disk. "It would be far more intrusive for me to find it on my hard drive."

Glenn offered from across the house, "Couldn't he have booted up from a floppy disk?"

"Not on my computer. All boot-ups require a password."

Not that my information is any more sacred than anyone else's, I've made it a point to keep my PC from being tampered with because I can.

I only wish my house had been so secure.

The floppy disk contained four files. One was named "sharp.exe," an executable program, so I ran it. The floppy drive whirred. The screen went black for a moment, then a photo image revealed a photograph of a knife, displayed on a piece of white cloth.

Matt and I stared at the screen while my printer worked on the color image. It looked like a plain kitchen knife with a corroded blade. Meaningless without context.

Unsure what to do next, I tapped the space bar, the enter key, and finally the page-down button, which changed the screen to the next image, which was a pencil or charcoal sketch of two people on the floor, a man and woman, drawn in detail. On the floor nearby was a knife similar to the previous photo image. There was what appeared to be blood on the floor and on the woman. The edges faded to white.

The third image was a color photograph of a nude young woman, laid out on some surface covered with a cloth, her slashed throat gaping open. The focus was haunting. She should have been bloody. Instead, her skin was clean and pale.

I swallowed hard, struggling to keep both hands from reaching for my own throat to make sure there was no blood. Irrational, yes. Controllable, no.

The screen went black. I copied the image files to my hard drive and gave the disk to Glenn. "Get us color prints as large as they'll print clearly. Then send the disk directly to Quinton Gresham at the FBI Computer Analysis Response Team, and tell him it's from me. He can work on the details." I printed the address from my contacts list.

He nodded, tucked it into an evidence bag, and closed his cases to leave. "Sorry about all this," he said. "Maybe we should have collected the guns."

"Why would you even think about it? But I've got something you may want."

Going to the spare bedroom closet, I reached behind a box of books to a fireproof safe. I spun the dial combination and pulled the door open. I browsed folder tabs to one labeled "Firearms" and pulled it out, looking for papers on the missing gun. Attached was a small manila envelope with two bullets and casings.

I shut the safe door and tried to stand up, but under the crushing weight of emotions, I wilted to my knees, tears in my eyes. I was being manipulated by a maniac who now had one of my guns. I very well could have sat there and bawled, but I heard MaryAnne's voice in the kitchen. I knew if she found me crying, she'd want to stay.

Struggling to my feet and to regain my composure, I stopped to check my face in the bathroom mirror, then joined them in the kitchen.

"Ballistic comparisons," I said, handing Glenn the envelope. "I hope you don't need them."

He nodded solemnly, fearing the same thing I did. There's something uniquely nauseating about having a gun stolen – hopes it doesn't get used in a murder.

MaryAnne separated my groceries into groups – refrigerator, freezer, canned and dry food, and toiletries. She helped me put everything away while Matt squared things with Glenn Corbitt.

"I won't stay," she said when we were done, handing me my car keys. "Gerald brought your Suburban, so he's waiting for me. Make a list of anything I've forgotten. I'll check again tomorrow when I get ready to do my shopping." She hugged me. "Call if you need anything."

I thanked her again.

Glenn took his leave as well.

Not even three o'clock, and I was exhausted.

Matthew went to his car and returned, handing me my Glock in its shoulder rigging. "Sorry, I meant to tell you I took it from EMS and put it in my locker. We got a little side-tracked."

I felt vaguely more at ease.

We went through a criminal complaint report for the stolen gun.

Then he sat with me on my sofa for a long time, not saying anything while I cried. I must have dozed off – the next thing I knew, he was paying for pizza.

He sat down the box and got a roll of paper towels from the kitchen as well as two bottles of Lowenbrau Dark I hadn't seen MaryAnne bring in.

"I don't know you well enough to know where to start with this case, Julie. Help me out. I have to learn what someone else either knows or could find out about you. Like you say, knowing why he picked you may help figure it out. Can you do that? Tell me who you really are, from the beginning."

CHAPTER 14

"Oh, sure, Matt, you want to know everything? The history of Julie Ann Madigan, Day 1 to present." I took a bite of pizza.

"No, before that even."

"There isn't that much beer," I said gruffly. I got up to find some Tylenol for my headache but didn't find any in MaryAnne's restocked supplies. I didn't want to mix narcotics with alcohol, and I really wanted the beer.

"Okay, here's what I know about me," I said, eyeing the tape recorder Matt had placed on the table between us.

"Maybe there's something really important." He shrugged with a grin. "I can't take notes and eat pizza at the same time."

More past. Try for fewer skeletons this time."My father's parents lived near Detroit. We had visited them a few times when I was eleven or twelve. His father, Clyde Madigan, had worked for General Motors from his teens to retirement. June, my father's mother, died young, leaving three children, Jeff, Kate, and Thomas, my father," I explained. "I never knew much about his family when I was younger, other than my grandfather was a grouchy old man who would rather fish than just about anything else. My mother hated the water."

My mother was from Germany, or more specifically what became West Germany within months of my birth. My grandmother, Margot, was married to Julian Damrosch, who had suspected in 1936 what was ahead, so he sent his wife and two children back to Margot's family in Mannheim before Hitler's regime engulfed them all.

From what my mother told me, her father never returned. Her

mother refused to believe he might have been killed during the war, but she feared he'd been involved in Hitler's activities. Even though she never heard from him again directly, she received an occasional envelope of money dropped into her basket by a stranger who passed her in the market or on the street. She refused to spend it, uncertain of its roots and afraid of its strings. But she saved it for her children. That money paid my mother's way through nursing school at the Deaconess Institute at Kaiserwerth near Dusseldorf, then she moved back into her mother's home and worked for a local doctor.

"In 1957, there was an outbreak of flu, and many of the nurses at the Second General Hospital in Landstuhl were out sick, so a few local nurses were helping out. My parents met when my father was airlifted to the closest U.S. military hospital – Ramstein Air Force Base – for leg burns that had become infected while his ship, the aircraft carrier *USS Lake Champlain*, was in the Baltic Sea."

Apparently it was love at second or third sight. Dad said he spilled his soup the next day so she'd have to give him a bed bath.

"What a man won't do to get a woman's attention," Matt muttered, shaking his head.

"My dad was there for several weeks, and afterward, he vowed to come to Germany again when he could. He must have spent all his time writing to her and saved his paychecks so he could go back to see her. She still has all his letters tucked away in a trunk."

"Wow, that's love. My mom didn't even keep her wedding ring when my dad died," he mused.

"They married the next summer, when the *Lake Champlain* returned to the Mediterranean," I said, "and he managed six days of shore leave. But my grandmother was aging and ill, so my mother decided not to leave Germany until my father could be stationed back in the States. Then she learned she was pregnant.

"I was a bit premature, and my mother was in active labor in the backseat of my grandmother's car at the gates of the base. But because neither my mother nor my grandmother had any identification with them and could not prove that my father was a U.S. soldier, they were turned away. My mother nearly bled to death when the placenta ruptured before I was born, so the doctors did a hysterectomy, which explains why I'm an only child. And when my mother nearly died, my grandmother named me, so my original birth certificate read Julia Ann Damrosch, after my grandfather."

"Not Julie?" he asked.

"Nope. It seems like a minor thing, one vowel, but that's the way my mother wanted it – Julie Ann. But that name thing complicated the situation when Dad got ready to move us to the States because my mother's passport was already made out with her married name of Madigan. Took my parents weeks to get all the paperwork corrected with my 'official' name."

My father's next assignment, new family in tow, was Bremerton and then to Whidbey Island Naval Stations in Washington.

"Dad was one of those guys who was very smart about electronics but not so sharp on other things. He could wire an entire ship by himself but couldn't drive a nail straight. By the time he retired, he had worked his way into the cutting edge of the personal computer industry."

I loved being near the water in Washington, but they didn't think it was family entertainment. – my dad had spent enough time on a ship, and my mother never learned to swim. They were relieved when he was offered a job in Albuquerque when he was ready to retire from the military. I think it only took telling my mother there was very little water in New Mexico and no coastline to get her to start packing.

"Dad worked for an electronics company designing circuit boards and memory chips. Long before Silicon Valley was a booming computer capital, Sandia Digital Engineering was moving toward the changes in computing from vacuum tubes to transistors. Mom got her nursing license worked out and went to work at the University of New Mexico Hospital in the nursery. They bought a house in the Heights near Eugene and Menaul, not far from Dad's shop on Menaul," I said.

"So that's where you learned about computers, right?" Matt asked

I nodded."Dad taught me about computers as he learned. He was working on motherboards, trying to design more efficient processors. He helped me build my first computer when I was in junior high school. It didn't do much in comparison to today's processors and personal computers, but I was the first kid in school to have one. It was the size of an ottoman," I said with a laugh, then thought about how it ended. "I was sixteen when my father was murdered. I was actually there in the building when he was shot. Maybe that's when I decided on law enforcement as a career." My heart raced. "All those psychological exams asked why I wanted to become a police officer, and I always answered that I wanted to protect others."

It's a fact; it's just not the truth. I don't exactly know why I earned a badge.

I investigated my options with the state police, and though I might have been accepted to the academy straight out of high school, having a degree solidified my application, as did having completed paramedic school. While I was at the University of New Mexico, mostly what I learned was I really loved being in school. I finished my master's degree in psychology while I was at the state police academy.

The one case that boosted my career more than any education, however, was also the most disturbing incident I could have imagined at the time. Although I had transferred down to Otero County to a public safety position, I was in Albuquerque for a week-long training.

I had heard from my mother when she got home from work that night about a woman who'd gone into labor and had her baby all alone in a car that afternoon. Mom had been in the nursery when the woman and baby were brought in by ambulance. She said the mother had told her how she and her husband had been at odds over the pregnancy, barely getting by without the financial demands of a baby. Mom described how the new parents had cried together. The father had told the mother they would make it somehow.

I remember my mother saying how beautiful that baby was and how sorry she felt for the mother.

But the next morning, while I was flipping through the channels during breakfast, I heard the first details about a pregnant woman who had been kidnapped at knifepoint from outside the Kirtland Air Force Base clinic. What I learned later was how she was forced to ride around town for a while then was driven east into the Tijeras Mountains, where the assailant had cut her belly open and taken the baby, leaving the mother tied to the tree.

I called my mother into the kitchen in time to see a photo of a woman named Darcy Pierce flashed on the screen.

"That's her!" she exclaimed. "That's the mother."

Toast and oatmeal congealed into a rock in my stomach. I had to tell my mother what I'd heard on the news. The woman she'd felt sorry for wasn't a mother, but a murderer.

She was stunned and then plain pissed off. That was the first time in years I'd heard my mother stomp around the room, cursing in German.

I had to be at class at 7:30. Before the morning session started at the training, I was pulled aside by a captain, who asked if I would be interested in shadowing his detective on this same case. I was astonished, but eager to follow the case out, because of my mother's passing involvement.

I accompanied Criminal Investigations Lieutenant Manny Salazar in his car, following in the parade of vehicles out into the mountains.

Because of the circumstances, at least half dozen jurisdictions were involved: the Air Force Military Police, Bernalillo County Sheriff Department, Albuquerque Police, New Mexico State Police, the FBI, the National Park Service, etc.

Darcy, who finally confessed she had not given birth to the baby after extensive questioning by the hospital staff and later the police, led us up to where her victim, the baby's dead mother, was still tied to a tree. Her abdomen was gaped open, her clothes bloody.

Pierce had killed a woman to steal her baby. Not just killed her, but kidnapped her and then ripped her abdomen open with a car key, leaving her to die.

I'm sure being female was the biggest reason I was chosen, and I stayed in Albuquerque for two weeks, following around state police criminal investigators, special agents, warrant officers and medical examiner investigators, all as affected by the story Darcy told as I was and tried to never let it show.

I returned from that trip with a promotion to senior patrolman and my first boost up the career ladder. After more than two years of driving back and forth to Las Cruces for fire academy and arson investigation courses, I had just made sergeant when I met David.

"Why did you come to Michigan?" Matt asked.

"Timing. Dr. Katz offered me a job I thought I'd like," I said.

He laughed and got us each another beer.

"The rest you know," I said, finding the pizza long gone. "So tell me, has anything you learned about me made *you* want to start killing people?"

CHAPTER 15

I woke at dawn with stiff muscles and a headache. My ribs were tender. When I turned my head, I felt the bones in my neck grind slightly. Nothing new, just not comfortable.

Matt left sometime after midnight.

Coffee. I hope MaryAnne bought coffee.

I made my way to my feet, stretched and put on a terrycloth robe, and made a stop in the bathroom. When I looked in the mirror, the face looking back had dark circles under its eyes, like the same person I'd seen the last time I'd been in an Albuquerque hospital. I didn't like her – she had a lot of secrets, and now some of them weren't buried any more.

After searching all the kitchen cabinets, I gave up on finding coffee and opened the freezer looking for juice instead, only to find the can of Folger's stashed there.

Thanks, MaryAnne.

I scooped coffee into the filter basket and filled the reservoir with water, then sat down at the counter to wait.

The six minutes it took for the water to drip through the coffee seemed like an hour. I poured myself a cup, briefly considered topping it off with Irish cream. There was no sense looking. I walked through the house again.

My home.

Neither large nor elegant, it was big enough for my needs. But today, the rooms felt foreign. The walls seemed to close in around me, shrinking each time I made a lap, feeding the emotional violation of the intrusions.

Another cup of coffee.

Three is enough, don't you think?

Time for a shower.

No, maybe I should work out first.

Yeah, right. Not with cracked ribs.

Okay, the shower.

I realized my internal dialogue was becoming confrontational, and wondered if I should be concerned.

No, you should get the hell out of this house.

And just where should I go?

This self-discussion finally ended when I thought of leaving my house unprotected, although I doubted my presence would deter the man stalking me.

Instead, I showered, washed and conditioned my hair, shaved my legs as best I could with the sore ribs. At least I felt cleaner and more limber. I sat on a barstool, combing out my wet hair, an empty coffee pot witness to how much caffeine I'd consumed and now felt. My mind and heart raced, but my body plodded behind in fatigue and pain.

Though time ticked by in aching slow motion, I managed to stay home over the weekend with daily visits from MaryAnne and Matt, but I was going bonkers. Even the deputies sitting outside my house were probably less bored and cranky than I was.

Every time I walked to my study, I thought of the disk with the images of the knife and the dead woman. When I went into the kitchen, I thought about the PCP in my candy. In bed, I worried about bombs and dead bodies in barrels, or I dreamed about my hallucinogenic experience.

I needed to do something constructive, so on Monday morning, I called Matt and told him I was going to the medical examiner's office. I just didn't tell him I intended to sleep there in my office that night.

The deputy parked in front of my house followed me.

I nodded as he accompanied me inside and took a seat in the hall near my office door.

"I'm sure this is terribly boring for you," I said. "If you need anything, please ask Connie, our secretary. Have her order you lunch

– it's on me today."

He thanked me politely and waited until five when I refused to leave the building for the night. So he called Matthew.

"I'm perfectly safe here," I argued. "Safer than I would be at home." I was even able to control the urge to put my hand under my jacket on my gun while I said that.

"I suppose one can't debate that," Dr. Katz said, joining the argument with Matt in my office. "The building offers a layer of security you can't provide at her house."

Matthew rolled his eyes. "She isn't supposed to be working."

"What? You think one patrol car sitting in front my house all night is going to deter someone who really wants inside?" I asked. "Enough of this. I am as capable of performing the same threat assessment to my environment and responding to it as your deputy in the car. I'm actually doing everyone a favor. Saving tax dollars."

The police surveillance dissolved to an agreement I would call for an escort if I left the locked corridor.

That was fair albeit still inconvenient.

At least a bunch of cops wouldn't have to babysit me all the time, unwilling as I was.

After all, what better way to rattle me than by killing the officer sitting outside my house?

Monday night, I slept on the sofa in my office.

By Tuesday afternoon, Dr. Katz had a twin bed delivered to an empty office on the basement level, where access was restricted by an electronic key card. I shared the floor with the bodies in the morgue down the hall, but neither they nor I complained.

* * *

My first two days in the office were quiet. I spent them at my computer doing the previous week's backlog of reports to the state. Only working to keep my mind occupied, and lifting nothing heavier than my coffee cup. A *big* cup.

I think Connie switched me to decaf around noon.

By Wednesday morning, Connie had stacked my desk with mail, forms to sign, and a small Federal Express box addressed to me in care of the department from a Mrs. Dixie Gates in Grand Rapids.

I opened the box without thinking about poisons and bombs. Without thinking at all.

From beneath the packing paper I retrieved a baby food jar full of murky fluid. Tucked inside the box was a note, computer-printed on plain white paper:

Julia,

Since there has been no news of these cases, I must wonder if your fine investigatory senses are lacking. You may not be feeling up to par since your hospitalization, or perhaps you're not up to your regular duties yet.

You will find this specimen helpful in determining the cause of death of a young woman who died yesterday. Since you didn't realize we were playing a game, unfortunately, you've forfeited your turn, and I've rolled again. Perhaps the next victim could use a piece of your delicious white chocolate caramel candy.

Did you enjoy yours?

CHAPTER 16

I dropped into my chair, stunned and hyperventilating, staring at the paper on my desk and the jar.

Dr. Katz was as distressed as I was to realize the man who had drugged my candy and broken into my house was not content with mind games and making my life hell, but was apparently willing to kill to play this "game," as the note put it.

Matthew Shannaker was livid when he showed up in my office.

Tracking the shipment was fairly simple. Federal Express had shipped the package from a franchised mailing center two miles from the airport in Grand Rapids as ground service.

Kent County deputies were trying to locate the clerk for questioning.

I turned to tracking down the victim to which the note referred. Within an hour, I'd identified a likely subject who died Monday – Patricia Stowe, age 20.

Last week, severe nausea and vomiting had prompted her to go to her doctor's office. He gave her drugs to help the symptoms, diagnosing gastroenteritis with mild dehydration, and sent her home. Two days later, Saturday, her roommate took her to the emergency department where she was admitted. After developing a high fever and gastric bleeding, she suffered a cardiac arrest that failed to respond to resuscitation efforts. Cause of death was listed as acute kidney failure and sepsis secondary to gastrointestinal parasitic infestation causing dehydration, according to her private physician, who had signed the death certificate and released the body for burial.

The hospital laboratory had identified *Giardia*, a common

parasite in Michigan streams and rivers. The patient had been camping and canoeing the weekend before the onset of her symptoms. The diagnosis fit.

Dr. Katz requisitioned the body from the funeral home over the protests of both the family and her physician, who stood by her death as being caused by complications of giardiasis until a mention of homicide changed his mind. Checking the lab specimens and notes, we discovered there had been other unidentified microorganisms, but the labs were cancelled after the patient died.

I took a look at the sample from the jar and the lab specimens, then I dragged out a reference book the size of the Chicago Yellow Pages. I'm no microbiologist, but this parasite didn't look like anything native to the United States, and this girl hadn't been camping outside the local area code.

After digging through all our references, I called the Centers for Disease Control and Prevention in Atlanta, asking for assistance from someone in the Division of Parasitic Diseases. While the organism itself wasn't a cause for alarm, its use as a murder weapon got someone's attention. After some bureaucratic debate, I was told they were sending an expert to see the body and the sample. I was given peculiar instructions on care of the specimens, which I followed to the letter.

Before she left for the day, Connie told me she had received confirmation that Dr. McNeil would be arriving on an 8:30 flight the next morning, and she had made arrangements for someone to pick him up and bring him to the office.

I turned my attention to the second victim. Because of the reference to needing candy, I presumed symptoms relating to diabetes, so I contacted funeral homes, other ME offices, and then hospitals until I located someone who remembered an unusual case.

But this victim wasn't dead. She lay unconscious in ICU with high concentration dextrose solutions and insulin drips running into her veins to feed her organs.

Kathryn Leggitt, a 19-year-old Northwestern Michigan College student, had been found unconscious in a mall movie theater. When the paramedics transported her, her blood sugar was too low to register a number on the glucometer, even after two consecutive doses of concentrated glucose solution intravenously.

Her case was suspicious because she was not a diabetic. With no obvious link to Patricia Stowe's death, the connection would have gone unnoticed had the killer not sent a note.

Her doctor was hoping Kathryn Leggitt's brain had not gone without glucose too long. She had purchased a ticket for a movie 102 minutes long, and staff agreed cleanup didn't start for another 15 minutes before she was found. As yet she showed no signs of voluntary movement. Sadly, if her brain was permanently damaged, her healthy young body could maintain its current function for decades, dependent on tubes and nutrition.

I met Kathryn's parents that evening when Dr. Katz, Detective Brandan Callaghan and I spoke with them about our belief she was also an intended murder victim and explained we would be testing for the parasite we had previously identified. Permission was not required, but we believed it was a fair disclosure to her distraught parents that what they thought was an extraordinarily unusual medical problem was more likely a criminal act. We simply had no idea how it was done.

The tests for parasites in her blood and stool were negative. Later, I relayed this information to her parents, who had in turn explained their daughter had begun to demonstrate spontaneous movement in response to pain.

It was a glimmer of hope.

* * *

Thursday morning, when I woke in the basement office, I was thinking about the parasite and the young woman in ICU. I began to see this killer's ideas for creative methods might outrun our connections to find experts to assist us. The mental list of other similar methods of murder exceeded a dozen while I showered, until I was nauseated. The possibilities seemed endless.

I wrapped a towel around my hair and started to dress. Putting on my bra, I inspected the bruise under my left arm where my holstered gun had cracked the ribs. The skin was fading through the purple and green stages. Still tender, mostly toward the back. The cuts and burn on my hand and wrist were healing nicely, but I could tell it was time to remove the sutures.

No time to go to the hospital or clinic today.

One does not need a medical degree to remove sutures, only a little experience and pointy scissors. I had both, so I snipped eight stitches out and dropped them into the trash.

Another ugly scar, a mark of violence done for reasons I could not understand.

I stretched a large Band-Aid over it. Something else to cover.

The dark circles under my eyes required a little makeup to hide, and I used a little blush to offset the paleness. I combed and dried my long hair, then left it loose. With no chance of being called to a scene today, I had no reason to tie it up.

In my office, I tried to get settled in to another day's work, but I felt like I was getting nowhere.

Connie brought me a cup of coffee and a toasted bagel slathered in both butter and cream cheese.

"You're much too good to me," I said, taking a bite.

"Probably," she said, going back out my door. "But we both love it."

Instead of E-mail, I turned my attention to my mental list of ideas from the shower. I knew of various toxins from spiders and snakes and a couple of amphibians. Ingested or inhaled poisons that might include cyanide and phosgene. Even something as simple as mixing bleach and ammonia could be fatal. The list became depressing and expansive in the time it took to finish my bagel.

Connie buzzed me to say a Kent County deputy was on the line for me.

"I finally tracked down the clerk who shipped your package," he said after introducing himself. "Sorry for the delay. Yesterday was her day off. An older woman brought in a box that size already sealed up. The woman asked her to write the shipping label because she had forgotten her glasses. She says she thought it was weird that the woman was wearing gloves, but her hands looked gnarled and arthritic, like her grandmother's."

"That's great. Any other description of the woman's dress, voice or other mannerisms the clerk might think of may be helpful," I said, explaining what the package had contained.

He agreed to contact her later to see if anything else had crossed her mind about the incident.

Why Grand Rapids?

I turned my attention to Kathryn Leggitt's condition. I was digging through a text on endocrine disorders, trying to find something that made sense about her hypoglycemia when Connie knocked and announced Dr. McNeil's arrival.

I turned around from my credenza and stood up. My heart skipped a couple of beats, and my face felt like it turned crimson.

He extended his hand across my desk and took mine.

I shook hands with a man I hadn't seen in, what, twelve or more years? The math failed me.

His beautiful golden brown eyes locked my gaze.

"It's McNeeley, actually," he said in a smooth Southern baritone, a passing correction for Connie's benefit. He didn't blink.

"Coffee, Julie?" she asked, backing cautiously toward the door, probably clueless what was transpiring between the doctor and me.

It must look like an electrical storm. That's what it feels like.

His hand did not release mine.

I might have stood there with my mouth hanging open. Maybe Connie thought I was overwhelmed by his good looks. Many women have been. He was as gorgeous as ever.

I regained enough composure to at least answer Connie that I didn't think coffee would be necessary at the moment.

She exited, still looking puzzled.

"This is quite a surprise," I said, yanking my hand free.

"I must admit, it's less a surprise for me." He shrugged and pulled the chair closer to my desk before sitting. "I sort of assigned myself the case when I read the briefing and saw your name. At least I was prepared in case you turned out to be the same Julie Madigan I knew in New Mexico." He paused, his eyes still locked on mine. "Are you?"

Wanting to look away from him, I found I couldn't. "I suppose the answer could go either way, but I used to be," I said, wondering just how much of the Julie he knew was really left in my soul.

In a flash of memory, I saw our bodies wrapped together in the moonlight of a hot summer night. I blinked away the image I did not want to remember.

"Taylor Healey called and told me you were in the trauma unit at University after an assault," he said. "I thought about sending a card or flowers. Taylor said she wouldn't recommend it."

I could only nod. I finally remembered to breathe. "It's not a big deal, Jeremy," I said.

"I hope you will have dinner with me," he said, clearly looking at my hand for a wedding ring, "and maybe drive me around to a few sights while I'm here. I've never been to Michigan, but," he smiled, "so far I like what I see." Charm so pure he really couldn't help himself.

I swallowed and tried to remember all the reasons why I hated him. "This wasn't a social invitation," I said, attempting to be professional. "Provided the cat doesn't drop another dead bird on the doorstep, maybe I can arrange something."

The quizzical look on his face said he didn't know what I was talking about.

"You didn't get the case summary I faxed this morning? No, I guess you probably wouldn't have. Let's go to the lab." I suddenly needed to move away from the direct view of those soulful eyes. While we walked, I explained that the murderer's parasite sample matched the victim's, and then about the latest victim, Kathryn Leggitt. "She's had continued extreme hypoglycemia. If they manage to save her with her memory intact, she could be a very valuable witness. We're considering moving her to another city and announcing to the press that she also has died in hopes he won't try to finish the job. I've no doubt he could easily get to her."

No doubts at all, knowing how easily he got into my house.

"Profound and persisting hypoglycemia?" he repeated as if he hadn't heard any other details. "That might be even simpler to diagnose than your bug. May I use your phone?"

He placed a call from the laboratory and asked whoever answered to e-mail him information on a plant. He hung up.

"Something I recalled from a botany class," he said. "Akee is the fruit of the *Blighia sapida* tree, common in the West Indies, Jamaica, and West Africa. The seeds contain a toxic amino acid that is an inhibitory neurotransmitter, hypoglycin A, which causes severe hypoglycemia by inhibiting hepatic glycogenesis."

"That's very impressive, Dr. McNeeley, *whatever* it means. How do they save her life?" I asked.

"Doing whatever it is that's kept her alive so far," he said, ignoring the barb. "I'm not an endocrinologist, but Lori's going to send more information on it. It's a hunch, based on a probable West African source of your parasite, according to your description. Good eye for details – it helped a lot." He nodded to the lab. "I'm really anxious to see it."

After a quick examination of the body, I left Jeremy in the lab the rest of the day with the parasite.

Meanwhile, I sat at my desk, thinking about him.

CHAPTER 17

Years ago, Jeremy Cameron McNeeley had been a third-year medical student from Atlanta on academic scholarship at the University of New Mexico School of Medicine. But he grew tired of the manic schedule demands that really did very little to improve the quality of medical proficiency of the med students and residents, and the quality of care for their patients. So he pitched it all and became a paramedic instead. This, of course, infuriated his father and administrators at the school, but he felt that killing himself or a patient due to sleep-deprivation was irresponsible, and just because it had been done that way for years didn't make it right.

His father worked as a virologist with the CDC, though that hadn't even crossed my mind when I called yesterday. His mother had been a cellist in the Atlanta Symphony Orchestra. I got the impression Jeremy had not been a planned child, but he seemed to have had an extraordinary childhood, nonetheless. I'd only met his parents once in Albuquerque.

Jeremy had a stunning complexion that tanned dark. His eyes were almost gold, like a tiger's. He had a baritone voice with a Southern cadence like honey that sounded every bit the well-educated gentleman he was.

He was working for Albuquerque Emergency Medical Services when I started paramedic training at the University of New Mexico.

I think I fell in love with his voice on the EMS radio long before I ever saw his face.

He could have made a living in broadcasting. Or modeling.

Or in porn movies.

Given my full-time college load, I pretended to be much too busy to show any interest in him when I first began my 240 hours of paramedic internship. I chose to ride mostly on night shifts, and I was assigned to him and his partner, Taylor Healey.

In the quiet hours of the morning, Taylor napped on the couch at the Northside station. When I finished studying, my choice was to stay in the dark and be quiet or go sit in the ambulance with Jeremy and listen to the scanner. I began to choose the conversation. I liked talking in the dark.

He was almost too good looking to be discussing drunks and sick people. Talking about my career, my goals came easy with Jeremy. I understood why he quit medical school, although I'm not sure I would have if I were that close to the end. He learned why I was going to paramedic school instead of straight to the police academy. He taught me a lot about medicine those nights.

Probably no one was surprised except me when he asked me out.

Our first date started as a trip to the movies and was interrupted at the scene of a motorcycle accident at Lomas and San Mateo. With nothing but our hands, we managed until EMS and fire units arrived and took over. Too bloody to go anywhere in public, we retreated to my mother's house, where I gave him a terrycloth robe and dumped our clothes in the washing machine. We settled for an HBO movie and microwave popcorn for the evening.

My mother required convincing that the handsome young man with no pants had only honorable intentions, but I'd recorded the ten o'clock news segment for her, giving her the first look at her daughter working.

My first news footage. And like every piece of EMS footage of me since, my back was turned to the camera. Jeremy made a comment about my butt, which my mother pretended not to hear, but I remember she tried to hide a smile.

Over the next few months, we dated in a more traditional manner, without someone else's misfortune and blood interrupting our plans. We bicycled and hiked in the mountains. We went to movies, the state fair and balloon festival. The relationship became serious, despite my initial hesitancy to spend that much time away from school.

We dated about four months before we first had sex. I don't think he expected me to be the virgin I was. On the other hand, I was pretty sure he wasn't.

Since he shared a small house with a city firefighter, and I lived at home with my mother, we discussed getting an apartment. I wanted to finish the semester before moving, but we started looking for a place.

Then one night, after a particularly ugly ambulance call, he told me he was sorry, but he wanted to break up. He wouldn't give me a reason.

I loved him, and I was crushed because he seemed unconcerned how his decision affected me. Within a few months, he left town, and I hadn't seen him since.

That is, until Connie escorted the handsome CDC microbiology consultant into my office this morning.

CHAPTER 18

Aggravated how distracting Jeremy's arrival had been, I seemed to accomplish nothing all morning.

At noon, I chickened out. "Connie, could you order Dr. McNeeley something for lunch? I have to run a few errands."

I did have things to do, but I could have done them any other time or the next day.

Connie didn't need to know I was trying to avoid looking across the table at an ex-boyfriend who broke my heart years ago, or that I still felt like a jilted teenager about it apparently.

I drove to the bank and to my house for clean clothes, the assigned deputy in tow.

Shortly before five o'clock, I went back to the lab in time to introduce Dr. Katz to Dr. Jeremy McNeeley.

"MaryAnne asked me to invite you and Dr. McNeeley for dinner tonight. And she's making pot roast," he told me, waggling his eyebrows. "Dinner's at seven, but come earlier for drinks."

I wasn't really in the mood, but one does not turn down MaryAnne's pot roast.

"Well, that alters my plans for a quiet candlelit dinner alone with you," Jeremy said after Dr. Katz left. "I won't leave town until we do, either." He patted me solidly on the back then felt around. "Body armor and a shoulder holster? I thought this was an ME's office."

"Business has been a little risky lately," I said, trying not to wince at the pain in my ribs from the impact of his hand.

Before we left the lab, I told the deputy assigned to guard me on the afternoon shift that I would be okay without him sitting with me at Dr. Katz's table and promised to call when I was on my way back to the office. This was not in keeping with his orders, and so I suggested that he go change to an unmarked car and plain clothes, then meet us at the Katz's and sit out there and follow me wherever I might go. Not acceptable.

So, with the deputy following in a patrol car, I drove Jeremy to his hotel so he could change clothes for dinner. "Get rid of the suit," I said. "This is dinner with the family."

He seemed disappointed that I waited for him in the truck, though I didn't know what he thought the point would be for me to accompany him to his room.

When he returned, he'd left his professional intensity in his briefcase and his professional clothes in the hotel, but his personal curiosity remained intact as we drove out Old Mission Peninsula to the Katz's house. "What's the reference to the cat and bird you made earlier today?"

"The killer sees this as a game," I said. "Like a cat catches a mouse or a bird and brings it to the door. Not to eat it. Sort of a gift, I guess. To say, 'Hey, look what I can do and you can't stop me.' In fact, he was so certain we hadn't identified his work with the parasites, he sent *me* the sample, along with a hint about the next victim and the akee or whatever you called it." My voice took on a bitchy edge. I took a deep breath, trying to relax. "I'm sorry, between this case and the bomb –"

"What bomb?"

"You don't get CNN down there in Atlanta?" I barbed. "We're also working a case where a dying man was left chained to the floor of his barn. We found a trap door to a sub-room. After I went down, two bombs were detonated to destroy evidence and the victims."

"Victims?" he echoed again, ignoring my sarcasm.

I sighed. I did not want to discuss any of this. "There were four bodies stored in barrels in that hole. In acid."

"Didn't catch that news blurb."

I caught what looked like genuine concern.

"Okay, enough questions about work," he surrendered.

I highlighted a few local points of interest on Old Mission Peninsula, just to make conversation.

"Do you live near here?" Jeremy asked, not knowing the geography and economic borders of the Grand Traverse Bay area.

I turned up the driveway to the Katz home. "No, I bought a small house near downtown, not far from the offices."

"No roommate or significant other?" he said, watching me closely as I turned off the ignition and opened the door.

"I live alone," I said, trying to think of the most effective way to stop this line of questioning.

Gerald Katz rushed out the front door of their split-level home, saving me from saying something unnecessarily rude.

"Perfect timing!" he exclaimed. "MaryAnne sent me after more butter. Real butter, of course. Can't serve guests margarine for rolls, she says. Perhaps Dr. McNeeley will take a quick ride with me to the market? Julie, I'd appreciate it if you could keep her from calling me with the rest of her grocery list before I get out of the store, eh?"

Jeremy shrugged like a gentleman and joined Gerald.

They were pulling out of the long drive as I let myself in the house.

"Oh, Julie. I'm so glad you could come," MaryAnne said, coming through the living room to greet me. "You can taste the gravy for me. Gerald says I never get enough salt. You're looking better. A little color back in your face. How's the pain?"

"The ribs will hurt for a while, I'm afraid. I get tired quickly, but everything else seems okay." I followed her to the kitchen. "How can I ever thank you enough for being such a good friend during this? You couldn't possibly have done anything else for me."

A moment of weariness flashed on her face, barely visible to me as she turned away, with a pause as the smile returned to her face. "That's what friends do best – be there in the difficult times as well as the easy ones."

"I hope you'll never need me, but I'll be here for you, MaryAnne," I said, hugging her.

I took a seat at the breakfast nook in the kitchen where she made me taste the gravy. I suggested adding a dash more salt and then tasted again. "I think it's perfect."

She stirred it another minute and turned down the heat. She was pouring us each a glass of merlot when Kimberly Katz came hobbling into the kitchen in tears.

"Mom, where's Daddy?" She turned her foot up. A thumb-sized chunk of bloody wood stuck out from the arch.

"Oh my God, Kim, what happened?" MaryAnne said, sounding panicky. "Your father went to the store."

Kim was every father's nightmare: a drop-dead gorgeous redhead daughter who is intelligent, popular, athletic, and not quite 16. Except for her occasional adolescent silliness, she could easily pass for 19 or 20 with a little makeup and more sophisticated clothes. She looked her age this evening in navy sweats and an oversized hooded white sweatshirt with palm trees printed over the front and up one sleeve.

"We were gathering wood for a bonfire on the beach. I stepped on a branch or something." She was beginning to look pale.

"You finish up dinner, MaryAnne," I said, offering her the spoon back. "I'll go see what I can do about Kim's foot. I'm much better at this sort of thing than I am at cooking."

Mother and daughter both looked relieved.

I helped Kim hop down the hall to the bathroom, her arm over my shoulder for support.

With a slight smile, she commented that my gun holster must be hard to hide when I wore a bathing suit.

"Do you recall ever seeing me in a bathing suit?" I replied with a chuckle.

She hadn't. No one in Michigan had.

Well, Jeremy McNeeley was in Michigan at the moment, and he had seen me in one. And less.

But he hadn't seen all the scars I kept covered now.

I looked down at the large adhesive bandage covering the cut on my hand. More scars yet.

Kim laid on the floor and rested her foot up on the side of the bathtub, then directed me to the various first aid supplies as I assembled things I might need.

My first really good view of the wound revealed sand and a piece of wood the size of my thumb. "Wow, Kim. You know, this looks really dirty. Maybe we should take you to the emergency room and let them—"

"No, please!" she begged. "Just pull it out. You can do anything that needs to be done, can't you? I don't want to go the hospital."

I felt around the edge of the wound. "I'll try to take it out, then we'll see. Deal? This really ought to be irrigated so it won't get infected."

"Deal." She took a deep breath as I poured Betadine over the sole of her foot. "That's cold." She made a soft growling noise as I attempted to grasp the splinter with a pair of tweezers, which slipped off the wet wood.

"Sorry," I said. "One more try." I resorted to using my fingernails to grasp the sliver and pull it from her foot. "Better?" I asked, holding up the bloody fragment.

"I think I'm gonna puke," she said, closing her eyes.

"Take slow deep breaths," I coached. I handed her a cool rag for her forehead and then mixed an antiseptic solution and water in a basin I found. "Try to think of something else."

"Can I ask you a question? It's, you know, kinda personal. Mom would say it's none of my business."

"I think you know me well enough to ask personal questions," I said and eased her foot down into the water to soak.

"Well, I heard Mom and Dad talking one night. I didn't mean to eavesdrop, really," she said. "Dad said something like how much courage he thought it musta taken you to tell him about killing someone. Did you really?"

Great. Someone else who really didn't need to know.

"Yes, I did," I said. "Does that change the way you think of me?"

"I guess it depends on why. Was he a criminal?"

"He intended to kill me, if that makes him a criminal."

"Is that how you got the scar on your neck?"

I nodded, resisting the urge to tug my turtleneck up.

"Oh." She said quietly. "Even though he hurt you, did you feel bad about it? Killing him, I mean."

"I felt a lot of mixed-up things. I was angry about what he had done to me. I couldn't forgive him."

Truth is, I can't forgive myself.

I used a large syringe to irrigate the hole in her foot.

"I was really scared when Mom told us you and Dad were at the barn that blew up," she finally said. "They don't think Kayleigh and I should hear about all the bad things that happen."

I smiled at her. "Your folks are good people. I'm sure they don't want you and your little sister to grow up being afraid or feeling there's no good left in the world." I inspected her wound again. The skin around it was warm despite the cool solution I used. "The bad news is I think you need to get a second opinion, Kim. You should go to the hospital to get this cleaned out and x-rayed."

"And your second opinion says you should follow your first opinion's advice and go to the ER," Gerald Katz said from the doorway. "But your mother has dinner ready if you think you can wait half an hour?"

I was surprised when Kim looked to me for confirmation that this was an acceptable alternative. "Sure, but eat light. Remember, you felt a little nauseated." I placed a bulky dressing on the wound and extended a hand to help her up. "And don't put your weight on it."

She hugged me. "Thanks. You're pretty cool."

I think I blushed. "You're pretty cool, too." I helped her hobble down the hall to the dining room.

After everyone but Kim had stuffed themselves at dinner, Gerald took his daughter to the emergency department for x-rays and antibiotics.

I tried to leave then, too, but MaryAnne insisted on serving us all a brandy. She made polite conversation with Jeremy, discussing his mother's musical career and his first impressions of Michigan, still unaware I knew him. I kept not finding good places to interrupt and tell her.

She left the family room to answer the phone, leaving Jeremy and me alone for the first time that evening. I walked to the patio doors overlooking the bay, and he came over and stood behind me, looking out into the darkness. I began pointing out lights along the distant shoreline, trying not to think about how close he was.

Then he stretched his arms around my waist and kissed my head.

"Your hair is beautiful. You must not have cut it since I saw you last. It's all sorts of colors – gold and honey and amber and cinnamon. It smells wonderful," he said, burying his face in it on the left side of my neck.

I wanted to shrug him off, to yell at him he'd lost his chance when he walked away before.

But it felt good.

"That was Gerald," MaryAnne announced as she came back into the family room, finding me with Jeremy's arms wrapped around me.

CHAPTER 19

"They're on their way to the pharmacy." MaryAnne was very tactful, but dismayed to see us in such familiar contact.

"I should have told you and Gerald earlier that Jeremy and I have known each other a long time," I explained, pulling away from him and going back to the sofa. "We dated in Albuquerque fourteen years ago. Imagine my surprise when Jeremy showed up in the office today,"

She recovered her composure with elegance.

"Isn't it getting to be such a small world anymore? If I'd known, we could have done dinner another night. You two must have a lot of catching up to do, then?"

"I hope so," Jeremy said, sitting down beside me again. "We've both been through a lot in the past several years."

"Not tonight," I interjected. "I'd like to stay and find out how things went with Kim's foot, but I'm exhausted, and I have an appointment with the neurologist in the morning."

"Are you still sleeping at the office, Julie?" she asked with her motherly concern. She voiced a complaint during dinner that she'd rather I stayed in their guest room, but my concern for security included keeping her family safe.

"Yes, but hopefully not for long," I said.

Jeremy excused himself to the bathroom as I stood to leave.

"I almost forgot. Would you remind Gerald to have someone pick Dr. McNeeley up in the morning at his hotel? I won't have time before my doctor's appointment, and he'll probably want to get to the office early," I said, hoping to dispel her fears I would take

Jeremy home with me.

"Of course," she said, but I could tell she didn't buy my statement.

"I haven't had a chance to really talk to Jeremy. I loved him once, MaryAnne, but he broke my heart."

She nodded. "You be careful. A man that good looking could probably break mine more than once."

True to my unspoken intent, I dropped Jeremy at the Holiday Inn. He seemed a little miffed when I declined a drink at the bar. "I'm sorry, but I really am exhausted," I told him. "I'll see you tomorrow."

"What's wrong? Why the doctor?"

"I told you about the bomb," I said.

"You said there was a bomb. You implied it went off. I do not recall you mentioning you were hurt," he said. "Nothing serious, I presume."

I sighed. "Depends how you look at it. I woke up a day later with a few cracked ribs and a mild concussion."

He looked stunned, then took a breath as if he intended to start a lecture on my health.

"Look, I understand your curiosity and your concern," I interrupted. "We needed assistance to identify an organism in hopes we could narrow down its source, catch the killer, and to treat any other victims. Unless you can be our in-house expert on weird murder methods, help with the regular load of car crashes and UD's, check all my food for hallucinogenic drugs and the previously-mentioned miscellany of poisons or bugs, or help identify four bodies buried in barrels full of acid, then giving you the history of the rest of this month's medical examiner's investigations would be a waste of time." I sounded much angrier than was necessary, but I hated feeling pushed. "At least for tonight."

Jeremy sat without speaking for a moment. "I do have the expertise and connections to help, and the CDC will make me available for indefinite support. Anyone who would use *Bilharzia* and akee as means of homicide may have other nasty global aces to play."

"That's not my decision to ask you to stay," I said. "Nonetheless, the stories can wait."

He nodded and opened the door, then paused. "I thought about you. I didn't realize how much until it was too late." He seemed to want to say something else, but hesitated. When I didn't reply, he touched my sleeve, then turned and stepped out. "Good night."

His little revelation wound my pulse rate up. How dare he say he'd thought about me.

As I pulled out onto the street, my cellular phone rang.

"Madigan," I said after pushing the button.

"Ms. Madigan, this is Central Dispatch. The assigned officer wanted to ascertain if you were en route to the office so his relief can meet you there," a very disinterested voice asked, mixed with voices in the background.

I glanced at the digital clock on my dash. It was 9:18.

Not time for shift change.

Besides, Central Dispatch would have paged me to call for such a request. I carried a county pager, but the cellular phone was a private account.

I pushed the end button to disconnect the call without saying another word. At the next red light, I motioned the deputy up beside me.

"Did you have Central call me on my cell phone?" I asked.

"No, ma'am."

"Have Deputy Shannaker meet us at my office." I said, rolling up the window again.

We drove on to the Government Building Annex, blood pounding in my ears from something completely different than Jeremy's confession.

My phone rang again as I pulled up to the garage door entrance.

"I don't know what it's about," Matt was yelling at someone before he heard the connection. "Julie, what is it?"

"Now he's got my cell phone number and apparently knows I'm under police protection and sleeping at the morgue." I pulled inside when the sallyport door opened, making the connection crackle. "We're here. Call my office in five minutes."

The deputy escorted me up to the office and stood outside my door while I paced, waiting on Matt to call back. Ten minutes passed when I finally gave up and sat in my chair. I propped my elbows on the desk, massaging my temples, when I heard his footsteps marching down the hall.

Matthew dismissed the deputy for the night before he came in and closed the door behind him, leaning against it in the same sort of exhaustion I felt. "This is way out of hand." he said. "The phone company is working on the incoming number. What did he say?"

"Actually, he sounded like a woman, and I was almost fooled," I said, relaying the conversation.

"We need to get you away from here," Matt said.

I was about to either argue or agree – I wasn't sure which – when my fax machine rang.

We sat and watched the paper feed out the slot.

Dearest Julia Ann,

In a few days, I will be leaving town on another expedition, so you won't have to sleep in the office on my account. I do not intend you any harm, truly. I'm sure it will be clear before long. I'll have more photos for you soon. –

I wanted to scream. "How did he get all this information about me?" I exploded.

"Julie, if you weren't at home, it wouldn't be hard to guess where you'd stay. Most people would try a hotel or a friend's house. You aren't most people."

"But it means he's watching me," I argued. "And digging too far into my past."

"Spend the night with me at Mom's place – as a precaution. We can leave your truck here, hide you in my patrol car on the way out of the garage. Even if he's watching the building, he won't see you leave."

I nodded, too tired to argue. I grabbed my overnight bag and we left in his vehicle, though I had to share the backseat with Laser, who was torn between sticking his nose out the cracked window and getting his ears rubbed.

"I don't get why he is so focused on you," Matt said, eyeing me in the mirror. "Why the name thing? How would someone know to look for such information about you, much less where to find it? I wouldn't."

"Crap, I don't know, Matt."

"Well, maybe it's his tracking where he'll leave his own footsteps uncovered."

I wasn't convinced, but it was a good question – who would know?

"Julie, use all that psychological magic-wand stuff. What does your gut instinct tell you about him?"

"You really want to know?"

"Of course."

"My gut says he's been following my life for quite a while."

That was met with silence from the front seat. Finally, Matt said, "Okay, so why has this interest only recently surfaced? If this is his way to stalk you, why now? Why the victims?"

"The better question is why am I not one of them?"

"We can think about that tomorrow," he said, pulling into the driveway. Using the remote door opener, he parked in the garage of a three-story house on the east shore of Leelanau County, north of Traverse City.

I'd been inside Mrs. Shannaker's home twice before. The house was every bit as magnificent as its view of Grand Traverse Bay.

"Doesn't your mother feel lost in this big house all alone?" I asked, knowing she had been a widow for many years.

"I doubt she's ever here long enough to feel lost in it," he said, rolling his eyes. "She's in Europe this fall. Says she's spending my inheritance to save me the tax burden."

The wooden floors reflected light around the great room, an open area with a high wood cathedral ceiling and a walk-around stone fireplace larger than my living room.

I heard Matt scooping up dry dog food for Laser, then washing his hands before opening a bottle of wine in the kitchen.

I wandered to the far side of the great room to look east into Grand Traverse Bay, on the opposite shoreline from where I'd stood just hours ago on Old Mission Peninsula at the Katz's home, looking west.

I refused to let myself think about Jeremy.

"You've heard all about my life this week," I said, taking the glass Matt offered. "Tell me about yours. We've shared so little about ourselves and how we each got where we are. We only talk about the present. What were you like as a kid?"

"For that, we need the bottle," he said, tucking it into the crook of his arm. "Good thing my mother isn't here to get out the old slides and 8 mm tapes and embarrass me."

I followed Matt downstairs to the enclosed deck off the family room. The night air was cool but still.

He excused himself and went to change out of his uniform, returning in sweat pants and an oversized sweatshirt. He brought me an equally baggy and aged sweatshirt to wear.

"So," he said, as we settled comfortably in the darkness. "What is it you'd like to know?"

"Umm, what was it you said the other night? Everything? Or shall we play twenty questions?"

"Interesting idea." He thought for a moment. "But I get to choose what kind of questions."

I decided I could play along with this.

"First question must have a yes-or-no answer."

"Have you ever regretted becoming a cop?" I asked.

"No, although I promised my dad I wouldn't. Next question must be a favorite-something."

"What is your favorite firearm?"

"Hands down, a Sig P226 .40 caliber with a twenty-round magazine. That, in my opinion, is the perfect tactical weapon." He sipped his wine. "A best-or-worst question."

I paused to interpret the question's parameter. Best or worst what? "Who was your best friend in second grade?"

He tilted his head to look at me. "His name was Billy Hartman. We were best buddies until sixth grade when I saw him kissing a girl on the bus. I had a terrible crush on her. Good question. How about a how-many question?"

"How many serious girlfriends have you had?"

"Since the one Billy kissed?" he grinned. "Three or four sort-of serious. No one I wanted to keep, I guess. Or any who'd have me. Double jeopardy round, a category of your choice."

"Do you forgive me for not telling you about David?" I asked softly.

"Yes. I'm sorry I was such a jerk. I was upset you hadn't told me, that our friendship never included sharing something that tragic, that important in your life. And your career, too. I can understand why, but I felt left out." He squeezed my hand. "Another question. That one didn't count. It's not about me."

"What happened to your father? You've never mentioned him."

"You never mentioned yours, either." He countered, then he sighed. "That's a question I'd like to pass on for right now, if I may. I will tell you. Later tonight, if you want, but just not right now. I don't want to spoil a moment like this."

"Sure," I said, trying to think of another philosophical question. "What one decision would you change because it could change everything in your life?"

The silence hung between us until the only thing I could hear was my heart pounding in my ears and the waves lapping against the rocks below us.

"It has to do with my father, part of the same story."

More silence, so I decided to move on.

"Are you mad our relationship is only what it is right now?"

He stood up, then helped me to my feet, setting down our wine glasses. "No. I like the way things have been, Julie. I like spending time with you because you're smart and funny and compassionate. I like your brains and your heart," he said, lifting one hand and kissing my fingers. "I like all these things about you, but. . . Maybe it was just the secrets I felt, but God help me, I'm scared to touch you. Always have been. It's like I felt the ghosts or the invisible walls between us. More than anyone I've ever known, I wanted to love you, but I don't know if love is enough."

CHAPTER 20

I understood what he meant about being afraid. I knew the ghosts and walls of secrets I'd been hiding behind, and I hadn't wanted commitment. That was nothing new with me – Matt wasn't the only one kept more than arm's length away from my heart. I hadn't wanted anyone to get close enough to love me.

After a long silence, we sat down and he poured more wine, and then he told me about his father.

I tried to stop him, to tell him he didn't need to do this now, but he insisted.

"You need to understand this about me, Julie. You were forced to tell us your secret. It's only fair that you hear mine, too."

And so I listened to Matt's story.

"My dad had been a state trooper here since he came home from Korea. He was a quiet man with a very clear sense of right and wrong. He came to my room one night when I was fifteen, woke me up to talk. We'd been having those teen-parent fights about cars and curfews. Nothing really serious. I wasn't into drugs or anything, so I knew it wasn't about that. But it was serious, adult stuff, I could tell.

"After small talk about grades and school, Dad said he'd been having these headaches the last six months or so, and he'd finally gone to the doctor without telling my mother. But instead of the two-aspirin cure, a few tests later, the doctor had told my father he had a very large brain tumor that might slow down with aggressive treatment, but it would still continue to grow rapidly until it killed him. There would likely be some time toward the end when he would become demented or vegetative before he died, the doctor said. Dad was horrified about that."

I waited for Matt to tell me his father had committed suicide.

"We talked all night. He'd had made lists of things he wanted to tell me. Pieces of fatherly advice he wouldn't be around to give me later, like never to buy a Ford or a Beretta, and never shoot cheap ammunition. He gave me lists of things to be done around the house for my mother, like how often to paint or what year to re-roof. He told me he had bought the house for her and that he wanted her to stay in it as long as she wanted it, but he didn't want me to feel bad if she decided to sell it and move after he died."

I wanted to interrupt him, to console a friend who I'd discovered shared a coincidental grief with my own. My father died when I was sixteen, so I understood the loss a teenager could feel, what a lasting impact the loss has on someone so young. On the other hand, I envied Matthew that time his father had to share those thoughts with him – my father had only seconds as he died.

Matt continued. "Dad made me swear not to become a cop, to find something easier on the soul to do for a living. I promised, but we both knew I wouldn't keep it. He told me he wanted me to be around to take care of my mother, so I joined the Coast Guard for four years first."

I emptied my wine glass, waiting on him.

"Before sunup, while my mother was still sleeping, we loaded up his old Jeep and drove to a piece of land he and my uncle had bought to hunt on years before. Deer season was in full swing. Over my first cup of coffee, poured from a Thermos that had to be as old as I was, we discussed his plan. I was supposed to tell the authorities that I tripped and fell, and my gun went off, shooting him in the head. He said that way, he wouldn't suffer, and Mom wouldn't have to watch him die slowly during the months he might have left. Because his death would be ruled an accident, we would get all his benefits and the accidental death policy whereas if he committed suicide, the insurance wouldn't pay and his pension would be reduced. 'I know it's a hard thing to ask, Matthew, but I'm asking you to do it for your mother,' he'd said, 'for everyone's sake.'"

I had been holding my breath so long I thought my lungs would burst.

"So I did it."

"Oh, Matt." My hands covered my mouth and tears stung my eyes.

He continued on with details, presuming I wanted to hear them. His voice sounded more like he'd read the story in a book instead of having lived it.

"I shot him with a .30-06 in the right side of the head from about fifty feet. Afterward, I ran to his side and held him, waited for his heart to stop. I swear he squeezed my hand. It seemed like it took hours for him to die, but I didn't leave him. Then I dragged him to the Jeep and drove to a neighbors' house a few miles away. There was only a basic investigation, and it was done."

I was unable to speak.

"That answers both your questions. How my dad died, and what one thing I would change if I could."

We sat in silence, then he stood up. "Like I said, with secrets like we've both kept, I don't think love is enough." He left me there alone.

Alone to think about how difficult it must have been for Matt to hear I'd shot David.

Alone to consider the trust it took Matt to tell me his story.

Alone to wonder just *which* of those things it was he regretted or would have changed.

I was afraid to follow Matthew, afraid he'd tell me more things I couldn't stand to hear. Wishing he'd come back, and hoping he wouldn't. Stretching out on the coach downstairs, I tried to stay awake to think everything through, but I didn't last long. Despite all the unbelievable things the day and night had held for me, I fell into a dreamless sleep.

The smell of coffee and toast woke me the next morning, but I wasn't ready to face Matt yet. I hadn't had time to digest the story about his father, much less determine how I felt about it.

Or did I have to feel anything?

He had accepted the fact I had killed David, hadn't he?

Yeah, but shooting David was self-defense. Matt pulled the trigger with the intent to kill, a cold-blooded assassin. He killed his father.

That's where my emotions hit head-on.

I got dressed and went upstairs to the kitchen. There was a cup and plate in the sink where he had breakfast. But no Matthew.

After I poured myself a cup, I started searching for a phone book so I could call Dr. Harper's office. I was still opening drawers and cabinets when the phone rang.

And rang.

And rang.

I considered answering, stopped by the absurd fear it would be the killer –

Which one?

– saying he knew where I stayed last night, too.

After four rings, it quit.

The patio door on an upper level slid open then closed again, and footsteps coming down the stairs. Matt came around the corner of the kitchen. "That was Dr. Katz. He was worried because your truck was in the bay but you were nowhere to be found. I told him we'd be there in half an hour."

I nodded.

We stood in the kitchen avoiding looking at each other like liars who've been caught.

"You understand why I've never told anyone else what I told you last night, Julie, but I felt obligated to share my secret since you had no choice but to tell me yours. I needed to say the words, to remember again instead of keeping them buried, but it wasn't fair," he said, looking down at the floor. "I wish I hadn't told you."

"I'm sorry it happened to you, Matt. I can't imagine. . . " I raised my hands in surrender. "Honestly, I don't know what else to say."

Our pasts – the histories we'd both tried to hide – had ripped a horrific chasm between us.

Matthew drove me back to Traverse City and let me out beside the sallyport door. Neither of us said anything.

I hadn't bothered to hide in the backseat – we both knew we wouldn't do this again, so there was no reason to hide it.

"I was concerned about you." Dr. Katz was waiting by my truck when I got inside. "You could have left me a voice mail, you know."

Feeling guilty, I explained what had happened and the spur of the moment decision to go with Matt. I promised to keep him posted in the future.

At my appointment, Dr. Harper was not pleased I'd been sleeping at the annex building. He scolded me about working, then interrogated me about the headache I mentioned to the nurse.

"You don't understand," I explained. "I've had headaches since I ended up at the bottom of a flight of stairs with a broken neck."

He looked at a few more pages in my chart. "You didn't mention this the other day."

"The neurologist evaluated the headaches several times in New Mexico. Nothing specific was ever diagnosed. I live with them."

"How often?" he asked. "How severe is this compared to before the explosion?"

"No different. Most of the time, I ignore it. Sometimes, the pain is much worse. Sounds, lights, smells – I can't filter out anything. I'm no less miserable in bed than I am at work. Sometimes I end up taking narcotics when I can't deal with the pain any more, maybe once every couple of months. This headache isn't that bad."

He didn't ask me any questions about my memory or hallucinations or nightmares, for which I was grateful. We agreed I'd make another appointment if I needed to see him again.

I returned to my office and began making phone calls, starting with the intensive care unit. I was informed that Kathryn Leggitt was stable at her current regimen of dextrose and insulin. She had opened her eyes once but had not yet spoken. Improvement.

Next I called the FBI Violent Crimes Against Persons Unit at Quantico, Virginia. Another one of my contacts from the distant past.

"Hey, Julie! Nice to hear you're back to work so soon. I heard about the bomb. Hope you're doin' okay," Quinton Gresham bellowed, causing me to pull the phone away to save my eardrum.

I assured him I was doing better than expected.

"What can I help you with?"

Besides whispering?

I outlined the criteria for two database searches. One for disappearances of young women within a 500-mile radius, hoping for a hit on one or more of the victims from the farm, and the second for victims in either Michigan or New Mexico whose deaths did not involve the use of a hard weapon.

"Soft weapons?" he said, chuckling. "Good one."

"I don't know, Quin, how do you classify murder by biological means – natural things like microorganisms and trees?"

"Intentional deaths?" Sounded like he suspected my head injury caused mental impairment.

"He's killed one with a parasite, a strain that is not native to the Americas. CDC is working on the specifics. Another victim was poisoned by a plant that affects blood sugar. These wouldn't have been classified as crimes, except the killer was kind enough to send a note to identify his handiwork."

"So you want to search non-violent murders of young women, say under twenty-five?" he said, but not really to me. "For how long? Let's make it ten years."

I heard him typing, which he did with as much enthusiasm as he talked.

One last keystroke that sounded like a boulder crashed onto his desk.

"You know, there are poisonings and such, but you realize we won't have data for deaths not classed as foul play in the first place."

"It's a long shot, Quinton. I'm just looking for a pattern." I looked up to see Jeremy McNeeley standing in my office door. "Let me know what you find. Thanks." I hung up.

"Pardon my tactlessness and familiarity, but you look like crap this morning, Julie." Jeremy came in and sat down. "And, to drop another cliché, wherever you slept last night, you don't look like you enjoyed it."

Why would he wonder where I slept unless Dr. Katz had asked him where I was?

Several unprofessional responses came to mind, but I held my tongue.

"Spare me, *Doctor* McNeeley," I growled. "Anything new?"

"Not new, but definitive on both cases. This guy has done a lot of research and likely travels globally," he said, explaining that his hunch about the akee tree seeds had been correct, and the crawly little things were a match to a specific strain of a South African water-borne parasite found in a lake west of Johannesburg.

"Could we look for flights from there?" I asked.

"Don't waste your time. One connection through any other country would throw off a search, and you've no idea where he landed here. The number of people who've been in the South African areas would be huge and useless to investigate."

"If it's such a nasty organism, what would happen if it were released into a body of water here?" I asked, thinking of all the lakes and streams.

"You'd need the snails that go with it, which isn't a problem, I'm informed. The good news is this particular parasite doesn't fare well in the cold," he said. "And as you saw, there are similar bugs here in this country. We call them schistocytes, causing schistosomiasis. Not hard to treat. She didn't die of the parasite itself. She died of kidney failure from the dehydration, liver failure, and systemic infection from the GI rupture that allowed the organism into her bloodstream. She probably shouldn't have died at all."

I slumped into my chair, acutely aware of the creaking sounds it made, which were deafening inside my head. Without conscious decision, my fingers were rubbing my temples.

"Go take a hot shower, Julie. You'll feel better." His voice was soft and intimate. His prescription, perfectly correct. He left before I could argue.

I really *wanted* to hate him.

CHAPTER 21

A shower sounded great, but it had to wait.

Connie informed me that there was a luncheon briefing, so I had to get what was on my desk under control first. It was almost eleven o'clock before I went down to my temporary quarters and took a quick shower.

Just before noon, I walked the block between buildings with the officer escorting me. I wanted to get there early enough to get something to eat. Universally, emergency services people are motivated by food – we got lunch and a crowd for this debriefing.

I got in the line behind Glenn Corbitt.

Matt came in alone, still dressed in civilian clothes and didn't go through the buffet. He didn't acknowledge me, and he found a chair on the opposite side of the room.

When everyone was seated with sandwiches and soup, Nolan Forrester stood up at the tabletop podium and waited for the chatter to subside. He practically dripped FBI in his expensive charcoal gray pinstriped suit and crimson tie over a perfectly starched white shirt.

"Thank you for your time today. I realize you have important things to be doing, but we need to share information. For those of you who don't know me, I'm FBI Special Agent Nolan Forrester from the Grand Rapids office. I'd like to make it clear I am not leading these cases. I'm simply offering assistance and technical support to what could become a multi-jurisdictional investigation later. I have resources to offer – no more, no less."

Everyone who believes that . . . .

"This briefing will address two investigations. First the Tucker case: James Patrick Tucker died from drinking a potent acid, but autopsy reveals he had been starved and chained to the floor for days, and hanging from his hands before that. Dr. Katz's initial report is in your briefing packet, though other forensic data is still pending."

I noticed no one reached for the folders.

"Of four bodies found beneath the floor of the Tucker barn, three are confirmed female, with strong speculation the fourth is, too. According to Ms. Madigan's statement, there were five barrels, one empty, so we feel confident about the number of bodies, despite the damage from the bombs. The empty barrel may indicate preparation for a next victim. Ms. Madigan described the sub-level room before the explosion. This summary is also in your briefing packet."

I can't wait to read that.

"Someone made two attempts to leave messages at the scene, most likely Tucker. One, we think, refers to the bodies, and the other to the bombs. Both were incomplete. I believe techs have located a portion of board with the message in blood, so testing will be done to confirm the DNA was Tucker's. Unfortunately, there's also blood from those injured in the blast, so we will need samples from anyone who was there, if you'll drop by the lab and donate."

After a chuckle went around the room, he continued.

"The fire marshal tells us there were two bombs, which detonated separately. A preliminary report is included. One firefighter died as a result of the explosion."

As I looked around, I saw weary faces as stressed and helpless as I felt.

A detective I didn't recognize raised his hand. "If Tucker committed suicide, isn't there enough to close that case now?"

"Based on the phone call and the bombs, we suspect Tucker's death was orchestrated by someone else." Forrester's eyes found mine. "Someone who may also be involved in the other deaths."

Nods circled the room.

"What we don't know is a much longer list," Forrester continued. "Victim separation and identification could take months. We don't know what Tucker's role in their deaths might have been or why he tried to leave messages. It is unclear how the other victims in the barrels were killed, but evidence suggests the most recent victim's throat had been cut. I'll let Dr. Katz explain."

With that description, I felt Matt's eyes on me, but he turned away when I looked at him.

Gerald Katz described the separation and reconstruction of the skeletons, which had been turned over to the FBI. "Hydrochloric acid destroyed soft tissue and weakened the smaller bones, completely dissolving some, such as in the hands of the earlier victims. There is hope the recent victim's bones are all intact, possibly yielding suitable tissue for DNA. And one other tidbit, she had metal orthodontia in place, so we may get an ID from dental records eventually."

He sat down and Forrester continued, "Has any of Tucker's family been located?"

Matthew nodded and flipped through his notepad. "A younger sister, who arrived home in Phoenix from vacation yesterday. I spoke to her this morning and made arrangements for her to fly here. Sunday is the soonest she could make it."

"What did she have to say about Tucker?" someone asked.

"After she left home, she seldom heard from him. She returned to Michigan for the funerals of her parents, her father's in 1975, mother's in '79," Matt said, looking back up. "She said he seemed particularly paranoid about her visiting the farm the last time she was here, about three years ago. Despite obvious room in the house, he insisted she stay in a hotel in town, to the point of paying for her room. She wanted a few antiques from the house and the barn – toys and things for her own kids – but he told her he'd thrown all that stuff away. Being the suspicious type, she even joked with her husband when she got home that perhaps Tucker was making porn movies in the barn."

"Was he?" Forrester asked with a raised eyebrow.

"He did some sort of video production, but it seems legit if low-end. No evidence to suggest porn." Matt continued, still not looking at me. "Tucker told her he intended to renovate the barn and move his studio out there eventually."

Jeremy entered and took a seat across the room from me as Forrester wrapped up discussion about the Tucker case.

"Now, parallel to this case, one of the investigators injured at this explosion was drugged while in the hospital. Search of her house revealed that someone entered and left a written message about that incident. After she got home, it was determined the subject had been in her house a second time." Forrester extended his arm to me. "If you would care to elaborate, Ms. Madigan?"

I stood. "On the second visit, he left a computer disk with several images. He's also called and faxed me, revealing personal details about me that indicate he has done extensive research. On Wednesday, FedEx delivered a package containing a jar with a microorganism, accompanied by a note, explaining that since we, or specifically, since I did not recognize this dead woman's case as a murder and identify the cause of death, the evidence was provided and we were shown how the game is played. But I 'lost the round,' so it was his 'turn' again, and he suggested that a second victim could use a piece of my candy, which refers to how he drugged me in the hospital."

I looked around at faces all watching me.

Everyone except Matthew.

This wasn't just a stranger's case, like Tucker. Even without a badge, I was one of them, which made it personal.

"The second victim was admitted to the hospital with profound low blood sugar after being found unconscious at the mall theater. She is still alive and may possibly survive. As for the first victim," I extended my arm toward Jeremy in the same manner Agent Forrester had introduced me, "I contacted the Centers for Disease Control, and they sent Dr. McNeeley to identify this particular microorganism provided in the sample. He has been helpful in both cases."

Jeremy stood. "The sample of microorganisms is a genus of what we call *Schistosoma* in the United States, or *Bilharzia* globally. This particular species is from South Africa, where infestation is common. In fact, we have matched the water and the parasite itself to a specific region west of Johannesburg." He turned and wrote on the white board – *Schistosoma mansoni*. "I presume the parasite was brought over by plane in person, as the specimen wouldn't survive the freezing temperatures of a cargo hold during a commercial flight. However, it would do very nicely in a vial or bottle in the passenger compartment." He put a baby food jar of liquid on the table. "No one would have questioned a container like this in carry-on bag.

"According to the victim's laboratory reports, *Cryptosporidium* and *Giardia* were identified. These are local and fit with the patient's history of camping prior to the onset of symptoms. Ingestion of either organism can make one extremely ill, but *Crypto* would cause symptoms of diarrhea and vomiting with a minimum of two to three days, Giardia in seven to ten. Infestations of *Schistosoma* are typically through skin exposures, so the onset of symptoms is usually 30 days or more. However, if ingested, schistocytes could be fatal if not treated aggressively. I suspect she died due to the delay in seeking treatment once she became acutely ill. From what I read in her medical records, she was critically ill on admission."

He turned again to the white board and wrote the word *akee.*

"The source for the second victim's poison is also native to Africa as well as Jamaica, though the plant could be grown domestically in a greenhouse environment. The substance in question comes from the seeds of the tree and affects the hepatic –" He paused and looked at me, then amended his intended description into simpler terms. "It affects the liver's ability to store sugars, more or less emptying the body's supply of fuel. This patient was on a low-sugar diet, trying to lose weight, so she had poor sugar storage already. This contributed to her susceptibility."

I nodded approval of his explanation.

"Both of these poisonings could have been made with relatively little victim contact," he concluded, unscrewing the lid from the jar and dumping it into Brandan's drink. "As simple as that."

Brandan made a face, earning laughter that swiftly turned to groans as the magnitude of the issue became clear.

After a round-the-table summary of what tasks were in place, the meeting seemed to adjourn itself.

When I stood up, a wave of vertigo made me close my eyes and press my hands to the table for balance.

I hadn't been thinking about Matt's story, at least consciously, but in a flash of images, I saw a much younger Matthew Shannaker cradling the butt of a rifle against his right shoulder to take aim. I heard the sound of the trigger moving, the firing pin striking the primer, and the deafening crack as the bullet left the muzzle at over

2700 feet per second.

To me, it looked like an old blurry 16 mm movie they showed when I was in grade school. The vision took far too long to play out in my head, the details much too vivid, but it must have only lasted a moment.

"Julie," Katz spoke to me, his hand on my shoulder. "I'd like you to pick up a book in – Are you okay?"

I sat back down, trying to figure out what I had just seen. I nodded, jotted down a note on my packet. It was gibberish, but it looked like a good excuse to have been so distracted. "Sorry, it was one of those fleeting thoughts. You needed what?"

His look said he wasn't sure he believed me.

I started to speak, to defend my momentary confusion when another wave of mental images flew by. This time, dead women and knives.

The connection hit me like a fist in the gut.

I turned from Katz and grabbed Glenn Corbitt by the arm as he made his way to the door. "What about the girl?" I blurted out. "In the photo from the disk?"

Corbitt looked at me blankly.

I took his notebook. "The photos on the disk left at my house? There has to be a reason I received that particular photo. This girl's throat was cut," I said, flipping to the image from the disk. "What if she is the last victim, the one in the barrel? What if this is the same killer?"

This caught several people's attention, especially Jeremy McNeeley's. Forrester went to catch Matt Shannaker and Brandan Callaghan.

Finally the smaller group was seated around me, waiting for an explanation of my outburst.

Absent was Matthew.

I unlocked the rings of the notebook and spread out the photos Glenn had printed and enlarged. "These images were left for me on the disk. The knife, the drawing, and the photo of the body with her throat slit. I don't think this is a coincidence. What if this," I said, pointing to the photograph, "is that last victim in the barrel?"

"We can send the disk to the FBI lab for enhancement,"

Forrester said.

Corbitt smiled. "Julie had me ship it September 9."

"Quinton Gresham didn't have anything definitive this morning, but there was no link to the other cases, nothing to compare to," I said.

Callaghan sat back in his chair. "So if these cases are linked. . . " he said, letting the thought hang. He ran his hands over his face. "Damn. What else do you know about this intruder, Julie?"

Part of me didn't want to acknowledge the connection. The rest of me knew it was true. I couldn't imagine how I'd missed something so obvious.

"He left the disk, put a fish in my tank, and has called and faxed me with a reference to how my name was listed on my original birth certificate in Germany, and he's –"

Several of them started to ask questions at the same time about the situation, but Jeremy's deep voice drowned them all out.

"What kind of fish?"

CHAPTER 22

Faces turned, all giving him that same quizzical look, questioning how could a fish be the more important issue?

"A puffer fish, I believe," I said. "In my salt water aquarium."

"Puffer fish is eaten as a delicacy in Japan and the Eastern Oriental countries; however, parts of this fish are poisonous," Jeremy stated. "If he's leaving hints, he could kill his next victim with tetrodotoxin, which interferes with nerve signals and causes paralysis."

I felt nauseated at the new connection. "The fax said he was leaving, but that doesn't mean he hasn't already poisoned someone," I explained. "Maybe we should notify the emergency rooms and EMS crews about what they might encounter."

Dr. Katz nodded and made a note on his folder cover.

"We need to figure out why he's communicating with you, Julie," Forrester said. "If he's the one who killed Tucker and the other four in the barn, he must feel confident of his abilities to hide."

"Julie said it was like a cat leaving a bird, a kill not out of need but a presentation," Jeremy said. "He's spent a lot of time to research these unusual ways of killing. Time to use them."

"It's a huge change in killing methods if he had previously been cutting throats," I said. "Why would he switch?"

"He's proud of how the new ways are challenging you – stumping you. You may or may not get more clues like the fish. Or to pardon the pun, it might be a red herring," Detective Callaghan said.

Pun as it was, it broke the tension.

"The candy I received was a clue we didn't understand until he made a reference to the second victim needing some of it," I said. "Or maybe it was a scare tactic."

It damned sure worked.

They agreed it was prudent to follow the lead about the fish.

Leaving them in a loud discussion, I walked down the hall with Dr. Katz and my escort. Almost to my office, what felt like a bolt of lightning crashed through my skull, agony that dissipated just as quickly. I must have flinched.

Often, this type of pain was a precursor to a severe migraine, which I didn't have time for. My vision hadn't faded to shimmering lights yet, which was a good sign.

"Julie?" Dr. Katz said, touching my elbow. "Are you sure you're okay?"

"Headache aura," I said, knowing it would take no further explanation. I'd had several of them. "I'll be fine. You have something for me to do?"

He held out a piece of paper, a set of keys and a map. "An errand for you to run, if you're up to it."

I read the tight handwriting. "Pick up a book called *The Mayhem and Mystery of Murder* by Gordon Royce Elliott. Nelson Bain has it in Marquette. (Coincidence?) Have a little chat with him about the case. Make it a long weekend. Take your camera. You'll find great scenery around the coastline at the cabin. GK"

I nodded, knowing that his suggestion for staying over the weekend was not an option, and that it was useless to argue.

He continued. "Before you came in, Connie intercepted this note in the mail, referencing the book. I had her calling every bookstore in the state around until she found it."

In his scrawling on the map, he indicated there would be no fresh food in the cabin, but he had checked with a neighbor about the power.

"Sure. Beats sitting in the morgue all weekend," I said, beginning a mental list of things to take as I headed for my office, where I dismissed the deputy on guard.

First, I pulled a scene kit, so I could properly handle the book as evidence. I checked the case containing my own cameras and lenses to make sure I had plenty of film.

"I came to make plans for the evening," Jeremy said from my door. "But it looks like you're running away." He nodded toward the cases.

"Sort of, I have to pick up a book for Dr. Katz in Marquette."

"Can I come with you?"

The "yes" was out of my mouth before my brain had finished the admonishment *What the hell are you thinking?* "But it's more than five hours away, and I'm spending the night, so if you have any issue with that, speak up."

He shook his head.

What the hell am I thinking?

"Can you take these to my truck? I need to grab one other bag." I pushed the two cases across my desk toward him and handed him my keys.

In the hall, we parted, and I went to the room where I'd been sleeping and stuffed a change of clean clothes, toiletries, and my holstered Glock 17 into an overnight bag.

Jeremy stood waiting for me by the truck and loaded my last bag into the back without question.

I drove to his hotel and asked him if he had something warmer, explaining our destination.

"I have one pair of jeans and a couple long-sleeved T-shirts. Will I need goose down?" he kidded. "Are there polar bears and penguins?"

"For a Southern boy like you, it might be cold enough for goose down. There was still ice in Lake Superior in June this year." I pulled onto the bayside highway. "I realize you've never been north of the Mason-Dixon Line before, but Marquette averages over twelve feet of snow a year."

Probably the most snow he'd seen in his life was the weekend I'd taken him to Taos, where he spent the day in the bar at the base of Al's Run. Jeremy was not a skier.

He shook his head in disbelief. "What the hell do you do with twelve feet of snow?"

"Besides shovel it and blow it? Well, there's skiing, which is a shame. So much snow and no elevation. And snowmobiling, the speed sport invented to cull stupidity from the gene pool," I said. The sledding fatality rate was very high. "Those pesky trees and other fixed objects like to jump right out in front of drunken sledders racing from bar to bar." I pointed to the road ahead of us. "Sleds are also street legal, adding a traffic risk as well."

"That's absurd."

Sure, if you're not a sledder, it's perfectly illogical.

"Hunting is big here. Deer season is practically a religious event with communion from a flask," I continued, knowing I was not quoting the state tourism guides and was risking eviction to New Mexico if someone overheard me.

"I don't understand hunting. I think it's pointless to track and shoot an animal I'm not going to eat," he said.

"Who said anything about tracking? They dump out carrots, corn or apples into a pile for weeks before the season opens, then sit in blinds and tree stands, waiting for deer to come feed. Nothing sporting about that at all, in my opinion," I complained. "Might as well sit in the kitchen and shoot at your dog when he comes to his bowl."

My mind again flashed an image of a young boy shouldering his rifle, target in his scope, crosshairs settling on the side of his head –

CHAPTER 23

"– in a tree stand? Why would –" Jeremy's voice faded back into my thoughts.

I held up my hand for him to stop. "I have a theoretical question. How or why does the mind, when given only certain facts of an event, fill in other details?"

Jeremy's puzzled expression said enough.

"For example, I mentioned hunting and so you thought of tracking animals, right?" I prompted. "What if I told you about a car accident where a driver was decapitated. Close your eyes. What details does your brain give of that accident? What do you see?"

He rolled his eyes then shut them. "I imagine a car smashed under the rear-end of a semi. A red sports car, like a Corvette. The scene is dark, and there are flashing red lights bouncing off everything," he said, opening his eyes. "Why?"

"Okay, then how does your brain adapt to the new facts if I say it's a green Volkswagen bus that hit a bridge abutment in broad daylight?" I asked. "What do you imagine about the scene then? Your mind alters the image and reformulates those details you still don't know based on current data and previous memory, right? Do you still see the red lights still flashing on the patrol cars? How much of that process is purely imagination to create the image?"

"What are you getting at, Julie?" he said, head cocked.

Seriously questioning my sanity.

"I have this nagging image I can't explain, but I didn't see the real event. I think something is wrong with the version I see – like in a movie where someone injures his right leg but then later has a cast on his left. I have to figure out what's wrong," I said, stopping in front of his hotel. "I'll wait. I need a little fresh air."

He went inside without further discussion.

I strolled toward the beach, wondering why my mind kept showing me the images of Matt shooting his father. Given time to actually think about the memory's details, I was able to picture Matt wearing a hunter's orange cap with the ear flaps snapped up, a red and black plaid flannel shirt and an orange vest, a high-powered rifle butted against his right shoulder. But I had no previous memory or knowledge on which those details could be based. I'd never seen Matt dressed like that, never seen him shoot a rifle.

Jeremy was waiting for me when I returned to the truck.

"I'm sorry. I'm a little preoccupied with this case." I didn't lie. I was distracted, but not by the case he suspected. I started the truck and turned onto the highway that wound around the east side of Grand Traverse Bay.

We rode in silence for a long time as he took in the beauty of the lakeside. I saw nothing but the stripes on the pavement, fighting to keep visions of Matthew killing his father out of my head.

Small talk wasn't going to keep my mind occupied long enough for this trip.

"Tell me how you ended up at CDC," I said, hoping for a happier diversion.

Jeremy had been very passionate about medicine. I heard the same fire in his voice as he told me about his career with the Centers for Disease Control.

"I decided to go back to medical school and ended up at Tulane. During my residency, my attending diagnosed a woman with Guillain-Barré, but something about her story didn't fit. After I spent time really talking to her, I learned she'd been to Finland, her homeland, and to parts of Africa throughout the summer, working with children. I believed she'd contracted paralytic poliomyelitis. No one would listen to me, so I called my father. He sent out an epidemiologist. I was hooked when I found out I was right."

"I thought polio had been eradicated," I said.

"Not everywhere. Polio elimination was just certified in 1994," he said. "Small pox. There's something we think is globally eradicated, except for countries that might use it as a biological weapon."

"Lovely thought." I muttered. "So exactly what do you do?"

"My specialty is biological identification and epidemiology. I'm on a go-team whose members travel around the world to evaluate special circumstances. For example, the team investigated the 1984 biological attack in a small Oregon town. Members of a local commune contaminated food and drinks in 38 restaurants with *Salmonella* ordered from a laboratory in Maryland."

"Intentional poisoning?" I asked.

He nodded. "Political terrorism over building permits, mind you. Poisoning in 38 restaurants, caused symptoms in over 750 people with 45 requiring hospitalization."

"How does one order something like *Salmonella*?" I blurted. A voice in my head played an option. "I'd like a cheeseburger, a medium ice tea, and a large order of microorganisms to kill a thousand people, please. Oh, and could I get fries with that?"

Jeremy laughed. "Companies grow genetically pure strains of bacteria and viruses for research. Officially, the United States signed the 1972 Biological and Toxic Weapons Convention, calling for the destruction of all stocks of bio-weapon agents, as well as banning research and development of weapons such as anthrax, botulism and plague." He flashed his best bureaucrat smile. "But we must be prepared to respond to an attack or other outbreak." The smile dissipated. "The Russians built their research facilities on an island in the early 50's, but now the water is being diverted. If the Aral Sea goes dry, it could set in motion the release of plague, smallpox, anthrax, tularemia."

"Stop. That's depressing. I've learned more about germs this week than any healthy human should know," I said. "And this epidemiologist who forever changed your life – did you marry her?" I tried to hide the smirk.

"Um, yeah, but it's been over for about a year." He sighed. "How did you know?"

"Just a hunch."

"You got married, too. Did he change your life?"

Not nearly like I changed his. . .

I nodded. "Permanently."

I'd driven another six miles before he got the nerve to ask.

"Okay, so you didn't tell me about the bomb. Are you going to tell me about the husband?"

"Why not? I've had to tell practically everyone else I know in the last few days," I said, hating it. "It's one of those things I wish had never happened, but I wouldn't be in Michigan if it hadn't. This job is the best thing I've ever done for myself. Let's get something to drink, then I'll tell you."

When we got to Mackinaw City I parked to show Jeremy a view of the bridge from Fort Michilimackinac.

The Mackinaw Bridge is a five-mile-long suspension bridge connecting the lower and upper peninsulas of Michigan. At the highest point, it rises 199 feet above the Straits of Mackinaw, two lanes in each direction with the inner lanes being metal grate between the towers.

We bought a couple of soft drinks and a pound of fudge at one of the touristy places and found a picnic table where we could feast and marvel at the engineering.

The day was clear with visibility better than any other time I'd ever crossed the Straits. "What a place to commit suicide," he observed. "How many people jump a year?"

"Jumpers? I can't say I've heard of any. They only allow pedestrians on the Labor Day walk. A few workers have fallen, I think. And as far as I know, only two cars have ever gone off. One of them was suicide."

Overloaded on sugar, we climbed into my truck, and I pulled back onto I-75 northbound and headed over the bridge. Traffic was moving slowly due to perpetual maintenance, but this allowed Jeremy time to take in the experience properly. From the top is a spectacular view of Mackinaw Island.

I was about to tell him about the Grand Hotel there, where the movie *Somewhere in Time* was filmed, when he spoke.

"So did you really shoot your husband?" Jeremy blurted, his face growing pink. "I mean, that's what I was told."

Without answering until we were off the bridge, finding my hands gripped on the wheel so tightly my knuckles ached, I finally said, "Yes, I did."

He looked like he wanted to ask, but maybe he wasn't sure he *wanted* to know what came next. I watched him open and close his mouth twice before I let him off the hook.

"David Wesley was going to kill me – he said so. I don't know why he hadn't. Maybe he believed I was nearly dead, lying at the bottom of the stairs, bleeding. I don't remember how I got there." Without tears, but not without tension all through my body, I told the story yet again. "I managed to get my backup revolver. I raised it over my head to point it at him and fired as he tried to take the gun from my hands."

Jeremy was quiet, watching me.

I wished I could hear what was going through his head.

I wished I didn't hear what's going through mine.

"Why so long at the hospital?"

Without rolling my eyes at how casually he'd asked, I reported. "I had a seven-inch gash across my neck. Lacerations and contusions to my face. He dislocated and fractured my right shoulder. I had a cervical fracture and lumbar compression fracture. The list goes on."

He fell silent again for several miles, and I just drove, letting him put it all together.

"I'm really sorry," Jeremy finally said.

I shrugged.

"I mean I'm sorry I let you go."

Holding my breath, I resisted blasting him with fourteen years worth of nasty retorts, in hopes of finally hearing a true answer. "Why, Jeremy? What was the real reason you broke off our engagement?"

He stared out the side window, maybe struggling with an answer. Finally he turned to face me and said, "Because I was jealous of you."

"Jealous?" I echoed. I'd imagined a hundred other excuses from him, but never that one.

"I didn't think I could compete with the state police for your attention. You were destined to be fast-tracked up the ladder. Me? I'd dropped out of medical school," he said, sounding defeated, not defensive. "I didn't want to follow you around the state and be

Superwoman's lame paramedic husband."

"When you broke up, I hadn't even applied to the state, Jeremy," I said, getting louder with each word. "But you decided our plans weren't worth talking about, so you just dumped me? We hauled in a dying pregnant woman from a clusterfuck of a car crash at the most dangerous intersection in town, and while Kent's writing the report and I'm mopping blood out of the back of the rig, you say, 'Oh, by the way, it's over.' Because you were jealous of my career?"

He had no reply.

"Remind me later to tell you the rest of the story. We screwed up something else that night."

He nodded. "My ego was wrong, but I couldn't stand the thought of living in your shadow."

"I was so damned mad that you couldn't be honest with me, that you chose to walk away without explanation, without ever looking back at what we lost," I said, trying to be civil.

"Trust me, I looked back."

"No, you didn't. I was driven toward law enforcement, but I would have changed for you, for us." I paused. "For all three of us."

That news hung in the hum of tires on pavement and wind noise for a long time as the words sunk in for him.

"Why didn't you tell me you were pregnant?" His voice almost squeaked.

"I didn't know that night. When I miscarried at five weeks later, I figured if you hadn't changed your mind by then, you weren't going to."

"I kept thinking I'd be damned to try to change you. I'm really sorry." He paused. "But I've changed in these last years."

"We both changed. Not necessarily for the better."

He took a deep breath. "So be honest with me. Would you give me another chance? Can I compete against your deputy?"

I looked at him. "What makes you think –"

"I overheard him telling Dr. Katz you stayed at his place last night. I just want to know if it's serious – why you didn't ask him to come with you on this trip?"

"Matt and I have a platonic relationship," I said. *He killed his father when he was a teenager, so I don't think I could love him now even if I wanted.*

"So you don't love him? This isn't something to get even with him for a fight?" He smiled.

"This has nothing to do with Matt," I said. "The day you walked into my office, I swore to myself I wouldn't feel anything. I've hated you a long time for hurting me. When you put your arms around me at Dr. Katz's, I still hated you." I let that thought go and sighed. "I'm not sure I like where any of this is going."

"If you hate me, why am I here?"

Why had I had said Jeremy could come along, other than I felt safe with him?

"I think because you asked to go," I said.

Checking the map again, I drove twenty minutes before I turned off the highway and maneuvered my Suburban over the heavy undergrowth on the two-track that led to the cabin. When it came into view, it wasn't what I expected at all.

I expected a hunting cabin, rustic and bare necessities. But one look inside the door proved MaryAnne had been here. The living room furniture included two futon sofas and a recliner. The kitchen had an oak table and chairs, a small refrigerator, gas stove and a stacked washer and dryer. There were also two bedrooms and a full bathroom. Despite its lack of use, it was orderly and clean.

"Cozy, eh?" I said, making the tour. I went through the kitchen and out the sliding door to find a breathtaking view of Lake Superior with the late afternoon sun reflecting off the water.

I heard the door slide closed and soft footsteps as Jeremy came to the railing beside me. I watched the waves, pretending not to notice his eyes were burning holes in my soul.

Finally, Jeremy asked if I was hungry.

I'd forgotten there was no fresh food, so we scavenged the kitchen, finding an assortment of pasta and sauces. We even found a full wine rack.

Jeremy tried to open a bottle of merlot and pushed the cork into the bottle. I spilled a handful of angel hair pasta. And we laughed as the awkwardness faded and the tension relaxed.

I forgot about the past and the circumstances of his being with me until Jeremy brought it up after dinner when we sat in the living room with a fire blazing.

"So tell me about being in a halo," he said, pouring more wine. "That must have been tough for someone like you."

"Oh but I loved spending two months with my head hanging on four posts by nails in my skull," I said, faking a dreamy voice, then changing back to my own. "I'm sure it wasn't much easier on anyone around me either."

"Closest I can relate is a broken ankle. I was in a cast for seven weeks."

"Not even in the same hemisphere," I said, thinking back to the weeks of hell. "You can't imagine the complications of simple things like sneezing or brushing your hair. I begged my mother to shave my head, but she only came and shampooed my hair ever other day, taking hours to do what had taken me five minutes in the shower and ten minutes with a brush and blow-dryer. But since you brought it up, there's a part of the story that involves you, indirectly. About someone I met when they removed the halo."

CHAPTER 24

I'd spent weeks in various levels of hospitalization until the alleged good news – I could move to a rehabilitation center.

Great. Now I'll be stuck in a stinky nursing home with old people.

By then, the impromptu party by the nurses was probably a good-riddance celebration more than a congratulatory one. I really hadn't meant to be a miserable bitch, but after sixty-four days, I could not find any more pleasantries to share. They could medicate my pain, but narcotics couldn't reach what hurt most inside me – and no one could numb that.

"My first weeks in Desert Sun Rehab were a monotonous, exhausting blur," I told Jeremy, who leaned back on a pillow in the floor. "I needed assistance to get up and dressed, to get to breakfast, and then two half-hour sessions of physical therapy for my shoulder and lower back. Between, I was allowed a snack, a brief period to rest or nap. I had lunch and an afternoon social hour, though I preferred to sit in the spring sunshine alone. Then two more physical therapy sessions in the afternoon to work on general conditioning."

"I think I'll stick with broken ankles," Jeremy commented, reaching to tweak my toes.

"All that fun was interrupted for a short trip back to the hospital when it was time for my halo to come off, which meant a new phase of physical therapy to work on the muscles of my neck. The excitement of release from the halo turned to anger when I realized that I was too weak to lift my head from the pillow."

Jeremy nodded.

"That's where I met Scott Dunn, the hospital physical therapist," I paused, but saw no recognition in Jeremy's eyes. "He's someone from our past."

After the doctor had removed the device that kept my head still, Scott had explained he remembered me, only I thought at first he meant when the helicopter flew me in from Alamogordo, so I apologized and told him there was a lot about that day I didn't remember because I was snowed in morphine.

"But he said he didn't mean that evening. In his Scottish brogue, he said, 'I remember seeing you the night my own neck was broken in a crash. You were on the ambulance that night, taking care of my wife.' And suddenly the entire scene flashed in my head. We'd responded to the intersection of San Mateo and Montgomery, where Scott's Volkswagen Jetta got creamed on the passenger side by a full-size Chevy pickup."

Yep, it took a moment, but there was the connection I expected from Jeremy.

"Alice Dunn was our patient," I said. "And her unborn son." Tears ran down my cheeks as Jeremy sat, stunned at the story. "On the way to the hospital, she told us the baby's name – Ian. Alice died, but they did a c-section to deliver the infant. When doctors told him his son's lungs were not mature enough to survive, Scott asked them to bring the baby to him. He and Alice hadn't talked about naming the baby yet. 'I was going to lose him, too, but I didn't know what she wanted to call him. I'd hoped she'd told you, Miss Julie. Alice would know our son when he got to Heaven, you see? I wanted to know his name for when I get there, too.'" I paused. "You remember why we didn't go talk to him?" I didn't bother to hide the harsh accusation. "Why we failed to pass on her words to her husband?"

CHAPTER 25

Jeremy nodded – that was the night he dumped me.

"I'm sorry about Dunn's family. You're right. We should have talked to him." Jeremy reached out and emptied the wine bottle in my glass. "I'm sorry about everything that happened that night."

Not knowing how to respond, I said nothing.

My voice was tired after the long tale. Another chapter of my life I hadn't shared with anyone, not even my mother.

Jeremy went to open another bottle of white zinfandel, our third for the evening. Fussy Mr. California Chablis hadn't known they made wine in Michigan.

"That's one thing I always admired about you. You're good with people," he said when he returned, sitting down near my feet. "They're all impressed with you, the cops and the guys in the lab. They have confidence in you."

"I worked my way up here. Part of the deal when Dr. Katz hired me was not to reveal my law enforcement background. I did what I was hired to do and made a place for myself later as an ME investigator. Nobody fast-tracked me, as you put it. It wasn't until after this bombing case that anyone else knew I'd been with the New Mexico State Police, and that was by accident."

"Do you believe in accidents?" he asked, tilting his head in curiosity.

"There is always a margin of error or some element of preventability," I said. "I tried hard to prevent that one."

"No, I don't mean whether an event is preventable. I believe certain events happen because of circumstances we could control but elect not to. That we sometimes decide not to make a choice at all, then call it an accident when the obvious happens anyway."

"Are you saying I *wanted* to expose my past to everyone here?" I said, getting defensive.

"I'm saying you've been waiting since I showed up in your office for me to make a move so you can say no." He touched my hand on the chair arm. "And I've been waiting for you to say no so I can rationalize why I shouldn't bother trying again. But my being in Michigan, here with you like this, can't be an accident, can it?"

I blinked and looked away, swirled my wine, watching the candles and fireplace light sparkle in the glass. "It might not be an accident, but it's a train wreck in progress."

He nodded.

I leaned over and kissed him.

He laughed. Kept laughing. Rolling-on-the-floor, holding-his-belly laughing.

I didn't understand what exactly he thought was so funny. I was perfectly serious.

But he was snorting and rocking, tears running down his face. Then I began to laugh at him because he fell over on his side and bumped his head. Soon, we were laughing at laughing because it felt good.

Finally we came back to our senses, with a few regressions of giggles, both of us sprawled on the floor, faces red and damp.

My ribs ached. My sleeves were damp with tears. I rolled to my good side to look at him, still on his back.

His hair was mussed, and his cheeks were flushed. A smile lingered.

"Okay, so what was so funny?"

"You," he said, reaching up and touching my lips with a fingertip. "Watching you stacking up these stones that seemed to be falling at your feet. Like an old silent movie."

"I tried hard to push away the past," I said, not quite so amused now. "Including you."

"You always had the most beautiful laugh hidden behind that serious face. But it was the kiss. The only way this wasn't going to be an accident was if you made the first move."

It was no accident at all, I guess.

From the moment he shook my hand, I knew I couldn't stop feeling the way I had before, no matter what happened then or since. As much as I didn't want to feel anything because it was terrifying to acknowledge such vulnerability again, it was all fresh and alive in my heart.

Jeremy was right about the evening. I had been waiting for him to do something so I could shoot him down. Be in control.

I hadn't allowed myself to think about this possibility – that I would step around that wall I'd been trying to hide behind.

Since that night when Jeremy said it was over, since I'd expelled a bloody mess that was supposed to be our baby, I'd tried to replace what I had lost with work, with other men. Look what it had gotten me with David. I don't recall thinking about Jeremy again until Scott Dunn told me about his wife and son, which only reinforced the thoughts I didn't want to be in love like that ever again because it would only end in more pain. If Jeremy hadn't contacted me while I healed, I didn't think he would. I'd taken that and added one more rejection to the rest of the ugly scars I hid.

Now, in the midst of one of the biggest murder cases in the county's recent history, with Matt Shannaker's confession about his father, and with a killer stalking me, Jeremy stole back what pieces of my heart were big enough to grab.

I must be out of my mind.

I kissed him again.

He pulled me closer, and we held each other for a long time before he pulled the futon into a bed and spread a sleeping bag over us.

Despite a distant memory of passionate sex lingering between us, now there was the hesitancy of two people embracing for the first time, or more accurately, for the first time in a very long time. A precarious balance between urgency and intimacy.

Desperation and caution.

He slid his sweatshirt off and wrapped his arms around me. His skin was hot against my face and fingers. He seemed in no hurry to bare my skin, but moved his hands over the silk on my arms and back and caressed my face.

"You smell good," he said, running his fingers through my hair, lifting it off my neck and kissing me under my ear.

I must have flinched as his lips moved down toward the collar of my turtleneck.

"You don't have to hide the scars," he said, pulling away and looking me in the eye.

I nodded. "A few are still sensitive," I said, trying not to seem timid. "No one ever sees – " I let the words trail off.

"I'm more concerned with the scars on the inside, Julie," he said, leaning up on one arm and kissing me on the tip of my nose. "And the cracked ribs. I don't want to hurt you."

I reached up and turned off the lamp, leaving us in the light of the fire.

"I'll tell you if something hurts." I rolled over, straddling his thighs. "But don't treat me like I'm damaged." I sat up and pulled the turtleneck over my head and tossed it to the chair, leaving a sports bra.

He sat up, facing me, wrapping his arms around my waist. He slid his hand up my back and began peeling the cloth up.

I wrapped my fingers in his hair and pulled his face toward mine and kissed him until he pulled my arms up over my head with the tanktop and pulled me down with him.

He ran his hands through my long hair, letting it cascade around our faces, shadowing him from the fire, but his eyes still sparkled. Suddenly, our bodies responded to each other without inhibition.

After he pulled off my jeans and panties, then his own remaining clothes, he yanked the sleeping bag over us as he moved over me.

"I want you, Julie. I have prayed for so long I'd get the chance to hold you, to make love to you one more time, to beg you to forgive me."

I felt him hesitate, waiting for acceptance.

I wrapped my legs around his thighs, and ran my fingers through his hair, turning his face so I could see his eyes. "So beg."

* * *

Later, he turned to me in sleep, draped an arm over my waist, and whispered in the darkness.

Was it my name?

After a few moments in the absolute silence, I wasn't sure I'd heard him say anything at all.

I checked my watch; it was 4:36 a.m.

Hours till sunrise.

I sat up and stretched, pulled on my tank top and panties, and padded barefoot to the bathroom. The toilet flushing was deafening in the quiet of the cabin. Icy water from the tap numbed my fingers when I washed my hands and face.

Although I expected to be awake for the rest of the night, when I crawled back under the sleeping bag and Jeremy snuggled up behind me, I drifted off to sleep.

The next morning, I woke to the smell of autumn and a warm male body next to me. The fire had burned out, and the room was chilled, but it was toasty under the covers next to Jeremy. He was sleeping on his stomach, one arm hanging off the side. Sunlight gleamed in his hair.

I got up and made coffee, then showered. When I came out of the bathroom, Jeremy was sitting on the floor with his legs crossed, his back to me. Curious, I watched as he took a few deep breaths, raising his arms over his head with each inhalation, lowering them as he exhaled. He lowered his head for a moment as if in prayer. Then he stood up, bold and naked, turning to face me. "Oh, I didn't hear you come out of the bathroom," he said sheepishly. "Meditation."

I motioned toward the kitchen. "So long as you haven't given up coffee or red meat," I said, tossing him a robe.

He went to the bathroom, and I put on my jeans and poured myself a cup of coffee.

Last night hadn't been what I expected, but at least he didn't confess to killing anyone.

CHAPTER 26

After breakfast in a truckstop, we drove to downtown Marquette to a bookstore I'd visited several times before, thanks to Dr. Katz's friendship with the owner.

"Nelson Bain has a collection of books I think might interest you, too," I explained as we walked toward the front of the store. "Old medical books. He keeps a room for antiques and first editions. It's a fabulous shop."

We browsed the sales floor and drank hot chocolate from the coffee shop until Nelson could break away and greet us. He walked us to a back room where he presented the book Dr. Katz had sent me for – a yellowed, dog-eared edition wrapped in plain white paper. When more customers came in, Nelson returned to the front.

Jeremy browsed the books on the first edition shelves while I slipped on a pair of gloves and examined the Elliott book.

Gordon Royce Elliott, an early 1940's British physician, had collected stories of unusual methods of homicide, both fact and fiction, or more precisely reported and hearsay.

"There is a reference in here to using parasites. I wonder if this is his cookbook or just a ruse. I don't find akee trees," I said, after browsing the pages a while.

"Probably weren't called that when the book was written. Besides, it's only a poison when it's not cooked. I hear they fry the ripe fruit in butter in Jamaica. But like your bug being called something else in North America, akee might have another name if it's in there," Jeremy said, joining me with a couple of old books he wanted to purchase.

Finally Nelson was able to join us again, bringing more hot chocolate and a muffin for each of us. “Gerald told me a little about this case yesterday. I knew exactly what book he wanted after he began describing the two cases. Elliott lists some extremely unusual methods of poisoning, including the ancient standard of hemlock and honey.”

“Has anyone been in here looking for this book?” I asked.

“Not that any of us remembers, which makes this even more bizarre. I didn’t show we had a copy of it in the inventory, but I’ve seen it recently enough to have recognized it. It might have been on the shelf for several years, I couldn't exactly say.”

“Is it possible someone left it here intentionally?” Jeremy asked. “Just slid it onto a shelf when no one was looking.”

“Given the circumstances, it’s more than possible,” Nelson said, waving around to make his point. “Otherwise, I’d have said it came from a library cull or maybe from an estate.”

“No sense looking for fingerprints,” I said.

“Julie, you could pull prints till a thunder moon and never get them all and never get a match to your perp,” Nelson said. “I wish I could help you more. He’s playing a nasty game.”

“He sent us looking for this book for a reason,” I said. “But why here? He could have dumped it anywhere else in the state. Could have mailed it. I think it’s another demonstration of something he knows about me, that I’ve been here before. Rather than being a real clue, it’s something to make us, or me in particular, feel overwhelmed, which he has done exceedingly well so far.”

We talked a while longer, and I put the book in an evidence envelope before we headed forward to the main part of the store.

Nelson rang up Jeremy’s purchase, then he made me sign a credit slip for the Elliott book, refusing to let me pay for it and be reimbursed.

“I know how getting money from the county can be,” he said with a wink. “Good luck catching this bastard.”

Jeremy and I stopped at my truck so I could lock the book up. I drove us to the waterfront park for a stroll.

In the distance, we could see the steel dock where ships load hematite and iron ore through dozens of chutes. To the east, the abandoned wooden dock hunkered like a forgotten old man.

"It's pretty here," he said putting his arm around my shoulders. "No bulletproof vest today?" he asked, patting my back.

"In the truck, along with all my other gadgets," I smiled. "You know, I think the killer's probably telling the truth – he doesn't want to hurt me. I'm his playmate, his penpal. Maybe he feels some kind of connection to me. Maybe for surviving his bomb. He's certainly gone to great lengths to find out about me."

"Yeah, and he knows far too much."

"He probably knows too much about everyone chasing him," I said, changing the subject to something more pleasant. "I told you you'd like the store."

"How'd Bain get involved in this, do you think?"

"He and Gerald Katz went to college together in Lansing. Bain was a motorcycle cop until he got hit in an intersection by a teenager," I said. "Gerald introduced me when Bain visited Traverse City, and I made a few trips up here since. As for the book, I hoped it was a coincidence it was here, but I don't think so."

We walked on in silence back toward my truck.

"Bain said something about it being a game, too. Isn't that an odd term to use?"

"The killer called it a game, about taking turns. He very easily could have hurt me, but instead, he's sending me clues. He has nothing tangible to gain by killing these women except manipulating me. He also could kill a much greater number of people, but he doesn't. This isn't about money or even fame. It's sport. It's pure evil."

"Define evil," Jeremy asked as he opened the driver's door for me.

I'd had a long time to work out what it meant to me. "True evil acts without conscience or remorse, toying with or destroying the lives of others to cause pain and suffering, and takes immense pleasure from doing so," I said. "This man is evil."

"That's more than my dictionary says," he said with a chuckle, "but I guess it's true."

"Since my father's murder, I've defined evil by the crimes I've seen. Truly insane criminals may be violent, but they are seldom so creatively malevolent."

On the way out of Marquette, we stopped to buy something for dinner and more wine to replace what we'd consumed from the Katzes.

Back at the cabin, I bundled Jeremy up for an afternoon walk along the shore in a brisk wind. I knew he was cold, but I waited until he confessed he wished he had goosedown before turning back.

Jeremy fixed chicken and wild rice with mushrooms, and I kept the wine glasses full, the conversation carefully steered away from the case.

While dinner was in the oven, he led me to the futon and laid me down. "My heart melted when I saw you again after all these years." He stretched out beside me. "I know it's too soon, Julie, but I hope this is more than just a weekend fling. I hope you want it to be more."

"Those things about me you couldn't live with before haven't changed much, Jeremy."

"I know, but I have. Tell me you're willing to try, that you really want me. All I ask is an honest chance."

"What about the things I want from you, Jeremy? This can't be a one-way street," I said, but my words were muted in soft kisses.

And what did I want anyway?

* * *

After dinner, we cleaned up the kitchen and were getting into a feisty game of rummy when a car pulled up beside my truck. A Michigan State Police patrol.

Preliminary questions of identity out of the way, the sergeant handed me a fax page.

Been trying to contact you all afternoon. Call cell stat. Katz.

I checked my belt, but my pager was not there. Realizing I'd left it and the cell phone in the car when we got to Marquette that morning, I retrieved them and called the numbers repeated on the pager and caller ID.

"I'm glad they found you, Julie. Where are you?" Katz answered on the first ring, his voice edgy. "I've been calling for hours."

"I'm sorry. I left everything in my truck today when we got back from Marquette. What's wrong?"

"Well, it's Matthew. He didn't go to work today and wasn't at his apartment, so they had a Leelanau County deputy drive by his mother's house. Matt's patrol car was there, but he didn't open the door." Katz turned away from the phone and spoke to someone else about a map. "They called, and he answered, but he said he wasn't leaving and wouldn't talk to anyone but you."

"Me? About what?"

"After the sheriff called here looking for you, I tried calling Matthew to explain that I had sent you out of town for the weekend. He said he knew, because he'd followed you and Dr. McNeeley."

"He followed me?" I echoed in dismay.

I saw the alarm I felt mirrored on Jeremy's face as he listened to my side of the conversation.

"As far as Elk Rapids. He told me you were the only person he would talk to. He said he wanted to make things right with you, and to say goodbye," Dr. Katz said with a heavy sigh. "He said he would shoot anyone who came in to get him, so the department is standing by. We've sent a state police helicopter to pick you up at the parking lot of Benson's Excavating, two miles east of the paved road in twenty minutes. No, they say fifteen now. Have Dr. McNeeley drive your vehicle back. And Julie, I think Matt is very serious about this, whatever it is, just so you know. He hasn't answered the phone since."

When we hung up, I tried calling, but the answering machine picked up. I left a message that I was on my way back and would be there as soon as I could.

Jeremy drove to where the helicopter would pick me up. Two local deputies parked to illuminate the landing zone.

I sat speechless in the Suburban, trying to keep my hands from shaking.

"I'm sorry," Jeremy said as the helo came in to land, whirling dust around the cars. "I didn't mean to get between you."

"You don't understand. We didn't have anything but a friendship, really. I don't understand what this is about. What he said doesn't make any sense to me."

He shrugged.

"I'm leaving you the phone. Just get there as soon as you can." I squeezed his hand and got out as the blades began to slow. I handed him Dr. Katz's map.

The helo door opened and someone waved.

I looked at Jeremy who opened his door and tossed me the body armor from the backseat. "Go. Save him if you can," he yelled over the roar of the engines and blades. "But don't let him take you down with him."

CHAPTER 27

I had time to contemplate what to tell Matthew about Jeremy, but what could I say? Was Jeremy really even the issue?

The ride was choppy, and I couldn't see anything from my seat.

I didn't get to look out during my last helicopter ride, either. At least I'm not bleeding this time.

The pilot landed at the high school soccer field in Suttons Bay, several miles north of the Shannaker house. A state police officer drove me to the scene without offering an update. His silence didn't bode well, but I didn't ask.

Six patrol cars sat in the cul de sac in the darkness, no flashing lights to attract more attention than they already had, though I saw faces peering from windows of several houses nearby as we passed.

I got out of the car and was greeted by worried men.

"Julie, we don't know what's happening," Leelanau County Sheriff Bill Evans said.

We had met on a few occasions when I'd responded to calls in his county. Normally, he was easy-going and friendly. Today, a frown aged him ten years, which was hard to do. Bill was a short, stocky man with a snowy crew cut that offered the only semblance of maturity his baby face would ever have. He was in his fourth term as sheriff, and he barely looked old enough to drive his patrol car, except for the cotton-white hair.

"The first officer arrived about 1600 hours at Frank's request, but Shannaker wouldn't come to the door," Evans continued. "In fact, Matt yelled he'd shoot anyone trying to enter. Neither the doorbell nor the knocking bothered the dog more than a few barks then, but it began raising hell about an hour later, before anyone else arrived to back up my deputy. Matt hasn't answered us or the phone since."

I looked at Evans, at Grand Traverse County Sheriff Frank Lomas, then at Gerald Katz, who was there for support, I hoped, and not professionally.

"What do you want me to do?" I asked.

"I told them about your law enforcement background, Julie, and your friendship with Matt – and he did say he wanted to speak to you when I called him. I thought it would be in everyone's interest that your skills and judgment be trusted," Katz explained. "We're all working for the same goal here."

I nodded. "Same question, though. What do you want me to do?"

"See if you can get him to talk," Lomas said.

Since I'd left my cell phone with Jeremy, I borrowed Dr. Katz's and punched in Mrs. Shannaker's number. I could hear the phone ringing inside the house, but no answer, not even the machine now.

Strike one.

I went to the nearest patrol car and climbed in to use the PA. "Matt? It's Julie. I'm here, and I want to talk to you."

No response except from the dog.

"Matthew, if you don't answer me, I have no choice but to come in."

No response inside, but I received a flurry of looks of suspected insanity from the men standing nearby.

Strike two.

"Got any other ideas?" I asked them, getting out of the car. "Anyone got keys to Matt's take-home car? Doggy treats would be nice."

No spare keys.

Strike three.

I hope they still have my room in ICU.

I slipped on my vest, less than encouraged by its presence, pulled a holster from my pack and removed my Glock.

More questioning looks from the group.

"The dog likes me, but he will defend Matt," I explained. "Matt said he'd shoot anyone."

Lomas nodded that he realized I might end up killing one or both.

I borrowed a portable radio from one of the deputies and went to the front door. I knocked and yelled at Matt to come let me in.

No response except barking.

I tested the door, which was unlocked, much to my surprise. I took one last look at the worried men who were hoping I could pull this off, and stepped inside.

Laser came bounding around the corner toward me, barking but not in threat once he saw me. He stopped ten feet away, head down.

"Hey, buddy, whatcha doing?" I knelt and held out my hand and waited. "I came to check on you, take you out for that steak I promised. Come 'ere, boy. It's okay."

He looked around, then came toward me, hunkering down the last few steps. I saw blood on his muzzle and on his paws. He let me scratch his ears. If he was injured, I didn't find anything.

"Good boy. Stay," I told him, making the hand cues I'd seen Matthew use with him. Laser crouched down, eyes still meeting mine and ears perked, ready for another command. I stood up, repeated the directive, almost believing he would obey. With my first step, however, he scrambled up from the slick hardwood floor and took off through the living room toward the staircase.

"I'm in the living room," I reported on the portable. "The dog's got blood on him, but I don't see any wounds."

I blinked away another flash image of Matthew shouldering a rifle.

"Matthew? I'm coming in," I yelled.

Seeing no blood other than paw prints, I followed Laser's path left of the center fireplace and up the carpeted stairs to the main bedrooms. I heard on the radio that one of the deputies had spotted me through the windows from the kitchen.

"Matt? It's Julie. I'm coming up the stairs behind the dog, okay?" I called out.

I looked into the first bedroom and found no one.

As I came to the second room, the dog turned and barked at me. I smelled blood and gunpowder.

Blood spatter on the ceiling told the story.

In the dresser mirror across the room, I could see the puddle of blood on the hardwood floor under what was left of Matt's head. He was on his stomach, facing the bed, away from my view in the mirror. A shotgun lay next to the body, but he had fallen onto his hands. I could see the dependent lividity, where blood had pooled in his bare feet.

He was wearing the same sweatshirt I'd borrowed last time I was here.

What a useless observation. Get your shit together, Julie.

I approached the foot of the bed, careful where I stepped. The bed was a shambles.

Matthew is dead.

I swallowed, fighting a wave of nausea.

Nothing I can do. I couldn't have saved him.

I backed out of the room, calling Laser, who hesitated only a moment, then followed me.

There was one more bedroom and bathroom on this level. I made a sweep but found no one.

I started down the stairs, but my knees felt weak. I took a deep breath and held it as long as I could, then exhaled forcefully.

Matthew was dead.

The words rang inside my head like church bells, making me dizzy.

For the sake of argument, I made a brief search of the rest of the house, though for what, I don't remember. A suicide note, maybe?

"I'm coming out," I finally said into the radio.

I went to the door and slipped outside. Evans and three deputies stood a few feet from the entrance, out of Laser's sight until I closed the door behind me.

"He's dead, several hours, I'd say. It looks self-inflicted," I reported to Evans and Lomas, though neither looked particularly surprised. "Shotgun."

The ripple effect of that news moved through the four other deputies like an electric current. The other two returned to the front of the house.

"We need to get the dog out," Evans said. "Can you manage

that?"

"I suppose so. Where shall I put him?"

"Ms. Madigan," Sheriff Lomas said, "To be honest, I don't know. I was wondering if you would keep him for the night. He seems comfortable with you."

I nodded. I went inside and grabbed a leash from the cabinet where Matt kept Laser's stuff. I took a box of treats and what was left of a bag of food.

Laser came to me and allowed me to put a lead on him.

Ripping off a handful of paper towels and soaking them at the kitchen sink, I cleaned his paws and muzzle. Then without a fuss, we came out the side door from the kitchen, away from the crowd. He found a place to do his business, then eagerly hopped in the backseat of the state police car that had brought me from the helicopter.

I closed the door behind him and then rested my forehead on my crossed forearms against the roof, fighting gravity not to drop to my knees and sob. Other law enforcement personnel controlled their emotions when I could not, but I knew I couldn't watch while they carried out Matt's body.

Dr. Katz came and put a fatherly hand on my shoulder, speaking calming, supportive words I simply could not hear.

Tears still blurred my vision, and I wiped my face with my sleeve. Without looking back at the house, I asked the patrolman to drive me to the Annex.

Laser had been in and out of my office frequently and had claimed a spot there, too. He followed me inside.

I closed the door, and when I sat down on the floor beside my desk, he came over and put his head in my lap. I sat there with him, stroking his ears and talking to him. "You were a very good dog, Laser. I wish you could tell me what went on today." I felt the tears run down my cheeks again. Like the vision of Matt shooting his father, something about the story didn't make sense, but I was so overloaded, I couldn't figure it out.

What a pathetic scene, two Type-A personalities, law enforcement professionals in mourning, cuddled in the corner. At least dogs don't cry.

I woke when Laser raised his head to a soft voice, calling from the door.

"Julie?"

Unsure what Laser might do if someone entered, I got up and stepped into the hallway.

Katz and Deputy Callaghan both looked exhausted.

"No one heard the gunshot, Julie," Brandan said.

I didn't get it.

"Julie," Katz said. "The deputy stayed at the house after I called and talked to Matt yesterday. He stayed there until you arrived, but he never heard a gunshot."

Blinking, I tried to focus on what he said.

CHAPTER 28

"Not Matthew?" I repeated, my brain as stiff and unwilling to function as my muscles.

"No, we don't know who, but definitely not Matt," Katz said, sensing my relief.

"Remember, the deputy said Matt yelled at him not to come in?" Brandan asked. "But that begs the question whether Matt was involved in the shooting in the house."

My heart stuttered. I'd thought the fact Matt wasn't dead was good news, until that idea ricocheted though my head.

"Higgins and Scott brought the body in and started a trace evidence search," Katz said.

"But where is Matt?" It was the same stupid rhetorical question that we were all thinking.

"We don't know, Julie. Can I check your house?" Callaghan asked. "It's a wild shot, but he said he wanted to talk to you."

I went back into my office to get the keys from my bag, then remembered I'd left them with Jeremy. I dug in my desk for a spare set.

Laser followed me to the door. "Bet you have to go out, huh?" I said, rubbing his head. I opened the door but held his collar as I gave the keys to Brandan. "What do I do with the dog?"

"The sheriff thinks that for now, you're as good a candidate to handle him as any of us." Callaghan asked. "Laser likes you. Can you keep him a few days?"

"Sure. Let me know about the house?"

Callaghan nodded and left, twirling my keys around a finger.

"I need to take the dog outside," I said, trying to stretch my back.

"Dr. McNeeley is waiting in my office," Katz said. "But we need to talk first."

I looked at my watch, amazed I'd been asleep so long on the floor of my office. It was 6 a.m. I nodded and went to put a lead on the dog.

"Do you think any of this is really about you and him?" Dr. Katz asked as we took the elevator to the main floor.

"Him Matt or him Jeremy?" I asked, unsure how to answer.

"Both, I suppose. Matt does care about you," Katz said. "Now there's a dead man where we thought Matt would be, and Matt's gone."

Laser found the only patch of grass near the parking lot.

"My relationship with Matt was only platonic," I said. "Even that has been strained since Matt told me how his father died Thursday night."

After hesitating, Katz nodded. "I know Matt didn't accidentally shoot him."

"If you knew, why didn't –" I slumped against the building.

Katz explained. "I didn't know right away. Much later, after Matt became a deputy, I discovered that although he's right-handed, he is grossly left-eyed and prefers to shoot a rifle left-handed. In fact, he told me that when he started deer hunting with his father, Sam bought him a .30-06 with the bolt on the left."

Dr. Katz's story explained why my visual replication of the story seemed wrong. I'd imagined Matt shooting right-handed, but he'd told me he had an eye-dominance problem once.

"Matt said he tripped and fell, that he accidentally pulled the trigger. The bullet hit Sam in the right side of the head."

In other words, if Matt shot a rifle left-handed, he'd have to turn almost 180 degrees before kneeling to aim at his father.

A cold chill ran through me. "But you never took it to the prosecutor." It was not a question.

"No, I guess I didn't see the point so many years later," he paused. "Would you?"

I shrugged. "What a damned horrible thing to ask your kid to do."

He leaned against the wall next to me, and we contemplated in silence.

I was disturbed by one thought I couldn't bring myself to ask out loud – was he really a victim like we assumed, or had Matt killed the man at the house?

Finally, I called to Laser, who was sniffing around the curb, and we headed inside.

"I thought Dr. McNeeley's traveling with you might have triggered anger or jealousy. I interpreted Matt's statement as a suicide threat, but that isn't what happened." Katz slid his keycard through the lock. "Which leaves us to interpret the facts with very little information and a lot of unanswered questions."

His pager went off, so he went ahead of me.

I put Laser in my office, found a bowl in the kitchen to give him water, then I headed to where Jeremy was waiting.

"Julie, I am so sorry," Jeremy said, standing and holding his arms out to me.

"It's not Matthew. There's nothing for you to apologize for," I said without feeling. I wasn't mad, wasn't sarcastic. I was numb. I let him hold me for a moment then pulled away.

"I'm still sorry for how badly this hurts you, that you're involved in this."

I sat down.

"Julie," Katz said, rushing into his office. "Callaghan called from your house. There's a message on your answering machine he wants you to hear." He clicked the speaker button on his desk phone. "Detective?"

"Okay. Um, Julie, first I need to know if your outgoing message was in your voice or the automated message," Callaghan's voice boomed from the speaker.

"I use the automated message," I answered. "Why?"

"You need to hear your new outgoing message," he said, pushing a button on the machine.

A man's voice began. "I'm sorry. Julia is being a bad girl and is sleeping elsewhere with another of her men friends, so she can't talk to you. But I'm sure if you leave a message, she'll return your call promptly. She really does seem to be dependable, even if she's a bit slutty."

That's the voice of my stalker, I thought.

I was going to say something, but Callaghan continued. "I've recorded this to a cassette because I assume the messages are digital and will be gone if we unplug the machine, right? I'm bringing the entire machine in to process for prints and such. Here are the incoming messages. There are four on the counter."

The synthesized voice stated, "Message taken: Friday, at 5:21 p.m."

"Julie," Matt's voice said softly, "I saw you leave with that doctor, then Dr. Katz told me he'd sent you to Marquette for the weekend. I know you were upset about last night, but I can't believe you'd – Damn, I really need to talk to you. I'll –" The call ended with a beep.

"Message taken: Saturday at 2:14 a.m."

"Julie? What the hell is that message? Who is that? Damn, I bet it's the – Oh great." He paused a moment. "We really need to talk. I'm worried. About that message, about you leaving – this whole thing. Call me back. I've tried your cell phone but – Please, just call me."

"Message taken: Saturday at 5:47 a.m." There was no message in the slot, only static then a hang-up.

"Message taken: Saturday at 3:12 p.m. "Uh, hello. This is Jerry at Dillon's Pharmacy Photo Lab. I'm supposed to leave a message that there is a roll of film here for processing that can be picked up after 9 a.m. on Monday under the name of Julia Madigan. Thanks."

"End of final message."

"Have you checked your voice mail at the office yet?" Callaghan asked.

I hadn't. Not since Friday morning before the meeting. Only someone dialing my office number directly or asking to leave a message in my voice mail would be there.

"Don't. Let me duplicate it so we don't lose any voice print information if, well –" Callaghan paused. "Julie, there's also a note by your phone that says Matt won't be seeing you anymore. It says he'll be 'tied up for a while,' in quotation marks."

Matthew Shannaker had been kidnapped out from under the nose of a deputy sitting in front of Carolyn Shannaker's house yesterday. By a man we knew was capable of unspeakable evil.

"You need to leave, Julie. Get away from this killer," Dr. Katz said.

Jeremy nodded in agreement.

"Leave? He's made this about me. For all we know, if I stay, he may keep Matt alive," I argued. "Worse, if he knows so much about me, he probably knows something about all of us, including you. If his targets revolve around me, you might be next, Jeremy."

"Oh, I've already thought of that," he said with a wry smile, "as unpleasant as it seems. But I could take you somewhere he couldn't get to you."

"What about Matt?" I countered. "Photos are supposed to make us believe he's alive."

"You may be right," Callaghan said, "or we may get pictures of a body. Either way, we wait till tomorrow to see. The killer probably selected a pharmacy that sends its film out for processing on purpose. I'll try to find out where and get it back sooner."

"See? I can't leave," I said, desperately looking from Dr. Katz to Jeremy.

"Your call. How many other people will he kidnap or kill to play this game with you?" Jeremy asked, then raised his hands in defense when I stood and turned on him. "I'm not trying to be cold, Julie, and I swear to God this isn't personal. I'm concerned about you, here and now, more than I am about anyone else."

Callaghan's voice came from the speaker again. "He's right, Julie. It's likely Matt's gonna die if he hasn't already."

"Just like that, I should disappear in hopes this will solve itself?" I exploded. "What if – I mean, how can I –?" I sat down so hard it jarred my ribs. I wrapped my arms around my chest for support.

"How do we know torturing you this way isn't exactly what he wants? This could play for a long time," Katz countered. "If he took Matt, why would he stop there? Why not Jeremy?"

"Why not you?" I screeched. "What if I leave and he takes someone else because of it? It doesn't make sense to piss him off by disappearing."

"Based on Shannaker's response, the message was changed between 5:30 Friday night and 2 a.m. Saturday morning," Callaghan said, trying to redirect my anger.

"He had to have been in the house to reset the outgoing message and to leave the note. Why didn't he delete the message Matt had already left?"

"My guess is he meant you to hear it," Callaghan offered. "To confuse the facts. Look, Julie, Nolan Forrester and I both think your input has been extremely valuable in establishing the groundwork, but he feels it's in your best interest not to be involved in this investigation with Matt's kidnapping."

I was stunned. "Just how involved am I now, Detective Callaghan? I work for the ME."

"I know, Julie, and I think there is more you can contribute. There's a conference room at the station," he continued. "We're assembling everything we have there. My theory is that the suspect will keep feeding you information to lure you into the chase, which could be to our advantage. We want you to keep us informed, but not to act on anything. You understand?"

"Yeah, I get it." I stood up to leave. "If I won't leave, then I'm the bait."

CHAPTER 29

In the basement, I took a long shower and put on clean clothes. I stopped to take the dog out for a short walk and then put him back in my office.

Not bothering to call for an escort, I walked to the law enforcement center to find the conference room Brandan mentioned. The only thing I could do for Matt was look at the information and offer my opinion. I would do that, regardless what Nolan Forrester thought.

The case files had been delivered. Reports and photos from the barn, my house, Mrs. Shannaker's house, preliminary autopsies on the victims, even the transcribed statement I'd given about the barn that night in the hospital were stacked on conference tables around the room.

Going around, I scribbled notes on a legal pad about facts, evidence, witnesses, questions, connections.

I wondered if Mrs. Shannaker had been notified. Where was she? What would they tell her?

I dug out the bottle of Darvocet from my bag and took one and a couple of ibuprofen for my aching ribs and pounding headache. I hadn't felt this bad since I woke up in the hospital. Stress and emotional exhaustion were unmasking the pain.

Ten minutes later, Callaghan came in and opened a box with my answering machine in it, bagged as evidence. "I'm really sorry about all this," he said, "and despite Forrester's opinion, you are probably the best lead we have right now."

"Thanks," I said. "I think."

"And for what it's worth, I don't want to push you out of the case. I'm only trying to protect you."

He started a list of priority tasks for the team to work on. Many of the same men and women who had eaten lunch together on Friday would be returning in a few hours for an update about the newest twist in the cases.

Before, this had only involved someone they knew – me. Today, it involved one of their brothers.

A technician brought in a copy of the preliminary reports of trace evidence picked up at the Shannaker house. I made notes on the white board while Brandan read out loud.

"One neighbor said a strange boat docked at Shannakers' earlier in the day, but she doesn't know when it left. This is unverified, but the lab wanted us to have it anyway," Brandan said.

Nolan Forrester came in but did not interrupt.

"Obviously Matt's hair is throughout the house. There's a great deal of German shepherd hair, which has made collecting samples a bit cumbersome. A few hairs match the body for color and texture. There is also hair we presume is his mother's because of the length, about four inches. A few are presumed to be Julie's because of length and color, knowing she's been in the house recently. We'll need a sample for comparison, by the way," Brandan said looking up at me. "There were two hairs not matching presumed knowns."

"Just two?" Nolan asked.

"Short and apparently colored over a gray," Brandan said.

"Could lead somewhere," I ventured.

Dr. Katz and Jeremy joined us, and Brandan continued. "They found a size 12 generic tread pattern imprinted in the carpet in a few areas of the house with two slight smudges leading from the blood of the body, which seems to be a size 9. A set matches the victim's shoes. Boots in Matt's departmental locker are also size 9."

"The dog tracked several sets of bloody prints out of the room," I said.

"Yes, they used Luminol to illuminate where the loafer stepped on a bloody paw print and tracked it from the hardwood flooring out onto the back deck. When we processed the teak flooring, we also found sweaty barefoot prints, probably Matt's. Since there was a deputy in the driveway, they must have left via the dock. The Coast Guard is searching the shoreline now, but the witness could not describe the boat in detail," Brandan said, finishing.

Dr. Katz spoke. "The shotgun blast did not kill the deceased."

I slapped my forehead. "Let me guess. The bullet is a 9 mm Glaser Safety Slug?"

Forrester gave Callaghan a nasty look, and Brandan squinted at me suspiciously.

"Didn't Matt tell anyone that my 9 mm was stolen from the house while I was in the hospital?" I wanted to scream. "The report has to be in this mess of paper somewhere," I explained, waving my hands at the reams of paper surrounding us all.

Brandan began shuffling pages.

"There is extensive soft tissue damage from the shotgun, of course, which might also have been fatal, but x-rays show a bullet within the skull," Dr. Katz continued. "The angle of the head shot would be hard to figure, because of the shotgun injury; however, because of the dispersion of the round and the shot, as well as lack of obvious powder burns or stippling, the victim was shot through the orbit of the skull. The shotgun blast came from under the chin, loaded with buckshot."

"So the Glaser shot was the kill, and the shotgun was cover-up?" I concluded. "To make identification more difficult. The longer we thought it was Matt, the longer we wouldn't be looking for him. It bought him hours to get away."

"Glaser?" Jeremy asked.

"Glasers were designed in the 1970's for air marshals so the bullet would stay inside the target body rather than exit and puncture the hull of a pressurized aircraft. They are hollowpoints filled with lead shot suspended in liquid Teflon," Brandan supplied. "Maximum tissue damage and one-shot knockdown power. But the expense of Glaser slugs makes them uncommon."

Eleven of them had been loaded in the Smith & Wesson 5904 stolen from my house.

CHAPTER 30

Two hours later, I sat in the conference room alone.

They'd all left, but I didn't care. I felt deflated, looking around the table, stacked edge to edge with folders and photos and notes, at the white board and its questions and pieces of the puzzle. Plenty of data, yet it felt like shards of a crystal – there was no way to put it together.

A knock at the door startled me from my gloom, and I looked around to see Jeremy.

"I know you didn't have breakfast. I doubt you've eaten since supper last night." He motioned me to follow him, and we walked back to the Annex breakroom.

While I washed up, he cleared a breakroom table and removed from two grocery bags a casserole dish, a foil-wrapped loaf of fresh bread, salad, and a cake pan.

"MaryAnne?" I quizzed.

"Oh yes. She threatened me with bodily harm if I didn't personally see that you and her husband had a full meal." He smiled. "She's a formidable woman, like my mother, so I'll take her at her word."

We walked down the hall to the machines for drinks and found Dr. Katz, who was coming to join us for lunch, which we ate with little conversation.

"Tell MaryAnne lunch was delicious," I finally said to cover the hum of the wall clock roaring like a freight train in my head.

"Hmm, this beats our deli and take-out lunches. Think she'd do this every day, Julie?" Dr. Katz asked, slicing carrot cake for us.

"Yes, I do, and don't you dare ask her," I said. "She has quite enough to do feeding you and the girls without cooking for the rest of us, too."

"Wow, women really stick together about this cooking thing, eh?" Katz said to Jeremy.

After lunch, I took the dog for walk.

Laser seemed content to hang out with me. Because he knew he wasn't on duty, he was playful and friendly. We walked down to the beach where he tested the water but decided not to chase the birds. He barked at a few ducks that flapped into the water.

We were waiting to cross Front Street near the heart of downtown when Laser's head went up and he growled. As there was no one near us, I saw nothing threatening. He stood and took a step, following his nose.

I hesitated, looking at the cars, waiting for the light to change. I couldn't find what he was after, but maybe he could.

"Okay, Laser, go find." I didn't know if he even knew such a command, but I gave him enough slack in his leash to lead me for a block in the same direction as the one-way traffic, making me think he was trailing a car. At the next light, he seemed to lose interest.

I knelt down by him, petting him generously, with lots of good-dogs and atta-boys.

Unfortunately, whatever Laser had sniffed was gone, and I had no idea what he was following. But I felt goose-bumps on my arms, wondering whether it was coincidence.

With a shiver, I realized I was alone, seven blocks from the office without a radio, phone, gun or police escort.

Like an idiot with a bulls-eye on my forehead.

Back at the office, although it took a while, I finally focused on work and paid no attention to the clock behind me until the dog stood up and barked.

"What is it, Laser? Huh? Time for dinner or something?"

A confident *Woof!* answered me.

"Sorry, I forgot. I'm not much of a partner, am I?"

It was a quarter to four.

Brandan Callaghan had left a note on my door - *Tucker's sister is due in on a 5:30 p.m. flight. Would you be available to go with me to meet her?*

I tracked down Jeremy, who was hanging around in the lab, probably scoping microbes growing on this and that. I was afraid to ask. I explained I needed more food for Laser and asked if he could go to the store. "And chewy treats."

Jeremy took the keys to my Suburban and directions to a grocery store nearby.

I returned to my office to make a few calls and flipped through my mail with less enthusiasm than before that Federal Express package landed on my desk days ago. I was even hesitant to get my voice messages.

Callaghan called to see if I was ready to go to the airport. I told him I'd meet him in the sallyport in about fifteen minutes.

Jeremy brought in a ten-pound bag of dry dog food and two bowls. He eyed the dog suspiciously. "You wouldn't bite a hand that feeds you, would you?"

Laser sat obediently, tail wagging.

When Jeremy had arranged everything and poured water into a bowl for him, Laser turned to me, waiting for permission to eat.

"Go ahead," I said, trying to remember what command Matthew used. "It's okay." I nodded to him.

He stood, unsure.

"Eat up, boy. We've got errands to run."

That must have been enough encouragement. He went to the bowl and wolfed down the contents.

Jeremy sat in the chair across the desk from me and grinned.

"What?" I asked, seeing no big reason to smile.

"I wish you could see yourself the way I see you," he said sincerely. "You have such a sense of determination and self-discipline. I mean, this thing must be chewing you up, and you do show that once in a while, but you are so composed for the people you work with. Like taking the dog. It means a lot to them, I'm sure."

I shrugged, embarrassed.

"Really. And you're cute when you blush."

I haven't been cute since I was four months old.

I ignored him and started shoving paper into file folders.

When Laser was done eating, he came around to the side of my desk and sat.

"I guess you'll be okay in my truck with guests," I asked him, rubbing his ears. "You've had dinner, so no nibbling, okay?"

Jeremy walked out with me to catch a ride to his hotel. He even offered to take the dog while we met with Tucker's sister, but I wasn't sure how Laser would take to being with a stranger in another strange building.

Brandan Callaghan was waiting by my Suburban.

I couldn't help but compare Brandan and Jeremy as they stood side by side while I loaded the dog.

Brandan was compact and muscular, barely taller than me but solid though the shoulders over which his sport coat did little to conceal his holster. Jeremy was several inches taller, built more like a gymnast than a weight lifter.

"I was hoping you'd drive. Patrol units aren't comfortable, being locked in the back and all." Brandan nodded in the direction of his car. "Besides, mine's a mess."

"Sure. Nice of you to consider her feelings," I said. "I was going to drop Jeremy at the hotel on the way."

Brandan and Jeremy traded childhood geographical histories, so I learned Callaghan was from Traverse City, but had moved to California and worked six years for the Orange County Sheriff's Department before coming back. He told Jeremy he was married and had twin sons who were nearly eight.

In turn, catching my eye in the rear view mirror, Jeremy confessed to having a three-year-old daughter named Stephanie.

Always something you hide, isn't there, Jeremy?

I hadn't asked about children from his marriage. Did that make it fair nondisclosure?

When I pulled up to the doors at the hotel, Jeremy got out without further explanation regarding his offspring, waving a jovial goodbye to us as I drove away.

"Can I ask you something personal?" Brandan asked as I sat waiting to turn left from the parking lot.

"Depends on how personal, I guess."

"There's something between you and him, isn't there?"

"Dr. McNeeley?" I asked, hoping to sound innocent but failing. I made the left turn into heavy traffic. "Well, yeah. When I was in college, there was an engagement. He walked out. I wasn't expecting him to walk back in. It's been awkward."

"Were you and Matt romantically involved?"

I didn't answer.

"I mean sexually?" he prodded.

"That's way beyond personal, Detective," I growled, angry I was now obligated to driving instead of facing off with him.

"You're right, but hear me out." He held up his hand to stop my interruption. "My hunch is, for all the time you spent together, which was a lot, you never went to bed, or maybe just once or twice."

Silence was the only answer I could think of. I didn't know where this was going, but I didn't think I was going to like it.

He continued. "I've known Matt since junior high school. We don't really ever hang out together these days, but we are friends. My guess is if you don't know what I'm about to tell you, no one else knows either. It may be important to this case." He paused. "Am I right about your relationship?"

Whatever he wanted to tell me, I didn't want to know. Driving became less a diversion as I approached the intersection to turn to the airport.

"We never slept together, no," I finally said.

Brandan Callaghan took a deep breath. "I think that's because he is struggling with whether or not he's gay."

I hit the brakes so hard the tires chirped on the pavement.

Brandan hardly rocked with the deceleration.

"He's gay?" My voice squeaked.

"Maybe not what you're thinking. Something happened while he was in the Coast Guard. I'm not sure about the details, but it affected him deeply. It's become more difficult for him the last few years," Callaghan said quietly. "The dead man at Matt's house is Lance Parker. He was kind of a local gay activist, support guru."

"Okay," I said, trying to gather my wits, "but what's that got to do with the case?"

"I'm not sure. I thought you deserved to hear this first, before the team starts tearing his life apart for the sake of finding him." He looked away. "If it means anything, Matt does love you."

I made the circle at the airport and parked in a short-term space, struggling to erase the words that kept echoing in my head.

We got out, leaving the windows cracked for Laser.

"May I ask you something personal then?" I asked as we walked toward the terminal.

He nodded.

"How do you know Parker's gay?"

"Can we just say for now that I have it on good authority," he said. "I'll tell you, but I can't explain it before we get to the door."

I nodded.

September had apparently become the month for all of us to bare our secrets.

CHAPTER 31

Penny Daniels' bright green Grand Canyon sweatshirt made her easy to identify as she came from the Northwest Airlines flight that connected through Chicago.

I approached her and introduced Detective Callaghan and myself.

She did not appear timid or defensive, given her reasons for being in Michigan.

"Do you have any checked luggage, ma'am?" Brandan asked.

"No, just the one bag," she said, indicating her duffel. "Couple of weeks in the canyon makes you realize how much you can live without."

Brandan carried it for her as we walked to my truck, discussing the cool weather here as compared to Arizona.

"I was never so glad to get away from these winters," she explained. "I miss the mild summers now, but as a kid, between school and snow, winter seemed to last forever."

I explained I lived for many years in New Mexico, so the lengthy winters had been an extreme change for me, too, but I'd grown accustomed to them.

As we headed to the Annex for a brief interview, Brandan rode in the backseat with Laser.

"I don't know what all you want to ask me," she said, deliberately looking out the side window, "but there are things you should know about J.P. He was my brother, but we weren't close. I was four years younger, always in his way as a kid. He left home for about eight years, but when my dad's health got bad, he came back to help. I'd already moved west and had a family."

"We'll listen to everything you have to tell us. At this point, anything might be helpful," I said, hoping we could encourage an open dialogue that did not make her feel she was betraying him.

We went into the Annex to a small conference room where Brandan got us all a cup of coffee from a pot brewed hours ago.

"The bodies on the farm. How many?" she asked

"Four, we believe," he said. "In barrels under the barn."

I could tell he wanted to jump into our questions, but I was more interested in what she chose to tell us before we started asking things that could lead her.

"Growing up with him, I almost believe he could do something like that," she said, sipping her cup with a look of disgust.

I exchanged a glance with Callaghan. He nodded for me to respond.

"Why would you think your brother was involved?" I asked.

"Well, besides being a jerk," she said, setting her cup down and looking me straight in the eye, "I'm pretty sure there is one other body buried on the farm. It's nagged me all my life. Maybe I can help you find it and be done. I'm the only one left alive who knew about it." Penny explained how she'd secretly followed her older brother and their cousin one evening when the boys told her she couldn't go. "J.P. never played with me, and they didn't want me hanging around."

"Your cousin?" I interrupted.

"Yeah, my mother's sister's son. Mom brought him to live with us when my Aunt Angela died, and there was no one else to take him." She cocked her head in memory. "I hadn't thought about him in years."

"Where is he now?" Brandan asked, looking up from his notepad.

"After high school, he joined the military. He committed suicide. In 1972 or '73, I think."

Brandan and I both nodded.

She continued. "Anyway, that night, our folks had gone to a church potluck or something, and the boys planned to sneak off for another big adventure. I followed, hoping once they got where they were going, they'd have to let me in on their game or I'd tell on them.

"They walked to the southeast corner of the farm. I got scared when I figured out where they were headed. Old Man Farley was a wicked crotchety old man. I hid in the trees when we got close. Sure enough, Farley came out of his shack to run 'em off, but they didn't run. Instead, they charged him. It looked like they had hammers or hatchets. They killed him, I'm sure of it. Just beat him to the ground. I bolted home," she said and shuddered. "I worried about whether someone would find the blood or the grave or footprints, including my own. But there was a thunderstorm that night, which probably washed away any traces of what they had done. They must've buried him." She paused. "I don't remember hearing anything except that Farley was gone and good riddance. Even that was weeks or maybe months later."

"Maybe you could identify the area to search so we could find the body?" I suggested.

"If any of the old sheds or stuff are still standing," she said after a moment of consideration. "Is that anything like what happened to the people in the barn?"

"We don't know exactly because so much was damaged in the bomb blast," I said, feeling I had to let her finish the story before new facts distorted her memories. "We can drive out to the farm in the morning so you can look around."

She agreed.

"Penny, is there any significance to the orange barrels?" Brandan asked.

"No. A lot of the chemicals and stuff Dad used on the farm came in drums. There were always a dozen or so around in the barn."

"Yeah, but they were mostly metal, right?"

She nodded.

I looked at Callaghan, and he made a note to call for the lab techs to assemble metal detectors for our rendezvous the next morning.

"A preliminary search for metal in the area will be quick and easy," I explained. "But since the old man wasn't buried in a barrel, I doubt that will help find him. None of the other victims in the barn were in metal barrels." I turned toward Callaghan. "Call the electric companies and ask for a ground-penetrating radar."

He shot me an inquisitive look.

"Power companies use GPR to locate underground lines, pipes, water under pavement, and such," I explained.

"So you'd get an image of any skeletal remains?" Penny asked, sounding too excited.

"No, unfortunately, what you get is similar to what you get with weather radar," I said. "The returning waves will indicate metals, but it's actually showing the changes in density. There are almost always changes where something has been buried. And barrels would certainly return a different signal than packed earth."

We discussed the history of Penny's family farm a while longer, but no more details about her brother, so I suggested we take a break.

"Let's take you to your hotel to get settled in, and we'll pick you up for dinner at 7:30, unless that's too early for you with the time difference?" Brandan suggested.

"I didn't have lunch," she said. "That would be fine."

I drove her to the hotel, and we escorted her to the desk where Brandan checked her in.

"Take advantage of all the hotel amenities. I arranged for a room with a hot tub," he told her, giving her the key.

"That wasn't necessary," she argued.

"The last time I hiked in the Grand Canyon, I was so sore I wanted to sleep in the hot tub for a week." He smiled.

She took her bag and went to her room alone.

"That was thoughtful of you," I said as we left. "This must be hard on her, all these suspicions about her brother."

"Didn't sound like she was all that surprised about anything in the investigation."

"No, but thinking someone in your family is a bit strange or a jerk is vastly different than having to solve the puzzle of whether he's a killer."

I dropped Brandan at the sheriff's department so he could brief an on-coming crew at shift change. Feeling I had nothing else to offer, I went to my office to catch up on paperwork until he was done, but I accomplished very little as my thoughts rewound to

Matthew. My memories were like the flakes in a snow globe, whirling around my head.

Everyone was working on the premise that Matt was a victim, given the messages and note at my house. Disturbed about the story of his father, then the dead man at his house, a black question settled in my head – what if Matt was the man we were chasing?

CHAPTER 32

Over dinner, conversation started with Penny describing her family's vacation.

"Our kids are not quite to that age where nothing is fun because it's with their parents. Mark and I felt we had to do the big vacation before we lost the chance. We home-school, so we took our vacation later than regular students. Five days at Disneyland and the studios, ten days at the Grand Canyon. It was great."

Brandan told her about his twins, Vincent and Riley.

"Marissa is ten and wants to be a concert pianist. Jaralyn is six and wants to be a teacher and a firefighter and a ballerina and a veterinarian – you know the type," she laughed. "And Colby is twelve and thinks he rules the computer world, thanks to his Uncle J.P., who gave us a computer a couple of years ago. I'll probably have to bail him out for hacking the Pentagon before he's old enough to drive."

Even though the tales of their children were light-hearted, I felt left out of the family conversation. I didn't even have a pet, save the salt-water aquarium I kept.

Changing the subject, I asked if she still had any other relatives in the Traverse City area.

"No, I guess now that J.P. is dead, I'm the last of the Tuckers. My father had two brothers, both killed in the Korean War. That's how we ended up with the farm. It's been in my father's family for four generations. I think once my father had grown old chained to the land, he wasn't so disappointed his son didn't want to farm cherries and apples."

"After your parents passed away, what did your brother do with the land?" Brandan asked.

"J.P. moved back when Dad got sick, to help with the orchards. After my parents died, he leased off the best of the land to neighbors who were still farming and sold the hardwoods for cash. He couldn't sell the land without my approval, but he never asked. I didn't understand why not – I have no interest in living here again." She pushed her salad around on the plate without taking another bite.

"What did your brother do for a living?" I asked.

"J.P. had a job with a big graphic arts and video business in Chicago, so when he moved back, he started his own company."

"How was his business going, do you know?" Brandan asked.

"No idea. He had video stuff all through the house when I was last here, and he said he wanted to renovate the barn for his studio. He might have cleaned out the old junk, but it still looked so dilapidated I couldn't imagine him putting expensive cameras and computers in there. Had he done that?"

I shook my head. "It's all in the house."

The conversation moved back to how Brandan and Penny thought the bay area had changed over the years.

On the way to the hotel, Penny asked, "Are you sure it was J.P. in the barn?"

From the backseat, Brandan explained that the preliminary identification made against the driver's license was legal, though it was standard procedure to ask a relative for confirmation whenever possible.

She hesitated. "Do I have to see his body?" The question had probably been on her mind for days.

"No, we have photographs," he said.

"I know it's late, but I'd like to do that now," she said. "I don't want to wonder about it all night."

Brandan told me he had copies of the photos in his files, so I drove to the sheriff's department instead of the morgue, and we went to a small briefing room.

I sat with Penny while he retrieved the photos from the file.

"Dr. Katz generally uses photographs for identification for relatives. Then if the family wants to see their loved one, that can be arranged," I explained.

Brandan returned with a large manila envelope. He gave Penny the close-up and spread out a few others on the table.

I had not seen these photos, because I'd been in the hospital.

Tucker didn't look all that bad, but it was obvious his death had not been easy. His lips and chin were stained yellow from the acid.

Penny nodded then covered her face with her hands to cry.

As I scanned the other photos, without warning, panic raced through me. Images triggered a cascade of memories I could not control. My pulse rate soared.

I smelled the acid burns, the body waste, the inside of the SCBA mask. I saw the blood on the wood – smeared letters meant to warn us about the bomb. I saw, much larger than real, the explosive device next to the beam. I felt the stairway heave under my feet when the bomb detonated. I heard the deafening explosions.

None of what went on in my memory was visible in the images of Tucker, but the whole scene played in my mind.

I bolted down the hall, fighting to suppress a ragged scream.

CHAPTER 33

Brandan found me outside, bent over a railing, panting as though I'd run a six-minute mile.

"I thought you'd seen the photos," he said quietly. "I'm sorry."

I shook my head. "It's not . . . your fault . . . ." I took a deep breath and blew it out, hoping my heart would slow down. "It was like being there all over again."

"Let's take Penny to the hotel, then you can tell me about it."

When the dizziness passed, I followed him back inside and apologized to Penny for my wild reaction, but she didn't ask for an explanation.

Brandan drove my Suburban to take her back to her hotel.

We agreed I'd pick her up at nine o'clock the next morning to go to the Tucker farm.

She thanked us for dinner. Despite her cheerfulness with us through the evening, she now looked drained.

Much like I felt.

When he parked at the Annex, Brandan handed me back my keys.

"I still have to walk the dog. Poor guy's been locked inside far more than he's used to." I let Laser out the back.

"I'll walk with you, if you don't mind."

We strolled down the sidewalk toward downtown.

"Can you tell me what happened to you with the photos?" he asked in a curious tone. "I mean, from an outside, objective perspective?"

How do you explain a flashback?

“Have you ever been on a fire fatality?” I asked.

He nodded. “Once you've smelled it, it's unforgettable. It lingers in your brain.”

“Yeah, like that, only much bigger. The photos triggered a repeat of the explosion – some of the sensory information, some of the emotions,” I said.

“Matthew told me a little about the scene, especially about digging through the rubble for survivors,” he said. “For you.”

“Because I was unconscious, my brain is now collecting new facts and images secondhand. The emotional responses are tagged to pieces I haven’t yet connected consciously.”

“Are you sure you can . . . I mean, should you stay on the case then?” Brandan hesitated, trying to be diplomatic. “For your own well-being?”

“I’ll make a deal with you. Tomorrow I go to the scene for the first time. Then if you think I need to walk away from my regular MEI duties in this case because I'm not fit, tell me and I'll walk. But I'm not asking for FBI-Guy’s advice, okay?”

“Sounds reasonable.” He turned away, looking down toward the bay through the buildings. “Just for the record, though, Forrester’s been pretty fair with me so far in this.”

I wasn't willing to concede any points to Forrester unless absolutely necessary. Neutral was the best I could manage.

We walked a while in silence.

“What do we do if we find more bodies?” Brandan finally asked as we made our way back to the Annex.

“When. If Penny is right about her brother, a kill in his youth only means there are probably more murders as he got older,” I said. “Maybe between the old man and these four.”

“But Tucker’s dead. How does that work with the case now?”

“I wish I knew.”

We parted company before I got to the Annex.

Feeling I needed to resolve something tonight, I loaded Laser and drove to Jeremy’s hotel. The dog seemed content in the truck, so I cracked a window and went inside.

I stopped at the guest phone to ring Jeremy’s room, but there was no answer. I hung up and headed to the bar, passing up the night club with its loud thumping music.

He wouldn't be in there. In the lounge, where it was quieter.

I caught the bartender coming back from the club with a couple of bottles. I asked if there was a tall blond man sitting alone in the bar.

He nodded.

"Pour him a double of the best scotch in the bar and give him a quarter," I handed him three tens, "and keep the change. I'll be in shortly."

He shrugged and took the bills.

I went to the restroom down the hall then came back to the bar.

Jeremy would recognize this as our version of the scene at the end of "Top Gun" of the quarter in the jukebox playing "You've Lost That Lovin' Feeling." We must have watched that movie dozens of times together.

Sure enough, the bartender met me in the hall with a napkin with the words, "Is this your idea of fun, Mav'?" What Anthony Edwards had asked Tom Cruise as they flew inverted above the cockpit of the MiG in the opening scene.

I followed the bartender inside and asked for a cola as I went by the bar, then I slid into the booth opposite Jeremy.

Neither of us spoke till the server brought my drink.

"I'm sorry, Julie," he said, staring into the amber liquid in his glass. "I should have told you about my daughter, but I didn't know when or how, or if it was even worth discussing."

"Not worth discussing," I echoed, staring at him, lost about what to do next. "Do you have a picture of her?"

He pulled his wallet out of his jacket pocket and opened it to a photo of a blond-haired toddler posed with a Malamute. "Stephanie and Kodiak."

I handed it back. "She's beautiful, Jeremy. Why wouldn't it be *worth* telling me you have a daughter? You plan on keeping her a secret forever?"

He shook his head, struggling for words, and I let him flail around in his discomfort.

"I expected this whole thing with you would be a failure. That I'd come here and find you were happily married and had a family, so I'd finally have a reason to feel better about ending our relationship, or maybe to feel worse seeing what I'd missed. I didn't know I'd find you single and," he took a gulp of twenty-year-old scotch that made his eyes water, "I didn't know I'd still love you so much."

I stared at him.

"Sure, dinner, yeah. Then we ended up at that cabin. I figured I'd get to tell you I wanted another chance with you, and you'd tell me to go to hell. And I do, but –" He leaned his head against the wooden booth dividers and squeezed his eyes shut. "Deanna and I are still married."

More secrets, McNeeley? You bastard!

"You told me it was over," I finally said. "I somehow thought that meant you were divorced. My mistake."

"We only stayed together because of Stephanie. Deanna gave up traveling to be home with her. I'm away so much I might as well not live there. We quit sleeping together over a year ago –"

"Stop. Just stop it. I'm not interested in the rationalization of your marital problems." I stood up, but he grabbed my arm.

"I had no reason to leave her before."

"I didn't think you had much of a reason to leave *me* before, either, Jeremy." I jerked my arm away from his grasp, and even after several years of healing, I felt the muscles pull. Just like I felt my heart break. "But you did."

CHAPTER 34

Brandan was at the farm the next morning when Penny and I arrived. He had already started a crew with metal detectors around the house and barn areas.

Penny got out of my truck first and just stood, looking over the farm that had once been her home. She nodded a distracted answer to Brandan's greeting and query about the accommodations being satisfactory.

I suspected she was as apprehensive about the scene as I was, though for different reasons. Yellow tape still flapped in the morning breeze around the remains of the barn.

"You look tired," Brandan whispered to me, watching me watch her from beside my truck.

I felt as if I'd tried to slay demons all night. After all this time, I ought to be more adept at looking better the morning after nights like that.

"Didn't sleep well," I said, my eyes wandering to the remains of the barn.

"I wish I could make this better for you, Julie." He put his hand on my shoulder.

Yeah, I wish someone could make all of this better.

"You'll be okay," he said, somewhere between a statement and a question.

I think I nodded. Seeing the pile of rubble that had been the barn made me queasy. I wasn't even aware of the steely grip I had on the door till I had to pry my fingers away to walk with him.

I know the symptoms of critical incident stress – normal

physical, mental and emotional reactions to a particularly abnormal experience. I've certainly been through enough of those events, like my father's death or shooting my husband. Raw emotions that feel like all the insulation has melted away, short-circuiting every time one bumps another.

I might recognize the symptoms, but what did I really know about fixing them?

I should have realized, even before last night, I hadn't been doing very well emotionally with any of this – the bomb, Matthew's kidnapping, being stalked by a killer, heart-to-heart combat with Jeremy.

The last few days, I'd attributed the little bouts of rapid heartbeat and cold sweats to the stress of the case, not my uncontrolled emotional reactions to one incident or another. Did it matter?

We were about to find out.

Maybe I ought to step away.

The open earth and other odors of the barn were intense.

Today, my reactions were less dramatic, but still I felt a staggering sense of fear, not because of the bomb itself, but because I stood on the same ground as a killer who'd taken so many lives. Fear knowing that a monster was killing people in order to play his game and manipulate me.

I took a couple of breaths.

While Brandan returned to coordinate the ground search by the lab team, I walked with Penny toward the house.

She appeared to be concentrating on memories that had exploded as surely as the bomb had blown up the barn.

I followed her through a gate she must have opened thousands of times in her life. The metal hinges screeched loudly, though she didn't seem to notice.

"I can't believe it's gone," she finally said, turning to look toward where the barn had stood, her hands resting on the gate she had closed from habit. "That barn was the center of my father's world. He wasn't born to be a farmer, but he became one."

"Tell me about him," I said.

"He had brutal hands. Maybe there was love in his heart, but it was hard for him to show it, especially to us kids. He worked hard, and he expected those who ate at his table to work, too." She smiled. "I have trouble getting my kids to set the table or wash the dishes. Get them to milk a cow or hoe a garden every day? Then again, we didn't have cable television and video games. It's not the same world."

I nodded. My life was also very different than my parents'.

Penny turned toward the house. "It broke my mother's heart when we moved to Arizona after I got married. She spent her life trying to make this house a home. She should have been a model when she was young. She was so beautiful and graceful. Farm work eventually stole that, but not her love."

I felt her attention turn from the house and her memories to me.

Not a competitive size up, but more whether she could trust me with her secrets.

She pointed up to a window on the left side of the house.

"That was J.P.'s room." She paused and walked around in the yard, kicking at the tufts of grass, perhaps deciding if she should say what was on her mind. "I don't know if this means anything, but I'll tell you anyway. He came into my room one night when I was around eight or nine, maybe," she said softly. "I didn't know what he wanted, and he didn't exactly know what he was doing, either, I suppose. He threatened to take my birthday money if I made any noise. He fumbled around a while, then left. He didn't hurt me or anything, so I never told anyone. He threatened to come back again if I did." She looked away.

I had no way of knowing if the story merited digging for more details since she said it only happened once, but it didn't seem necessary to interrupt her thoughts.

We entered the house through the front.

"No one used the front door except for 'company' visiting, like the minister, or strangers," she explained. "Everyone else used the back door like we did."

The living room and kitchen lacked personality, much less style. The sofa, chair and ottoman were a matched set, plain dark gray, sitting on a beige carpet. A medium-sized television and stereo components were arranged in a wooden cabinet.

"He purchased the furniture about five years ago," she told me.

After seeing it, she recalled joking with her husband that her brother bought it at a thrift store.

The stone fireplace in the corner looked as though it hadn't been used in years. An ancient rack of elk antlers hung over the mantle, dusty and beginning to deteriorate. There were no photographs, no art, no knickknacks.

One corner of the room was dominated by computer and video equipment, the likes of which I wasn't familiar but could easily learn to envy.

Brandan had mentioned that the FBI was sending a specialist to investigate the computers for any possible evidence or clues.

I could see why Penny might kid about her brother making porn movies, as she had told Matthew on the phone. She might be right, I thought.

The kitchen was even less personal than the living area. Relatively new refrigerator and dishwasher dominated the room, out of place with the original range, cabinets and countertops. The floor was original hardwood with millions of footsteps worn into it, showing where the table and chairs had sat for most of the life of the house.

Here and there I noticed fingerprint powder. Short of fingerprinting every surface in the house, though, finding a usable print left by anyone but Tucker was another needle in a different haystack than the search going on outside, looking for more evidence on a 600-acre farm.

Thanks to Penny, at least we had an idea we would be looking for one more body.

"I really don't want to be in here," she said suddenly, going through the kitchen to the back door and out onto the porch. She sat down on the steps, and I joined her.

"I used to think my brother got in trouble to get their attention. My dad swore the best way to get J.P. to do something was to forbid him to do it. He was suspended from school in fifth grade for setting a fire in a trash can. The next year, it happened again, though they didn't catch him."

I made another mental check mark in the list in my head about

Tucker.

She pointed to where the barn had stood. "I used to spend a lot of time in there. We had all sorts of animals, but the closest thing we had to pets were the barn cats. Each year, I would pick out a new kitten to keep for my own, but Dad always got rid of them."

"Are you sure it was your father? Were there any unusual animal deaths around?" I asked.

"It was a working farm. Animals died. My father only called a vet for the milk cows. Anything else was sick or hurt, it either got better, it died, or he shot it." She ran her fingers through short, sun-bleached hair. "You think J.P. killed animals, too, don't you?"

"It's a common behavior in the childhoods of repeat killers," I responded without answering her question directly. "I'm trying to understand what he was like."

"A hellion," she said, turning away from me. "Did anything he damned well pleased. No rules, no fences. He was the kind of kid you'd hate to see your children bring home."

This was a subject I wanted to learn more about, but we were interrupted as Brandan came toward us, a cellular phone to his ear.

I heard him bestow his thanks to someone and disconnect. "MichLight and Power has two of these radar units on the way, plus four men to operate the equipment for us. They'll be here in half an hour. How'd you know about them?"

"I'm a resource idea collector," I offered. "It's my hobby to find out about other people's cool toys."

"Um, Detective?" one of the lab techs called to him. "I think we've got something."

We followed him to where the back door of the barn had stood.

"It appears to be a large round metal object," the tech said, pointing out a vague outline made of little flags.

"Let's dig it out. Same collection process."

They went back to work.

Penny and I walked on around the barn. I tried to explain what I had seen, where the new flooring and trapdoor had been. The floor was apparently new since her last visit.

Dangerous drop-offs and evidence areas were bordered by

yellow tape. I could see a technician down in the hole where the barrels had been.

My pulse skipped a beat, and I felt a shiver.

"The detective said you were in the barn when it blew up." Penny said softly. "That's what freaked you out last night with the photos?"

I realized I was holding my breath when my chest muscles began to ache. I could only nod.

"It must be hard to be here," she offered. "I'm sorry. For you and the others who've been killed."

I tried to empathize with her situation and forget my own, but thoughts of Matthew drifted around me as I imagined him digging through the rubble of the barn to find me, of what he must be going through – if the monster hadn't killed him yet.

I turned and looked away, hoping to keep control of emotions running like a herd of wild horses through my soul.

By the time the radar crews from the power company arrived, I'd pulled myself together. Their teams followed us as Penny gave me directions around the orchard away from the house. When we parked, she pointed to where she thought the body would be.

"What we're looking for here," I explained to the technicians, "is a body buried in a shallow grave 20 years or more ago. Much less than six feet most likely, but certainly no deeper. Please watch for any metallic objects, hatchet or hammer heads, too."

One of them explained that they didn't get a first-hand image, that the signal was recorded and interpreted by a computer.

"I understand. I wanted you to know as much about this scene and what we are looking for as possible." I left them staking out a grid.

"I appreciate the way you've treated me during this," Penny said on the way back to the house. "I'm not sure what I believe about J.P., but you don't judge me by him."

I nodded. "You aren't the criminal, and being related to someone who's being investigated doesn't change who you are. I'm interested in the facts you can provide us, whichever direction those facts point us. All we ask of you is to help us find the truth."

"Aren't truth and fact the same?" she asked, skeptically.

"No. Even having all the facts doesn't mean you have the truth. Truth is often more and sometimes even quite different than the facts that make it up. You can't always prove the truth without facts."

"I guess they call that faith, right? Believing in what you can't prove?" She smiled. "It means a lot to me that you want the truth."

"It was true that the world was round long before anyone could prove it was a fact," I said.

CHAPTER 35

I returned to the office after dropping Penny off, and Connie presented me with a cup of coffee at my desk.

"A detective called and said the film at the developing lab was blank. No signs of any pictures at all, as if it were never exposed," she said.

Disappointed, but not surprised, I leaned back in my chair.

"Are you feeling okay, hon'? You look pale."

"Having trouble sleeping."

Grandmothers know a half-lie, but she let it slide.

Laser crunched a serving of dry food while I dialed my voice mail. Three messages.

"Julie, it's Mom. I hope you're doing okay, dear. I called your house, but the machine didn't pick up. I wanted to talk about us getting together for the holidays again. I'd love for you to come down, but I know you are so busy. I was thinking maybe if you can't get away, I could come up there to visit you instead. Think about it and give me a ring. I love you, bye!"

Love you, too, Mom. Later.

Next message.

"This is Jeremy. I heard they found something at the farm, so I know you'll be busy. I wanted you to know I rented a car, and I changed hotels." He left the phone number and room number. "Call when you get a break." A short pause. "Please."

A long string of profanity unfairly involving his family heritage crossed my mind.

Next message.

"Julie? Hi, this is Kim Katz. I need to talk to you about Mom, but please don't tell Dad I bothered you, okay? It's really important or I wouldn't ask. I get home from school after four o'clock. Call my phone, okay?" And she gave the number.

I considered this secrecy of Kim calling me from school at lunch. She sounded worried, and I wrote myself a reminder to call her.

But her message gave me another idea about phones and secrets.

I'd been trying to figure out how the killer had learned my cell phone number, then it occurred to me it was in the filing cabinet next to my computer at the house, right on every monthly statement.

In fact, there was probably a great deal he could learn from perusing my files, the tidy accountant that I am.

I could change the address for all my bills to a post office box, but then I decided the horse had already left the barn. So what if he knew I ate at Pizza Hut weekly, shopped at Tom's Market and Horizon Books, and banked at Traverse Credit Union?

My bank accounts!

My pulse rate skyrocketed.

A round of phone transfers later, I spoke to the branch manager. Explaining the break-in at my home, I asked him to take a look at recent transactions in my accounts.

After a debate whether he should freeze my accounts and other normally helpful options, he began reading dates and amounts of checks, deposits and transfers of my checking account in the last two weeks. To me, it all seemed normal. Most of my bills and payroll are paid on automatic transfers.

"I don't see any unusual activity in the checking account, Ms. Madigan," he said. "I could fax you a statement summary, but it's similar to the previous month. Same number of electronic drafts and deposits as the prior month, three ATM withdrawals in late August, several in September so far. Let me check the other accounts."

I heard the tapping of keys.

Sounds like he could use a Mavis Beacon course in typing.

"Nothing in the CD account," he declared, tapping some more. "Only a $755.38 deposit into your savings account on September 5. No other user activity."

I didn't make a deposit on September 5. I was in the hospital.

And wasn't $755.38 a weird number?

"I need to know if it was cash," I stated, less courteous by the minute.

"One moment." More keyboarding. "It was a drive-through deposit at the downtown branch in cash."

Seven hundred fifty-five dollars and thirty-eight cents had to be intentional– but why?

Insurance.

I had received a $5380 check from a disability policy at work, plus the $750,000 life insurance benefit from David's death with the ironic accidental indemnity clause. Move the decimal point to get $755.38.

Okay, David's death was hardly an 'accident,' but that isn't the point.

How would someone find that insurance information?

I called Brandan to let him know what I found out.

He agreed it was interesting, but being so intentional, he agreed it would not likely provide any clues.

"And hey," he added before I hung up, "the radar team at the other site thinks they've located something, but we're going to finish up the first barrel before we start another scene. Great idea, Julie. I'll get back to you."

I groaned and crumpled into my chair.

So much information.

An overload of old evidence that doesn't lead anywhere.

Some of the scenes we'd looked at were more than twenty years old. He set Tucker up to die and then reported it, but was it to intentionally lead us to the bodies? If he wanted us to find the barrels, why blow them up?

Then another voice in my head boomed.

He doesn't care what we find because he doesn't believe any of it will lead us to him. He's letting us bury ourselves in his past so we will overlook his present.

I didn't know how to find his identity except through his clues. But I thought about a question Matt asked – why had the killer chosen me? Had he crossed paths with me before?

I scribbled down the thought before I lost it again to check old cases in New Mexico.

Yeah, like I'd find a murder if the weapon as obscure as parasites or South American tree seeds or whatever those things were. The FBI hadn't found anything yet.

Maybe he'll tell you about them next time he calls.

A disturbing thought I wanted to escape so I went down the hall to see Connie about another idea.

"While I was in the hospital, did anyone you didn't know call about me?" I asked, taking a piece of candy from her dish.

"Well, I don't think so, but let me look," she said, leafing through her call and message book. Meticulous woman she was, she recorded incoming calls even if the caller was put through to someone in the office, providing us all with documentation of communications. She flipped back to the week after the explosion, then ran her finger down a list of names. "I don't see any names here I don't recognize. Several here for Dr. Katz from the media." She turned the book toward me to scan.

"The media never contacted me. Isn't that odd?" I asked.

"No, Dr. Katz made one statement then deferred all inquiries. The press release only stated that an investigator was injured. With that, the media focused instead on the firefighters."

I thanked her and turned to go.

"Oh, and Dr. McNeeley called for you about an hour ago. I transferred him to your voice mail, but he left a phone number in case you wanted to contact him today."

Not damned likely.

CHAPTER 36

I dialed my boss's secondary phone number, the one the kids used.

"Kimmie," I said. "It's Julie. What's wrong?"

"Thanks for calling. I was afraid you'd think, like, I'm just a kid or something." She was almost whispering.

"We're friends, so you can call me any time. Now, what's all the secrecy? You said it was something about your mom?" I sensed insecurity.

"You know, you kinda get a feel for what someone is really like, and it's different than what they're like at work or in public? Like Mom has always been happy and, you know, upbeat?"

"She's always very positive and cheerful," I agreed. "A modern day Mrs. Cleaver." I figured the reference whizzed right over Kim's head.

"Lately, when she thinks no one is looking, she's really down. I heard her crying in their bedroom when I came home from school a few days ago. She's always okay before Dad gets home, so I don't know if he's noticed," she said. "And sometimes she stops what she's doing and looks, you know, dazed."

I considered the brief glimpse of weariness I'd seen the night Jeremy and I were over for dinner. "You shouldn't jump to conclusions, Kim, but I understand you're worried. What would you like me to do?"

"I don't know. I was hoping you'd know what was wrong."

Poor kid.

"No, unfortunately, I don't. I can talk to her and see if she will tell me what's going on, but maybe it would be better if you tried to talk to her," I suggested.

"What would I say?" Her voice squeaked with doubt. "I'm still her kid."

"Find a time when you two are alone, then say what you said to me, about how she's always been very upbeat, but lately you've noticed she's been down. Ask her if she wants to talk about it. She might say no, at first, like sometimes you say everything is okay when it isn't. At least she'll know you've noticed and care enough to ask. She might have to think about it a little, but maybe she'll talk to you later about it."

What kind of advice was that? My mother asks if I'm okay, and no matter what, I always say, "I'm fine, Mother. Really."

"If she doesn't, will you talk to her?" she asked, sounding desperate. "I'm afraid something's wrong, like they're going to get divorced or something."

"I don't think they're getting a divorce. Your parents seem wonderfully happy together to me," I offered, hoping I wasn't wrong. I had noticed nothing amiss with Dr. Katz lately, but I'd been occupied with many other issues. "Take a day or two to find a good time to talk. If you don't get anywhere, call me again, and I'll give it a try, okay?"

She agreed.

"How's the foot?" I asked. "I'm sorry we left the other night before you got home from the hospital."

"They cleaned it out with a Waterpik, isn't that weird? They didn't sew it because they said it might still get infected. I got a tetanus shot, a bottle of horse pills to take, and crutches."

"Be sure to take all your pills," I cautioned.

"Yeah, I got that lecture," she said. "I didn't want the crutches, but by the next day, I couldn't stand on that foot, much less walk all day at school. But this guy, Bret, is in almost all my classes, so he's been carrying my pack, mostly because I couldn't lift it after they gave me the tetanus shot. Dang, what's in that stuff, rocks?"

I laughed.

"Bret's cute but not as good looking as Dr. McNeeley. Wow, he's gorgeous," she whispered.

"Yes, he is, isn't he?" We shared a moment of teenage giggles. "I dated him when I was in college," I explained.

"Think you'll get back together?"

"At this point, I don't know."

See, there's his wife and daughter.

She made a sigh of teenage love that I almost envied. "Thanks, Julie. I'll let you know what happens."

When I hung up, I thought maybe I should talk to my own mother, if for nothing else, to tell her everything was okay.

Really, Mom, everything here is fine. Just fine.

Except of course the crime rate here has risen dramatically, and I don't feel safe in my own home.

I dialed my phone card number, feeling even more disgusted, thinking how my credit cards and other information had probably been compromised, too.

My mother's machine picked up, played her cheery message, and beeped.

I hung up, discouraged. Somehow I could not bring myself to say everything was fine, but what should I say?

Gee, Mom, I'd like to see you for Thanksgiving, but there are all these men in my life. One apparently likes sharp objects and has kidnapped Matt, who's a very good friend, but we haven't slept together. I'm all screwed up about him because he killed his father. Oh, and then there's Jeremy, who's here helping to solve part of the case, and I was falling in love with him again, until he told me about his wife he hasn't gotten around to divorcing and a cute little girl. And then there's . . . Oh never mind. I'll bring the cranberry sauce and pumpkin pie, okay?

I'm fine. Really, Mom. Just fine.

I looked at the note I'd scribbled earlier about similar cases I'd worked. I certainly didn't remember anything like these.

Names, some addresses even, were as fresh in my mind as the day I wrote them on the report. Other names and faces I've completely blocked due to the horrors associated with them.

But surely if I'd worked a murder where a victim's throat was cut, I'd recall something about it.

My own case notwithstanding.

I do remember something about that, even if I don't remember it all.

Which only begged another question I hadn't thought of in some time.

Knives weren't David's style. I didn't even know he owned the bloody hunting knife they told me he dropped in the kitchen sink. I had no idea why he used it if his intent was to kill me. There were four other firearms in the house besides the two I'd been wearing. Why a knife?

My train of thought derailed when Connie rang me on the intercom and announced a call from Penny Daniels.

I took a deep breath before answering, aware how fast my heart was beating, thinking of David again..

"Julie, you asked me to call if I thought of anything else," she said. "I don't know if it would be helpful or even if they're still there, but my mother used to keep diaries. She told me before she died that she kept the full ones in a box in the attic. That's one of the things I wanted to find when I was here last, but J.P. wouldn't let me go up there. He said he'd cleaned out the attic, too. Would you look?"

"Why don't you go with me?" I offered. "You have a better idea of what you're looking for."

"I – yeah. Yes, I'd like that," she said, sounding like she had to convince herself first.

I told her I'd pick her up at the hotel in the next half hour.

I had one more task to tackle – checking my e-mail in hopes of having a response from the FBI on the photos.

Although I had dozens of e-mails waiting, most were routine department notes or responses, but one was from Quinton Gresham from Quantico.

His message read much like he spoke. "Hey, Julie! Got that disk you wanted processed. The photos themselves are still running through the image computers for enhancement, but I also found one deleted image file that had been partially overwritten. I'll process it, too, after the others. It's not great, but I'm attaching you a copy so you can compare it to your evidence. Keep me posted – QG."

He'd always loved those initials, the joke being that he was as opposite from a GQ – *Gentleman's Quarterly* – model as possible, weighing more than 300 rotund pounds.

I downloaded the attachment and waited as the graphics program started, chastising myself for not looking for deleted files.

PC files are not actually erased when they are deleted; the name is altered, which only removes it from the directory list. The actual contents remain until overwritten by other files or by formatting the disc.

I watched as the application opened the file Quinton sent me. It seemed to be missing about a third of the pixels, the tiny blocks that make up an image. What could be identified, however, appeared to be another victim of a throat slashing, but this was different in two ways.

First, the blood wasn't cleaned up like the woman on the disk – this victim was bloody, slumped against a wall. And second, the victim appeared to be male by the clothing – I could make out a tie on a white shirt - though there was a towel or something thrown over the face.

I glanced at my watch. Twenty minutes to go get Penny.

Flipping through my Rolodex, I found a number and dialed.

A deep serious voice answered, "Rader, Internal Affairs."

Eric Rader had been the state police post commander when I worked in Alamogordo. He was now a Deputy Chief in Santa Fe. He was the only one who had stayed in contact with me after I moved to Michigan, calling occasionally to say hi and catch up.

This was a favor I hated to ask.

"Hi, Eric. It's Julie Madigan. Got a minute?"

His voice changed to a softer tone. "Hey, lady! Of course. How are you?"

"I'm alive," I said, though I figured there were bets being placed on that in an office pool, even as we spoke. "But I'm in a situation here, and I could use your help."

I tried to summarize our investigation and my unique connection to it.

"Wow. Life in the big city," he quipped.

"So I'm left with this nagging question of whether I've crossed paths with this killer before. Do you remember any calls like that?"

There was a brief silence. Eric had been the investigating officer who wrote the final case summary for David's shooting because it involved a member of his division.

"Besides the obvious," I added.

He knew the facts of my case. Probably better than I did. We never talked about the investigation. Somehow the badge had been too great a shield between us, even after I left the department.

"I don't remember anything like that, but I can check the database. There might be something in a related case," he said.

"No, Eric, that's okay. I probably ought to go through the regular channels to do that."

"Nonsense. They've finally finished cataloging open cases in the last 25 years. Hang on. I'll load up a search."

I heard the clicking of a keyboard for several seconds.

"I'll never be as good with a computer as you," he said. He paused, then seemed to be talking more to himself. "Nineteen statewide cases in the last 25 years. Hmm, more than I'd have thought. Now, how many were you involved in?"

More clicking. Another pause.

"Madigan, Julie, and Wesley, Julie." He hummed as he clicked the keys a few more times. "This will take a few minutes to actually do a search for your name in any field of these cases. Must be a pain to change names. I'm glad you went back to Madigan."

Like I'd keep David Wesley's name after what he did to me?

"Speaking of names, Julie, I've been meaning to call you. This woman I've been dating the last year or so, Samantha? I finally got the guts to pop the question, and she was crazy enough to say yes," he said in his out-of-uniform shy voice, something not many people ever heard instead of his booming baritone in-command voice. "She hasn't set a date yet – I just asked her give me two weeks' notice so I can be there."

Married? At least someone had bright news.

"Now what about you, Julie? What's happening in your life?"

I laughed with the irony of how twisted things were. "My personal life mirrors how complicated this investigation is. I called the Centers for Disease Control about a victim of a parasite, also related to this case. Believe it or not, the consulting physician they sent was Jeremy McNeeley. And that's just one facet."

Rader and I shared lots of pieces of our lives over coffee on midnight shifts in the New Mexico desert, so he knew who Jeremy was.

He whistled. "Complicated, indeed. Your life always makes mine seem so simple," he teased. "Okay. Two cases in the database. Let me look."

I waited as he skimmed the fields.

I had seen this database as it was being developed. It didn't contain huge hunks of information for each case, only pieces that could be searched and compared, such as dates, investigators' names, locations, victims, types of crimes, and so on.

"One is your case, 1991, Otero County. But the other. . ." he trailed off, still reading. "Your name isn't listed with the investigators, but it must be in the file somewhere. Just a second. No, this was in Albuquerque in November of 1976, but I don't see the matching criteria."

A shiver went through me.

"Eric, the victim was Thomas Madigan – my father," I said, stunned. "Maybe my name is in the file somewhere, but the criteria must be wrong. He was shot."

"Might be a coding error, data mixed up with your case." Silence as he read further. "Yeah, here we go," he said. "This lists you as a primary witness. The cause of death is exsanguination from a GSW to the lower abdomen. There's nothing noted here about a neck wound."

"The femoral artery had been obliterated by a bullet," I confirmed. "But why is my father's case even in this database?"

"His murder is still unsolved," Eric said. "It's supposed to be listed. Yours, however, should not."

CHAPTER 37

"Can you tell me more about these journals?" I asked Penny as we drove toward the farm. "You said they were your mother's back to her childhood?"

"She and her sister both kept diaries as girls. Mom kept writing after she married, even after she had us. She told me once she'd kept Angela's books, too, but I never saw them. Maybe she gave them to Anthony when he was old enough."

"Anthony?" The name didn't make a solid connection to anyone for me.

"My cousin, remember? My family took him in after my aunt died."

"You said he committed suicide, right?"

"He was in his twenties, in the Navy," she said, as if it held no emotion at all. "I don't think he took more than a duffel bag when he left. He was always different, distant."

When we arrived at the farmhouse, Brandan brought us the house keys from where they were digging near the barn.

The scenes they were processing at the farm had progressed slower than anticipated, due to being second to current cases under investigation, but Brandan said he was sure the barrel would be out of the ground by noon the next day, barring rain. So far the weather had cooperated, much to everyone's amazement. He headed back that direction.

Penny and I went inside, turning on lights as we went.

Houses feel different after their occupants are dead, almost as if the building knows it's been abandoned by its residents and begins to settle and decay as quickly as the human body. The furniture sags. The air smells musty, feeling dense and heavy. The lights appear less bright.

Of course, this wasn't scientific. It's a sensation I noted in homes of the deceased, even if the death happened elsewhere. Very different from a home where the residents were simply away when I entered, say on a burglary call.

This house definitely had the feeling of the dead.

Flat surfaces smudged with fingerprint dust added to the emptiness.

I followed Penny up the stairway to one end of a narrow hallway. She pointed out that her room and the boys' room had been separated by the stairs to the attic. The bathroom and her parents' bedroom were on the other side of the hall.

She stopped to look inside the master bedroom, which was as plain and tasteless as the downstairs areas.

A plain blue cotton comforter lay smooth and straight. Curious, I lifted its edge and found white sheets tucked tight at the corner. I saw no other such obsessive tendencies toward neatness in the room. Several paperback books were stacked on the bedside table, including Stephen King's *The Stand*, a bookmark poked out from the middle. Next to these was a cup of what might have been coffee several weeks ago. The evaporated black sludge had an oily film with clumps of bluish-green mold floating on it.

That takes a while to grow, I thought, having left the carafe in my coffee maker too long.

Still, in contrast to the bed, the dichotomy of dust and green coffee slime itched in my brain.

The phone also had a layer of dust that matched other untouched surfaces nearby. His business involved daytime customers, so he probably took those calls in his office. Didn't anyone ever call him at night?

"Was J.P. in the military?" I asked, trying to figure out the contradiction.

She laughed. "Not that rebel. He'd refused to follow an order if someone told him to take his next breath."

The dresser was cluttered with loose change, pocket items. A small cedar box sat in the center, closed.

"My father's," Penny said, seeing where my attention had focused.

I tried to lift the lid with my thumbnail, but it was locked. I had a sudden urge to get it open, imagining a stash of jewelry or other personal belongings of the victims inside.

"Where's the key?" I asked.

"My father kept it hidden in his bottom drawer, thinking we wouldn't find it. He put his Sunday suit accessories in the box – tie tacks, cufflinks. And his pictures of us kids. He kept a cloth wallet thing I made him when Mom taught me to sew. It was really ugly." She smiled. "Military things. Just stuff."

Maybe for a moment, we both got lost the memories of our fathers and the memorabilia we knew they held closest. After my conversation with Eric Rader about my father's murder, I felt especially sensitive.

I imagined she might feel that way, too, being back in this house.

Penny took a breath and pulled open dresser drawers until she found the ring box hiding the key.

As much as I wanted to know what was inside that wooden box, I knew the best action was to let the crime scene techs dust it and mark it as evidence. It would serve no one if my curiosity caused critical evidence to be inadmissible.

I called Callaghan's cell phone and asked him to send up someone with an evidence bag.

"Why? Did you find something?"

"A box and a hunch," I said.

He said he'd be right up.

I looked around the bedroom again. "Did you ever talk to each other?" I asked.

"I called him, usually at Christmas and his birthday, because he was the only one left," Penny said. "Then I'd swear I wouldn't call again because all we ever had to discuss was the weather. Last time we talked was in March, I think."

When Brandan arrived, Penny showed him where she found the key, then she and I headed to the attic while he collected the box.

"I don't get it," I said as we climbed the stairs. "Parts of the house are fastidious, but others are not. Which was your brother, a neat freak or a slob?"

"I thought he was a slob," Penny said. "When I was here last time, it was clean but messy. Cluttered like the living room, but not dirty. Anthony was the neat one. They had many a fist fight over that when they were young."

I looked down at the steps as we climbed. Like those I'd descended in the barn, there were no footprints despite the dust on other surfaces.

The contrast bothered me. A bed made so neatly my mother would be proud, but dirty dishes growing science projects on the table next to it. The bathroom was renovated, but with minimum effort to make it usable, not aesthetic. Same with the work in the barn. The flooring was perfect, but the shoring of the walls in the chamber below was only functional.

With that in mind, I wasn't sure what I expected to find in the attic. It was, however, a stereotypical jumbled dusty place depicted in Hollywood's melodramatic movies where an awful secret waits in the shadows. A small shuttered window let in enough light that I saw the string hanging from a light fixture at the top of the stairs. Penny pulled it without looking, a familiar action she had done so many times that her body had not forgotten the mechanics.

She stood at the axis of pathways through boxes and old furniture. After sneezing twice, she apologized for her allergies. "Looks like J.P. put more stuff up here. This could take a while." She turned around slowly, looking for something familiar, a place to begin, then worked her way toward one corner, opening boxes as she went, dismissing most. "You should look, in case there's anything of use to the investigation," she suggested.

I didn't know what to look for, but I nodded.

As she went, she pushed several boxes to where I could browse them, but remained focused on finding her mother's diaries, despite frequent sneezing and nose-blowing. She stopped to find her nasal spray. "I forgot to bring a new bottle," she said, sounding congested. "This stuff is magic, except of all things, it smells like flowers. How stupid is that?" She held it up so I could see the label.

"Yuck," I agreed. But it had to smell like something probably, so flowers beat cow pies.

Penny used the spray and snapped the cover on before tossing it into her bag. "I know we're not supposed to, but I share my daughter's prescription sometimes when I travel. I don't need it in Phoenix, but Michigan autumns and old dusty boxes make me miserable."

Perhaps in sympathy, I sneezed.

Most of Tucker's boxes were packed loosely, with no sense of order – clothes mixed with cassette tapes and a few eight-tracks, family photos and childhood art projects.

I scanned books and magazines I came across, looking for references to violence, criminal investigation or pornography, but found nothing out of mainstream publication though he appeared to be a Stephen King fan.

Twisted stuff, but not necessarily an indication of a killer.

My search was interrupted when Brandan called up the stairs. I excused myself and left Penny to her excavation.

"You need to see what's in the box, Julie," he said when I met him in the master bedroom. "Not what I expected."

Using latex gloves, he lifted the wooden lid, revealing a stack of photos – maybe a dozen.

"I don't want to handle them here, so I don't know what's below this first one. Recognize it?"

The top picture was of me, getting into my Suburban in front of Matt's apartment.

CHAPTER 38

My eyes rolled up as I squeezed them shut. I nodded my head and groaned. “No wonder he went for Matt. See the dent in the bumper and the tailgate on the driver’s side? I was rear-ended in February 1993. It took three weeks to get it into the shop to be fixed. This was taken during that time.”

Seeing the photo made my stomach churn. Each new link to me withered my sense of control and safety, tightened the windlass on my fear for Matt.

“Let me know what you find upstairs,” Brandan said. “I’ll bag whatever you think is pertinent. Hell, I'll empty this house and look at everything. Say the word.”

“We won’t find anything he didn’t want us to find,” I said, nodding at the box. “And none of it will help catch him.”

I left him and returned to the attic, where Penny was sitting near the light, reading. “I found them. They were in two different boxes, her childhood diaries in one, and journals she wrote later in the other. Will I be able to take them?” she asked. “Or anything else?”

“This being a criminal case,” I said with a shrug. “I don't know much about probate in this state. Did your brother have a will?”

The property had been left to Penny and her brother jointly by their parents. Because she brought papers to support that, ownership of the real property wasn’t in question, but the disposition of her brother’s belongings and contents of the home might be.

I went downstairs talk to Brandan about what Penny wanted from the house, and he said he’d get an answer.

“Maybe we should ask her to take the journals to the hotel

tonight to browse, even if she can't take them home with her," I suggested.

Brandan agreed, following me back into the attic. "Is there anything else you want from the house besides the journals," he explained, "so I can ask. If there's a delay, at least those items can be taken into police possession instead of being left in the house where they could be stolen."

"There really isn't much here I wanted except these journals." She seemed disappointed that there was so little left of her childhood.

I helped her repack the books into a single box that weighed about 25 pounds, and Brandan carried them to my Suburban.

When I locked the house behind us, Penny looked relieved.

"I can't tell you how much we appreciate you flying to Michigan. Your information and insight have been very useful," Brandan said. "There is a good chance we'll find the body of the old man you told us about. The ground-penetrating radar maps should be ready by morning."

She nodded.

"Before you leave, could I ask you to take the time to write a brief statement about that night you saw the boys kill the old man, details about what you saw? Nothing fancy – just handwrite and sign it," he explained. "Since we can't prosecute J.P. or your cousin for the murder, your statement doesn't need to be formal, but we'd like to close the case officially."

"I'll do that tonight," she agreed.

After Brandan set the box of books in my truck, he rubbed Laser's ears. "Is she feeding you T-bones and fresh rabbits? You shouldn't have to eat regular ole' dog food, should you, boy? You make her give you the good stuff."

"Before you give him any ideas," I said, pushing Brandan out of the way and closing the doors. "Coming to dinner with us?"

He declined, stating he had a lot of work to finish before getting the team's efforts shut down for the night. "The guys working on the barrel want to stay till they're done. I guess I can't blame them. We may do that, since the rain looks to be holding off."

"Can I bring food out?" I asked.

His face lit up. "I'll ask around and call you in a little while, okay?"

Penny declined dinner, too, saying she'd rather spend the evening reading. I encouraged her to order from room service or delivery from a few of my favorite restaurants.

After I dropped her off, I went by my house to grab more clean clothes and to feed the fish before going to the office to shower. I was almost ready to leave when my cell phone rang.

"We decided to stay late," Brandan said. "We could use food and drinks for seven people. Everyone is fine with sandwiches, maybe subs or burgers. Could you arrange that?"

"I'm not having dinner with Penny, so I'll take care of it right away."

Having been stuck on all-day-all-night scenes, starving, I understood. Providing a meal was the least I could do for a crew who really wanted to stay. I called a diner known for its burgers and milkshakes to place an order.

I poured Laser a bowl of food and put water in a leftover whipped cream bowl from under the sink. "You behave while you're here alone," I told him. "Don't let in strangers."

After a noisy drink, he went to his favorite corner in my den and gave me a look that said he would be right there when I got back, intruders or not.

I put a cooler in my truck, stopped for ice, bottles of water and soft drinks for later, and was on my way to get the burgers when my phone rang again.

"Julie, can we talk?"

Jeremy McNeeley.

What is there to talk about?

"I'm on my way to take food to the crew at a scene right now."

"Can you pick me up?"

I felt my eyes roll. "No."

"After? Maybe dinner?"

Despite my anger, I agreed to stop when I was finished, though I didn't know why. "In an hour. Don't bother dressing up. I've been digging around in a dusty attic this afternoon." I disconnected.

Seven hungry people were gathered at the back gate of the Tucker house when I arrived. Brandan passed out the burgers and shakes, with the news I'd brought extras in case anyone wanted seconds.

"How's it going," I asked Brandan as he took a giant bite from his burger. "How close are you to getting the barrel out of the ground?"

Broad smiles all around told me they were very close, but no one interrupted their chewing to say. Finally Brandan swallowed.

"I think we're set to raise it in an hour or so. We've got lights set up, and we'll call Dr. Katz when we feel it's safe to open."

"Safe?" I asked, working on a chocolate milkshake so thick the straw collapsed.

"Given what happened in the barn, we thought it prudent to have a bomb squad expert take a look before we open it. That would be Theron's job," he said, nodding toward the man with the haircut of an ex-Marine sitting a few feet away from me. "Theron Howell, state police bomb squad, this is Julie Madigan, deputy medical examiner investigator. She's the only one who saw what was in the pit in the barn."

"Nice to meet you." Theron extended a scarred and deformed hand to shake. "Pipe bomb, 1987," he said when he saw my eyes drop to his hand. "Keeps me focused."

I nodded.

"We can swap bomb stories someday over a beer," he said, nodding his head toward the barn. "I'd say yours trumps mine – much bigger crater."

"I'm not missing any fingers, but it's a deal."

"Let me show you something," he said. He picked up his milkshake and headed out toward his vehicle, where he opened his trunk and turned his back to the group.

"They tell me you were on your way out of the hole when you saw the bomb," he said. "Or one of them, anyway. You're lucky. If you'd been down in the hole, you wouldn't have survived the blast."

"So I'm told. I feel pretty lucky," I said, rubbing the sore ribs, "that any of us survived."

"No. Everyone is fortunate that both bombs went off at almost the same time. They were meant to go off separately," he said, locking eyes with me to make his point. "Completely separately."

I nodded that I understood.

Howell lifted a lid of a box in the trunk, showing me debris he'd collected from the bombs – pieces I did not recognize, even when he pointed out and described various components. "I think the first bomb was set to detonate after the call to 911 brought initial responders to the scene – to kill EMS, fire rescue, deputies – you understand? I suspect the second bomb was meant to take out everyone who responded to the first explosion, those looking for survivors. Either the first one didn't work right, or the second one went off prematurely."

The milkshake congealed in my stomach.

"Why?" I asked, my throat constricted in fear of the implications. "We thought the bombs were to destroy evidence. This is completely different."

I'd asked, but I had a feeling I didn't really want to know the answer.

"In most cases, a bomb is a political statement. It's power. Terror around the world." He let me think about that a moment. "There were about 3,100 explosive and incendiary incidents reported to the feds in 1994. Not unfounded bomb threats, fireworks injuries or accidental explosive events. Real terrorist-type bomb and explosive events in this country you seldom hear about on the news. The difference is, bombers like Timothy McVeigh still leave the scenes."

The images of the Murrah Building in Oklahoma City haunted me and practically every other American who owned a television set five months ago.

"Wow." What else was there to say?

I glanced back at the technicians. Most had gobbled down their half-pound hamburgers and fries and were fidgeting, waiting for word to get back to work.

"Do they know about this?"

"About the barn bombs, yes. They're digging in a very old site so I can't imagine there'd be anything active from so long ago. Then again, I'm still here – age doesn't make a bomb safe."

Safety. The concept slid into the mental column of incomprehension.

"I didn't want to make you jumpy, but I thought you should

know what my impression of the two bombs meant."

"Uh, thanks. I guess." I smiled. "But I'm still jumpy."

"That can't be a bad thing."

The crew gathered up trash and stretched. I doubted any of them had thought about food since breakfast, but the break and nutrition would stave off any thoughts of quitting before this phase of the project was done.

Brandan walked me to the truck. "I'll keep you posted on what we find. You're taking Penny to the airport tomorrow, right?"

I nodded, finishing my shake with slurpy sounds.

"I talked with the probate judge and the prosecutor. She can keep the diaries," he said, "and anything else from the house that does not appear connected to the investigation."

"I'm sure she'll appreciate that."

I returned to Traverse City, calling Jeremy to let him know I was on my way. I didn't know why, except I didn't like the way things had ended the night before. Walking away just seemed too trivial for the damage caused by his lies. Maybe I was just looking for a fight.

In the fifteen minutes it took to get to his hotel, I replayed the conversation about his wife, infuriating me more, until I considered not stopping at all. When I pulled up to the registration parking area, Jeremy was outside waiting.

"Thanks," he said, climbing in.

I hit the accelerator before he had buckled his seatbelt.

"I know you're mad –" he started.

I pointed a finger at him. "Oh, no, McNeeley. I'm way beyond mad. You told me you wanted another chance with me, but somehow you conveniently forgot to mention your wife and daughter. I won't be a pawn in your marriage or your excuse for a divorce."

He'd mentioned dinner on the phone, but all I wanted was to go home, so home is where I headed. He could order pizza if he was hungry.

I hit the garage door opener button on my visor before I turned into the driveway and barely slowed down to pull into the garage, coming to a hard stop. I yanked the keys from the ignition and growled, "Don't bang the bike."

Jeremy got out and stood next to my motorcycle.

"Hmmm, very nice," he said.

For some reason, the Harley-Davidson "thing" about me seems to surprise a lot of people.

I'm sure a good many other "things" about me would surprise them, too.

I walked around the front of my truck and the motorcycle toward the kitchen door while he drooled on the chrome, mumbling something asinine about women on Harley's.

I ignored him.

The chain-drive garage door opener makes so damned much racket I can't stand the noise. I usually have enough time to get out of the truck and get both the deadbolt and the doorknob unlocked before the automatic light goes off, then I hit the button to lower the door and hurry inside the kitchen to avoid the noise

But with Jeremy in the mix, I lost several seconds of that time.

I'd unlocked the deadbolt but hadn't gotten the key in the doorknob when the light went off. Standing in the darkness, he was suddenly right next to me, so I had to reach around him to push the button to close the garage door. The light came back on, and the door clattered shut.

As I turned to finish unlocking the door, Jeremy grabbed my left arm.

"Julie, I love you," he said in a desperate voice I barely heard.

In pure reflex of anger, I turned and connected flat-handed to the side of his face with a slap that burned my right palm.

It had to hurt – it rocked him back on his heels.

Astonished, I tried to jerk away but stumbled on the doorstep.

Jeremy had not let go of my left arm and, perhaps sensing I was falling, he grabbed at the other arm and pinned me to the door, holding both my wrists against my chest.

The only reason we didn't fall to the kitchen floor with him on me was because I hadn't turned the doorknob.

I tugged at his grip without result.

The garage door closed.

"Did that make you feel better?" His words echoed in the sudden silence.

Too angry to speak, I struggled to yank my arms free, but he stretched them over my head, leaning close, which angered me even more.

"You think hitting me is enough?" He let go of my hands and took a step back. "That's the best you can do? Hit me!"

I slapped him again in a white-hot rage.

He stood there, waiting as a bright pink handprint spread across his face.

"Is that it?" he whispered, his eyes watering. "Did you hear me, Julie? I love you."

When I pulled my arm back to hit him again, he caught my wrist and turned to the shelf next to the door and picked up a box cutter, holding it out to me. "If you can't tell me you love me, you might as well cut out my heart," he said, pointing it at his chest.

My vision went red then black. My mind strobed memories.

I squeezed my eyes shut, trying to turn away. Stumbled again, falling against the doorframe. In fear, I pulled my arms up toward my face.

What if everything I remember after David cut my throat has been a dream, and I'm still lying on the floor, bleeding to death?

I began to slide down the door, cowering, but Jeremy stepped forward again and pushed his legs against my buckling knees to hold me up.

He tossed the knife onto the shelf and took my face in his hands. "Damn it, Julie, I love you," he whispered. "I have never loved anyone the way I love you."

He kissed me, cradling my head.

"Just tell me –" he said, but his words turned to more kisses.

I opened my eyes, finding that nothing had changed. I was standing in my garage. In Michigan. Being held by a man I used to love.

All I could do was cling to him to keep from falling, my weight almost pulling us both down to the floor. I was afraid to let go of him. My heart was racing so fast my chest hurt.

Finally he picked me up and carried me to the bedroom.

CHAPTER 39

Long after midnight, I slipped away, leaving Jeremy sleeping in the jumble that had been my bed.

After we'd drifted to sleep, flashes of David attacking me surfaced in my dreams, leaving me emotionally hollow and wide awake. I curled up on the sofa in my den, trying to figure out exactly what happened tonight with Jeremy, but I was too tired to make sense of it.

Jeremy came around the corner through the kitchen. "May I join you?"

I nodded, and he sat down close to me.

I touched his cheek where I'd struck him. "I really didn't mean to hit you. The first time."

"I know. It's okay."

"No, it's not okay," I said. I didn't understand the rage and violence.

He turned to face me. "I knew you were angry. I shouldn't have grabbed you. I only wanted you to say you loved me."

I couldn't say the words he wanted to hear.

"I know you probably don't want to hear about this," he finally said, "but I talked to Deanna today. I told her about you, about everything. We agreed on a divorce without a fight. We'll have to find a way to work things out about Stephanie for her benefit. There's nothing else worth fighting over. All I'm asking is that you consider giving me that chance after the divorce is settled."

"Damn you, Jeremy," I whispered. I took a deep breath and let it out slowly.

No question. I hated him.

And I loved him. The idea that, despite him walking away, I could love him so completely, so desperately, was overwhelming. And terrifying. Yet it felt good somewhere inside, too.

But could I – did I even want to – forgive him for hurting me? How could I trust him, knowing what he'd done to his wife and daughter?

Matthew's words echoed in my head. *Was love really enough?*

Neither of us spoke again. Too little to say, or maybe too much.

I curled against his warm naked body, wondering what to do next.

I'd always loved him. Even when I hated him most.

Was it enough?

* * *

Penny declined breakfast when I called, saying she wasn't feeling well. Maybe the grief over her brother's death was finally taking hold. I encouraged her to order room service and told her I'd be there in an hour – after I dropped Jeremy at his hotel.

He didn't mention the events from the night before, and not wanting to start a conversation we didn't have time to finish, I didn't either.

I started a pot of coffee and took a quick shower to wake up, and he brought me a cup into the bathroom where I was drying my hair.

"I went to the cupboard, but the cupboard was bare," he chimed over the noise "What's up with that?"

"You don't want to know," I said loudly, then whispered to myself. "Just pray the coffee isn't contaminated."

I dressed in black jeans and a dark gray turtleneck pulled over the ballistic vest. When I was lacing up my black work boots, Jeremy sat down across the living room from me.

"I bet you look fabulous on that Harley," he said. "When did you get it?"

"In 1987," I said. "After my promotion to sergeant."

It had been the first year for the Heritage Softail, the FLST, a step on the upward climb for Harley-Davidson, back when you could find a new Harley on a showroom floor. Five years later, all the yuppies wanted one, and they were scarce.

"I'd never've guessed you liked motorcycles," he said, shaking his head. "Or that you'd made sergeant."

"There's a lot about me you'd never guess, Jeremy," I said, pausing to look up at him. "Some of it you may still not like much."

* * *

When I called from the lobby, Penny asked me to come to her room.

The woman who answered the door was not the same bright-eyed, energetic woman who had stepped off the airplane a few days earlier. She looked tired and pale.

"I was up all night reading, and there is something I think you should see," she said, picking up one of the journals and flipping to a bookmark. She handed it to me. "My mother wrote this."

October 12, 1960

I can't believe what's happening! The Detroit police called to tell me Angela had been killed by her husband. Murdered! Why? I don't understand. They say she's dead, but that's all they'll say other than it was her husband.

Bob Bock was a bastard to Ang' but I never believed she was in danger. The police want to know if we can come get Anthony. Not tonite. I can't drive now. My hands shake so bad I can hardly write, but I have to do something or else I'll scream and scream. Nick isn't home yet with the car anyway. I said I'd come tomorrow.

I finally got my nerves settled enough to call Momma in Florida. She said the police called them, too, but she didn't know any more than I did. I heard Pa bellowing in the background, yelling that Angie got her throat slit like a pig, and it was a shame that bastard son of hers wasn't home to get it, too.

As much as my heart aches, I told Mom I'd said my last words to my father for being such an arrogant selfish bastard, that it was all his fault this happened to Angela in the first place – he gave her no choice but to marry Robert Bock. Mom didn't argue. She didn't say a thing – just hung up.

Only one of them is dead, but tonight, I lost everyone else in my family with one phone call.

Tear drops had discolored the paper and smudged the ink in a few places. The heartbreak was visible in the handwriting as well as the words.

Penny touched the pages as if she could comfort the writer. "They didn't even have a real funeral for Angela, she wrote later. My mother drove down state to get my cousin, and that was that. She never mentioned my aunt or uncle, or my grandparents again." She looked up at me, changing subjects. "Anyway, the news this morning said the girl they found in the barrel, that her throat was cut. Could it be my uncle?"

"Your uncle would be pretty old to be kidnapping young women now, but it's worth looking into. Does the journal mention what happened to him? Was he convicted?" Despite my doubts, I felt my heart rate increasing.

"Mom never mentioned him to us at all. I skimmed through the rest of that book and the next, looking for more about him. She wrote a lot about how my cousin was adjusting, how she tried to make him feel at home, and about how J.P. and I treated him. I remember feeling jealous of Anthony sometimes because she tried so much harder with him, but I didn't know what happened to Angela except she died. No one told me."

I realized how much of a shock this must have been, even though it happened when she was so young. "It must have been hard on your mother to bring a child into her home when he reminded her of so much hurt."

"Or maybe that was the only thing she had left." Penny zipped her bag closed. "I'm ready to go. Are you sure I can take these?"

"Brandan said the judge agreed," I said and carried it for her as we walked to my truck.

"I'm afraid something in here might be important, and I don't want to be responsible for reading and interpreting every word. After last night, I'm not sure I want to read it at all, not right now."

"I understand. I could make photocopies for us, then ship the books to you, if you'd like."

"Would you? I'd feel a lot better about that," she said, clearly relieved. "I already feel like I've been run through a mill saw."

Laser barked a friendly greeting to her as she got in the truck.

"What a good boy you are," she said. "I brought you a treat." She pulled a wrapped piece of bacon from her pocket and broke it in half for him.

He delicately took it from her fingers and practically swallowed it whole, then sat down patiently, tail thumping hard against the backseat, waiting to see what he would have to do for more.

"Does he know any tricks?" she asked me.

I smiled. "Well, he's a police dog, so I don't think his tricks are the entertainment sort."

"That's okay," she said, offering him the other half. "But that's all I have."

I started the truck. "Penny, I appreciate you taking the time to come and help us with the investigation. I know we kept you from another couple of days of work."

"Oh, that's okay. Everyone needs a vacation after a vacation, right?" she half-joked. "I was leery I'd be forced to say things about J.P. You know how lawyers can take anything and make it sound like something different. But you listened. I hope you get to the bottom of this. I know my brother did some awful things, but I really don't want to believe he could have killed all those girls."

"Something in human nature keeps us from believing the very worst," I said, "until we have proof, and then sometimes longer still. Parents believe their children. Spouses believe each other. Trust is destroyed and rebuilt in both the tiniest and the largest of steps. But it is forgiveness we struggle with most."

She nodded, as if not exactly listening to my words. Maybe she was struggling to forgive her brother for things he'd done to her through the years. She wanted to believe he wasn't a monster, but there were so few answers. All of this must have complicated her grief.

"Well, it's the truth we want to find," I said. "We could say he did kill them since he is dead, too, but that would leave a guilty man to murder again if it's not true. As I said before, truth can be greater than the sum of its facts."

"I'm most afraid to find out he's so evil."

"Evil is choosing to hurt others and enjoying doing it." I pulled up to the curb at the Cherry Capital terminal. "You've lost a brother. No matter what he may have done, he was still your brother. That is a fact, and it doesn't change. I'm sorry you lost him," I said.

I walked to the ticket counter with her and was surprised when she put down her bag and hugged me. "Thank you for everything, Julie."

"Keep in touch," I told her. "I'll send the journals as soon as I can."

She smiled. "Whenever you're done with them. I'm in no hurry."

I drove from the airport out to the Tucker farm, pondering Penny's idea about her uncle.

Could there be a connection?

CHAPTER 40

I reached the farm a little past eleven, in time to see several technicians eating lunch in the shade of a tree.

Brandan looked up from where he and several others were squatted, looking into a hole. He stood and came to meet me.

"The scene here is clear. No bombs. We're ready to open it when Dr. Katz arrives. Maybe another ten minutes. Great timing," he said. "And I'm ready to send a team to dig at the other site. The radar team marked off two distinct places for us. Fantastic idea to call the power company, Julie." He clapped me on the back.

My ribs only hurt a little through the vest.

We walked around the barn debris to the hand-dug crater almost twice the diameter of a barrel centered inside.

"Unless there are holes in the bottom, it seems intact and sealed."

"I'm not sure that's an advantage," I said, my nose twitching. "Who's going to the other site to start digging?"

"Benton, Cook and Perron. Benton is a great ground tech."

"I'll get them going if you'd like," I offered, and he accepted.

I gathered up the trio and rode with them in a county van to where Penny had witnessed a murder so many years ago, explaining what she had told us.

"Both boys involved in this crime are dead, but while you're digging up bodies on this property, we should get them all and clear as many cases as we can," I said, wondering how many more we might find. Too many already.

I reviewed the site map and the markers placed by the power

company team as they interpreted information from their computers and applied it to the gridded area of ground.

They began their task, and I wished them luck.

I walked back to the barn, enjoying the cool fresh air and autumn colors.

September turns the corner to autumn, when maple leaves begin to blush, ever-changing until crimson saturates the landscape like blood. The height of the color change is beautiful, but I love those first subtle changes, starting with the first little airbrush of red on green. The part of autumn I don't like is the loss of daylight. By Christmas, the sun sets before five in the afternoon in Michigan.

When I got to the barn, I saw the technicians gathered around the barrel, which had been lifted from the ground by a tow truck. Apparently the bottom was intact, but my nose suspected the crowd would back away when the barrel was opened.

I caught Callaghan's eye, waving as I got into my truck.

At my office, I put in a call to the Michigan Department of Corrections, hoping to get information on Bob Bock – Robert, I presumed. I was glad his name wasn't Bob Jones or William Smith because I had no date of birth, middle initial or other information about him. DMV didn't make a match, but that only meant he didn't have a current driver's license in Michigan.

Several transfers and explanations later, a call was directed to someone else who might be able answer my questions.

I love bureaucracy.

I spent a few minutes relaying again what I knew about Robert Bock, which included an approximate age and date of the crime.

I left my number and was told the information could take a day or so to retrieve.

A day? I tried to reiterate that a police officer's life was at stake, but my plea fell on deaf ears.

"Lady, it's not like I've got these files sitting in a cabinet behind my desk," the voice said, becoming less patient. "Someone has to go find them in a warehouse."

I hope I said goodbye with sufficient courtesy that my request didn't get filed into the trashcan under the kid's desk.

Needing distraction, I opened the box of Sally Collins-Tucker's journals I'd carried in from the truck and picked up the book on top.

How weird Penny must have felt, reading from her mother's childhood and adult years. There were probably family secrets that Penny would rather not know.

Encouraged by my father, I started journaling often. Since his death, most of my writing has been about the black holes in my life, captured in song lyrics and poems. I've spewed a lot of the ugly emotions from my father's murder, about Jeremy when he left, and about David's attack in those journals. Though the ink did not incinerate the pages, some passages still ignited the anger in my soul years later.

Sally used her journals to work out problems in her life, which documented the issues of Angela's death and of bringing the young boy into her own family. I skimmed entries, sympathetic to her heartbreak. And for Anthony's, too, though she found his lack of grief to be distressing. She noted on several occasions how unemotional Anthony seemed to be about the loss of his parents and his upended world.

I have tried to explain that his mother died, and his father can no longer keep him, but Anthony shows little interest in what happened to either of his parents. From what Angela had told me, Bob never paid attention to the boy, but I know she adored him. I think I need to talk to the minister about this, because it doesn't seem normal that he doesn't miss them.

Did she even know what normal grief was for a seven-year-old? I wondered. Grownups have so little understanding about how children grieve, which is a travesty for the entire family in the middle of a crisis.

Did she ever tell him how his mother died?

I kept reading.

Anthony got in a fight at school yesterday. The teacher sent home a note saying he'd given the other boy a black eye for making fun of his father being in prison. To my knowledge, Anthony didn't even know that, but people do talk and children listen more than we know. I went to the school and talked to the principal, who felt it was important to enforce the rule against fighting, but he wasn't going to punish the other boy!

This isn't about life being fair, I told him. How much should we allow one to make fun of another before a victim is allowed to stand up and fight? I asked. Is it okay to pick on a child because one of his parents is dead or black? Okay to make fun of a crippled child? How about laughing at the boy whose father is screwing the school secretary?

Ha! That hit the mark.

I left and took Anthony with me, talking with him on the way home about what had really happened with his parents. Anthony said he knew his father had killed his mother. I wish I could tell him Bob wasn't his real father, but I have no answers about who his father was. I guess it doesn't matter now.

CHAPTER 41

Around 4:30, I needed a break from the journals, so I took Laser out. We met up with the morgue crew as they unloaded the body from the farm.

"Pretty amazing find out there," Katz told me. He described the condition of the body inside the barrel and his initial findings – young female, adolescent probably. Not quite mummified, but close. Clothes mostly intact. A bracelet with a couple of charms on it. "Hopefully we can match that to a missing person's report. There was no acid, and once sealed, there were no bugs or moisture. I suspect her throat was cut."

He excused himself to accompany the techs to the morgue.

I had more work to do and nowhere else to go anyway, so I returned to my office. I tossed Laser a chewy bone, then scavenged my desk drawers until I found a granola bar.

Supper or lunch, I don't remember.

While I was downstairs, my mother called. Apparently she and Connie had a bit of a chat. They became friends during Mom's last visit to Michigan. Part of Connie's shorthand message included "NM or MI for Thkgvg?" followed by a smiley face and her own addition of big letters - GO. Connie obviously approved of my trip to Albuquerque for the holiday.

Another message slip indicated I'd missed a call from the Department of Corrections in Lansing concerning Robert Bock. *Damn, alone in my office all afternoon and I'd missed the one call I'd been waiting for.* After business hours now, that call would have to wait till morning.

Disappointed, I worked on cleaning up. My desk looked like the paper fairy had vomited. An hour later, I'd only managed to shuffle papers into fewer piles, accomplishing one stack to be filed and another to go to the shredding bin behind Connie's desk.

Giving up on the organization project, I answered my direct line only to hear Jeremy. Wasn't I was supposed to still be mad at him?

"How was your day?" he asked.

"Long," I said, leaning back in my chair. It screeched. I scribbled OIL CHAIR on my calendar pad. "Yours?"

"Didn't do much. Drove around and got lost in someplace called Benzonia. The natives were nice enough to point me in the right direction. Very pretty."

"Your instincts taking you south like the geese?" I chuckled.

"Maybe. Let's go to dinner."

"I'm exhausted. How about meeting me for breakfast?"

"How about we have it brought to our room?" he suggested.

"Sorry, not tonight. I –" I trailed off, looking at my fax machine, flipping up the page in the received bin that had been empty before I went down the hall just minutes ago.

In plain block print, the page read: *Your deputy isn't dead yet, Julia. I'm waiting till you find the key to your soul so you can save him. It's in the blood.*

I whispered a string of profanity. "Gotta go." I crashed the receiver into the cradle to disconnect and paged Brandan through central dispatch.

I scanned the page again while I waited, finding a bogus phone number programmed for the sender, wondering whether the call itself could be traced after the fact.

My phone rang in less than two minutes. "Detective Callaghan."

"I received a fax about Matthew." I read him the statement.

"I'll take that as news he's alive," he said, "but is that supposed to be another clue?"

"The key to my soul?" I asked. "No idea. Maybe it's an allegory or a metaphor."

"Julie, I wasn't a literature major. Does your soul have a lock? Give me an example."

Not a bad interpretation.

"Rather than meaning a real physical key, it may be a symbol used to represent an abstract idea, like the dove means peace," I explained. "He's proven locks on my house don't mean anything to him. What kind of key relates to blood?"

"Evidence. DNA. Crap, I don't know," he said and sighed. "Forrester is officially taking over the investigation. Even if this hadn't become a federal case with the kidnapping, we don't have the manpower to keep this search up without more assistance." Brandan sounded disappointed.

"Help is help, Brandan. So long as someone finds Matthew, it doesn't matter." I hoped that didn't sound as desperate and helpless as I felt.

"Yeah, I know. I'll pass this on to Forrester, or I can give you his office number."

"I should call him." I heard music in the background as he flipped through his notes. "Where are you? You should be home, Brandan."

"That's the pot calling the kettle hot, right?"

"My bed is downstairs. I'm a lot closer than you are."

"Call Nolan, give him the scoop. Then come down to Benjamin's, and I'll buy you a beer."

As tired as I was, that sounded good.

I called Nolan Forrester's number, spoke briefly with the agent who answered, sent the fax that I'd just received to their office.

Benjamin's restaurant was three blocks away, close to the police and sheriff's department, which made it popular with cops. The jukebox was never too loud to have a conversation, always loud enough no one could overhear. It was a friendly sort of place, not too bright, not too dark. The air wasn't clouded in smoke. The beer was always cold, the popcorn fresh, and burgers cooked the way they were ordered. And although the place was supposed to close at eleven, Ben always stayed open as long as there were customers, switching to non-alcoholic drinks after 2 a.m. by law, but still serving appetizers. He carried take-out bags to patrol vehicles double-parked at the front door at any time of the day.

That was good for business.

Three blocks or not, I drove. And I took the dog. It was time I paid off that steak.

CHAPTER 42

No one paid any attention to Laser coming into the restaurant with me.

"I was afraid you wouldn't show," Brandan said when I found his table. "What can I get you?"

"Something American in a bottle," I replied, looking at the Killian's next to his half-eaten chicken sandwich.

Brandan went to the bar and came back with a bucket filled with ice and four bottles.

Laser curled up at my feet. He'd been here before, probably more often than I had.

I took a bottle and unscrewed the cap. "Cheers," I said, clinking my bottleneck to Brandan's.

"S'lainte," he said with a smile.

A server stopped like a race car at a pit stop.

"A cheeseburger for me, and a rare steak for my friend here." I nodded to the dog beneath the table.

He scribbled my order on his pad with a nod, then zoomed on.

The place was busy.

"You sound bummed about the FBI stepping in," I said, taking a handful of popcorn from the bowl between us.

He shrugged.

"Bottom line, it's just about finding Matt," I said, and I wanted to believe that, but my imagination painted ugly pictures I tried to blink away.

"I appreciate the help, but it's as if no one believes we could do it without the suits."

Law enforcement ego is a fragile thing.

"The nastiest case I was ever involved with had badges from seven agencies – city, county, state, FBI, Air Force military police, U.S. Forest Service, and the tribal police." I took another swallow of beer. "Lots of ego fluffing and head butting, but the suspect was already in custody."

"Any clues about the key to your soul?" he asked, changing the subject.

I yawned. "Sorry. It's been a long day – sorta slipped away from me."

He nodded and tried to hide his own yawn in response.

"No, but I bet you're on the right track," I said. "What kind of blood evidence do we have? Anything with DNA come back yet?"

"You know how backed up the state system is – critical evidence is tied up for months." He shook his head and took a drink. "Take a guess what it means."

"The phrase sounds familiar but just out of reach. I'll have Connie do a literary search tomorrow. Or maybe the FBI has a match for similar themes." I turned my bottle up, distressed to find it empty already. I took the other from the bucket and wiped the ice chips off with a finger.

Ben came by with a chunk of meat on a platter and set it down in front of Laser. He ruffled the dog's ears and said, "Just the way you like it." He straightened up and looked at me. "Matt will be real happy to hear you treat his partner so good."

News of Matthew's disappearance had circulated in the bar, but given the number of cops in and out of Benjamin's in a day, I shouldn't have been surprised.

"Thanks, Ben," I whispered, barely able to speak at the latest flood of worry over Matt.

He nodded and retreated behind the bar.

"He's pretty attached to all of us," Brandan said. "We're family, regardless of breed."

"Looks like some species get better service than others, though," I quipped, trying to find more solid conversation.

"I checked your office voice mail. There was nothing from Matt or from the – " he hesitated, "you know."

"Hard not to call him a monster, isn't it?"

"I had something a little more colorful in mind, but we're in public."

We let that hang with Bob Seger singing "Against the Wind." It seemed to be a fitting soundtrack for the moment.

Ben brought my meal, another serving of fries for Brandan, and two more bottles of beer in a new bucket, taking away the empties.

I squirted mustard on the bun, found a way to wrap both hands around the burger without dumping its vegetables, and took a bite.

Brandan spoke as I chewed. "You asked me about the other victim at the Shannaker house?"

I nodded.

"It was personal. Lance was an –" Brandan paused for effect, "acquaintance." He gave me a moment to connect the dots that he was also gay.

I nodded again, still munching.

"Molly and I married because we were very good friends and because we both wanted children. Neither of us wanted to put our personal lives on the professional firing range because of *those* facets of our lives."

I swallowed, shrugged and stuffed my mouth again.

Brandan laughed. "You took that pretty well."

Not wanting to talk with my mouth full, I smiled until I could speak. "Your life is none of my business. You're willing to make that compromise so you both have what you want."

"Our kids are the center of our lives. It's been good." He eyed me for the final verdict.

"As long as you don't care who I sleep with, Brandan, then I'm okay with your secret."

* * *

Wednesday morning, my alarm had beeped for six minutes when I finally fumbled for the snooze button. I rolled onto my back and began the process of waking and stretching, realizing how much I liked the total darkness the basement room provided.

Maybe I'll blackout my bedroom windows.

In my office, I had a voice mail from Jeremy.

"I can't make it to breakfast," he said. "CDC is doing a consult on an infection in Arizona. I have a teleconference in an hour. I've got to read the prep." He suggested we should try for lunch and that he'd call me.

That was fine with me. I helped myself to Connie's muffins and a cup of coffee on the way to my office. I was anxious to return the call to the Michigan Department of Corrections and see what had become of Robert Bock.

In a nutshell, I learned Bock was convicted of first-degree murder and given a twenty-four-year sentence. He served fourteen years in the State Prison of Southern Michigan in Jackson County with eventual parole.

I received a fax copy of his visitation records, which for fourteen years, was almost empty. His sister visited two or three times a year. One of the few other visitors he had was in June of 1971, A.R. Bock, son.

Anthony Robert? I made a wild guess at the middle name being the same as the father's.

But A.R. wasn't his biological son, according to what I'd read in the journals from the attic. Angela was forced to marry Bock after she got pregnant. Angela's sister wrote that she didn't know who the boy's real father was.

The records clerk couldn't tell me much more about Robert Bock, but she did mention I could check with the parole officer in Wayne County, where the case was transferred upon Bock's release in 1975.

A call to the Wayne County Parole Board was another not-today answer. The officer who handled Bock's parole had retired and moved to Florida years ago.

On a whim, I called the Detroit Police Department records division, though I doubted they had computerized closed crimes that old. The clerk who answered was a pleasant elderly-sounding woman.

I began reciting what little I had put together about Bock when she told me she remembered the murder.

"You do? Can you tell me who the lead investigator was?" I

asked, genuinely impressed.

"No, not those details. I'd have to dig out records for that kind of stuff," she said. "But I was workin' here then. I don't remember 'zactly everything, but folks talked about him killing his wife like that for a long time."

"Killed her how?" I asked, afraid I already knew the answer.

"They said he'd been tryin' to have his way with her, you know what I mean, and then he took a knife and cut her throat," she said. "When she didn't show up to school to get the little boy, his teacher walked him home and found that bastard with blood still all over him."

Angie got her throat slit like a pig.

My hand went to my neck. When I tried to speak, my voice sounded choked. I coughed to cover my distress. "Could I ask you look up that detective for me, Lanelle? I believe there's a possible link from this man's son to other crimes."

She assured me she would find it before the end of the day and let me know.

Our conversation left story fragments floating around in my head, but I had a feeling that the new information would lead me somewhere.

Probably somewhere I don't want to go.

Needing to get out of my windowless office for a while, I stopped to ask Connie if she'd send Lanelle a small gift of appreciation. "Very helpful people deserve a little kindness in return," I said.

"Does that mean you'll buy me a car?" she asked with a wink.

I headed to the breakroom for more coffee. When I turned the corner, I saw Dr. Katz was in his office with the emergency department physician director.

"Julie, I was just about to page you," he called as I passed by. "I'd like you to hear Dr. Channing's assessment of a patient who presented to the ER last night. He knew we were looking for unusual cases."

Dr. Katz made the informal introductions, then asked Dr. Peter Channing to continue.

"The patient is a 46-year-old male who had eaten from the

Primo Pizza buffet with his wife and two young children. They'd been eating about twenty minutes when he suddenly developed difficulty breathing, followed by what the wife thought was heart-related because he grabbed at his chest. He collapsed within a minute of the onset of his symptoms."

"Okay, then what?" I asked.

"Paramedics found a mixed presentation. He had wildly variable heart rate from 50 to 140, BP barely palpable at 60, flushed skin, and almost no respiratory effort. He became briefly combative with a little oxygen then unconscious. They intubated him, called for orders. Without a twelve-lead EKG, I was hesitant to order epinephrine for an allergic reaction, given the possible cardiac component. They were only six minutes away, so we waited."

Sometimes it's better to run to the hospital for more tools and help than to stay on the scene and keep trying to figure out what's happening. I nodded agreement so far.

"When he arrived, we decided it was more likely anaphylaxis and gave him some epi and also initiated antihistamines and steroids."

Allergic reactions can be mild to severe but not life-threatening. Anaphylaxis causes airway constriction, vessel dilation, and can be fatal.

"But the patient didn't respond," I ventured.

Dr. Channing shook his head. "We admitted the patient to ICU on a ventilator, but he's shown no improvement in the last twelve hours."

Dr. Katz raised his eyebrows at me.

"Fish, you think?" I asked, answering his silent question.

"There was no fish or seafood on the buffet," Dr. Channing said, "according to the manager."

"Of course not," I said under my breath, "that would be the trick, wouldn't it?"

I know who else had dinner there last night, but no one can provide a description.

"No one else was sick, right?" I asked.

"Not that we were made aware of," Channing answered. "Nothing like this."

"Would you interview the patient's wife?" Katz asked.

I nodded. Dr. Channing gave me the patient's name and ICU bed number.

On the way to my office, I considered the significance of a poisoning that caused such confusing symptoms. My first hunch, the poison of a puffer fish, was based on the little fish in my tank. Puffer fish neurotoxin causes progressive symptoms from the tingling lips and mouth to full paralysis and respiratory failure in minutes. And it's so toxic that only a small amount would be necessary.

I pondered the setting – a restaurant with a buffet. An ideal place to drop a small piece of fish into a mixture such as potato salad or a Caesar salad.

CHAPTER 43

Gretchen Ledbetter, the patient's wife, was sitting in the ICU waiting room alone when I found her. She looked like she'd stayed overnight in one of the chairs designed to keep people from sleeping in them.

I introduced myself, but the part about the medical examiner's office visibly upset her.

"I'm not here because the doctors have given up on your husband," I said, trying to allay her panic. "After talking to the emergency room physician, I think we are in a position to offer ideas about what happened to Mr. Ledbetter. By figuring out what happened, the doctors can better help him. Okay?"

She nodded.

"Let's start with your dinner out," I said. "What's routine for you, and what was different last night?"

"We go there once a week to the pizza buffet – everyone gets what they like. Hayden – my husband – and I usually get salads, too. That's what we did last night. He fixed his plate while I got the kids settled at the table, then I went to the salad bar to fix mine. A while later, he went for seconds," she said.

"They do have a great salad bar and pizza," I agreed, hoping to make this feel more like a pleasant conversation than an interrogation.

"We were eating when he made a sound like he was in pain." She closed her eyes and cringed. "He grabbed at his chest at first, then his throat like he was choking. He couldn't speak, but he kept breathing okay for a few minutes. I thought it was his heart."

I waited for her to continue.

"I yelled for someone to call 911, then I helped him to the floor so he wouldn't fall. He seemed to get weaker every breath. When the ambulance arrived, I was sure the oxygen would help, but he started fighting them. Then he just . . . stopped."

"This isn't easy, I know, but your description is very helpful. Maybe you can remember exactly what he had on the salad each time," I prompted.

"He likes a lot of stuff," she said, her eyes moving around an imaginary scene in her mind. "I didn't see him make the salads. Lettuce, of course. There was cheese, carrots." She thought a minute. "Red onion, radishes, I think. Sliced hard-boiled egg. Clumps or whatever you call them of broccoli," she said, waving her hand helplessly. "The kids call them trees." Her eyes teared again. "He always uses their Italian dressing. Topped with sunflower seeds."

"Anything like cottage cheese or pudding?" I asked.

"On the second trip, he got potato salad. He said it's like his grandmother used to make – chunky with mustard."

I remain composed although I wanted to stand up and dance. I was sure it was the potato salad. Purple onions and eggs for color in a chunky texture and strong taste that would easily disguise a small chunk of fish dropped in.

"I know you are exhausted. Someone's keeping your children?" I asked.

She nodded.

"After the next visiting hour, take a little time to go home, have a hot shower, and go see your kids. It will do you good to breathe fresh air."

"But what if . . . " her voice trailed off.

"They tell me everything is stable. Take an hour or so. You have to take care of yourself. Your kids need you, too."

She thanked me. "You think what I told you can help him?"

"No promises, only a little hope."

"I'll take all you can give me."

CHAPTER 44

Taking the shortcut through to the emergency room, I saw Dr. Katz speaking with Dr. Channing and another physician I didn't recognize. The discussion appeared serious. I intended to pass by, but Dr. Katz waved me over to join them.

We were standing at the end of the hallway connecting to the main hospital, blocking traffic, but they were oblivious to this.

Dr. Katz introduced me to Dr. Isabella Valiquette, a small woman with hair tucked into a severe bun that pulled her face taunt. She recounted her patient's history for me with a rolling Spanish accent.

"My patient is a 28-year-old woman I saw eight days ago with a sudden onset of vomiting and cramps for about 24 hours," she explained. "After she was hydrated, I asked her to follow up two days later. She canceled the appointment because she said she felt so much better."

That's not unusual for patients, I thought.

"But Monday, she called again, complaining of worsening GI symptoms, a rash, pain in her legs, and burning in her feet. I was out of town, so they waited instead of coming to the hospital. This morning, she became confused and disoriented, unable to walk. Her family called 911," Dr. Valiquette concluded.

"And how is she now?" Dr. Katz asked.

"I suspect she'll be on a ventilator by the end of the day because of the ascending paralysis. It progresses like Guillain-Barré syndrome, but it's too fast."

A woman in a lab coat spoke from outside our circle. "Excuse me?"

Thinking perhaps she needed to get through our cluster to the main hallway, we separated to make room for her to pass.

"I'm sorry to eavesdrop. I'm Olivia Palmeri, from the lab. I drew blood on this patient earlier and saw her chart," she said with some hesitation. "I think she has classic symptoms of heavy metal poisoning."

Eyebrows went up in surprise all around. We exchanged looks.

"Such as lead or mercury?" Dr. Valiquette replied.

"Actually, I suspect thallium," the tall auburn-headed woman answered, more sure of herself now that she had our full attention.

"Like thallium from the cardiac cath lab?" Dr. Channing asked.

"Maybe. Or non-radioactive thallium was a rat poison," Olivia said.

"Do you think it is related to the other cases?" Dr. Katz asked me.

"Maybe." I didn't want to think about the possibilities.

Had I missed a clue about this?

Dr. Channing's bushy eyebrows scrunched together, creating a deep vertical crease on his forehead. "What *other* cases? You mean the anaphylaxis patient I told you about?"

"Well, yes. And a young woman who was admitted with the severe hypoglycemia last week, who was poisoned with a plant that alters glycogenesis," Katz offered, only fueling the fire.

I tried to step in the middle of the conversation. "We think these are victims of a man who is looking for very out-of-the-ordinary methods to kill. Heavy metal poisoning would be unusual enough – "

Channing interrupted me in a demanding voice. "You issued a memo about unusual symptoms, Gerald. I don't recall you mentioning homicide. How long were the ED docs going to be in the dark?"

"We were not trying to keep you in the dark," Katz replied. "Should I have started a panic about this? Have you all chasing zebras, as you put it?"

Channing had no reply. Looking down the hall of the emergency department, all he could see at the moment was zebras.

"Actually," Olivia said, more to me than the physicians, "I think

I can answer a couple of your questions about the thallium, if you have a minute."

I nodded.

Peter Channing latched back onto Dr. Katz like a terrier as we turned to escape.

I followed Olivia to the hospital lab, deep in thought about this victim.

"You don't recognize me, do you?" she asked as we walked through the halls. "I live across the street from you."

I hadn't until she asked, but I remembered chatting with her last summer in the yard.

Livvie Palmeri and her little boy had moved to Traverse City after her husband was killed overseas in a military exercise. She had been in her third year of medical school at Duke University and pregnant. She'd finished the year, but with a newborn and another year of school to go plus residency, she could not manage. When her mother offered to help take care of the baby, Livvie moved here and turned her focus from surgery to pathology. In the meantime, she took every opportunity to learn all she could from her time in the lab.

I got the impression that Olivia absorbed the ink off the pages of all the books and manuals available to her as she explained how acute thallium poisoning caused a progression of unpleasant symptoms, very similar to what the patient had suffered. Although some symptoms were also noted with other heavy metals, thallium fit all this patient's symptoms and presentation.

"It might not be a zebra," she said, "but it's got all the right stripes."

CHAPTER 45

Jeremy knocked on my office door an hour later. "I was hoping you could get away for a late lunch."

"I'm starving," I said, picking up a stack of envelopes and folders. Pointing to the box that Penny Daniels had left, I asked Jeremy if he'd carry it. "I need to ask Connie to send it out for photocopies. Then we can leave."

He picked up the open box. "What are these?"

"Journals belonging to Sally Tucker, mother of the man in the barn," I said, shutting Laser in the office. "When his sister came here to identify Tucker, she wanted to look for them. She was going to take them with her, but I'm afraid she felt we expected her to read them and report back on any clues."

"Didn't want to read the family secrets, I guess," he ventured.

As we walked down the hall, I explained the convoluted connections to our case involving Matthew and the poisons. "After reading some of them, Tucker's sister suggested maybe her uncle, Robert Bock, had something to do with these murders because he killed his wife the same way. I called the prison, but he was released on parole 20 years ago. His parole officer retired and was in Florida, last anyone knew."

Jeremy placed the box on a table near the secretary's desk.

"Connie, can you see about getting these books photocopied, whatever makes them most legible. Enlarged single pages, legal size, I don't care. But we should keep each book separate."

With a purposeful nod, she picked up the phone. "Will tomorrow afternoon be soon enough?" she asked as she dialed the last number.

"You and your memory. That's fine," I said with a laugh. "We're going to lunch. Can I bring you anything?"

"No thanks, dear," she said as the phone connection took her attention.

Of course not. The woman's desk was better stocked than my kitchen pantry, even before the crime scene techs emptied it. Soups, crackers, candy. What wasn't here was in the breakroom refrigerator.

Jeremy and I walked to Benjamin's. Our conversation drifted from the weather to fishing in Lake Michigan and its rivers, about which I could offer little except I'd been told salmon fishing was fair here.

"Salmon?" he asked.

"I don't understand either," I shrugged, having grown up believing salmon needed to live in salt water most of their lives. "Something about importing salmon to control a nuisance fish."

We kept walking.

"Speaking of fish, we have two more weird cases through the emergency room," I explained. "A sudden onset of respiratory failure and paralysis after eating at a buffet. My guess is that it was puffer fish meat, as you suggested."

"I don't think CDC can help there."

"The other is what looks like heavy metal poisoning. They're running tests, but thanks to a lab employee, the current theory is non-radioactive thallium," I continued as he held the door open for me. "The classic signs, I'm told."

"One of the so-called near-perfect poisons," Jeremy agreed.

We took a seat near the windows.

"And you want to know where the thallium came from? Not a chance," he said.

"Why not?"

"It's still used as a rat poison in other countries. No problem to buy it and bring it in."

"Damn." My shoulders sagged. "Where can you get it?"

"Sorry, I don't have Miss Connie's memory. But considering your other poisons, South African nations wouldn't be out of the question," he said. "There are treatments, if the exposure was caught quickly enough."

"I don't think so." We needed a change of subject before I broke into tears. "And what have you been up to this morning?"

"We're investigating a primary amoebic meningoencephalitis. The child died this morning."

"Oh." Nothing against Jeremy and his profession, but I didn't feel like having another microbiology lesson, especially over lunch. "Everything on the menu is good," I said, changing the subject. "Even the salmon."

Conversation dragged as we both seemed distracted by the cases in our heads. We ate without talking about work or our personal lives, though I couldn't remember when we finished eating what those topics had been.

We were about to leave when Ben came to our table and gave me a take-out box.

"Scraps for the dog," he said. After hesitating, looking from me to Jeremy and back, he took a breath and asked, "Is there any word on Matt? I mean, I've heard nothing."

I reached out and touched his arm. "Not that I know of, Ben," I said. "But there are a lot of people looking. And praying."

For whatever good that does. It didn't save my father.

He clamped my hand beneath his and nodded, then walked away.

Jeremy and I left the restaurant and headed toward the office.

"I can't imagine how much this would tear me apart," he asked as we walked. "How do you deal with all this?"

"Like on the ambulance, when there's something really bad, your brain and your hands do their jobs without letting emotions interfere." I stopped to lean on the cement railing of the street bridge over the Boardman River. "I'm running on autopilot, doing my job, but there are moments I think this thing could break me."

And it might, before it's over.

"You can still leave," he suggested.

"No. I can't."

Maybe he had intended to convince me otherwise, but I turned and began walking.

I heard him hurry to catch up with me.

"Julie, you can't take responsibility for this."

He touched my arm, but I shrugged his hand away.

"Don't talk to me about responsibility," I growled at him, mad again about the wife and daughter.

We walked in silence to the parking lot where he got in his car and left without saying goodbye.

In my office, I dumped what looked like half a roast into Laser's dish. "Ben sure likes you, doesn't he?"

While I was gone, Connie had taken a message from Lanelle, my new connection in Detroit. I returned her call and learned she had located the case file and even gone to the trouble of looking for detectives' addresses from the retirement benefits office.

"The detective on this case is no longer living, you see," she said. "But I got the address of the first officer on the scene, if that'd be helpful to you."

"Certainly," I said, writing the information down. When I was done, I sent Connie a network message, asking if she had sent the gift I'd asked for.

Connie replied she had not.

"Make it something really nice," I wrote back as Lanelle continued with details she'd dug up about the officer.

Kelly Christopher Adams, now 78, lived a little more than an hour away. He had retired to fish and play golf, and when his health declined to the point of needing assistance, his son placed him in a prestigious home. After suffering a stroke in 1992, K.C. Adams required full-time support.

I called the number Lanelle had given me, and a woman's voice answered the phone. I told her my name and that I wanted to speak with Mr. Adams.

"Does he know you?" she asked. Her voice sounded formal, almost British.

"No, he doesn't. I'm with the Grand Traverse County Medical Examiner's Office. I was hoping to speak to him about a case he worked on many years ago."

"Well, he doesn't hear too well on the phone. Could you drop by and visit him in person?"

"I'd certainly like to do that. Is there a time today that would be convenient for him?" I asked, hoping I had a chance.

"Except for meals and his massage therapy at one, he doesn't have anything scheduled today. Would three o'clock be suitable for you?"

That would be perfect, I told her. She gave me directions.

"Is there anything I might bring Mr. Adams in consideration of his time?"

She chuckled. "He might be a smidgen friendlier if you presented a six-pack of beer, I suppose. Something cold, canned, and American."

It was my turn to laugh. "I think I can budget that."

I paged Brandan Callaghan, who called promptly from the farm.

"I was about to call you," he said, chomping a piece of bubblegum loudly in my ear. "We uncovered the skeleton in the grid where Penny Daniels said."

"Is that supposed to be good news or bad news?" I asked.

"Touché. We're waiting on Dr. Katz. What's up?"

I explained the steps from Penny's mother's journals to Robert Bock and the murder of his wife, his prison term and release, and his parole. "Penny thought it was worth mentioning when she read how he killed her aunt in the journals." I paused for effect.

"And?" he asked.

"He cut her throat."

The gum smacking ceased. "Interesting. And where is the criminal in question today?"

"No one knows. His parole officer retired and headed off to the Gulf, but I think I'm onto something at least as good. I know how busy you are digging up bodies, though," I teased.

"Come on, Julie. Don't make me beg."

"You're no fun. How about an appointment to interview the first officer on the scene? In two hours in Cadillac?"

Cadillac is a small community southeast of Traverse City.

"Oooh, that's good," he said. He blew a bubble that popped loudly in my ear. "That's really good. Pick me up."

CHAPTER 46

As I drove onto the farm where the barn had exploded under my feet two weeks ago, I realized I didn't feel as anxious as the first time I came here with Penny.

Like Pavlov's dog, positive conditioning is a good thing.

No one was around, so I went to the search area on the back of the property and parked next to the other vehicles.

Brandan waved me to join the crowd standing around an open grave.

Always curious about skeletal recoveries but having no formal training, I got out of the truck and joined the group peering into a shallow grave.

After twenty years, the bones were stained with the dirt that covered them. The soft tissue had long since become part of the food chain. Most joints were held together only by the soil supporting them. The skull, almost completely uncovered, showed several depressions.

"There are fractures in the right ulna and several bones in the hand," Dr. Katz said. "Probably defense wounds, based on the description given by the witness."

A technician stepped to the left, and I saw a blade next to the pelvis.

"Why would they leave the ax with the body?" someone asked.

"I suspect the handle was broken. There's no evidence of it in the grave," Katz explained, "so it might have been tossed elsewhere. The boys would have been in less trouble when it turned up missing than if they'd brought it home broken."

With his crime scene in good hands, Brandan excused himself and left with me to go talk to Mr. Adams.

"What made you think of talking to a patrolman?" he asked as I drove toward the road. "Is there really any chance someone as old as this Bock guy could do these crimes?"

"There has been very little physical violence. Poisonings are effortless, but the knowledge required to research, obtain, and deliver them effectively puts the criminal's maturity at over thirty, don't you think?"

"Okay, but what about the computer technology? Wouldn't that point to someone younger?"

"Bock'd be around the same age my father was, and he was a computer geek before the term was even coined. Only takes motivation to learn."

For the next 45 minutes, our debate continued. In Cadillac, I stopped at what Michiganders call a party store. While Brandan went to the restroom, I bought a six-pack of beer for Mr. Adams and had it placed into a paper bag. I also bought a couple of bottles of water and a candy bar for Brandan so his stomach would not keep growling while we were talking to our host.

We arrived at a new bright yellow complex that looked more like a resort than a nursing facility. The building was surrounded by an elegant manicured lawn. Inside, the hotel feeling continued, with bold carpeting, colorful furniture. The smell of something Italian lingered in the air from lunch, making my stomach rumble.

I checked in with the receptionist, who rang Mr. Adams' room, giving my name to the person who answered. She led us down a hallway to a room near the end, knocked softly, and then left us when a tall black woman opened the door.

"Julie, I am Mr. Adams' personal assistant, Bobbi," she said with a lilt I guessed was Jamaican. She invited us inside.

I introduced Brandan, and she seated us in a large living area, which opened onto a shaded patio overlooking a courtyard with more exquisite landscaping.

I handed her the brown bag. "A small token of our appreciation."

"Thank you. Make yourselves comfortable, please. I will take care of this and bring Mr. Adams to see you in a moment." She left us.

"What the hell kind of gift do you buy at a party store for a man you're going to interview about murder?" Brandan whispered harshly.

I shrugged. "American beer."

He rolled his eyes, but his lecture was interrupted as Bobbi rolled Mr. Adams into the room in a wheelchair.

We both stood as she wheeled him to the empty space next to the sofa.

"Pah, sit down," he barked.

Brandan introduced us this time. We shook hands and sat back down.

Though Adams had once been linebacker size, his skin sagged on his bones, leaving him with a slack, wilted look. Unhappiness seeped through the deep wrinkles of his face like water from a rocky crag. But his eyes showed a clear mind.

Brandan started to explain that we wanted to know about Robert Bock, but Adams interrupted him mid-sentence.

"You come here thinking you can dig through my brains like an old file cabinet? For thirty-some years, people nosed around, asking questions about one rat bastard or another. That case got too much publicity then, and I ain't gonna start it back up. It's all dead." His voice was gruff. After what I presumed was decades here, Michigan had not erased the more southern roots from his speech.

I tried again to explain we were following up on murders, but he cut me short, too.

"Young lady, I don't know what you think y'er gonna find, but it's not what you want."

In a moment of frustration, I stood up and yanked down the collar of my turtleneck and bent over in front of him. "Someone likes doing this to women, Mr. Adams." I did not move away. "If Bock has been killing women the last twenty years like he killed his wife –"

He tried to interrupt me, but I kept going.

"– then maybe you'll understand why we need the missing pieces. After she was murdered, Angela Bock's sister took her nephew to Traverse City. Just for sport, Anthony and his cousin

James Patrick murdered an old man who lived on the edge of the family farm when they were young teens. We are currently digging up that body and working to identify a young girl who also had *her* throat cut. Nearly three weeks ago, we found J.P. shackled to the floor in the family barn, dying of an ingestion of acid so strong we had to use a special liner on the table to do an autopsy. Beneath the floor, I discovered four more bodies stored in barrels of acid, dating back years. One of them with her throat slit. Then the barn blew up." I should have stopped, but I figured I might not have another chance. "Now someone is killing random people in our community with some very disturbing methods. Kidnapped one of our deputies. We're looking for someone linked to these murders."

Adams finally put up his hand to stop me. "Missy, you are dead wrong about Bock killing anyone but his wife."

I sat down, hoping he'd continue.

He shook his head in resignation, staring at me with icy blue eyes. "Bock killed her. Damned near cut her head off in one motion," he said grimly. "He kept swearing he didn't remember doing it, but he managed to hide that knife. We never did find it. That's the only reason he got second degree instead of capital murder."

"Never found it?" I asked in amazement. Could it be the knife in the image on the disk left in my house?

"Nope. We even had the bloodstain where the handle had landed on the floor, but that didn't match any other."

"Any guesses what kind of knife it was?" Brandan tried again to join the conversation.

"Why do you think I remember anything about this case at all?" he demanded of Brandan.

"Because, Mr. Adams, I've carried a badge long enough to know there are things you see that you can never, ever forget, sir," Brandan answered solemnly. "I don't think I'd forget seeing a young woman lying in a pool of her own blood, slashed open like a butchered deer."

Adams' face softened. He nodded.

"Bock was tried and convicted of her murder. Spent his time in prison. He walked out early on good behavior in 1975, checked in with his parole officer, rented himself a room for a week, and then disappeared," he said, then paused, scowling at me. "No one missed him until he didn't show up to meet his PO ten days later. Parole officer reported the violation, figured Bock jumped, left the country, maybe. No big deal – it happened a lot, and good riddance," he said. "Except a few days later, me and my partner got called to a body in an alley. No ID, but I knew. Bock's throat was cut clean through to the spine. One whack," he said, as if he had seen it yesterday.

"You identified the body yourself?" I asked.

"The day he killed his wife, I watched an emergency room quack sew up a nasty cut on the back of Bock's head with black twine," he said, spreading his finger and thumb as far as his arthritis would allow, indicating the size of the injury. "This dead guy was bald, so the scar showed up good."

"So he couldn't have killed the victims we're working now," I concluded, "but who killed him?"

"To be honest," Adams said, "there was no evidence and damned little effort to find out."

"No one investigated his murder?" Brandan asked.

"Oh, on the surface. Interviews, scene search for prints and weapons – didn't find a thing, Adams said. "Autopsy showed the obvious. We called it a down-and-out ex-con who ran into an enemy from prison. I sure didn't give a damn."

"Why not?" I asked finally, more than curious.

"He's dead, so you think you know how the story ends, Miss Madigan," he said my name like it tasted bad, "but let me tell you how it began for my family."

CHAPTER 47

"For fifteen years, I'd patrolled the streets of Detroit with only one promotion under my badge," Kelly Adams started. "In the summer of 1960, my wife died giving birth to our third child. I was working rotating shifts, but not a one of them gave me time to take care of my children.

"Abigail, my sister, was ten years younger than me, a schoolteacher who'd never married. I begged her to move in to help with the kids. She agreed and transferred to the school in our neighborhood. She was a Godsend." His voice reflected a note of sadness. "I never coulda raised those kids alone and done right by any of them.

"I was back working days and had been on duty almost all shift when we got a call for an assault. Me and Bill Petty rolled up, and I found my sister being tended by neighbors, all of whom were pointing us to the other side of the street.

"'She says there's a man in there with blood all over him!' someone yelled. We went into the house with our weapons drawn. Robert Bock was sitting on the sofa with his hands covering his face, his pants still around his ankles. Blood all over him, all over the room. And not ten feet away, the body of a woman with her throat gaped open.

"He was confused when we ordered him to stand up and put his hands on his head. Finally, Petty jerked him to his feet, then cuffed him and searched him. A large scalp wound bled, but already clotting.

"Petty searched the rest of the apartment then went to the patrol car to request a homicide team. I stayed with Bock and tried to avoid all the bloodstains. The smell was so overwhelming that I gagged. I'd never seen anything like that. You could tell where he'd cut her throat - the heaviest blood spray was around the sink - the window, cabinets, counter, dishes in the drainer," he explained, his eyes focused somewhere beyond the room where we sat. "It looked like she fell right there.

"Petty came back inside, and I went to find out what my sister was doing at a murder scene. As soon as she saw me, she ran into my arms. Words sobbed out about a boy she had walked home when his mother didn't come get him. She said, 'I looked. . . in the door. . . and saw. . .. I saw the blood and . . .' She tried to finish but passed out right there on the street."

I could think of no good response. Apparently neither could Brandan.

Mr. Adams' eyes focused back on me. "Abigail was so disturbed by what she'd seen, she couldn't go back to school, couldn't do much of anything. When the attorneys called her to testify, she couldn't do it. She was hospitalized with a nervous breakdown during the trial and then several more times over the next few years, but she never got better. She finally checked into a motel one night and swallowed all that crap the damned doctors had gave her. Her note said she left the house because she didn't want the children to see her dead."

A long ugly silence settled in the room.

"So, it might not'a been ethically or morally right not to look for who killed him, but I plain didn't give a damn he was dead," Adams stated.

Bobbi appeared with frosted mugs of beer for each of us.

I thought beer would hit the raw spot in my gut just fine, so we drank.

After time to wind down from the tension, we thanked Mr. Adams for the opportunity to hear his part of the story. He asked if maybe we'd let him know how it finally ended one day.

I promised to do so, and we said our goodbyes.

"I'd go crazy if I ended up like him, stuck with a good mind in a broken body," Brandan said when we reached the late afternoon sunlight. "It's just storage, no matter how nice it looks."

"Having spent a little time in a place like this," I agreed, "I can only hope I never have to do it again."

Brandan didn't ask what I meant.

I stopped again at the same party store on the edge of town, this time to empty my own bladder and grab a drink.

The shifts at the store had changed since our first stop. The man behind the counter was unshaven. His faded red and black checked flannel shirt was frayed at the cuffs and collar, sprouting little tufts of grayish thread that matched his stubble.

I smiled because there was something about that look that reminded me of my father on weekends.

Back on the road, the conversation turned back to the dig on the Tucker farm, the contents of the wooden chest, and other pieces of the puzzle.

"The photos had been fingerprinted and yielded two partials but no hits," he told me. "We scanned the originals then sent them to the FBI lab in Virginia. We sent the blank film, too. I think it was probably a handling issue by the laboratory, but I'm curious whether it was an accident."

I cocked my head in confusion.

"Your friend Quinton Gresham says that film exposed in a camera will have distinct frames, even if accidentally exposed to light during processing. If someone in the lab saw images on the film he liked and swapped our negatives for a roll he'd opened and exposed before developing it, we'd have no exposure frames."

"What can we do about that if it was exposed accidentally?" I asked.

"Nothing, but if there are frames, then we'll lean on the lab a little." He leaned his head back and closed his eyes.

I didn't say anything, and as I expected, within a few minutes, Brandan's jaw relaxed in sleep until I stopped at the first red light, still several miles south of the bay.

He'd been having those bizarre mini-dreams that naps cause, seemingly important revelations that evaporate when you open your eyes.

"Can I stop to get you a bite to eat before I take you to the farm?" I asked when he'd quit stretching like a cat. "You probably haven't eaten all day except that candy bar."

He checked the clock. "Nah, I ought to get back before they close up for the night."

"Why don't you call? Maybe they already lifted the skeleton and shut down."

He took out his phone and dialed, talked to the shift commander and discovered the team had indeed disbanded early for a well-deserved evening off.

"You were right," he said. "Why don't you drop me off at my house? I'll catch a ride to the farm in the morning. Then both of us can take the night off. You could use the break, too."

He gave me quick directions to his home, which wasn't all that far from my own.

"Go home, Julie," he said when I pulled up to the curb in front of his house, "Relax and enjoy an evening."

"I don't feel like I can go home alone," I said, "I mean, not knowing who might have been visiting while I've been gone. My cubby hole at the Annex is not exactly the Ritz, but it's secure."

"Then go check into a hotel with a hot tub, get a bottle of wine, and order room service, whatever would make you feel better. Go dancing with the dashingly handsome Dr. McNeeley." He winked. "I suppose that might improve *my* spirits. Quite chummy, you two."

I could tell the ribbing was good-natured, and he was comfortable with me knowing his secret.

Things are way past dancing with Jeremy.

"Jeremy and I were engaged at one point," I said a little bitterly. "You caught the part about the kid?"

"Like a bolt of lightning. I was glad someone got out of the car. Things were about to get ugly."

"Yeah, but you missed the confession about the wife."

"Ouch."

"I like the hot tub idea, though. And a quart of ice cream. I'll have to take the dog, though. I can't leave him in my office all night."

"Dogs like ice cream, too, don't they?" he asked as I pulled up to curb in front of his house.

"Yes, but dairy products give them horrible gas."

CHAPTER 48

I headed to the Annex to pick up Laser, who'd already been locked in my office all afternoon. Just as I pulled up to the sallyport, my cell phone rang.

"Hello?"

"Hello, dear. Hope I'm not interrupting," my mother said cheerfully.

"Not at all. I'm on the way to pick up the dog."

"Dog? When did you get a dog?"

"I'm pet-sitting, Mom. Laser is Matthew's police dog," I said, not wanting to explain all that on my cellular phone. "Matt's, uh, out of town for a few days."

"Oh," she said, relieved. A pet would interfere with her plans to get me to New Mexico for the holidays. "I wanted to see how you were doing. Are you back to work?"

"Of course. When could a little concussion keep me from working?" I asked, joking.

"That's the sort of thing a mother worries about, you know."

"I know, Mom. How are you?"

The conversation continued with no break in sight, so I parked outside the sallyport and chatted for a while.

I don't call as often as I should. My work hours and days off don't match hers.

They don't really match anyone's. I work all the time.

She asked about the bombing, and I told her I shouldn't discuss it.

"I'm headed inside for the evening. If you can give me an hour,

I'll call and tell you everything," I offered.

"Oh, that's not necessary, Julie," she said. "You're still working on it, though?"

"Among other things. Today we recovered the body of an old man that two boys killed and buried thirty years ago."

"How awful! It sounds like you've been run through a mill saw these last few weeks."

What an odd phrase. I always thought it was a "saw mill." Where have I heard that?

"Well, it's nice the victim will have a proper burial now," I said. "I guess no one missed him enough to wonder what happened at that time."

"How'd you find him?"

"Mom, I really shouldn't talk about it on a cell phone. Let me go inside and call you."

When I got to my office, Laser seemed happy to see me, even though he'd been cooped up all afternoon. I was thankful he didn't bite my leg off.

I called my mother back, and we chatted about the bombing, and how we found the body of an old man two kids had beaten decades ago. "We used a type of radar that penetrates the ground to find the grave and the ax head next to the body."

"I've never heard of such a thing," she said. "Wouldn't a metal detector find that?"

"The metal, yes, but we didn't know we'd find any, and they've been digging up all sorts of other metal things, too. The ground-penetrating radar actually gives an image of density, sort of like weather radar does with clouds."

"Imagine that!"

Actually I had.

"I should let you go. Are you coming home for Thanksgiving?" she asked.

"I'll work out being there somehow. I think by then I could use a break." That was no lie. "I'm thinking of driving, though. I can afford the extra days and could use the solitude. Love you, Mom."

Maybe I won't still be dog-sitting by then.

I found a note from Connie that she'd taken Laser for a walk just before she left.

"Umhmm, so don't give me that abandoned-dog look," I scolded him as I gathered his accessories. "She probably gave you treats, too. You'll be too spoiled to go back to work with Matt." The words caught in my throat. I clipped the unnecessary lead to his collar, put his bowls and bag of food in a box, and started for the door.

The phone rang.

Unsure why I would bother this late, I answered. "Grand Traverse Medical Examiner's Office."

"Why Julia, how nice to catch you in. I'm wondering if you solved the next two cases I left for you."

My heart skipped a beat.

"You mean your last two victims who showed up in the emergency department? I think so."

"Do tell." His voice was gritty, harsh.

"I think you dropped a chunk of puffer fish or other fish poisoned with ciguatoxin into the potato salad at the salad bar, causing the rapid onset of anaphylaxis and paralysis."

"Good guess, I'll give you one point. But you had a hint. And the other?"

"I think the next victim will die of thallium poisoning."

"Thallium? Interesting idea. Sorry, incorrect. That makes you only half-right. You realize today is the autumn equinox – half day, half night? You've a lot to learn about halves."

"Such as?" I asked.

"Oh, you'll see. Sorry about the answers, though. Half-right isn't good enough. You lose your turn again. Good night, Julia."

The connection dropped, dead as the next victim would be.

"Shit."

I dialed the FBI number Brandan had given me, got another anonymous agent who took a message for Nolan Forrester about the call. I hung up and started to leave, but saw the red light on my phone blinking, indicating a new message while I'd been talking.

I wanted to walk away without checking.

Really.

But I couldn't.

I sat back down and dialed.

"Welcome to Audex," the pleasant woman's voice answered through the speaker. "Please enter your. . . " I entered more numbers at the prompts. Finally, the system voice told me I had old and new messages. I picked up the receiver.

Yeah, no kidding.

One old message was a business issue that could wait, had been waiting, state mandatory disease reporting database stuff. I was probably only three weeks in arrears with it now.

Next was Jeremy.

"Julie, it's me. Look, I'm sorry about what I said at lunch. I understand you take everything that's happening very seriously and that you feel responsible for trying to put an end to it. I guess what I was trying to say is that you can't blame yourself for what this guy is doing. I'm afraid that you'll. . . well, I'm just afraid. Call me when you get done today." The message was recorded an hour after he drove out of the parking lot.

And next was MaryAnne Katz.

"Hi, Julie. MaryAnne here. I was wondering if perhaps we could get together for lunch one day soon. Our anniversary is coming up, and I need your help to set something up. Oh, and it's a secret, so don't tell Gerald, okay? Hope you're feeling better."

A surprise party? No. . .

I hung up the phone after erasing the messages, immediately thankful I hadn't been using the speaker when I looked up to see Gerald Katz in my door.

"Do you have a moment?"

"Of course," I said. "Come on in."

He did, closing the door behind him and sat down across from me at the desk.

The dog, sensing another delay in escape from the building, returned to his corner.

"How are you feeling?" he asked. "Really."

"Pretty good. My ribs still ache. I've had a few headaches, but that's nothing new," I said. "Anything on the cases in the emergency department?"

"Tests for heavy metals will take another 24 hours or so. The anaphylaxis patient is improving, as is the young girl. Any ideas from Mrs. Palmeri or Dr. McNeeley?"

"Thallium could be brought from lots of other countries. Doubt it could be traced. Ditto the fish meat or live fish. The only thing we can presume is that this guy travels globally." I shook my head. "There are a lot of toxic substances he can choose from."

"I keep waiting for a patient with a bark scorpion sting or Gila monster bite," he said, not quite joking. "We'd never get antivenin from Arizona in time. Or other poisonous animals – cone mollusks, for example, or those tiny little jelly fish you hear about."

I nodded. "I wonder if there are victims we've missed," I said, thinking I should tell him about the phone call I just received from the killer.

"Me, too," he said, distracted enough to fiddle with the carved alabaster box on my desk. "Julie, I need a big favor," he began reluctantly. "I hate to ask. . . "

"Sure, what is it?"

He nodded, but didn't seem convinced.

"While we were at the hospital this morning, I saw MaryAnne in the hallway headed toward the cafeteria. Maybe she didn't see us because she didn't mention it when I called later to tell her what time I'd be home today, since we finished the recovery of the skeleton early. I went into the hall to catch her, but she went to the mobile MRI unit. I did something I probably shouldn't have done. I waited until I heard it start up, then I went in the control room on the auspices of chatting with a radiology tech about scanning skeletal remains. They were running a chest scan on MaryAnne. "

That might explain MaryAnne's less-than-cheery moods Kim called me about.

"Okay, so what can I do?"

"Would you invite her to lunch in the next few days and mention in passing that you saw her at the hospital when we were in the ER?" he asked. "She wouldn't think so much about you asking."

"Sure. In fact, she left me a message today saying we should have lunch." I wanted to tell him his daughter had called me with her concerns, too, and from where I stood, they all added up to bad news.

CHAPTER 49

The knot in my stomach tightened at the thought that something really might be wrong in the Katz family. Knowing MaryAnne as I did, I knew she would dismiss any attempts they made to find out what was amiss, but both her husband and her older daughter had noticed.

I remembered that the night Jeremy and I went over for dinner, I'd seen one fleeting moment of weariness she'd hidden at the last moment.

What did MaryAnne say about someday needing a friend?

"Are you heading home now? I'll call and ask her to lunch. I'm telling her you're on your way home, too," I said.

"No, I've got to – "

I interrupted him. "No! How late are you already? Go home and have dinner with your family and relax for an evening."

He took the scolding well for being my boss.

I picked up the receiver of my phone. "Go now," I said, shooing him toward the door. "Fifteen minutes, you'd better be home." I began dialing.

He got to the door and turned as MaryAnne answered the phone.

"Hello, MaryAnne. I just picked up your message, and I'd love to have lunch."

He was still standing at the door.

"Fifteen minutes, Dr. Katz. Out!"

He smiled and left.

"Yes, I'm kicking your husband out the door now." I chatted for several minutes about how much of a strain these cases had been on us all, and then I mentioned lunch again.

MaryAnne suggested we meet on Saturday while Kimberly was at the pool taking a lifeguard class.

"Lifeguard?" I asked.

"She thinks it would be cool to work for the parks department this next summer as a guard on the beach. I wish she would find something else to do," MaryAnne said. "I think she's discovered boys. Why don't I call you Saturday morning and make sure you're free? Then we can settle on a place and time."

"That would be great," I said.

After our goodbyes, I hung up.

Seven o'clock. Where had the time gone?

Thinking it was time to make peace, I called Jeremy at his hotel to see if he'd eaten or had plans for the evening.

"No, I was waiting for you to call," he said. "I've been working on the etiology of the amoeba in Arizona. The bad news is that the mother has become ill, too."

"If it's so rare, it seems it would either be very easy or virtually impossible to trace how they were infected," I ventured. "Which is it?"

"Unfortunately, we're leaning to the impossible side of the scale."

"Well, I'm looking for a comfortable room with a nice whirlpool tub and a pint of ice cream. What can you do for me tonight, McNeeley?"

"You bring the ice cream. I'll fill the tub. I knew I could lure you with bubbles. That's why I changed hotels."

"Had to be a reason."

"Better view here, too."

"I'm still stuck with the dog," I admitted. "I could probably leave him with the jail crew tonight."

"No, bring him, too. I won't tell if he won't."

A half hour later, I showed up at Jeremy's hotel door with a 95-pound police dog and a box containing bowls, a serving of dry food and leftover steak bone from Ben's, two pints ice cream, and a bottle of citrus-scented bath oil.

"Mmm, my favorite," he said, unpacking.

"Beef bones?" I joked. "Extremely rare?"

"No, lemon Julie a la nude."

Jeremy filled Laser's water bowl, then placed it and the empty food bowl near the door. "You know what's in the wrapper, don't you?" he asked the patiently waiting dog, tail pounding against the carpet.

"Woof!"

"Is that one woof for yes and two wooves for no?" he asked, winking at me as I was pulling off my boots. "Wooves is plural for woof, isn't it?"

"Woof!" Laser and I said together.

Jeremy plopped the bone down into the dish. "*Bon appétit*!"

"That's it!" I exclaimed, watching Laser get up and go to the bowl. "That's the command Matt uses when the dog can eat."

The memory sent a chill down my spine. "Sorry."

"Julie, I don't expect you to stop talking about people in your life. Matthew, David, anyone else." He came to me and pulled my turtleneck over my head and tossed it on the bed, then began peeling open the Velcro strips on my vest. "I always wondered why you never talked about your father."

"Stop," I whispered. "Please don't dig tonight. I came here to get away from. . . all the death."

He tossed the vest into the chair and stepped closer, wrapping his arms around my waist from behind. His hands were cold from handling the ice cream. "No digging, I promise. Thanks for coming by."

He unzipped my jeans and wiggled them down over my hips and then left me to the rest.

I poured the oil into the water and settled into the bubbles.

Jeremy handed me my ice cream, then undressed and joined me in the tub.

"So what would you like to talk about?" he asked.

"I don't know." I spooned up a bite, then spoke around it. "Tell me about your daughter."

"Stephanie Marie, who'll be four in December. And she's the smartest, most beautiful little girl I've ever seen. I mean, I'm a proud daddy and all, but from the day Steph was born, I knew she was different somehow. She never cried, slept all night almost from the start," he said, though his voice descended from pride to pain.

"That's normal behavior," I said.

"Yes, but she started doing all the cognitive things babies do just a little earlier. Even though she crawled at six months, she didn't try to walk until she was fifteen months old. She began speaking words at sixteen months, real words. And weirdly enough, although Deanna didn't believe me, when we sat and read to Stephanie, I thought she was teaching herself to read."

"That's incredible. A child that age couldn't really learn to read, could she?" I asked.

"Yes, she did," he said, sounding sad. "But it seemed, I don't know, wrong somehow. I did a little digging behind Deanna's back, to see if I was right."

"Why would you have to do that?" I didn't understand at all.

"She didn't believe me. Said I was nuts. One of the child psych guys told me about the signs of hyperlexia, compulsive precocious reading, and I went numb all over. I convinced Deanna to have her formally tested, and when they told us the diagnosis, they said we had to find a way to control her reading."

"Why wouldn't you encourage her skills? What am I missing here?" I asked in confusion. "Isn't that a sign she could be a genius? I mean, look at her parents, for God's sake."

"It's not that simple. There's a fine line between genius and madness. Children with hyperlexia often become so engrossed in the world of words in their minds that they shut out the outside world, like a form of autism. They have difficulty learning verbal language skills for conversation, and they withdraw from social interactions. We had to put her in a social environment that lacks the opportunity for her to pull away from other kids into written words. Try telling that to a daycare operator."

I sat stunned, chilled despite the hot water bubbling around me.

"So what are you doing for her?"

"Sounds weird, but we have to limit the reading material she has available, but she reads anything. Cereal box labels, billboards and other signs. We've even had to lock up the telephone books."

"Wow. . . " I said, lacking any other words. "I could read when I got to first grade because my parents taught me."

"She can read the words, but she has no comprehension beyond the basics of her regular vocabulary and language skills, which are now behind."

I looked at Jeremy and saw all sorts of complications to being involved in his life, because he obviously loved this little girl with all his heart. Where would I fit in? How could I have any place in his world?

"Stephanie goes to therapy for what they call cognitive behavioral intervention, to work on her social interaction and language and learning skills. It looks cruel."

I stuffed another spoonful of ice cream into my mouth, so I wouldn't have to speak. All I could think of was how he and his wife would add divorce to a little girl's problems.

Maybe he read my mind, or my face.

"My daughter doesn't really know who I am, Julie. I'm someone who sits at the dinner table once in a while, who drives her to and from her therapist's when Mommy can't. I'm like the words she can say but doesn't know the meaning – there is no connection. She calls Deanna 'Mommy' but has never said 'Daddy.' She can read me the morning paper, but . . ."

He looked away, but I saw the tears roll down his cheeks in his reflection in the mirror.

"I'm so sorry, Jeremy."

"It breaks my heart that I can't reach her. I know I was gone a lot but . . ."

I took our cardboard ice cream containers and set them on the ledge. Then I turned and wrapped my arms around his neck, letting him sob against my shoulder.

Finally, his tears stopped. He took a deep breath.

"I really needed that," he said in the quiet left when the pumps cycled off. "I try to pretend it doesn't hurt."

"We all pretend things don't hurt," I said, stroking his sweaty hair off his forehead. "If we couldn't pretend, we'd eventually run away from everything else that might hurt, too."

His eyes met mine. "You think?"

I nodded.

"Where'd you get so smart?" he said, pulling my wet ponytail around and splashing my nose with the tip.

"I had to learn to pretend a long time ago."

"When?" he said, sitting back. "When your father died?"

I floated across the round tub from him and turned the jets on again. "When I was fourteen and had a crush on a guy who didn't know I existed."

He raised an eyebrow. "And?"

I picked up my ice cream and took a bite, though there was already a pool of liquid around the frozen glob. "He was a junior, a basketball star and a photographer for the school paper. I'd been asked to pose for a clothing ad, and he did the shoot at the mall. He was good, and I was impressed by the way he could pose me and make me look pretty, and he was very complimentary, so I thought he was interested. He didn't even notice me at school a few days later, as if I evaporated when he developed the film."

"Your first broken heart?"

I finished the ice cream and tossed the container into the wastebasket near the tub. The spoon missed. "The first until my father was killed, then I didn't want to get close to anyone else." I looked away. "Till I met you."

"And I broke your heart, too."

"No, you smashed it to dust with a sledge hammer and then took a blow torch to it. I was left with a blob of molten slag." I flashed him a sardonic smile.

"I'm sorry. Walking away from you was the stupidest thing I've done in my entire life."

I shrugged.

Jeremy took one last bite of his ice cream and set his container aside.

"I'll make it up to you, somehow." He pulled me toward him by my feet, floating me over his legs onto his lap.

"You can't make up for the past, Jeremy. If you really want to accomplish something, it starts today."

"You're right." He scrunched his eyebrows together and studied me for a moment, then asked, "Will you ever be able to tell me what happened, Julie? I mean all of it? Tell me about the scars on the inside?" He traced a finger down the surgical scar on my shoulder, causing a shiver.

I turned and asked my reflection in the mirror. "Is there something fascinating about hearing me relive my tragedy?"

"We all slow down and look at disasters. Maybe that's when we take time to whisper to ourselves the 'There but for the grace of God' lines."

"I don't believe in God anymore," I said. "The truth is, there are parts of it I won't tell you or anyone else. But there are parts I can't tell. Like the gory details of how I ended up bleeding at the bottom of the staircase of my townhouse. I know David slit my throat because I have the scar to prove it, but I have no memory of him doing it," I said. "I don't remember everything that happened."

He nodded.

I slid away from him a little. "But I had a little flashback in my garage the other night when you picked up that box-cutter." I said quietly.

His pupils dilated as his brain searched for a memory.

"Oh shit, Julie," he said, his hands banging his forehead. "I didn't – You – I mean, I'm sorry. It never crossed my mind that – I was desperate to get you to say . . . something."

I reached down between his legs, grabbing his testicles, digging in my fingernails and squeezing hard enough to get his undivided attention.

"Jeremy Cameron McNeeley, if you ever pick up a knife in anger in my presence," I said squeezing a bit harder, "these will be the first to go when I take the knife away from you. And I will take it. Do you understand?"

He swallowed hard. "Perfectly."

I released my grip. "Yeah, and you thought I'd suddenly swooned over your declarations of love," I said with a half-grin. "You had absolutely no idea, did you? That's the only reason I didn't castrate you while you slept."

"Never. Really, I. . . " He stopped when he saw me smiling in the mirror. "I'd have deserved it, too."

"That's a fact."

"I'm sorry. Again." The pain showed clearly on his face. "I can't imagine what you've been through."

"No, Jeremy, you can't. But I won't tolerate you treating me like I'm damaged or fragile. You can't dance around everything, but you need to know that I can't always either."

"Maybe remembering would be good. Maybe then the nightmares would stop," he said.

"What nightmares?" I challenged.

"I've slept with you enough to know when you have bad dreams, Julie."

"I don't want to remember. I can't put into words what I saw in my head when you picked up that knife, but I felt all the fear and pain. I can't go through that again. It takes all my energy to stay in control sometimes."

Jeremy opened his mouth to say something and then closed it abruptly.

"What? Yes, I was offered counseling, and I did go a few times. I quit when it came down explaining all the details I remembered ending with the question, 'How does that make you feel?' If I knew that, I wouldn't need counseling, would I? I refuse to keep vomiting this stuff up. I did quite well on my own."

Liar.

"What about using hypnosis to help you find out what really happened and –" Jeremy could tell he was about to cross a line, so he stopped.

"No."

"I'm not criticizing, but can the truth be any worse than what you imagine in its place? Like you asked me about the car crash, remember?"

"Jeremy," I said, holding up my hand to stop him. "I woke up in ICU, not knowing what was real and what wasn't."

"Well, days in the hospital all blur together, Julie."

"I don't mean blurred time, Jeremy. Let me give you another example. In February 1992, Monica talked me into going with her to Lake Tahoe so she could ski. Four-day weekend. I don't remember a single moment of it. Not where we stayed, what we ate, who drove, anyone we met. She raves about that trip, but I can't even tell you if I enjoyed it. I remember nothing."

His expression said he understood. His eyes were skeptical.

"What if things I think are memories are dreams, or things I've thought were dreams are real? Either way, I don't want to remember them. I have a degree in psychology, Jeremy," I said, standing up and stepping out of the tub, dripping water and bubbles. "I'm still worried this is how people go insane."

CHAPTER 50

I stood in the shower, unbraiding my hair and lathering it with hotel shampoo, then I closed my eyes and rested my head between my forearms against the cool tiles, letting hot water cascade down my back.

How many other holes were there in my memory?

Four years ago, when my husband had nearly killed me, the day began with an argument before I left work. David started telling me about some top-secret imaging system he'd caught wind of at the base and how it could be the most important tool to come along in law enforcement since fingerprinting and DNA identification. He called it ghost imaging – a computerized reading of the changes in a bioelectrical magnetic field left by living organisms because of the iron content of the hemoglobin in blood.

David explained how the military would use it for tracking.

I'd laughed, not so much because I doubted the concept was possible but because David had told me other loony stories about similar "top secret projects." I considered that, if this one really worked, the military would never let it into the public sector any more than they allowed the use of high-resolution military satellite images to solve crimes such as kidnapping, which could be useful.

Not amused, I snapped at him, "You're not supposed to discuss that sort of thing with me, David. Why do you keep telling me this crap?"

I read in his brown eyes that he considered my reply insulting.

David would not stand for being trumped in anger. No matter

what I was upset about, he always worked himself into a rage all the hotter. If my anger was directed at him, he'd find a way to make it my fault.

"I don't care about these projects," I'd said, trying to defuse him.

"Sure you do, and you sell the secrets to the Germans."

"That is not true, and you know it!"

"They have copies of schematics and research, so it's true someone sold them secrets, took the money. You went to Germany, remember?" He grinned like a maniac. "I can prove it was you."

* * *

A hand on my shoulder startled me. I spun so quickly I slipped and almost fell.

Jeremy's arms steadied me.

"Julie?" Jeremy said. "Are you okay?"

I turned my face to the spray of water to hide my tears. I meant to say yes. Another part of me silently screamed, *No! I'm not okay! How could I possibly be okay?*

I don't know if I nodded or shook my head, but he left me alone in the shower, alone with a stream of memories I didn't want to remember.

Finally, I rinsed my hair and turned off the water. I wiped a clear spot on the steamed mirror and looked at the face staring back at me. It was thinner than a month ago. My eyes looked haunted, restless. Sleep kept my body going, but my mind often refused to rest in those precious hours, picking through endless details and creating nightmares.

Working on a mystery, goin' wherever it leads...

Great. Now "Runnin' Down a Dream" was stuck in my brain, another song playing on the endless loop of the soundtrack music for my life. Somehow, "Running on Empty" seemed more appropriate for the moment, so I hummed a few bars of Jackson Browne, but the internal player went right back to Tom Petty.

Steam erased my face in the mirror, which suited me fine.

I wrapped the towel around my hair and opened the door.

Jeremy sat cross-legged on a towel on the floor, stripped down to his shorts. His back was straight and his eyes were closed. His hands rested palm up on his knees, thumbs meeting his middle fingers in a circle. He inhaled deeply, held, then exhaled.

Jeremy McNeeley's really into yoga?

I put on my underwear and tanktop, and then stretched out on the bed to watch.

After a few minutes, he opened an eye and asked if I'd like to join him.

"I guess," I said. "What do I do?" I pulled the towel from my head.

He asked me to sit with my legs crossed with my back to his. I did. We interlocked our palms together at our sides.

"This is a relaxation exercise. Clear your mind of everything except the sensation of motion and the breathing. Now, inhale and lean back against me as I move forward. When I inhale and lean toward you, you will exhale."

I did as he instructed, and we moved fluidly, bending around the other, stretching, relaxing.

"Now, close your eyes and concentrate on nothing but breathing in and out with the movement, and the sensation of our skin touching, the vertebrae sliding past each other."

With no awareness of time, we spent almost half an hour in the exercise. Finally, when we were both sitting up, he told me not to open my eyes, to sit, rest my hands on my knees, and bring my thumb and index fingers together in a loose circle, palms up. He coached me through more breathing exercises, and then asked me to open my eyes.

Instead of leaning against me, I was surprised to find him sitting in front of me.

"How do you feel?" he asked.

"Relaxed. Peaceful."

"Good. Then crawl into the bed and close your eyes."

No argument there.

He dimmed the lights and tucked the sheet and blanket around me, made sure my pillow was just so. Then he pulled the covers from my feet and alternated massaging each.

"You will sleep tonight without any bad dreams. Nothing will worry you. You will rest. Your body will heal and restore itself. . . " His soothing voice whispered as I faded to sleep.

Hours later, I jolted awake, hearing a knock at the door.

Jeremy threw the sheet over me and answered, accepting a room service tray that included a pot of what I hoped was coffee.

He set the table while I went to the bathroom to wipe the sleep from my eyes. The face in the mirror looked less desperate than it had the night before.

We sat down to breakfast.

Jeremy had ordered an extra portion of ham and an egg for the dog.

"You are definitely spoiled," I told Laser as he watched Jeremy scrape the food into the dog's dish. "Go on, eat up. We have another long day ahead of us."

"Did you sleep okay?" he said, sitting back down next to me.

"Better than okay," I said, biting into a slice of toast with blackberry jam. "That's some voodoo you do."

He only smiled.

"Especially the feet. Wow. . . "

"I learned yoga while I was in med school. Keeps me balanced. It's a mixture of several practices of yoga I found worked for me," he said, as if that explained everything.

It didn't, but I didn't ask. I don't have to understand the internal combustion engine to drive a car, so long as it gets me where I'm going.

"I've got a ton of work to get started this morning," I said when we finished, "but I appreciate the bubbles last night. And the yoga."

"Any time."

Laser and I headed outside, with a brief stop to unload my arms before finding him a small patch of grass out of the way of pedestrians.

Instead of going straight to the office, I detoured by my house to change clothes. Wearing the same outfit two days in a row makes me feel grungy. People probably already wondered where I slept.

I put on a maroon silk turtleneck shirt over my vest, followed by a blazer, black jeans. When I slipped on my hiking boots, I saw that my broken toes had transitioned from purple to an ugly yellowish-green color.

After a little makeup, I figured I was presentable.

All this, and it was only a quarter till eight. I actually felt good.

CHAPTER 51

Laser scarfed down the crunchy nuggets I'd poured into his dish, despite having had breakfast at the hotel.

"You eat like Matthew," I whispered, fighting the tears that stung my eyes at the thought of him.

"Good morning, Julie," Connie said from my door. "Your photocopies are here. There are several boxes. Will the dog be okay for the delivery person to bring them in your office?"

"I think he's full. But while we're on the subject, would you call the sheriff and see if he's come up with any alternatives for Laser? He's a great companion, but I'm not a very good hostess," I confessed.

She returned to her office and probably dialed the phone on Frank Lomas' desk. Connie knew everyone in town and all their phone numbers, it seemed.

A young man wheeled in four boxes on a dolly and stacked them in the corner of my office. I signed for them, and he left.

After an hour's sorting and filing the contents of my perpetually full in-box, I went to find Dr. Katz, who was in the largest of the autopsy rooms, examining a victim from a car crash the previous afternoon while a young intern examined skeletal remains in a corner of the suite.

"One of those cases where the patient insisted he was okay," Katz explained, looking at the ribs with the skin laid open in the standard Y incision. "He refused treatment and transport by ambulance, went home for a nap, and didn't wake up for dinner." Katz nodded to an instant photo of the car, taken by paramedics on scene.

"What a shame."

"The wife has already invoked attorney," he said, his twisted phrase analogous to summoning lawyer-demons of the almighty dollar, "for wrongful death. The fact that he refused to be evaluated or treated after crashing into the back of a tractor-trailer at 45 miles per hour will likely be irrelevant in a court of civil law."

Dr. Katz and I shared only the average malice toward lawyers in general, but so much of his time was spent on the stand between two of them trying their damnedest to twist his testimony to prove their respective sides, despite the legal concept of *res ipsa loquitur* – that the obvious facts speak for themselves.

"I arranged lunch with MaryAnne for Saturday," I said as Dr. Katz removed the sternum and the section of ribs from the chest wall, placing the piece on a side table. I could see bruising where the chest had hit the steering wheel. "No airbag," I observed, leaving us two parallel topics of discussion.

"No, and I suspect the seatbelt was improperly used, too," he said, pointing to a bruise and abrasion on the left upper arm. "Yes, MaryAnne mentioned it over dinner. I wish I could put all the pieces of her mystery together so easily," he said, looking up at me. "I'm worried."

I nodded.

Katz turned his attention back to the chest cavity full of blood, feeling around inside as he suctioned the fluid away.

"Kimberly called to ask if you and MaryAnne are getting divorced. I said no, of course, but whatever the vibrations are, she feels them, too." I said, stepping back. "MaryAnne tells me Kim is signed up for a lifeguard course. Her baby is growing up."

"That's the truth." He smiled and pointed to a reciprocating blade saw on the table. "Should any power tools come up missing from here overnight, I'll be taking random samples home to show all her boyfriends how I'll remove their appendages if necessary."

I laughed. "That's the trouble with having beautiful daughters."

"Pretty mushy in here," he said, changing subjects again. After suctioning, the container held almost three liters of blood. "He bled to death, and no one saw a drop. Bets on a torn aorta?"

The heart hangs from the aorta like an apple on a fat stem. A tear from extreme deceleration can empty the circulatory system in minutes.

"Not after seeing a chest full of blood. Definitely a tear," I agreed, watching as Dr. Katz continued retracting the lungs to reveal the heart tucked between. "But my first guess was a cardiac contusion, based on the bruised ribs."

"I think we're both right," he said.

I stepped closer, and he showed me first the small hole in the aorta where the carotid artery branched toward the head, and then two dark purplish marks across the heart - bruises from where it struck the ribs on impact.

"Since he obviously survived long enough to get home, he might have survived had he gone to the hospital," Katz concluded.

Might.

This caught the attention of the intern, who also came to look.

Dr. Katz started his lesson. "A chest injury of this sort might not cause the patient serious shock symptoms until the blood loss became critical, so the ER doc might delay imaging."

I couldn't help but join the discussion when I saw doubt in the young man's eyes. "The math of the matter is that while size matters, speed kills. Doubling the weight of a baseball doubles the impact energy. Doubling its speed quadruples the energy. It's an exponential increase."

Dr. Katz nodded, then removed the heart and continued to assess the injuries, changing conversation topics yet again. "Detective Callaghan stopped by this morning to check on the skeleton and see if you had any more ideas about where to dig. I told him I'd have you call."

"We could turn over every clod on that farm and be as likely to find a body under one as the next, but I'm guessing we won't find any more. I think we were expected to find the barrels underneath the floor. The barrel outside the barn door was luck. The old man's body – that was icing, thanks to Penny."

He nodded again.

"She left the journals her mother wrote for me to make copies. Apparently her parents took in her cousin Anthony after his mother was murdered by his stepfather, who did prison time and then wound up dead himself shortly after parole. Both the mother and stepfather had slit throats."

Katz looked up, interested. "And this cousin is where?"

"Committed suicide when he was in his early twenties. Penny's the only member of the family left. So unless we get something else urgent, I'm going to scan those journals for more clues."

Connie paged, asking me to return to my office, so I excused myself.

Sheriff Frank Lomas was waiting for me at her desk.

"I'm sorry I've left the dog with you so long," he apologized. "I've got another deputy who can keep him now. You don't know how much it's meant, knowing you were taking care of him."

"He's been no trouble, but I'm not paying him the sort of attention he needs. I think he feels out of place not working. He'll adapt to someone new," I said, opening my door and calling the dog.

Laser came and sat down by my feet, looking like a child being sent away to summer camp.

"Time to go to work, buddy. You have to earn those steaks you've been wolfing down."

"If you spent anything on him, I'll reimburse you –" the sheriff began.

"It's not necessary, really. I'm glad I could do something to help."

I haven't done much to help find Matt. Feeding the dog is the least I could do.

Frank's eyes met mine for a long moment, and I saw deep exhaustion.

He nodded.

I clipped the lead onto the dog's collar. Laser looked offended.

"I'll walk you out," I offered, handing him a piece of paper. "I made a list of commands I know. Most are German, a few are French."

He thanked me again.

"Frank? How long have you been with the department?"

"Since 1971. I've been in Grand Traverse County my whole career."

"Your deputies think very highly of you. That's not common," I said.

"My wife died of cancer in 1987. We never had children. Those deputies are my family. Each moment Matthew Shannaker is gone tears away another piece of my soul. God help us, I intend to see him found. Then maybe I'll retire and move somewhere I can fish in the warm sunshine all year. I can't take this anymore."

Not knowing what else to do, I hugged him.

When he was gone, I returned to face the piles of paperwork on my desk. I was too distracted to be doing anything requiring my full attention, so I filed cases and answered some email.

I was packing the box of journals to ship to Penny when Jeremy came into my office.

"You need food," he declared.

"Yes, I do," I said. "Let me tape this up first."

I pulled a roll of clear packing tape over the top of the box, shivering at the screeching sound it made, like nails on a chalkboard. What an obsolete reference in the age of dry erase boards, I thought. Did schools have chalkboards anymore? Did students go pound erasers on the sidewalks? Did the writing on the board disappear for days after the janitors wiped them down with that oily stuff?

"Where's the dog?" he asked, interrupting my childhood memory.

"Gone back to work," I said with a sigh of relief. "Sheriff picked him up a little while ago."

I stuck the shipping label on top and then handed the box to Jeremy to carry to Connie's desk.

"Geez, what's in here?" he asked as I closed my door behind us.

I laughed. "It's the very same box of books you carried out to Connie's desk for me yesterday for photocopies. I'm sending them back to Penny," I explained as we made our way down the hall.

Jeremy looked down at the label and stopped dead, staring at the label. "Oh, shit," he muttered through a grimace, slouching against the wall.

"What?" I asked, trying to take the box from him, worried he'd hurt his back or worse, from the sudden paleness of his skin, that maybe he was having a heart attack.

He jerked it away. "Tell me where to put this."

"Next to Connie's desk," I said, bewildered as he stomped down the hall.

He practically dropped the box and shouted to her, "Don't ship that!" as he grabbed my arm and hauled me toward to door.

"What is going on with you?" I demanded again, trying to wrench my arm from his grip.

"There's a connection," he said as he dragged me out of the office and to the stairs.

I finally wrestled my arm free as we left the building, mostly due to the serious looks of concern Jeremy earned from two deputies, who were about to intervene on my behalf had I not waved them off and retrieved possession of my extremity. "What are you talking about?"

"Penny Daniels, 40 or 41 years old," he said, heading to his car, "lives in Phoenix, mother of three kids, just had a vacation at the Grand Canyon and Disneyland? Same Penny Daniels?"

"Yes, the same Penny Daniels whose brother died in the barn that blew up. She was here until a few days ago."

He dug his keys from his pocket and opened the trunk. "Do you remember the case I told you about at lunch yesterday? CDC was contacted to make a definitive diagnosis. It was *Naegleria fowleri*."

Bugs again.

"Which is?" I asked sarcastically, expecting a microbiology lesson.

"Rare, but almost always fatal." He let this sink in. "The child that died yesterday morning? Her mother, Penny Daniels, is also sick."

CHAPTER 52

I slumped against his car, feeling helpless.

"How do you get this. . . this. . . whatever it is?" I asked.

"Amoeba," he supplied. "A free-living amoeba that thrives in the soil and in warm stagnant waters such as ponds or hot springs. When it enters the body through the nose, it migrates along the olfactory nerves into the brain, causing headache and fever, and a rapid progression into coma. Diagnosis is usually postmortem. They confirmed it on autopsy of the girl."

"And Penny? If they already know what it is, they can treat her and –"

He shook his head. "She's already comatose."

I could hardly breathe. Someone else would die because of my connection. "So where did they catch this, this . . . " I stuttered.

Amoeba sounds far too benign.

"We don't know."

"They were exposed before Penny came here, right?" I asked, grasping at any glimmer of hope. "She wasn't feeling well when she left."

He shook his head. "According to the timelines, the daughter was ill first. We think her exposure was Sunday or Monday."

"But Penny was still here then, so they were separated." I couldn't help rubbing my own nose with the back of my hand, thinking about his description.

"The mother wasn't exposed until after she got home."

"She got it from the daughter?" I was trying to follow the invisible lines between the dots, but nothing made sense.

"No, it's not contagious. The other two kids and husband seem fine."

I gave up on the microbiology lesson. "How did you get involved in this?"

"I've been consulting on other cases. After the *Bilharzia*, I asked the director to keep me informed of any unusual microorganism cases," he said. "This was very unusual. There's only one case of *Naegleria* infection last year. One case compared to over 1200 cases of *Cryptosporidium*, *Schistosoma*, *Campylobacter*, and *Shigella*, and the rest of the water-borne organisms."

"This can't be a coincidence," I said, hoping he would disagree.

"Because this case was in Arizona, I didn't make a connection. There must be one, though." He dug through a briefcase for a folder, which he handed me. "I'm really at a loss here, Julie. What the hell are we supposed to do?"

"Keep fighting, I guess." I flipped through the pages of information about the patients and the amoeba.

Ugly bastard of a bug.

Reported cases of primary amoebic meningoencephalitis, or PAM for a much-appreciated acronym, caused by *Naegleria fowleri* seemed to have common sources grouped under the heading of recreational waters – lakes, rivers, springs, etc.

"So," I said, turning to Jeremy, who was kneading his neck with both hands, "if I were to look for this amoeba, besides these warm water spots, where would I find it?"

"The amoeba itself isn't rare, only the infection. You'd never guess where I'd go look for a specimen." He laughed.

I rolled my eyes.

"Sorry. Believe it or not, you could probably find it in the tubes of water used to balance the centrifuge for blood samples in the lab."

"No way," I said skeptically.

He raised his right hand. "Serious. I don't know why, but that's what Dr. Archer told me – you'd probably find it in at least one lab in town."

"Would it be possible to determine where it came from?"

"I doubt it, and it wouldn't prove anything. Unlike the *Bilharzia*, it's native to many places in the U.S."

"Can they do anything for Penny?" I asked, desperate for even a glimmer of hope. "I really liked her."

Jeremy shook his head slightly. "They'll try, but I don't think so. I'm sorry."

"You have to leave," I finally said. "You have to go get your family and take them– "

"Deanna already took Stephanie somewhere safe. I'm here for the long haul with you."

I wanted to argue. Really.

His confidence and courage made me feel like a child, but I was terrified Jeremy would end up wherever Matt Shannaker was because of me. But I realized there was one other person who had no idea what was happening to me and who would also be a logical target.

And then I sneezed.

Two ideas collided in my head like electrons at critical mass."I think I know how he did it!" I slammed the trunk and dragged Jeremy back into the building in quite the same hurry he'd led me out. Neither of the deputies gave our passing a second glance with me pulling him by the arm, but the mad dash past her desk exasperated Connie.

In my office, I pulled a drug reference book off the shelf of my credenza and flipped through the pages until I found the name I wanted, and then slid the open book across to Jeremy, pointing to a drug.

Then I picked up the receiver and dialed directly.

One ring.

Two rings and a connection.

"Hello. You've reached Dagmar's answering machine." She must have other messages or it would have rung four times. "I'm not available, so leave a message at the beep. Have a wonderful day!"

"Mother? Are you there? I have to talk to you. Please call me as soon as you get this message." I checked my watch. Not time for work yet. "Page me if I don't answer my cell phone," I said, and left the numbers, barely finishing before my time was done.

I disconnected and dialed another number direct.

Two rings and a switchboard operator answered, "University

Hospital, how may I direct your call?"

I asked for the nursing supervisor by name.

Vera Samualson answered on the third ring.

"Vera, this is Julie Madigan," I said, trying to sound calm. "I need to speak to my mother, is she working? It's urgent."

Vera was one of Mom's best friends, so no further explanation was needed.

"No, she's not here, Julie. She traded her shifts today and tomorrow to go to Ruidoso with that gentleman she's been seeing. I expect she'll be gone all weekend. Are you okay?"

Gone? What gentleman?

"Oh, yeah, Vera. I remember. No, there's nothing wrong. I just. . . " Couldn't tell her the truth. "I was trying to make reservations to fly down at Thanksgiving and found a really good deal, but I wanted to check it with her," I lied. I doubted it sounded convincing.

"We'll be happy to see you. You make the arrangements. I'll see that everything works out with her schedule, okay?"

She must think I'll need a ride from the airport, I thought. Big deal.

"Ask her to call me as soon as she gets back, okay?"

Vera promised and started her goodbye.

"Do you know him?" I asked, interrupting her.

"Pardon?"

"This gentleman. Have you met him?"

"Well, no, I haven't. I've heard a bit about him, but I don't think she's even mentioned more than his first name to me."

I'd like to think that was strange, but since I was unaware of any other relationships my mother'd had in the last twenty years, I couldn't say.

"Oh, she hasn't told me much about him, either," I said, trying not to sound as defeated as I felt. "Do you remember his name?"

"Let's see. . . Emerson? No. . . Everett, like Chad Everett, the television star." She laughed. "I guess that shows my age, huh?"

"Okay, thanks, Vera. I hope to see you at Thanksgiving."

I traded the rest of the goodbye pleasantries and hung up.

I plopped down in my chair, only now aware I was still standing behind my own desk.

Jeremy sat across the desk from me, but I couldn't remember seeing his face during either call – the ideas had become so separate in my mind.

"She's apparently gone to the mountains with a man she's been dating," I offered when he gave me raised eyebrows. "She called me last night but didn't mention leaving."

"Did she tell you about him before?"

"Except for the one time I called and he'd answered, no. She hadn't shared any other details about him or their relationship with me."

That was fair. I didn't share my personal details with her.

"What did you talk about when she called last night?" he asked.

"She wanted to know about the case. The bomb thing. She asked a lot of questions. How was I feeling? When did I start back to work? Did we have any leads? She even asked me about the dog, but I said I was keeping him for a friend, which was true."

"You can play fact or fiction with her, but she can't hide secrets of her own? Did you ask about him?"

So much on my mind, I hadn't given it another thought.

"You think she might be in danger if she's out of town with someone she knows?" he asked.

"I don't know. At the risk of sounding paranoid, what if the suspect has been able to get into her house? He had no problem getting into mine," I said with utter resignation. "Or into Penny's."

I pointed to the book to explain my theory.

"Penny used a nasal spray for allergies when she was here, and she was almost out," I explained. "Her daughter uses the same stuff."

Jeremy's eyes got wide. "Oh, hell, that would be a perfect delivery system."

CHAPTER 53

I had no appetite when Jeremy mentioned lunch again.

"You still need to eat," he insisted. "I keep hearing about this famous white fish here. Where's the best?"

"Fish doesn't agree with me," I confessed. "I'm a red-meat carnivore."

As always, Connie had a list of favorite restaurants. She recommended a lakeshore restaurant overlooking West Bay, so that's where I took him.

Jeremy ate his fish and chips while I picked at a BLT that tasted like cardboard and settled in my gut like a rock sinking in the bay beyond the windows.

Fleeting ideas we couldn't discuss in public blasted through my brain until I found something we could talk about. "I talked to Eric Rader, the post commander when I was in Alamogordo. Now he's a gold badge in Santa Fe. He ran a state database search to find homicide victims with cut throats. There were a fair number in the computerized records in the last twenty-five years. Two of them cross-referenced my name. One was my own case."

"Why yours? You weren't killed, and your husband's death wasn't ruled a homicide, right?" Jeremy asked.

"That's not the point," I said, but it did snag in my brain for a moment. "The other case in the database search was my father's murder."

"You told me he'd been shot," Jeremy said, eyebrows moving up and then back down into a frown. "Now I'm even more confused."

"Yeah, he was – " I said, my voice trailing off as memories began to play in my head - blood on his khaki pants, on the floor. All over my hands. "He was shot. . . " Those three words echoed in my head, ringing true, but for the first time in years, I doubted what I remembered.

"Julie?" Jeremy said, startling me back to the present.

I blinked away the vision. "He was shot," I repeated.

That was a fact.

Was it the truth?

"He was shot," I said again, enunciating it slowly as if saying it again could convince me. "The cause of death was exsanguination from a gunshot wound to the femoral artery. But his case came up in the database search for knife wounds to the neck or throat."

Jeremy looked puzzled.

"Eric thought maybe it was a coding error. There isn't any extensive text with the database. The codes provide general information so you can pull matching files," I said, rubbing my temples.

The more I thought I knew, the less sense any of it made.

We both stared out the windows across the bay, struggling with the new questions.

Jeremy watched with interest as the tanker ship *Great Lakes* came about to dock her port side on the pier just north of the restaurant.

"In the dead of winter, I've seen fisherman stay out there while that ship cracks the ice around them. It's insane," I commented.

"Not if the fish are biting," an amused voice said behind me.

I turned to see Brandan standing there.

Jeremy motioned him to sit down, but he waved it off and looked at me.

"I hate to interrupt your lunch. Connie told me where you were," he said. "The FBI leaned on the manager and staff at the photo processing center, mentioning obstruction of justice charges for everyone on the payroll. Suddenly the guy's son confessed and produced the negatives and not only the original machine prints, but some good enlargements, too."

"What are they?" I asked, reaching for the manila envelope in his clenched hands.

"Not here. I just couldn't risk leaving them in the car. Come back to the task force room. We need to talk. Twenty minutes?"

The sound of the blood pounding in my ears drowned out all the voices in the busy restaurant.

"Is it Matt?" My voice squeaked.

Brandan's head nodded only slightly. He pulled his aviator sunglasses down and turned to leave.

Jeremy's face tightened.

The server was nowhere to be seen, so I tossed down enough cash to cover our lunch, and we left.

When I parked at the Annex, Jeremy went to my office to return a phone call to Atlanta about the nasal spray, and I walked over to the Law Enforcement Center without him.

Brandan waited in the task force room, along with Nolan Forrester. Another man I didn't recognize sat in a corner with a laptop. Suit said FBI.

Brandan emptied the envelope onto the conference table and spread the photos out, arranging enlargements under the regular-sized prints. "These are in the order of the negative," he explained.

I viewed them from left to right. Some were images we already had seen, like the unknown female victim on the disk. I kept scanning until I came to images that were ghastly familiar.

Feeling my stomach contents churn, I muttered something profane and bolted for the door with my hand over my mouth in hopes I could make the restroom down the hall.

I left the men standing there thinking I'd blown lunch after seeing the images of Matthew with blood on his face and shirt, but it wasn't that at all. It had been the photographs probably none of them had recognized that had sent me running.

Brandan must have lost the coin toss or short straw or whatever method they used to decide who got to check on me.

I'd finished puking when he knocked on the women's restroom door and then came on in.

"Julie, you okay?"

"Nope."

That always leaves them wondering what to say next.

"What can I do?" he asked, opening the door to the handicapped stall to find me with my butt against the wall, leaning over the toilet.

He went to the sink and brought me a handful of wet paper towels.

"Thanks."

I wiped my mouth with one and tossed it into the toilet, then flushed it. I stood up, still feeling swimmy-headed, and wiped my damp forehead with the other. Then things got gray again, and I thought it best to sit down for a minute.

The toilet looked handy.

"Sorry, I should have warned you about the pictures of Matt," he offered.

I ignored his apology and leaned forward to put my head between my knees. After a few breaths, I sat up and thought maybe I could stay that way.

I went out to the sink, washed my face and rinsed out my mouth.

Brandan handed me a roll of breath mints.

"Thanks." I took two and chewed them up.

We returned to the conference room to where the others were awaiting news of my condition and its cause.

Jeremy had joined them.

"Ms. Madigan," Forrester began, "You need to understand our position with this case. You have obviously become far too emotionally involved to objectively –"

I bristled.

Brandan winced and Jeremy took a defensive step back.

"Excuse me, Special Agent Forrester," I interrupted, taking a substantial step forward into his personal space, putting me eye to eye with him. "I don't pretend *not* to be emotionally involved. But let me ask you something. Do *you* know anything about these photographs except those of Matthew Shannaker?"

"No, but we are working on the –"

"No, but? Well, Mr. 'No-But,' you just keep working on them. You obviously don't need an emotionally unobjective woman to identify victims for you or tell you when and where those *other* photos were taken. The FBI has a lot of really high-tech resources. I'll go back to my office and file death certificates, like I was doing before I got called to that barn. I sure don't need to look at any more gory photos." I turned to leave.

"You *know* who they are?" he said, trying hard to sound objective and unemotional.

I kept walking.

"Ms. Madigan!" he barked.

"Go to hell," I said over my shoulder. I almost made it to the door.

"Ms. Madigan," Forrester said again in quite a different tone of voice. "I'm sorry."

I stopped but did not turn around.

The tension was like clotted blood on a wound.

"Julie?" Jeremy asked quietly.

I stood with my back to all of them, slowing my breathing, trying to think of objective and unemotional reasons why it would be a career-limiting move to shoot an FBI agent.

Finally, I turned and went to the table and took a deep breath before I looked at Jeremy, Brandan, then Nolan.

"I didn't ask to be a part of this," I stated. "This is personal to me because it revolves around me. But I'm not one of your agents, Forrester, so don't think you can pull out your FBI whip and make me perform like a circus lion. Stick your hand back in my face and I'm liable to bite it off."

He nodded.

I took another breath and pointed out photos as I talked. "This is the female victim on the disk. This one is the deleted image from the disk, processed by the FBI lab, with most of the missing pixels. It's familiar, but I don't specifically recognize it. This one of me next to my truck at Matthew's place is a duplicate of one from the cedar box at the Tucker house, which dates surveillance of me back almost three years."

No one interrupted me.

"These at the beginning of the roll, I don't recognize," I said, sliding a pair of photos out of the lineup and pulling them toward me. "But these? I can tell you lots about these two."

The looks from the three men ranged from confusion to disbelief as I continued.

"These photos were taken March 7, 1991, in Alamogordo, New Mexico. The woman with her neck slashed is holding a Smith & Wesson Airweight .38 Special with two rounds fired from it in her left hand. Two Glaser slugs that ended up in his chest," I said, pointing to the photo of the man. "Fired from an arm's length away. It was fatal."

I saw Jeremy make the connection, and he mouthed a rather colorful profanity that indicated he now understood why I had reacted the way I had toward Forrester.

"That's me there on the floor, bleeding to death, Forrester. That man was my husband." I let that sink in. "These were taken moments after I shot David, while he was still alive, it looks like. I couldn't see him after he fell because my arms collapsed across my face, and I couldn't lift them because of the broken shoulder. Maybe I passed out again. See how David is looking up toward the camera? Window of opportunity would have been seconds. Maybe a minute tops. No more."

I looked around at the three men.

"I didn't know anyone else was in the house. The 911 call came from the air force base. Ironically, thanks to David, the house was bugged."

Hmmm, an emotional and not very objective crowd. Even Mr. No-But looked a little stunned.

Jeremy looked like his fish wasn't agreeing with him.

Suddenly, it made sense why my case was listed in the unsolved database. They hadn't identified the other person who was present. Why hadn't I known about that?

I watched Jeremy study the photograph of me and cringe. The prints were reproductions, maybe photographs of photographs, making them grainy. I understood why no one recognized me.

Seeing the injuries David had inflicted still make me queasy.

In a move I didn't expect, Jeremy came and put his arms around me. "I'm sorry. I had no idea."

"Yeah, me either," I said, shrugging off his embrace, not wanting sympathy. "Do you understand now, Forrester?"

"We needed your assistance to interpret this information to identify him, yes."

"Yes and no. See, you need to keep thinking current events, which is the key to finding Matt, and that's the priority. The rest of this crap is old news – it's not going to identify or catch him," I explained. "He gave us this. We can assume he killed the other victims. Whether you can prove it isn't even an issue now. Saving Matt is. So is keeping him from killing again."

I looked up to see them trying to follow the logic.

"Who is the one man who could have taken all these photos, who could have killed all these people?" I asked. "Who has connections to everyone, including me? That's who we're looking for. Finding the answer to why I'm his focus is crucial to identifying him."

Forrester held up his hands in protest. "As far as we know, you are as much a victim here as Shannaker, if not the primary target. We can't risk him driving this investigation in order to get to you."

Brandan turned to face Forrester. "Sir, I'm inclined to think that if we exclude her, we're done getting any more information at all. All the clues, like the photos, the hints, the bugs? He's sent it all to get her involved. She is his sole contact. This has nothing to do with anyone but Julie. If she's locked out, there's no telling what could happen."

"There's more," I said.

"More what?" Forrester asked, eyeing me critically.

"What about the next two victims he called me about?"

CHAPTER 54

"What? He contacted you about more victims, and you just *guessed* about them?" Forrester bellowed as I'd tried to explain. "When was this?"

"Last night before I left. And what the hell would you like me to do when he calls, hang up on him?" I countered without anger, safe from his tantrum. "He asked if I'd figured out his next two victims. We knew he poisoned one with puffer fish – he left one in my aquarium. The other, I guessed was the patient seen in the emergency room with symptoms suggesting thallium or other heavy metal poisoning, which fit," I said. "When he asked if I solved the other, I picked that. He said, 'Interesting. No. You're only half-right so you lose your turn again.' And hung up."

"And when did you plan on reporting that information to the rest of us?" Forrester asked through clenched teeth.

I glared back. "I *did* report it. I called your office last night after I talked to him. It's not my problem your staff doesn't give you your messages. Exactly what else would you like me to do? Sit by your side and give minute-by-minute reports?"

"By God, if that's what it takes," he roared, slamming his fist into the table.

"I tried calling you before, but you weren't in then, either, and no one in your office seemed to care when I got a fax about Matthew. You didn't call me back."

"What fax?"

"The fax about the key to my soul, the blood."

Nolan whipped to the agent in the corner, who only shrugged.

"Maybe the thallium victim is just a coincidence?" Jeremy said, trying to interrupt the argument. "What about Penny Daniels and her daughter?"

"Penny?" Brandan asked, recognizing the connection.

"Damn, it must be," I said, feeling nauseated again.

Taking a half hour, we swapped information about Penny Daniels and her daughter, my most recent conversation with the killer, the previous fax that Nolan had missed, and the details surrounding Matthew in the photographs that might lead to his whereabouts.

We concluded that somehow there were links between the deaths of Angela Bock, Robert Bock, Penny Daniels, and James Patrick Tucker. Add to that those women in barrels and the old man on the family property, and suddenly everything revolved around the Tucker family somehow, until we got to the 1991 assault against me by my husband.

"David lived in Michigan before moving to New Mexico, so was there a link there I didn't know about?" I suggested.

"That's a huge leap," Brandan replied. "And there's little way of chasing that down."

Finding another dead end, we seemed to collectively slump.

"Part of the 'game' seems to be whether we figured out this spider web of connections," I said. "So if he calls again, do I reveal what we know or do I wait?"

They voted to hold the ace.

"He keeps offering vague hints," Brandan said. "Let's see what more he'll give you."

That decided, Forrester took one more swing at knocking both me and Dr. McNeeley out of the investigation, which earned him more ire.

"Nolan, the only reason I'm part of this investigation is because I have a few answers – I was the only one who'd seen the pit in the barn," I said. "But you can't have it both ways. You can't throw me out of the ballpark then expect me to come in to pinch hit, too."

"It's for your protection," he said, trying to sound reasonable. "We should get Dr. McNeeley back to his job at CDC as well."

"Nice try," Jeremy said, standing up. "But you didn't invite me here so you don't get to decide when I go home. I might not have any more official ties to this investigation, but I'll be staying with her."

Forrester opened his mouth to argue, then shook his head. "You could be dead wrong."

Jeremy shrugged. "So far, she's the only one he doesn't seem to want to kill. Leaving doesn't appear to be any safer than staying."

I stood up, reached over to pick up the enlargement of the photograph of me, my arm over part of my face, my wrists bound together. My neck wound gaped open about an inch, pooled with dark blood running down onto the floor beneath me. What was visible of my face was bloodied and bruised, swollen. My right shoulder was grossly out of its socket and broken. The gun dangled from my fingers against the floor.

"Bastard," I whispered, letting the photo drop to the table, and walked out of the room.

I worked in my office the rest of the day, avoiding more bad news until I was paged to the hospital to meet with Dr. Valiquette at four o'clock.

"There is nothing we can do for this patient, unfortunately," the doctor complained. "Organ failure is imminent."

Olivia Palmeri's hunch about the thallium had been correct. The question was how and whether this case was truly related.

If this were a random poisoning like the puffer fish incident, we were probably never going to find the source. The substance could have been delivered in either a powder or a liquid in practically any food.

Like the PCP dose in my candy, I'd consumed all the evidence.

I went to find Olivia Palmeri in the lab.

"How big would this thallium dose be to poison someone?" I asked.

"Concentrations vary," she said. "Depends what it was. I wasn't able to narrow it down to any closer than a few grams. As little as one gram can be fatal."

I smiled. "Grams is close enough. Thanks, Olivia."

I headed to the lab door.

"Everyone calls me Livvie," she said, walking with me on her way to another task. “So, um. The man I've seen at your house recently. Your brother?” she asked, a little shy.

“No, he's an old flame who fanned back up in a whirlwind, you might say,” I joked.

Jeremy does attract attention.

She nodded, looking disappointed. “Oh, I see. Just curious. See you around, then.”

When I got back to the Annex, Connie had left for the day, but I had voice mail.

“Julie,” Jeremy said. “We have to talk. Something has happened.”

A hundred things could have happened since lunch and the meeting after, and given the tone of his voice, not one of them could be good. My stomach twisted tighter.

Jeremy was officially no longer on the case for the Centers for Disease Control, but unwilling to leave my home. He kept his hotel room, but had been sleeping in my bed.

I picked up the phone and called home.

“Hello,” Jeremy said, on the third ring.

“Sorry, I just got back from the hospital. Why didn’t you call my cell phone?”

He paused, “I didn’t want to interrupt your day.”

“Your message made it sound important.”

“I guess it is,” he said, providing no clues. “But it can wait till you get here.”

I sighed. “Jeremy?”

“We can’t do this on the phone, really.”

CHAPTER 55

I pulled into the driveway a little before six. Inside, I dumped my stuff on my desk and found Jeremy in the kitchen.

"The first thing I have to do," he said, sitting down next to me at the breakfast bar, "is say I'm sorry, which must be getting pretty redundant."

Now what, I wondered. News of incurable cancer . . . mob ties . . . he lost my winning hundred million dollar Lotto ticket?

"Tell me." I had no patience for small talk.

"I came back to the house after the meeting. When your phone rang, I answered without thinking about it. 'You have no idea who she really is, no matter how long you've known her or how many nights you sleep in her bed,' a male voice said. 'Go to her bedroom. To the left side of her closet is a gray plastic bin. Her journals are in there. I thought I'd be giving them to the deputy, but you'll do just as well. I've marked passages you should read, and then you'll begin to understand.'"

Jeremy said when the connection broke, he realized he'd only said hello. He tried to think what my journals could have to do with any of this, and he considered calling me or Detective Callaghan. While pondering that, he decided to figure out whether the call was a hoax, whether the books were where he'd been told.

In the gray box were my journals, just as the caller had told him, along with other school yearbooks, photos albums. On top of the stack was a printed list of dates, which Jeremy discovered corresponded to the dates of the seven journals in the box. He followed the list's instructions to specific dates, starting in late 1991.

A blank business card bookmarked where he should begin.

"I didn't want to read them, but I kept thinking this must be some mistake, some kind of joke."

It wasn't. I flipped the first book he handed me to where he began.

September 4, 1991 – I made my appearance over at Monica's house for her party, then disappeared while everyone seemed occupied. No one was going to miss me. Invisible – that's the way I feel.

I took off, driving. Going anywhere but home, where I've been cooped up for weeks. I'm officially free from rehab and PT/OT, though I'm not physically as good as I might get, but the rest is up to me.

Mother's idea of a celebration gift was a membership at a 24-hour gym. I'll go, mostly because it's time away from the house and necessary for me to get back to work, but I'm likely to go in the middle of the night when there are fewer people there. My physical prognosis is good, but a long way off yet. Socially, I'm still on life support. Emotionally, I am just brain-dead. Like being on a roller coaster ride in a blindfold, I sometimes feel the sensations of cresting at the top or hitting bottom – otherwise, I have no sense of which way I'm headed except that it's too fast and I'm not in control.

I refuse to talk to another shrink. It has less to do with admitting I've got a problem than it does with having the problem carefully analyzed, documented, and then discreetly and "anonymously" reported to everyone else, including NMSP, by someone who has no frame of reference for my experiences. Mostly I'm tired of the very idea of answering all the same damned questions about what happened to me, ending with the same ultimate question, "So how does it make you feel?"

How is it supposed to make me feel? Am I supposed to feel normal?

I don't want to feel ANYTHING anymore. Not even normal.

Another card said to jump ahead.

I scanned my handwriting in between markers, knowing what it said, but found nothing of real interest. When I went to the next bookmark, I realized where this would all lead.

Last night. . .

After I left Monica's, I drove around a couple of hours, south to Belen and back. I was cruising east from Old Town, past the university on Central, thinking I wasn't ready to go home.

On a whim, I turned left into the parking lot of a bar where I'd been once on a stabbing call.

I parked well away from the entrance toward an adjacent furniture store that's been going out of business for the last three years. On the other side of the lot is a small motel advertising triple-X rated movies in flashing red neon. There was a streetlight on the other side of the street, about 150 feet away, so I was sitting in shadows.

I sat there for a while, watching in my mirrors to see if there were people moving around in the parking lot. Not many. The few obviously drunk and rowdy sorts stumbled toward their cars, ready to contribute to the after-midnight Albuquerque fatality statistics.

Finally, I got out of the Wrangler and headed to the door. The music became more deafening with each step, drumming through my bones up to my skull. As I reached out to pull the door open, it swung toward me in a whoosh of stinky smoke and cheap booze.

Why do I go to bars anyway?

In the doorway stood a man so broad-shouldered, I couldn't have squeezed around him to go in, had my intentions not vaporized like the cloud of dust I kicked up when I skidded to a dead stop.

Everything about him screamed bad attitude. His body language may have been convincing to some that he was shit-faced drunk, but the look in his eyes told me he was stone-cold sober. Even in the shadow beneath the black Stetson hat, his eyes locked my gaze until I turned tail toward my Jeep like a rabbit from a wolf. Running wouldn't help if this devil in faded jeans gave chase.

I'm not even sure he took a step from the doorway to reach for my arm when I turned, but suddenly his hand was wrapped all the way around my right arm, just above my elbow, in a grip that did not cause pain but indicated the profound ability to do so.

"I'm sorry, ma'am, did you want to go in?" he asked, mocking me.

I tried to yank my arm from his grasp, but his body hardly registered the motion.

"No? Then let me walk you to your car," he said, directing me toward my Wrangler as if it had a homing beacon flashing in the darkness.

There was nothing except the hand on my arm to exhibit any sort of threat. No reason to be afraid really, except I was in a poorly lit parking lot of a seedy bar in a not-so-upscale part of Albuquerque, being escorted away from the only people who might be able to protect me, though even that was laughable.

Before I could think to initiate any further physical response, he stood beside me next to my Jeep.

"Open the door," he said quietly, propping one elbow on the roof.

I reached out and pulled the door open.

"Get in," he said, letting go of my arm after nudging me toward the seat.

I slid in behind the steering wheel.

"A little advice, Blue Eyes," he said, moving inside the path of the door when I reached to close it. "One, lock your car or it might not be here next time."

I couldn't bring myself to turn and look at him again, so I nodded. I didn't know what I expected, but a lecture wasn't on the menu.

"Two," he said, pulling the buckle so I could take it, "always wear your seatbelt."

I pulled it across and clicked it into the receiver at my right hip. Then I didn't know what to do with my hands, so I dropped them in my lap and stared ahead.

He was silent for a moment, watching me. He was so tall, he had to lean down to see me inside. He reached in and turned my face to his with gentle fingertips and waited until I looked up into his eyes.

"Three, you should think about why you came here tonight. Maybe I'm wrong, but if you sleep on it and decide you really should have walked in that door for some wild reason, then you call me. I'd

like to hear it."

He handed me a business card with nothing but a handwritten phone number, closed the door and walked away.

So, it's almost 5 a.m., and I've had four hours to think about why I considered going into that bar.

In nothing but sheer defiance, I picked up the phone and dialed the number.

Two rings.

"Yes."

Same calm voice. No indication of surprise. No question. No expectation.

"Who are you?"

"My name is Zach."

I didn't know what else to say.

"Who <u>are</u> you?" I asked again.

"Someone who didn't rip you into bloody fucking rags and leave you dying in the alley," he said in a calm smooth voice with a slight cadence from south Texas or Louisiana.

Silence lasted a long time. I realized I was holding my breath, unable to speak.

"Disappointed I didn't?" he asked.

While I was struggling with what was supposed to be an obvious answer, he simply hung up.

Was I? A chill ran through me. The answer was the key to my soul.

Although Jeremy explained how he wanted to know more about this incident, a card tucked tightly into the binding referred him on to the next book, in January 1992. He browsed between the cards but found no further reference to the mysterious man, so he picked up the next journal.

Only one line caught his eye: *They call this survival, but it's like dying and never quite getting to dead.*

CHAPTER 56

"By then, I was hooked. I had to keep reading," Jeremy said.

"Why?" I demanded. "What possible reason did you have to pick them up at all?" But I knew. The killer was trying to show him who I really was.

Tucked into the journal, another card prompted Jeremy ahead to mid-January.

This section I knew by heart, but I read it anyway. It was less a reflection of what happened than a detached accounting, like I had watched it instead of living it.

Monica and I went out to that new cowboy bar last weekend to see an up-and-coming singer whose career I suspect won't outlast the bar itself, which changes hands and names about once a year. Not bad, but no personality. And louder ain't better.

Monica danced with a couple of guys, but she had to work early in the morning and left around eleven. I stayed because I was bored, and at least there were people to ignore here. I sat in the booth in the corner toward the entrance, refusing dance invitations of those few concrete cowboys who ventured far enough into the shadows to find me.

I'd had one beer when we first came in and half a dozen refills of the no-name cola stuff that comes from the spigot with the other mixers and tastes like crap. No one but me and the server knew I wasn't drinking alcohol, so it could have looked like I'd be pretty drunk by now. I kept paying, because my glass stayed full. The waitress brought the beer ordered for me by a real dude-looking guy (or maybe I mean "dud") a few tables away. I nodded but left it untouched. On her next pass, she took it away with a smile.

I'd had enough with one beer, but after all the liquid, I thought I'd hit the restroom before I left. Heading across the bar to the restrooms in the opposite corner, I tried to avoid the congregation around the center bar and the racetrack dance floor. The lighting faded away toward the back where the walls are all painted black and decorated with neon light designs.

I was almost past the rear bar when I felt a hand wrap on my right arm.

I wheeled around with full intentions of dropping its owner with a knee to the groin, except I found myself face to mid-chest with. . .

Zach

. . . who wasn't about to be kicked, easily turning me away from him with his fingers again wrapped around that spot above my elbow where the nerves compress against bones.

Even if I'd had a clear shot at his crotch, he could simply have squeezed and dropped me to the floor in agony with almost invisible effort.

"'Evening, Blue Eyes," he said in a casual baritone I heard over the music. "I see your taste in entertainment has improved a little."

I instinctively jerked my arm, but only succeeded in proving I could not remove it from his grip despite several more months in the gym. The effort was not only wasted but painful.

I was irritated, but not afraid.

No other pleasantries. No friendly advice this time.

Instead, the hand drove me like an errant child through the hallway past the restrooms and out an emergency exit, the sign above the crash bar clearly stating an alarm would sound.

It did not.

There were a couple of guys standing out behind the refrigeration units and stacks of bottle crates, smoking or something. Neither gave our passing a second glance.

Zach led me past them, and when I thought to turn and ask for help, his fingers at my elbow tightened, convincing me that not only was that a bad idea, but that I would be unable to speak if I tried.

He led me toward a car so average it would have been

impossible to find in a crowded mall parking lot. About ten years old. Dark, but in the tungsten lights, there was no way I could tell what color it was. Four doors. I couldn't identify the make or model, and I should have been able to. Yellow New Mexico plates, but I couldn't see the numbers.

I felt the panic rise.

He opened the back door on the driver's side, and with the slightest pressure, indicated I should get inside.

No. Worst place to end up is inside the car.

With one more yank, I pulled my arm free of his hand and sidestepped left to escape.

I didn't even sense him move, but suddenly I was wedged between him and the car, his bulk easily pinning me, one hand pulling my ponytail, the other wrapped around my throat, His fingertips pressed against the red scar under my left ear and on the carotid artery hard enough my vision wavered.

What didn't surprise me was how easy it was for him to make it look like I was there willingly, like we'd escaped the crowd for a little privacy.

He leaned down and whispered in my ear.

"Get in the fucking car, or I'll drop little pieces of your body on the freeway from here to Los Angeles like so much roadkill." Then he tilted my face up to his with his hand and kissed me, hard, biting my lower lip, staring straight into my soul with dark green eyes.

I gasped and tried to pull away.

When he straightened up, I saw the two bouncers or whoever they had been, were gone. I didn't see anyone else.

He pushed me into the backseat of the sedan, then wiggled his way in to sit beside me, his legs barely fit behind the front seat, pushing me toward the passenger side. In the time it took him to get settled, the two men who had been outside the door when we left the building reappeared and got into the front seat.

I scooted to my right and reached for the door handle beside me, but there was none. The driver started the car and headed out of the alley.

In a string of profanity that would have made my father blush, I reached forward and tried to grab a handful of hair of the man sitting in front of me then slammed my left elbow into the big man's solar plexus when he reached for me.

Both tasks failed, owing to the short hair of one and the quick reflexes of the other.

The driver stopped the car so the shotgun passenger could join us in the backseat, though he seemed to do so with resentment.

"Where to, Z'?" the driver asked as we approached the entrance ramps for both east and westbound I-40.

He looked at me and laughed. "Looks like it could be a long evening, Dom. Guess we better go west. Can't have her screaming at the apartment all night."

Jeremy wanted to read more, I'm sure, but the tale ended.

I had not written the rest of what happened. The next entry in the journal wasn't for three weeks, with no explanation of the gap, nothing to tie the events together.

The card referred him to the next entry toward the end of the same book, which began when I was getting ready to move to Michigan.

Jeremy thumbed forward through the book but found no further mention of Zach or explanation of what had happened that night.

"After that, your mood was so somber and heavy, like breathing was a huge effort," Jeremy said. "It's a textbook description of depression. I didn't know what else to do. I finally put the books down and called you."

The killer left the rest of the surprises for me to explain.

CHAPTER 57

I stood there looking at the journals and gray plastic bin Jeremy dragged out of my closet. I felt so overwhelmed by the naked feeling of knowing two men had read them, but keenly conscious of an entirely new emotional issue brought to light with Jeremy.

I didn't need to read my words about Zach and what had happened the rest of that night. The entry in the book ended with the drive westward in the car with three men.

Obviously, the story did not.

Jeremy wanted to know not only why this particular passage was being dragged from my skeleton closet but what really happened, but I couldn't tell him.

You don't share some secrets with anyone.

What I hadn't written in my journals and what I couldn't tell Jeremy was this:

West of Albuquerque, there are endless starry skies over nothing but empty miles after sunset.

I couldn't estimate how far we drove, about a half hour I guess. The lights of the city were no longer glowing behind us.

Panic overtook my good sense, and I began thrashing around, trying to kick, though the left side of my brain knew there was no way I could overpower either man, much less both, to get out of a car moving at freeway speed.

Zach, or whatever his name was, finally shouldered me against the seat. "Knock it off before you get hurt," he growled.

Several miles later, the driver took an exit onto the access road and then turned north several miles later, ending up at an isolated house surrounded by moonless black.

The driver got out and opened Zach's door from the outside first, then the other guy's, who turned and swung his legs out the door.

"Give him your boots," Zach told me.

I didn't move.

"Give me your boots or I'll take them off you the hard way," the other guy repeated, reaching toward me.

"Fuck you," I said, jerking away.

Zach, who was still trying to get his legs wiggled out, swung his right arm over my head, pulling me into a chokehold.

I made the mistake of reaching up with both hands to pull, but he snatched my left wrist in his right hand, immobilizing me further.

Then I heard the *snick* of a switchblade next to my left ear, and he flashed the knife just into my field of vision.

"You'll let Pauly pull those boots off without a fuss, or I'll start right now," he whispered.

I froze.

Mentally. Physically.

There was no flashback to previous events. Just brain lock.

My boots came off. I don't remember how.

Somehow, Zach unfolded from the car and then pulled me out and swung me over his shoulder, easily carrying me into a house where the lights were now on.

He set me down on my socked feet and stood over me, towering like a father over a misbehaving child. Like a god over a heathen mortal.

I could barely stand.

I had to remember to breathe.

The driver walked by and handed him a pair of handcuffs.

With a wiggle of his fingers, Zach motioned for me to extend my arms.

Dumbfounded, in terrified resignation, I simply offered up both hands. I felt the warm metal click into place over both wrists simultaneously.

Smith & Wesson cuffs, Model 100. Blue. Very used.

Then he reached into my hip pocket for my keys, and without

hesitating, he used my own S&W key to double lock the cuffs.

How would he know I carry a handcuff key?

He told me to sit down, and I slumped into the sofa behind me and watched as they knocked about the house, taking turns in the bathroom, getting drinks and snacks.

My ears were ringing, my heartbeat pounding in a high pitch so loud I could hardly hear their voices.

They ignored me, unconcerned I might step outside in the dark without a hint of which direction was which, into cactus, bear grass, rattlesnakes.

Snakes? It had to be near or below freezing. I'd die of hypothermia before I'd be bitten by a snake.

Discharging all logic, my mind had snapped to the conclusion that the worst possible outcome was likely – I'd be dead or dying by sunrise, having begged to live and prayed desperately to die – and no one would have a clue where I'd gone from the bar. Chances were good that my Jeep wouldn't even be there come morning.

So why not risk a run into dangers less than certain death? I took another look out into the darkness.

"I'll leave 'em in your trunk, Z'," one said, picking up my boots on his way out the door.

"These, too," Zach said, tossing him my keys.

The trunk. Probably where I'll end up, I thought.

How convenient. I should have run.

After the other two men got in the car and drove away, Zach came toward me, extending a hand to help me stand up.

"The bathroom is this way, Blue Eyes," he said, leading me down a hallway. "Towels and stuff, if you want."

Towels?

I closed the door behind me. There was a window, but it was too small to climb out. Same escape situation, barefooted and lost. Fall and break a leg, then he probably wouldn't even kill me. He'd leave me to die.

I unbuckled my belt, wiggled down my jeans, and finally urinated, remembering the bathroom was where I'd been headed when this began.

It took me a minute to figure out how to wipe since my hands were cuffed. *Like it matters.*

I flushed. Stood up and managed to get my pants up and my belt buckled. I ran a washcloth under cold water and wiped my face and neck. I sipped from the tap and then looked up at myself in the mirror, considering my options.

Didn't have any, short of bashing my head into the mirror.

The door opened.

"Out," he said.

He guided me down a flight of stairs toward to a more lived-in, comfortable area, maybe a family room or a den, with dark wood paneling and dim amber lights. He turned me to face him, an arm's length away.

"You remember me?"

"Yeah, from the bar on Central."

He tilted his head, "Remember what I told you, when you called that morning and asked who I was?"

I nodded.

"Do you believe I could do what I said? Or what I described at the car tonight?" he asked, holding his arms forward as a physical example, towering over me by close to a foot in his boots.

I just shrugged.

"You realize I can do absolutely anything to you I want to do, and you can't stop me?"

I looked away, feeling faint.

He took a step forward and wrapped his large hand around my throat tight enough to make my vision dim. "I can," he whispered, leaning close to my ear. "And I could do a lot worse to you than David Wesley did."

In a surge of adrenaline, my head snapped up involuntarily to his face. I pushed away from him with my arms, only because he let me.

He laughed at me.

I'd only managed to back into a wall.

"Wesley didn't do shit to you compared to what I will, Julie."

I was more astonished that he knew me, knew about me, than I was afraid of the threats.

He bent down and tossed me over his shoulder again and carried me through another doorway into a dark room, oblivious to my kicking and beating his back with my cuffed hands, and tossed me onto a bed.

"By the time we're done, Wesley's domestic violence assault will seem like a preschool birthday party."

I could barely see his silhouette in the light from the other room.

He kicked off his boots and peeled off his shirt, stopping once to grab my foot as I tried to scramble away, and then he crawled up on the bed, straddling my thighs, immobilizing my legs.

After I connected a two-handed swing and left a nasty scrape across his chest with the cuffs, he unbuckled my belt and put the chain between my wrists under it and buckled it back, securing my hands at my waist.

"Now, let's see what makes her scream," he whispered, leaning forward, unbuttoning my shirt and pulling it open, tracing the scar down the middle of my chest with a fingertip, causing a shiver I could not prevent.

I turned my head away from the light, hoping he couldn't see my face. My heart was pounding so loudly in my ears, it almost drowned out his whispers.

He reached into his hip pocket and pulled out a knife. Not the switchblade he'd had in the car. A folding hunting knife, which he held close to my face as he leaned down, taking a handful of hair in his other hand. Slowly, he swung the polished blade open with his thumb in front of my eyes.

The click as it locked open sounded like a cannon.

My brain and body reacted to the knife. In response to the next flood of adrenaline into my bloodstream, my pupils dilated, and I saw details about him and the knife not visible seconds before. My heart rate spiked again, preparing my body for a fight. But my muscles could not organize any sort of response against an opponent twice my size, sitting on my legs, with one handful of hair and another with a knife in my face.

My mind had already surrendered when he teased the knife blade against my cheek and lips.

I gasped for air, otherwise frozen in terror.

"I could start with your pretty face," he said in a singsong voice, pulling the blade flat to my jaw, sliding the tip against my chin and nicking the skin, then letting the metal trace on down my jaw to my neck under my left ear.

I closed my eyes and swallowed hard, but my mouth was dry.

"Oh, but this would be the most fun," he laughed.

He yanked tighter on my hair, pulling my head back, and dragging the point of the knife to the scar on the left side of my neck, where the sensitive nerves burned under the touch of the blade.

"Want me to do it again, Julie?" he whispered. "One swipe against your throat," he said, pressing harder, "and you can lie in a pool of your own blood again. Dying slowly."

The scream came from deep inside me – guttural and desperate, unlike anything I'd ever heard before. I flailed, trying to kick and hit, recklessly unaware of any injury I might be causing myself.

I screamed until I was almost choking, all fear and fight.

Finally, still restrained under his weight, I was exhausted. I felt like a gut-shot deer run down by a dog, collapsed and panting, wild-eyed, waiting for the final shot.

The hunter had no weapon.

He lay beside me, whispering into the night. "I know about the demons, Julie. They may not ever go away, but if you keep chasing them, you'll find them," he said softly. "Letting them kill you is still suicide."

CHAPTER 58

No, I couldn't tell Jeremy McNeeley all of that, so I explained what I could.

"Zach was a DEA agent working undercover in Albuquerque. He and the other two had been working a ring of cocaine dealers around different bars, just being part of the crowd. The first night I saw him, one of them recognized me from the Darcy Pierce case in Albuquerque when I came toward the bar. Nothing but coincidence. But when Zach came out to intercept me, he recognized me, too."

Jeremy listened as I told him about the aftermath of Zach's sister's rape.

"She went through these stages, he said. First not wanting to be alone at all, then not at night. She had an alarm installed, changed the locks every month. But Zach said after about six months, she suddenly changed. When she started staying out all night, he followed her to places where she knew she would be at risk. She was eventually murdered behind a liquor store."

"What did that have to do with you?" Jeremy asked.

"He watched Zoe commit suicide by letting the criminals kill her. He said I had the same look in my eyes as the night he confronted her about it. Prowling, he called it."

"Prowling," he echoed in a strangled voice.

Whatever emotion ran through Jeremy – maybe not fear but close – I could smell it on him.

"It's hard to describe," I said. "Not really looking for trouble, but putting yourself in places and situations where there is more likely to be a threat to your safety. It's similar to other risk-taking behaviors like sky diving or –"

"Like hell it is!" Jeremy exploded out of the chair, muttering medical school definitions of rationalization, displacement and avoidance as he paced. He was correct about them, but they didn't exactly apply.

I got up and got a beer for each of us, finally crossing paths with him in the living room. I sat on the love seat, facing him in the recliner when he finally composed himself enough to sit.

"Is that what you were doing at the bar that night – what you wrote about in your journal?" he finally asked, putting the pieces together.

I nodded.

"Why?" he asked, calmer.

I wasn't sure I could explain.

"We used to talk about adrenaline rushes, right? That jacked-up feeling when you're running hot, working a code? Some people become addicted to that rush, whether it's gambling, sex, danger. I think I was an adrenaline addict long before I met David, but it got out of control after I shot him."

Jeremy stared at me, but nodded for me to go on, swirling the beer in the bottle.

I took a breath and continued. "I've been hooked on that rush as long as I can remember. When I was about 13, my father and I drove up on a crash. He told me to stay in our car while he went to help, but I got out and stood with other people who stopped but couldn't do anything. I remember this feeling inside me I couldn't explain – like butterflies. The man in the car had been ejected during a rollover and was almost dead when my father got to him. I didn't see much directly, but hearing Dad tell about it later only heightened my experience."

Jeremy nodded.

"When I found my father in his office after he'd been shot, you can imagine the overwhelming dump of adrenaline. The whole event was so charged with emotion that each time the detectives questioned me, the rush hit me again so hard, I could barely control myself – I'd get all jazzed, unable to sit down and have a conversation. I had to move. When we were done, and sometimes even before, I had to run.

I could run for miles then just drop," I explained.

Jeremy finished his beer without responding.

"That rush is as much as I know about being high, but I liked it. And because so many people wanted to talk about Dad's case, I had to learn to stay cool because my mother started talking about sending me to a shrink. Then I noticed that rush sorta faded a little each time, so I stopped talking about it except when I absolutely had to. Saving it all for myself. Later, I learned new ways to turn it on and enhance the burn. Even now, like your yoga makes you relax, I can think about that day and set off another blast of adrenaline."

"I don't understand. Why?"

"I like the rush," I repeated. "Gambling addicts don't gamble because they like poker or slots. Sex addicts don't have sex for love. It's not because I liked reliving the moment of finding my father bleeding to death, or any of the dozens of other close calls. It's the exhilaration of knowing how close I came to dying."

He nodded.

"After the emotional and chemical kick of having a gun held to my head, shooting David, what else could possibly cause more of an adrenaline high? But because I was stuck in a hospital room, I couldn't enjoy the rush, and later it came laced with depression and a horrible guilty self-deprecating loathing." I emptied my beer bottle and ran my thumbnail under the label around the neck. "Zach recognized that. He called it suicide by fate. But because he had the guts to make me face it, it doesn't control me like it did."

"You mean you still . . . " Jeremy hesitated.

I looked up, and our eyes locked.

Everything between us rested on how he accepted this one answer. We both knew it.

"Do you?" he asked.

In my mind, I heard Matt's words again, about love not being enough.

I inhaled to answer, but Jeremy held up a hand to stop, shaking his head. The change in his attitude sucked the air out of the room.

Jeremy backed down from wanting to know the truth.

I stood up, suddenly needing to tower over him.

"Yes, Jeremy. I still fight this demon the way an alcoholic fights a bottle. Yes, sometimes I drive, looking for places with that very thought in mind. *What if I park here and walk through there*," I said. "But you know something? The reason I don't actually stop the car is because I've seen something most addicts don't – I've seen the demon I can't kill. But I don't chase it anymore, either. The only reason I understand that is because Zach had the guts to show me the demon's face by holding a knife to my throat and asking me if I really wanted to die."

Jeremy looked bewildered, but I couldn't stop.

"You can't imagine this. That's why it's so hard to live with this secret. Wouldn't it be more socially acceptable if I'd taken up a risky sport like rock climbing or parachuting? People understand that. Maybe say, 'Oh yeah, it's just residue from this trauma in her younger years. . . '" I paced now. "I'm not *permitted* that luxury. Even people who say they love me can't accept this. And hiding it nearly killed me."

I turned my back on him, looking out into the backyard but seeing nothing.

"So what about the cop? Where is he today?"

Where indeed?

"Zach? He's wherever the DEA sends him, and screw you for even asking. I haven't had to apologize for being married or having children somewhere. You want to talk about *my* life? Fine. This is about me. Today," I said, pacing in front of him. "You've offered afterthought apologies since you got here for every one of your heartbreaking little secrets, and my feelings be damned, but they're all still today's news."

He tried to interrupt me, but I whirled back to face him and jerked down the collar of my shirt to reveal the scar.

"I didn't ask for this, and I'm tired of defending myself for having survived it and for living with its consequences the way I do. If you can't live with my secrets, then get the hell out of my house and out of my life, Jeremy. You thought I couldn't change my future for you. I sure as hell can't change my past." I realized how close I was to launching the beer bottle at the wall above his head. It seemed like a perfect way to punctuate my last sentence.

He stood up and stepped toward me.

I took a breath and moved backward.

"You can't heal the scars, Jeremy. You can't erase the memories. You can't reprogram my emotions. Just like you, I'm a package trip, with all the baggage. Take it or leave it," I said quietly. "But you need to understand why this killer told you to read my journals because, like Forrester, you don't get it. There's no use threatening to kill me – I still don't give a damn. The only way he can hurt me is by threatening or killing people I care about."

CHAPTER 59

I set the bottle on the table, turned and went to the garage.

I didn't know whether he would follow, but we both needed time to cool off. I turned on the overhead light and took a polishing cloth from a bag on the shelf. I needed to focus my attention on something small, detailed and inanimate. Something I had control over. Something calming.

Motorcycles offer endless chrome to polish.

Sitting cross-legged on the cold concrete floor, with a rag and tube of expensive polishing stuff that probably only bikers and car nuts would buy, I let my brain separate details and sort emotional reactions from logic and facts.

What Zach did for me was so deeply personal that I couldn't journal it, for which I was relieved now. I might have found words to write about him at the time or later, but I would never want to share them. I was utterly relieved the story was unwritten for the eyes of a killer as well as for Jeremy.

I couldn't tell Jeremy where Zach was today in my life any more than I could say where he was in the country. All I knew was Zach had changed the way I looked at myself, and I was thankful for what he'd done for me, even if it was unorthodox, like the rest of that night in Albuquerque four years ago.

After Zach uncuffed me, I cried myself to sleep in his arms as he stroked my hair and held me, telling me over and over that everything would be okay. Then he tucked me in and quietly slipped away.

He woke me later and helped me to my feet, leading me to the bathroom where he'd run a bath and lit a dozen candles for me.

"I won't come back unless you call," he said, closing the door behind him.

My mind felt still sluggish with the lack of sleep and the waking up, from leftover chemicals of fear and release. Muscles ached, weak from the struggle.

But I was alive and whole.

I stepped into steaming water scented with magnolia and vanilla. A half-dozen fat candles cast dancing shadows on the walls.

He could have done anything, as he'd said. Without a single weapon, he could have easily broken bones and dislocated joints with little effort. Given the knife, the possibilities were endless.

In my post-recovery condition, I was physically unable to resist any physical threat, though I probably would have been relatively helpless against someone his size at the peak of my career, once restrained in the car. So I didn't exactly understand why I was sitting in bubbles instead of lying in a pool of my own blood in the trunk of his car.

"Hello?" I called quietly, testing to see how far away he was.

"Yes," he said, like he'd answered the phone that first time when I'd called the number on the card. Not a question. Just a statement.

Not far away.

"Would you bring us something to drink and come talk to me?" I asked.

"Hot tea?" he offered.

I guess I was expecting beer. "Um, yeah. Sugar, please."

While I waited, I drained a little water and filled more hot water in. He knocked a few minutes later and waited.

"Come in."

The candles whiffed in the draft from the door, and the breeze chilled me slightly, soI settled further into the deep bubbles and water.

The room was dark despite the candles because they were set so far away from the tub. I wondered if this had been intentional.

He was still wearing jeans, but he'd put on a different long-sleeve shirt – a soft faded denim with the sleeves rolled up to mid-forearms. He had buttoned several but not all the buttons to pull it closed over his broad chest.

I guessed it was his favorite, though I don't know why that even crossed my mind, except he looked so comfortable in it.

In the candlelight, I saw his hair was damp, and I presumed he'd showered while I slept.

From a small tray he'd placed on the vanity, he handed me a large mug with a tea bag still steeping. I dunked it a few more times, then lifted it out to the saucer he offered for me to drop it on. He extended the sugar bowl and spoon to me. I added one spoonful and nodded.

He pulled the tea bag from the other cup, stirred it with the same spoon, and sat down on the floor against the door. As far away from me as possible. His face was barely illuminated in the flickering candlelight, but still it was the best chance I'd had to look at him without fear or confusion.

"Thank you."

He merely nodded and lifted his cup toward me.

"Is your name really Zach?"

"So my mother tells me," he said, smiling a bit lop-sided. "You don't recognize me?"

"Should I?"

He nodded. "You may not have ever known my real name. When I was a kid, everyone called me Cubby."

"Cubby . . . Samualson?" I exclaimed.

Vera Samualson was one of my mom's best friends, but her kids were so much younger than me that the friendship of mothers hadn't crossed over to their children.

"Oh my," I said in a slow Southern drawl, "and didn't you grow up just fine."

"Since you last saw me at your father's funeral, yeah, I've grown a little."

"Two-and-a-half feet, I'd say."

He laughed. "Probably. You grew up pretty nice, too."

I turned away, feeling my skin flush even more.

"Why the elaborate ruse? Why didn't you tell me who you were that night?"

"I had this feeling when I saw you at that bar that you weren't interested in meeting old acquaintances. You wouldn't have believed me if I'd told you I knew why you were there."

I looked down to my cup, then shook my head. "So how did you know what had happened to me? Last I heard anything about you, you'd moved to Houston."

"Right after I started at the DEA, I came home on a short break, and Mom told me. I visited you in the hospital. You were still in Trauma ICU."

"I don't remember."

"You were pretty drugged – she warned me before I went. You woke up long enough to ask me who the hell I was."

"Sorry. No offense."

"None taken. You didn't know me."

"Why?" I asked. "I mean, why did you come to the hospital?"

"I wanted to see you," he said, as if it explained something.

"And what about seeing me at that bar?"

"Actually, because you sat in the parking lot so long, Pauly ran your plates and recognized your name. We didn't think you were part of what was happening, but no one knew. When you came toward the door, I had to intercept you. What was going on inside, we didn't need someone else with a badge interfering," he explained. "Then I saw your eyes."

I nodded, though I didn't really understand.

"I followed you home that night."

"Followed me home?" I repeated.

"You drove around aimlessly for another hour. I sat two houses down from your mom's until you called me."

"No shit? I guess I missed that." Pretty plain to see where my head really had been. "So you decided to kidnap me the next time you found me alone?"

He shrugged. "After I followed you a few more days, I got a feel for what you were doing. I knew I was right."

"For crying out loud, it's not like you're easy to disguise! Really?"

"Yeah, really. Mostly by car – you did a lot of driving," he said. "I kinda led my mother into a conversation about Dagmar and then you. She told me how your rehab had gone, that your mother was worried about you. Mom speculated your career with the state police was over, even though no one had mentioned it formally."

"I'm sure a lot of people were discussing it," I said.

"I didn't talk to anybody at the department or anyone else about it. I let my partners know I wanted to find you and that you were leave-of-absence state police. Didn't say why, and they didn't ask. Dom saw your Jeep at the bar last night and called me. I took a seat by the one place I figured you'd go eventually – the restroom. If you hadn't, I'm afraid you'd have found your Jeep had a flat tire. Oz asked you to dance once, but you declined." He smiled. "He said you were polite, though."

I couldn't help smiling, too, so I hid it behind the cup. "That's quite a screenplay."

"I was half-afraid you'd start a brawl in the bar or that maybe you were carrying. When I grabbed you and you didn't scream, I figured I might get you out to the car without you making a scene, though God knows why. I really expected a struggle."

"How far would you have gone?" I asked softly.

"I didn't know." He hesitated but didn't look away. "Not until that kiss."

I blushed, despite the hot water already reddening my skin. "No, I mean how far would you have pushed me physically?"

"There's not much I wouldn't have done to reach you. I didn't know how this would work out, but I knew I only had one shot at it. I wouldn't have really hurt you, Julie, I swear," he said, then paused. "I only knew I couldn't wait for you to let someone else hurt you."

I believed he was telling the truth. "I don't know what to say. You showed me something tonight I wouldn't have believed possible. I thought I was long past the point of caring."

"You must be good at hiding it. People who love you don't see it either."

"I don't want anyone to love me. My life has been hell the last year."

"I once read Hell is where the sadist must be nice to the masochist," he said, getting to his feet. He paused before opening the door. "I'd say we're both damned."

And then he left me alone in the candlelight, wondering what he meant.

I shampooed my hair, and then emptied the tub, drying on a huge fluffy towel that I wrapped around me.

I blew out the candles, and left the bathroom in wisps of smoke, opening the door slowly.

The dim amber lights in the family room helped illuminate him sitting in the oversized chair beside the bed.

I went into the bedroom and closed the door, leaving us in the light of one candle on the table next to him. I moved to where I was standing at his feet.

"You have to understand something, Zach. Whoever you are, you terrify me because you've seen something in me no one else can see," I whispered. "You see the secrets I try so desperately to hide."

He extended his hand and then pulled me closer when I reached out.

I sat on his lap, straddling his thighs as he had mine. Leaning forward, I ran my hands up his chest inside his shirt, unbuttoning it. My fingertips moved up his neck to his face. I traced his goatee and ran my fingers along his jaw and back into his thick dark hair.

Then I blew out the candle.

"I don't want anyone to love me," I said in the darkness, barely whispering, "but I need to know someone can still want me, that I'm not too. . . broken."

"Oh, Julie," he said, like his heart had just shattered. "I –"

I covered his lips with my fingers. "And I don't want your words."

I kissed him tentatively, lips scarcely touching at first. He responded, not the possessing way he'd kissed me in the parking lot. Gently, but desperate and barely in control, yet it left me trembling.

He slid his hands up my outer thighs, under the towel to my waist, his skin cool against mine.

The kiss lasted until finally he pulled us up from the chair, holding me against him, and carried me to the bed, unwrapping the towel. He peeled off his shirt and jeans.

Then in the total darkness, he made love to my body so tenderly he left me breathless and in tears, leaving no doubt he didn't need words.

Later, as light began filtering into the window, we lay tangled together, his arm wrapped protectively around my shoulders. He pulled the blanket over us, then smoothed my hair from my forehead.

"Zoe once tried to explain what she was looking to find when she went prowling, but I couldn't make sense of it. She said the only time she might ever feel alive again was if she was on the edge of dying."

I nodded, but didn't look up.

Zach had read the words carved in my soul.

CHAPTER 60

Zach had fixed breakfast as the sunlight peeked over the Sandias through the kitchen windows. He told me more about Zoe, that four years before, he watched his twin sister take the same long hike off a short pier.

"I worked for the Houston Police Department," he explained. "She was a graduate student at Baylor, a perfect life. Then she was raped. She was devastated initially, of course. I tried to help, but maybe it made things worse. I stayed at her apartment about three weeks, trying to help make her feel protected or at least like she might survive, whatever that means. She attended rape prevention and self-defense courses, went to counseling. Everything anyone suggested, she did." He shook his head.

Words failed me, hearing his story.

"The only thing I learned was that men have no clue how to deal with rape victims. That's a big plus with DEA – no more rape cases. I don't think I could process another." His attention drifted a moment and then he stared at me. "Ever."

He served me bacon and fluffy scrambled eggs with onions, jalapenos, mushrooms, and avocado slices on top.

"I thought she was doing better after a month or so. Then, she went from the obsessive self-protection behavior that sorta made sense to cycles of extreme risk-taking. I couldn't imagine *me* doing the things she did. She started going places she'd never gone in broad daylight – cruising parking structures, walking around the eastside neighborhoods with gangs, walking the strips where the prostitutes hung out. I caught her one night, leaving her address and an apartment key under the windshield wiper of a car at a porn shop parking lot. That's when I lost my head and confronted her. She completely shut me out after that."

Silence hung for a few bites, each of us recalling a past that could not be forgotten.

"I have no idea what she endured during that time, whether she was ever actually. . . with anyone. I tried to understand, to help. Zoe couldn't explain what she was doing – it made no sense to me," he said, his voice tight. "She was killed eight months later, beaten and raped in an alley around the corner from a liquor store." He paused, pushing the food around on his own plate, but no longer eating. "I heard the call go out, and I just knew it was her. Detectives tried, but no one could keep me from looking. Bastards stuffed her behind a trash Dumpster."

"I'm so sorry, Zach." I reached out and put my hand on his arm.

"After she was murdered, I began to feel what she was going through. I went crazy, you know? I finally understood what it was like not to care if I lived or died. I began to see that same look in the mirror. Her eyes," he said, leaving the statement unfinished. Instead, he pulled his shirt open, revealing a shotgun blast pattern on his upper chest and shoulder. "I nearly cost my partner his life. That's when I applied to the DEA, thanks to a guy I went to school with here."

He pulled his shirt closed and buttoned a few buttons.

"Will you promise me something?" he asked.

"No," I said. I chewed another mouthful, almost shivering at the feeling that he could see through my skin. "What?"

"Zoe went in and out of this in cycles. When you feel like going prowling, will you call me? Talk to me. I know you think you can't tell anyone else in the world about this, but you can tell me. Just talk about it first?"

"Right, so you'll come kidnap me and scare the hell out of me again?"

He raised an eyebrow, trying to hide a smile.

I thought about it. "Maybe."

* * *

When Zach dropped me at my Jeep later that morning, he made sure his partners had aired the tire up for me, then he left me with a gentle kiss.

I went home, not knowing what to expect from my mother after being gone all night.

She was still lounging in her robe at a quarter till eleven, which wasn't unusual, but she didn't look like she'd slept well.

I came in and poured a cup of coffee and sat down with her at the breakfast nook.

"I'm sorry I didn't call and tell you I wasn't coming home last night," I said. "By the time I realized I wouldn't be in, it was already very late, and I didn't want to wake you."

"Julie," she said over her half-rim reading glasses, "You're a grown woman. The only reason I was worried is that you don't normally stay out all night, not that I care if you do."

"After Monica left the bar, I ran into a couple of cops, and we went to one's house for the evening, and it turned into breakfast."

Okay, so it wasn't exactly the truth, but the facts were more or less correct.

"Don't you ever meet normal everyday people – salesmen, doctors, theologians?" she asked still pretending to browse the paper, then looked up at me. "No, I guess you don't, do you?" She smiled. "You are who you are. I still love you."

"I'm not a preacher's type, Mom."

"No, nor preacher's kid's type, either, I recall. Reverend Harrison was quite relieved when his son finally got over his crush on you in second grade. Something about a frog in the boy's lunch box, wasn't it?" She raised her eyebrows.

I feigned innocence, but we both knew it wasn't a snake only because I couldn't catch one.

"Well, it sounds like a nice diversion from your usual ho-hums. Cops? People you knew before?"

"Sorta," I said, sipping casually. "I ran into Zach Samualson. Have you seen him lately? He's a big boy." I had to suppress a grin.

"Cub? I haven't seen him since Zoe's funeral, I guess." She went back to her newspaper.

"I don't think you told me about her murder," I said.

"No?" she said. "I probably forgot to mention it."

She browsed the pages while I nibbled on a muffin, but she finally lowered them and said, "I know this has been very hard on you, Julie. I wish you'd talk to a counselor."

"Mom, don't –"

"No, please just listen. When I buried your father, I hurt so bad I couldn't breathe, but I still had you to take care of. I wanted to help you, but I couldn't fight with you about it."

"Fight about what?" I asked, trying to remain open to a conversation I didn't want to have.

She made a sound of exasperation.

"Everyone made such a big deal about how I was supposed to feel about Dad's murder," I countered. "People told me I had to be strong for you when Dad died. No one else had been through what I had. No one else hurt like I did, not even you. At first, everyone asked if I was okay. How was I supposed to answer that? If I said yes, then they went on about their business. If I said no, they didn't know what to say next. After a few weeks, no one asked me anymore, like I was supposed to be okay again by magic."

"I never knew what to say to you, what to do for you," she said, but then her tone changed. "You had always been so much like your father. I was torn between keeping you close so I would have the little pieces of him I saw in you and pushing you away so it would quit reminding me of him. I'm sure I did both. I could not imagine how it was for you. I probably didn't do the right things for you because I didn't know what to do."

I still didn't know what to do for me.

"You were at a point in life when you wanted to be comforted like a child, but you felt you had to be an adult. You always acted so much older than your age," she said. "Seeing what David had done, I was terrified of losing you, too. All I could think about was Stoney and all the blood on you. And forgive me, I prayed that you'd live so I could find a way to finally reach out to you and make up for not being there when your father died. If there is nothing else good to come of this, let it be that we are closer. We're all we have, Julie."

I reached out to her. She took my hand in hers. The skin was warm and soft.

"I'm sorry I've been so hard to take care of, Mom. No two people grieve alike. Adults don't know how kids grieve. Losing my father was so much different than you losing a husband. And it's different with David."

Yeah, it's very different when you kill your husband. But I was there as they were dying. You weren't, Mom.

I couldn't say that to her.

"I can't imagine what it's been like."

She never could imagine what it was like for me. From the time the police went to the door to notify her about Dad while I sat in the back of the patrol car, to when I refused to leave the cemetery at his funeral.

At my father's service, I had demanded a shovel from a rather flabbergasted funeral director, and made him lower the coffin while I watched. Then I stood on the edge of the hole, shoveling dirt onto the coffin, insisting on filling in his grave myself.

That pushed Mom over the edge.

It bothered the funeral director, to be sure.

I closed my eyes as I remembered the smell of the freshly turned dirt. I hadn't planned it. As a kid, there were no words to explain it, but I felt I had to do it.

I'd run away and left him to die, so it was my responsibility to finish this.

Mom tried to stop me, arguing that people were waiting for us at the church. That I was getting dirty. That I was making her crazy.

I refused to listen to any reason.

Finally, Dad's older brother, Jeff, came and asked if he might help me. I nodded, so he got another shovel and took off his jacket.

As we worked, he talked about Dad's determination and integrity, about what a good brother and friend he had been. Finally, when I dropped to my knees in physical and emotional exhaustion, Jeff helped me to my feet. On the way to the car, he said, "He was so proud of you, Julie. I'm sure the memory of your face and your love will give him eternal joy."

Those were comforting words, if you looked at it from my father's point of view. *What about my memory of his face, those last minutes, the blood and fear. . .*

Jeff asked the limousine driver to stop at the house so I could change clothes. I don't know what my uncle said to my mother while they were alone, but when I came out, she was calm. I suppose I was, too.

I don't remember the rest of the day.

CHAPTER 61

In the floor of my garage, polishing chrome, I let go of those memories.

"What should I say?" Jeremy asked from the door. "Besides I'm sorry. I feel like that's all I say to you, but I am."

I shrugged, unable to look at him. Another apology would make everything melt away too easily, and this one we were going to have to fight out the hard way. I kept polishing the muffler, but I could see his reflection.

He leaned against the kitchen doorway, watching.

"I can't pretend I understand it right now," he finally said, sitting on the step. "But I'll try."

A number of ugly responses raced through my mind – "Can you only pretend later?" or "What if understanding doesn't help?"

I managed to not say any of them.

"I have a lot of questions, though, Julie."

I dropped my hands to my lap and slumped. "I don't have all the answers. And the answers I do have? Some of them I can't tell you, and a lot of them you aren't going to like anyway. Are you always going to blame me?"

Jeremy's head jerked slightly before he spoke, betraying his defensive reaction. "I don't blame you for what happened."

"No," I said, getting up. "You blame me for how I've survived it, how I managed to cope with it. You can't accept who I am as a consequence."

His anger deflated a little. "Same consideration as before. Divorce final, case closed, maybe you can tell me things when and how you want, and we can talk on our own terms, instead of on a battlefield." He took a step closer and reached out to run a finger along the black tank. "If it's still worth something to you to salvage, it is to me."

"Loving someone shouldn't be this hard, Jeremy," I said, crumpling the rag and tossing it onto the shelf. "Facing the past isn't supposed to hurt like this."

CHAPTER 62

The phone rang.

Summoning a ghost by speaking its name.

As foggy as I usually am at two in the morning, I was instantly awake when I answered the phone, my heart racing at the sound of Zach's only word.

"Hey."

The call sounded distant, cellular maybe, hollow and noisy. At first, I thought he was in a bar, but there was no music.

"Hey," I replied, getting up, wrapping my flannel nightshirt around me and making my way out of the bedroom with the cordless handset.

Except for the background noises, there was a silence on the line. I knew something was wrong in Zach's world.

I got a glass of water and went to the den and settled in on the loveseat with a blanket.

Still silence. That was okay. We'd been here before.

I steeled myself for something dreadful to come from the darkness, out of the silence. Something needing translation to words.

Down the hall, from the spare bedroom, Jeremy came to check on me.

All he whispered was, "Are you okay?"

I nodded, though I wasn't sure. A shiver ran through me, making my skin prickle.

Whatever was wrong on the phone, this was the first time I'd considered Zach and Jeremy in the same context – men who had shared my bed.

What the hell was I thinking?

Jeremy left me in the darkness.

I listened to the phone, hearing distinct voices here and there, but no clear conversation. Keyboards. Radios.

A police station?

I could hear Zach breathe once in a while, a deep sigh hiding what he still hadn't found words to say.

Finally, I heard the noises change. Papers shuffled. Something banged, slammed shut. A chair squeaked and crashed. A door whooshed, then footsteps down a long empty hall.

He took another deep breath. He was listening to me breathe, and I was listening to everything.

Another door, then he was outside.

"Where are you?" I asked.

The car door slammed. "Largo. St. Pete, Florida." Halfway across the country from Albuquerque.

No idea how long he'd been there instead of in New Mexico.

I heard the engine rev. I guessed it was a Mustang, probably a convertible, given the sound of the wind. That was his favorite, despite the cramped space for a man who stands six-foot-six.

He made a little small talk about the weather, whether I'd talked to my mother lately, but I could tell his heart wasn't in it. Like the other noises around him, my answers were mentally filtered. Even when he asked what was going on in Michigan recently, I didn't mention what had happened to me in the last few weeks because this call wasn't about me.

Zach needed something.

I needed to listen to find out what.

First, he needed to find the words. I understood. If he'd shown up at my door, we'd be in bed, tangled in the sheets and long past tears before he'd let me see the wounds inside him.

He parked and killed the engine. He actually got out of the car to walk.

"I'm on the beach," he said. "It's empty."

"Mmm, barefoot on the shore, that sounds good. Warm sand between your toes," I began. I closed my eyes. "I can hear the surf. There must be a cool breeze ruffling your hair tonight. You probably need a haircut, don't you? Untuck your shirt, Cowboy."

"I need you." Another deep sigh.

"I'm here. Let's walk down the beach." A nice mental image, for me at least. "Wrap your arm over my shoulder as we walk, so I can be close. You've been on my mind."

You've no idea how much tonight.

"Yeah," he said. "You, too."

I could tell he walked a while further, then sat down. I heard that ragged, raspy sigh again.

"Zach, I'm here. Take my hand."

"I. . . Oh, fuck, Julie. . . " he sobbed.

All I could do was listen. Finally, I was able to put together most of his story from the pieces between bouts of tears.

It started with what was supposed to be a meth lab bust at a house. A team of DEA and Pinellas County SWAT deputies coordinated a tactical assault after a neighbor's call indicated that there had been young children living in the house, but she hadn't seen them the last two days.

The bust had gone okay, but several involved suspects were not taken into custody. One woman, when separated from the other five, told officers that her two small children had been taken from her after one of the dealers thought she had narc'ed on them. She gave police the address of a warehouse in South St. Pete where she thought the two missing suspects might be hiding, in hopes her children might be rescued.

An immediate turn was made to that location, where an entry team, including Zach, located the fugitives. Unfortunately, in retaliation for the raid on the house, the two men were in the process of torturing both children.

When the tactical team approached, one of the men stood on a stack of crates, holding the small boy by the nape of his ratty shirt and overall straps, shaking him like a rag doll, waving a pistol at him. Daring the men at the door to shoot him.

Approaching from a row of windows and seeing that the child's lower arm had already been cut off, two officers stood up and fired through the glass.

Zach was one of them.

The laws of physics being what they are, a bullet fired through a pane of glass is almost certain to deviate from its original course.

The intended target, a full-sized adult at 25 feet, waving around a limp three-year-old boy, took one of the first two bullets in the calf.

The other bullet, fired from outside the windows, ballistics still pending to determine whose gun fired it, had deflected and struck the child.

Not that it mattered. The missed takedown with the first shot only served to incite the suspect to shoot, first the boy, then the officers, who returned fire.

The suspect was wearing better body armor than any of the agents on the scene. He took seven hits by multiple officers before a head shot dropped him.

Despite the chaos around him, the medic on the team tried desperately to save the child's life, but the hemorrhage from loss of the arm alone had already caused shock. The three or four other gunshot wounds were fatal.

A little girl's scream from farther back in the building drew the team in search of the other child they might yet save. Four officers bolted through the maze of deserted machinery and junk, looking for . . . something.

And then Zach's story stopped.

I held my breath.

Whatever played out in his mind, words failed him again.

I understood.

Some memories need no further description, and words can do no justice. Like the Challenger shuttle launch several years ago or the Murrah Federal Building only months ago, words were inadequate. Those images can never be unburned from your memory.

"We screwed it up so bad, Julie," he sobbed. "We killed those kids."

I let him cry a bit. "Zach, when did this happen?"

"Two days ago."

So I figured he hadn't eaten, hadn't slept. He'd been questioned repeatedly.

Had anyone asked him or the others how they were? How they *really were?*

No. I doubted it. If someone had asked, it was damned certain no one wanted to hear anything but the standard, "Just fine, really, sir."

Shit.

"Z'?" I paused. "How are your guys?"

"Pauly took a hit in the leg going in. Ankle. Could be EOC." End of career.

"Anyone else hurt?"

He made a sound I took as negative.

"And what about you?"

"I'm blown, Julie. Fucking wasted."

"How can I help?" I asked softly.

More silence. "I probably shouldn't have called you like this, but. . . I was locking up my gun. I had to hear your voice."

"What?" I sat up. "Why?"

"They didn't take my badge, Julie. It's not that. They think the shooting was clean, I guess."

I waited.

"I left it so I wouldn't use it." He let that thought hang in the air between us, a desperate silent plea for help.

"Zach. . . what. . . Tell me what happened."

"That little girl was– " He made a sound like a wounded bear. "I've never seen. . . " he trailed off as his mind replayed it for him again.

Tension knotted my muscles, waiting for him to continue.

"No," he said, as if shaking the visions from his mind, letting anger replace anguish. "What that bastard was doing to that little girl, I'm surprised four men didn't unload every last round into him and send someone for more. As bad as Pauly was hurt, man, he'd have crawled out to the truck and dragged in a box of ammo with his teeth."

"Oh, Z', I'm sorry. What can I do?"

"I dunno, but I need help. I'm far enough gone to know that." The anger faded back to pain.

The despair in his voice broke my heart.

"This isn't your fault, Zach. You guys didn't cause this - you tried to save them."

He considered this. "Yeah, I guess."

"No one will hurt those children again," I said. "I wish you hadn't waited so long to call me."

"I couldn't do it yesterday. IA and debriefings and crap. They grilled us over and over."

"That's Internal Affairs' job."

"Trying to keep your shit together until everyone's through picking the wounds and digging through your soul. Damned if they don't act like we were. . . " He sighed again.

"Zach, if they don't ask the hard questions now, some asshole's attorney's gonna push buttons later. Let it go. They just want the facts. Hopefully it's all done."

"Yeah. I know." He took a deep breath.

I could sense him relax a little in the next pause.

"At least we don't have to live here. The deputies, this ain't goin' away for them," he said, the Texas drawl a little heavier than normal. Another deep breath. "I'm glad I caught you at home tonight."

"Me, too."

"I called twice last week, but either there was a freaky message on your machine about you being a real bad girl, or no answer. I made a couple of calls and got a little of the story. So I have to ask, Blue Eyes. What's it like to have a real monster?"

I could almost hear a smile in his voice.

"Oh, it's very interesting. A monster of my own," I chuckled. "Didn't think of it that way. A monster that blew up a crime scene under my feet. Who managed to drug me while I was in the hospital. It's been a wild ride –"

He interrupted. "Hospital? No one said anything about that."

"Bump on the head," I said evasively. "The monster visited my house several times while I've been away, leaving me little presents. And he sends me hints and evidence about our current investigation."

"Sounds like I should take notes," he said, kidding.

"The monster, as you call him, has kidnapped and is torturing Matt Shannaker, one of our deputies."

"Your friend? Damn, Julie. I'm sorry I joked about it," he apologized.

"But somehow, this is all focused on me, people I know. It's a mess."

"I think my source missed a few important details. Are you okay?"

"Yeah, but we can catch up on my case in daylight. Right now, I'm worried about you. Will you be all right? Really?"

He groaned as he stood up, "Yeah, I need to take some time off. Go home and see. . . *shit!*" he said suddenly. "Whatever happens, J', I love you!"

"What?" I said, my ears trying to make sense of his words over noises. But I didn't hear an answer.

I heard gunfire.

I heard him get hit, heard the bullets knock the breath out of him, and heard him fall.

"Zach!" I screamed.

CHAPTER 63

I heard Zach mumbling. To me, to God. I couldn't tell.

"Zach, where are you?"

I knew he was on a beach in Pinellas County, Florida, but that included miles of shoreline.

"Can you hear me? I don't know where you are, Zach. I can't help you! I need you to talk to me!" I begged.

Jeremy loped into the living room and sat beside me, but said nothing.

I motioned for him to bring me my cellular phone. I didn't know how else to help, but I guessed I'd have to start with Pinellas 911 and go from there.

How the hell do you call 911 in another state?

Zach could die before I could communicate with anyone who could find him.

I kept talking to him, trying to get him to answer.

But as I listened, I heard more gunfire, further away. Several different guns.

And then I heard more voices, coming closer. I heard Zach say, "'s okay, J'."

Tears in my eyes, "Zach, can you hear me?"

"Not very well, after," he groaned, "after you've been . . . screaming in my ear. Here. . . "

There was rustling on the line.

"Who is this?" a voice asked.

"Julie Madigan. Who is this?" I demanded in return.

"It's Domino. I'll call you back," he disconnected, just as I was taking a breath to start asking questions.

I dropped the phone to my lap and sat, trembling.

Jeremy wrapped the blanket around us and pulled me against him. He didn't ask questions.

I sat speechless for a while, looking for words, like Zach had. When I found them, I hardly had the energy to say them. "I just listened to Zach Samualson get gunned down on a beach in Florida," I said as tears burned my eyes. "I don't want to do this anymore. I want to do something where nobody dies."

I turned and buried my face in the blanket and cried for a while. After I'd used up all the tissue, I stood up and paced, trying to put together what I'd heard on the phone.

"Zach called me from an office, but then he went out on the beach without his gun because of a shooting incident two days ago," I said out loud to myself, looking out the window into the backyard. "Why doesn't that make any sense?"

Jeremy opened his mouth to join the conversation, but I must have made some gesture that told him to shut up. I don't remember doing it, but he fell silent.

I thought about what Zach had said about his gun. I initially presumed he meant he would use it in anger, but was he suicidal instead? Imagining what had happened 1500 miles away, I paced, recreating the conversation in my head.

Jeremy watched me.

"You must think I'm crazy."

He shook his head. "You process things through in a particular way. It works. That's why you're good at what you do."

After ten minutes of pacing and talking to myself, I'd come to two possible conclusions why Zach was on that beach without his weapon. I didn't care for either one of them.

I sat down next to Jeremy, waiting for Domino to call back.

It had been almost an hour, and I cuddled up next to Jeremy, who'd fallen asleep.

When the phone rang, I was immediately awake and on my feet.

"Madigan."

"It's Domino. He's okay. They're going to take out a piece of shrapnel in his neck. And he's getting some blood."

"Excuse me?" I shrieked.

"He's going to be okay, Julie."

"Hey, *going to be okay* is a lot different than *is okay.*"

"Julie, look, I got there and found him belly-down in the sand in a puddle of blood. I thought he was dead except he was talking. To you. He rolled over and handed me the phone and then he sort of passed out. The medics were right there. They put him on a backboard and hauled ass to the heli – hospital and –"

Give him credit, he almost got it.

"To the helicopter? Domino, they put him on Bayflite?"

That I'd pulled the helicopter name out of thin air seemed to have stunned him. I only knew because a friend in Albuquerque, Taylor Healy, had worked for Bayflite out of Bayfront Hospital in St. Petersburg before moving to New Mexico. I'd heard the name enough to be certain.

"You think you ought to bullshit your way past me? I heard the bullets hit him, Dom. I heard him drop. I deserve the truth. I'm too damned far away to do anything to help him right now. At least tell me the truth."

"You're right. I can't explain it all, okay? He'd been shot in the neck, right behind the left ear. I saw him go down and thought he had to be dead or a cripple or *something really fucking bad*, you know?" His voice trilled an octave higher.

"Take a breath, Dom. It's okay. Go on," I said, hoping the story didn't get any worse.

"They said the bullet went almost all the way through his neck side to side, but they said it didn't hit any bones, nerves, big blood veins or harteries," he said, missing the word, but making his point. "Or his throat, you know, his windpipe? The medics said that as much as he was bleeding, they expected him to die before they could get him to the chopper. Looking at where he fell on the beach, I figured I'd have to call you and tell you he was dead. I stood out there, shoveling bloody sand into HAZMAT bags, thinking what I'd say to you. They'd send brass to tell his mother, but I knew I'd have to tell you."

A shiver ran through me. "What about the shooter?"

"He went to the morgue. Multiple hits, not a prayer," he sort of laughed. "Kevlar wasn't his saving grace like it was Zach's, who also took two to the chest without penetration, but they'll leave bruises."

"Dom. I have to know. Zach told me he left the station without his gun. Was this –"

"Julie, stop. You'll figure it out or Zach can tell you. I can't talk about it now," he said in plain warning. He took a deep breath. "Listen. I'll put him on a plane as soon as the doc clears him. Go meet him in Albuquerque or somewhere, okay? He needs downtime." He paused. "We all do."

"He was telling me about the kids. I'm sorry, Dom."

"You know the last thing he said to me before they loaded him? He told me if he died, to make sure you know he loves you."

I couldn't say anything. I felt tears spill down my cheeks. "I know. I can't leave right now, Dom. I can't get away from this investigation. Take care of him, please?"

I hung up.

When I looked around, I realized I was alone in the den. I wasn't sure when Jeremy had left or why, but at the moment, it didn't matter. I curled up with my blanket and closed my eyes, trying to shut out the newest scenario in my head now, playing in full bloody dying color, even though the only input had been audio.

I couldn't stop the visual clips of what my imagination created. Couldn't stop the echo of gunshots ringing in my ears. Couldn't stop those desperate words Zach said as he thought he would die. Those three words I thought I never wanted to hear him say. Words I hadn't ever wanted so desperately to say back.

CHAPTER 64

In my office a few hours later, with a cup of coffee steaming its way to a caffeine and sugar buzz I desperately needed, I found the red new-message light blinking.

I hit the speaker button and dialed through the sequence of buttons to finally hear the two new voicemail messages.

Who did they get to record that? I wondered. Does she get royalty for every time it plays?

"Hi, honey," the most familiar voice in my world interrupted my wandering thoughts. "I checked my messages tonight from Ruidoso and found out you'd called. I hope it's about travel arrangements for Thanksgiving. I'm so excited you're going to come. I can't wait for you to meet Everett. He had to drive down this weekend to his cabin to show workers plans for renovations, so I rode down with him. We'll be back Sunday evening. I didn't want to wake you up, and you were already gone this morning when I called. Let's talk soon, and we'll make all the plans, okay?" She made a kissing noise. "I love you, sweetie. Bye!"

Recorded last evening about eleven o'clock. Nine in New Mexico.

I shook my head and laughed. "Who are you and what have you done with Dagmar?" That was definitely too bubbly for my mother. But at least she was safe. I needed to call her. I wondered why she hadn't paged me like I'd asked.

I hit the button to save the message and played the next.

Mundane work stuff. It would be a long day.

I sat staring at the walls around me and focused on a framed cartoon – the only thing I'd taken from my father's office after he died.

Done by Bill Mauldin, who had done hundreds of cartoons about military life in World War II, it showed two soldiers ducking bullets, one saying, "I feel like a fugitive from th' law of averages."

And with that, I was suddenly lost in memory of the day my father was killed. . .

"Hi, Dad!" I'd said, coming around the corner and nearly bumping into him and several other men in the company. "Can I work on my computer today?"

"Sure," he said. "I think I have a new memory configuration for it."

He often boasted in the office that his 16-year-old daughter was learning his craft.

From somewhere between the first huge computers built of vacuum tubes to the silicon chips of 21st-century PC still to come in his mind, I think the rapid technology progress fascinated him. Companies like Microsoft and Apple were the latest tech magazine gossip in the break room.

But to me, I simply wanted something no one else had yet – I was going to be the first kid in school with a "personal computer."

I bounded down the hall toward the workshop, a room in the back corner of the building, where I was "upgrading" an Altair 8800 PC, a kit computer someone had brought to the shop for work and abandoned. With Dad's guidance, we experimented to see what else in the inventory might work in it without electrocuting ourselves.

I worked on it till six o'clock, long after everyone else in the office had left for home.

Mom worked the evening shift at the hospital, so there was no hurry to leave. We'd stay until I came to a problem we couldn't solve or he finished whatever he was doing and interrupted me, then we'd go pick up a pizza.

I liked our Friday night arrangement. I hated high school football games. My friends didn't go. Monica was out at her family's ranch with her horses getting ready for a show or something. Lisa was out with the boyfriend of the week. I chose to hang around my dad's office when I wasn't working at the bookstore.

The Sandia Digital Engineering building on Menaul could be accessed through the main entrance at the front, where a secretary greeted customers. Electronically locked doorways opened to either side of the waiting area, turning to parallel halls that made a square at the back of the building. The two restrooms were outside the security doors, but someone had created an access from the men's room through the general supply closet to the back hallway.

Police later suspected the perpetrator had entered the building sometime after lunch and hidden in the supply closet, after the receptionist had left work early due to illness. He could not have entered the building after five as the security system automatically locked all the doors, two front, two back.

Likely, the suspect was not aware anyone but my father was in the building – he predictably worked late on Fridays, seemingly alone. From an observer's standpoint, it probably would have been difficult to know I was there. I generally parked on the side opposite from the employees' lot, which was always full because it was so small, so I left the building by a separate entrance when we left at night.

That night, I heard a brief low conversation and thought perhaps my father was on the phone. Nothing out of the ordinary. I didn't get up to investigate.

Next I heard two voices, and a door slammed shut.

Then there was a gunshot.

The sound took a moment to register in my brain. When I realized what I'd heard, I went running toward his office.

When I got to him, he was alone, slumped against the wall next to his desk, having fallen out of his chair. His hands pressed against his right groin, blood spilling over his fingers.

"Julie, run for help!" he pleaded. "Out, go out the east side. Go!"

I put one hand on his hands, to help hold pressure. I didn't need to go anywhere. I could stay and help him.

"I'll call an ambulance," I argued, looking around for his phone. "I can't leave you –"

"If he comes back, he'll kill us both, Julie. You have to go. Now!" His eyes fluttered, but he tried to push away my hand.

"No, Dad!" I helped him lie flat, horrified at the pool of blood soaking into the carpet. I heard another crash in the hallway.

"Go!" he demanded.

I ran.

By the time the police arrived, the man who had shot my father had simply walked out the other side of the building and escaped.

When the ambulance crew got to him after the police had secured the building, my father was dead. We were told there was nothing that could have been done; he'd bled to death in just minutes.

There was no question about the murder. The police had a cassette tape my father had been using to dictate his notes. He hadn't thought to turn it off when the intruder startled him.

Their conversation, the gunshot, my screams, and my last words with my father were all recorded, as were the killer's words. But the police would not let us hear the tape, nor give us a clue to its content, citing it was evidence critical to the identification and prosecution of a suspect.

My world had changed with a gunshot.

CHAPTER 65

Midmorning, Brandan Callaghan called me to the briefing room to look at a new photo. He and Nolan Forrester had spread all the available case photos out on the table again.

There was the one image on the negatives from the perpetrator that we were still unclear about. We all agreed it was the same victim as the incomplete file on the disk – the male victim, sitting on the floor, leaning back, a wide gaping wound across the left side of his neck, blood spilled down his shirt.

My hand went up to my own neck. I tried to stop the reflex but was no more able to do so than to stop a knee jerk.

"You don't recognize this?" Forrester asked me.

When I looked up at him, I could tell he was studying me for a reaction I had not yet given.

"Other than the match to the partial disk photo, no."

He punched a button on the telephone.

"Could you ask our guest to join us?" he asked.

I looked around at the men in the room with me, confused.

A moment later, New Mexico State Police Deputy Chief Eric Rader marched into the conference room, in dress uniform, briefcase in hand. Everyone stood, and introductions were made.

I made my way around the table for a brief hug, tossing office etiquette aside.

"Eric? What is this about?" I asked. "Why have they dragged you all the way up here?"

He looked at Forrester for an answer.

"Dr. McNeeley mentioned yesterday after you left our meeting that your father's murder was entered into the criminal database as having similar injuries to other victims of this killer, and so I contacted Chief Rader for clarification," Forrester said, turning to Rader. "We presented Julie the photo you brought, Chief, but she doesn't recognize it either. Could you explain for us where it was taken?"

"Um, yes, sir," he said, indicating I should sit down, then taking a seat beside me. "Julie, you asked me to do a search on old cases that matched your killer. You excluded your father's case as a mistaken entry. I pulled the case files anyway to look. Then Agent Forrester called me."

I nodded.

"The image you have," Rader said, placing the partial image from the disk next to the other print, "is a background match to the crime scene photos of your father's murder. Only the killer could have taken these photos."

"No, I was there!" I gasped. "That's not how my father looked when I left him!"

"You also left the scene before the killer did, Julie. We know from the tape that the killer returned to him and took photographs, after he . . . used the knife."

"No one would ever tell us about the tape," I said, anger rising.

Rader continued. "Because of the tape, investigators knew why, but apparently hit a dead-end as to who killed him. Initially, they kept the information confidential for trial. The cause of death was still listed as the GSW, and the neck wound was not to be revealed either."

Forrester took over the explanation. "In the last 24 hours, the FBI has linked more pieces of the investigation, including those Rader had brought with him from New Mexico. DNA analysis of bloodstains in the barn shows a maternal genetic link between the unknown subject's blood and Tucker's – cousins. However, there is a closer genetic link between the UnSub's DNA in the Tucker house and yours. We believe the perpetrator's goal in involving you . . . " he said and paused, unsure how to complete the sentence.

. . . in the blood.

"Julie," Rader said softly, putting his hand on my forearm. "We think your father was also this subject's biological father."

Halves.

If this were true, the killer was my half-brother.

CHAPTER 66

Dozens of pieces of the puzzle fell together in my mind, almost too rapidly.

"That explains the fax about the key to my soul and the blood," I said. "Sally's diaries. I think there is another connection between these murders and the Tucker case. Tucker's mother, Sally, kept journals. When we asked Penny to come here regarding the investigation, she located those journals in the attic of the house. We had them photocopied."

Brandan nodded for me to continue my theory.

"In them, Sally talks about taking custody of her nephew after her sister's husband, Robert Bock, slit Angela's throat. I tried to track down Bock, only to find out from the first officer on the scene that Bock had been murdered after he was released from prison. Someone had cut his throat and left his body in an alley. Same officer found the body. They didn't do much of an investigation for personal reasons."

"That's kind of a coincidence," Forrester remarked.

"I doubt it was coincidence," I said. "I think it was intentional to leave the body at the right place and time for that same officer to find."

Dr. Katz interrupted. "Wait. I thought this nephew was dead."

"Penny said he was dead," I said.

That made it a fact, but was it true?

"Bock was not Anthony's biological father," I continued.

"Anthony Bock reportedly died of a self-inflicted GSW outside of Las Vegas, Nevada, in 1973," Brandan said. "I couldn't think of a better alibi, myself."

"Meaning what?" Dr. Katz asked.

"I think it was less difficult for a man to disappear or to assume a different identity at that time," Forrester answered, and he nodded to the silent agent who had been parked in a corner, plugged into a laptop every time I'd seen him.

"Perfect. He could be anybody then," I said. "And he's getting rid of people who can tie this all together. That's why he killed both his cousins,."

Mr. Silent Agent in the Corner spoke up, reporting in a monotone that the death certificate for Anthony Robert Bock, Petty Officer Third Class, U.S. Navy SEAL, based at Coronado Naval Station, San Diego, was signed by a justice of the peace, not a medical examiner, July 16, 1973. The body was several weeks old by the time it was found a hundred miles west of Vegas, but there had been a note. The gun and the appearance had seemed ordinary enough for a suicide, according to the report, so there was no further investigation. His VW Beetle was abandoned in a parking structure at the airport about the same time. He paused and kept reading to himself.

"His car didn't get to Vegas without a driver," Brandan said. "How'd they figure that?"

No answers.

"A Navy SEAL wouldn't kill himself," I said. "That means he's got even more skills than the chemistry and bugs. That's where the bombs come in."

"Five bucks says the dead body wasn't Bock's. Who would he pick up to kill?" Brandan asked me.

"Someone with no family, no ties, and someone with the best credentials to meet his needs. Doesn't mean he's using the same name now."

"Check for missing persons in that time frame," Forrester said to the Agent in the Corner.

"How do you look for a missing person who isn't missing?" I said in total exasperation. It felt like I was in a room with three-year-olds. "Don't you get it? He provides information he wants us to have and watches us scramble to figure it out, but it doesn't matter. It's useless. He's still playing the game. The question is why me. If he's killing all these other people – people in his family – why hasn't he killed me?"

"Or why didn't he kill you the first time?" Rader suggested.

"He took those photos of me after I shot David. Maybe he thought I would die, so he left me?"

Eric Rader shook his head. "No, Julie, not *that* time. When he killed your father, he as easily could have killed you then, too."

Blood ran cold in my chest.

"So why didn't he? Is that on the tape?"

"Not exactly. He mentioned you as if your existence surprised him. He asked your father how he'd like it if someone got you pregnant and left."

I closed my eyes to the overwhelming amount of information I did not want to hear.

"I have a question," Brandan interrupted my thoughts. "The barn explosion, you had the weekend off, didn't you?"

"Yeah, why?" I said.

"Remember what Howell said? He thought the secondary bomb was set to injure responders who would come to the scene after the first explosion?" he asked, referring to the conversation I'd had with the expert from the Michigan State Police Bomb Squad. "What if this bomb was supposed to kill people who were there investigating, but he assumed you wouldn't be there?"

"Leaving me to pick up all the pieces. Again, I have to wonder why," I said.

Putting all this together led us no further to the most important questions: Who was this killer? Where was Matthew Shannaker? Who was the next victim?

Unfortunately, we all agreed my mother was as likely to be high on this list as anyone else now.

I explained her absence, which prompted Rader to initiate a BOLO in New Mexico statewide, a "be on the lookout" alert to locate and detain her in protective custody, specifically in the Ruidoso area where she told me she was.

"She has to be one of his next victims," I argued with Forrester and Brandan.

"Well, she'll be one of the last," Forrester concluded.

“That’s comforting,” I said sarcastically. “Why?”

“There are too many other targets nearby to manipulate you here. I think he’ll bait you with her in the end.”

“What’s that supposed to mean?” I demanded.

“He may threaten to harm someone else if you try to alert her or to move her somewhere safe, for example.”

“So what do I do?” I stood there looking from face to face.

“You do what you have to do. We understand that every decision you may have to make will be under extreme duress and your actions chosen with prejudice,” Forrester said. He looked around, then said quietly. “Just do the right thing if you get the chance. And in the end, no matter what the question, the answer is self-defense.”

I left the conference room alone, walking like a robot, unaware of my surroundings in any emotional way. Processing data for threats, like the robot on Lost in Space, waiting to flail my arms and yell, “Danger, Will Robinson, danger!”

Back to my office, to my semi-safe environment. At least I felt I could control the flow of information coming at me from the outside.

My message light was blinking. There were several written messages Connie had left on my desk as well, all ME business.

I dialed the voice message system, entered the numbers, and listened.

“Hey, Sweetheart, I wanted you to hear it from me I’m alive and doing well,” Zach’s voice said, scratchy and hoarse. “I’m sorry about what happened last night, that you heard it.” He paused a second. “I meant what I said, Julie. We need to talk. I’ll call you in a few days when I get out of the hospital.”

Nine o’clock this morning.

I was prompted to save or discard the message. I discarded it.

Part of me wanted to go see him, to make sure he was okay. That was the logical, medical part of me. I didn’t want to think about the other parts, those that made my heart race and my knees weak. What had I been thinking the last few weeks? The last three years or more?

The next message was from my mother.

“Julie? What on earth is going on? I called to check my voice mail this morning, and Vera had left several messages. She called again early this morning to say something happened to Zach! I've called, but I haven't gotten through to find out. Is that why you were trying to get in touch with me? Anyway, here's where I can be reached until Sunday afternoon or so," she said, reading a number. "That's Everett's cellular phone. It doesn't work well at his place, but leave a message. We'll be coming into town again later for dinner or something, I'm sure. I'll check my mach –"

The recording system interrupted her with the time warning.

"Anyway, honey, I hope everything is okay."

She was alive! The recording was made this morning at 9:30, while I was in the meeting. Half an hour ago. It was two hours earlier in New Mexico.

I hung up on the next message, not even registering who it was. It would wait. I dialed the cellular phone number I'd scribbled on the note pad.

Recorded voice mail greeting said, "Sorry, the number you have dialed is no longer accepting calls from people trying to track it down. Please check your voice mail, Julia."

I stared at the handset as if it came alive in my hand. Long enough the call disconnected.

I dialed my voicemail back and listened to the next unplayed message.

What I heard chilled my blood.

He'd called only a few minutes after my mother had. "Don't bother to trace the number or triangulate the signals of the cell phone. The phone was stolen to start with, and it will be in a thousand pieces under a tire somewhere before you hear this. I'll tell her I must have lost it," a calm voice said. "We'll have ourselves a wonderful weekend together, your mother and I. Or maybe we won't. That depends on you, Julia.

"By now, you figured out that everyone dies badly but you. I'll leave you with your demons and more secrets you think you hide so well."

I buried my face in my hands, and tears poured down my cheeks in silence as the voice continued after the time warning.

"I want you to know I'm the only one in your life who can tame those demons. I can give you power. You'll understand soon. You were not ready before. I'm sorry I had to hurt you to make you see how much power I have, but you bleed so beautifully. I'm thinking your lovely mother will, too."

The call ended.

I could not help myself. In one swift motion, I cleared my desk onto the floor and screamed like a pitiful wounded animal.

CHAPTER 67

I felt more like a human after Eric Rader explained everything he'd put in motion – the resources of the New Mexico State Patrol and agencies who offered up manpower and equipment – to find my mother and the monster that had her.

Eric left me alone to pull myself together for a while but came by later to ask if I would have dinner with him. I told him I didn't think I could eat and got the "starving-won't-help" lecture. I conceded.

"Why don't you ask Dr. McNeeley to come, too," he offered.

"Things are a bit unsettled between us right now. I don't think he likes me very much today." Actually, I was unsure if Jeremy was still in Michigan. He'd already left the house when I woke this morning on the couch. "It's not like my life was all that simple before, but then Jeremy showed up, all gorgeous and helpful, sweeping me off my feet again despite my initial resistance. Then he got around to confessing that he isn't divorced from his wife, and he has a daughter."

"Um," he chuckled. "Okay, I can imagine that would cause a little friction."

"And last night, I got a call from this DEA agent I've sorta been seeing occasionally. He was sitting out on a beach in Florida, telling me about a horrible bust down there, when he got shot." I cringed as the memory played again. "And the last thing I heard him say was that he loves me."

"Is he okay?"

"Yeah, though I feel like the bullets went right through my own heart when I imagined him lying in the sand, bleeding to death," I said, trying to put it out of my head. "It's all a mess. Now about dinner. Fish?"

"Of course," he said. "Why do you think I always jump at the chance to leave the desert?"

So we went to dinner at a place Connie recommended in Leelanau County. Despite having no appetite, it was good company and conversation.

I asked about Samantha and their wedding plans for the following spring.

"Well, we're going to move it up to Christmas," he said between bites. "I think it's important we're married before the baby arrives."

That was the first joyous news I felt I'd heard in weeks. "That's wonderful, Eric! Congratulations."

He actually blushed. "I'd still like you to come to the wedding, if you can make it."

Christmas still seemed an eternity away, but I promised to try.

I dropped Eric at his hotel for the night since his return flight was at 6 a.m.

I drove home, needing sleep, but I didn't get it. Tossing under the covers, I lay awake thinking about my mother's situation. Hoping she was safe.

After dozing off around 4 a.m., I slept until 9:30. When I got up, the Saturday morning was clear and bright, unusually warm for September.

Sunshine, and I could only feel dread without being able to do anything about it.

I called MaryAnne to see about our lunch date.

We discussed it and decided to meet during Kimberly's class. MaryAnne had errands to do, so she chose a place downtown, a small deli where a friend of hers worked.

"I didn't know about this place," I confessed as we went in. "We order out a lot, and this is definitely going on our menu list."

"Gerald would like it, too. We haven't been here together yet. He'd probably like the turkey, bacon and avocado sandwich," she said, pointing to the item on the takeout menu her friend Debby had brought for me.

"Mmm, me, too," I said, and that's what I ordered.

After a bit of chitchat and gossip, I finally thought it was a good time to ask Dr. Katz's question.

"I was over in the emergency room a few days ago for a case, and I thought I saw you go by in the hallway. I'm sure you didn't see me, but when I looked down the hall, you were gone already."

"Oh, that," she said and took a bite of her chicken salad.

I almost thought she was going to bypass the whole subject completely.

Finally, she looked up at me and said, "Remember when you were at the house that night for dinner, when Kim hurt her foot?"

I nodded and took a bite. Fair is fair.

"I told you I might need a friend like you someday. I think it's today."

I swallowed long before I had chewed up the mouthful of sandwich and almost choked. After I'd washed it down with half a glass of tea, I told her I meant what I said.

"I found a lump and had a mammogram, which showed something very suspicious, so my doctor scheduled an MRI. That's when you saw me."

What does one say to news like that?

"I'm sorry, MaryAnne. Have you told Gerald?"

"No, I wanted to have a little more to go on before I said anything. I love him but he gets so clinical with things like this. Now I'm so terrified, I don't know what to do." Tears formed in her eyes. "I'm scheduled for a biopsy in ten days."

I reached over and put my hand on hers on the table.

"What can I do?"

"Kayleigh is staying with friends tonight. Could you pick up Kim at the pool and take her out for a milkshake or something? Gerald should be home after noon, and I'd like to be able to talk to him alone."

"Of course. You know, Kim's noticed something is bothering you, and so has Gerald. I'm sure once things are out in the open, you won't feel quite so overwhelmed. Everyone will have a shoulder for you to lean on," I said. "Including me. Whatever you need, okay? Like you made me promise in the hospital, anything – just ask."

She smiled and wiped away a single tear.

An hour later, I picked Kim up at the community center pool. We stopped for milkshakes and a burger for her, and drove out M-22 north to the park next to the marina. We walked out to the breakwall to enjoy the sunshine.

"I had lunch with your mom today. I think I know what's been bothering her. You and your dad have both picked up those feelings. He asked me about it, too."

Sensing there was bad news ahead, Kim turned and walked along the edge away from me, then turned around.

"She's sick, isn't she?" she asked.

"Well, they aren't sure yet. She needs more tests, but there is a possibility, yes. She asked me to pick you up so she could finally talk to your dad today while you and Kayleigh were away. I think she needed a few hours to let down her Supermom mask and talk to him without having to feel she has to be strong for all of you right now. I would tell you the details, but I think she'd like to tell you in her own way."

Kim came toward me. "Thanks for helping me, though."

I hugged her. "You're very welcome."

The embrace was interrupted by a shout near my Suburban, a man was bent over near a large dog, waving at us.

"Help! Please, help me!" he yelled again. "My dog collapsed!"

Kim took off and raced toward him, and I followed with no hope of catching up to her.

As Kim reached them and fell to her knees by the dog, the man stood up and pointed a gun at me, still a few yards away.

Focused on Kim, I didn't recognize this motion as a threat until the last moment when I instinctively turned sideways. I felt the hit in my left hip. I yelled at Kim to get away.

In incredible slow motion, I watched as he pointed another weapon at Kim, hitting her in the thigh. I expected to see an explosion of tissue and bone from her leg, but after blinking again, saw only a feathered tail of a drug dart.

The scenario became very clear as I hit the ground and began to lose consciousness.

I heard Kim's cries, and I struggled to reach out, to crawl toward her, to find a way to help her.

And then came the blackness.

CHAPTER 68

In slow motion, I became aware of noises around me, but my mind had trouble processing the information. My eyes were sticky, my mouth dry. I finally lifted my chin from my chest and looked around, though my vision remained blurry. My back and neck hurt, and when I tried to lift my arm to rub the sore muscles, I found my wrists handcuffed to the arms of a chair.

The sound of the breathing in the distance changed in response to the noise the cuffs made. From a soft snoring sound to a weak cough.

I jangled the cuffs again. "Kim?" I yelled. "Kimmie, are you here?"

"Julie?" a hoarse voice called from somewhere behind me. "Is that you?"

A moment passed as my brain put a name to the voice I had not expected. "Matthew?"

"Are you hurt?"

I bit my tongue to make my mouth water before I started coughing.

"No," I said, panic growing in my guts. "Kim, where are you?"

"Julie, I don't think she's here."

Apparently the shock to each of us about the presence of the other was so disturbing neither of us spoke for what seemed like a long time.

"How did you get here?" he finally asked.

How *did* I get here? Where was *here*?

"I don't know," I croaked, dry again. "Where's – "

"Shh," Matt said, whispering. "He's coming."

"Who?" I asked, as if it might possibly be anyone else.

"Shhh!"

Eventually, I heard footsteps approaching. A door screeched open then closed. Heavy footsteps on soft soles.

"Good afternoon, Julia," a male voice said, still about ten feet away, out of my vision.

"My name is Julie."

"That's not the name you were given at birth. I like Julia better."

I tried to turn to see him.

"My name is Julie," I repeated. "My grandmother misunderstood naming me after my grandfather, Julian."

"Unfortunately, I was mis-named as well. My mother named me Anthony, after my father," he said, "but that wasn't his name. I never understood how she got that confused. Maybe you can enlighten me."

"My father's given name was Thomas Jackson," I said with determination, "but his friends called him Stoney, short for Stonewall. Maybe your mother heard 'Stoney' and thought his name was Tony."

"Stoney?" he sighed. "How quaint. So you do know."

"You think my father raped your mother, leaving her pregnant, and then disappeared back to the navy. I don't happen to agree, but thanks to you, there's really no one left alive to ask now, is there?"

"I know what she wrote in her journals about him. God knows what else he might have done until he met *your* mother, but later you came along, the near-genius golden child of two doting parents - something I never had." He paused. "How does it make you feel to know I'm your half-brother?"

"What should I feel, Anthony? Love, hate? I have no connection to you at all except through your victims. That makes you an evil bastard."

"A bastard, indeed." He laughed. "You and I are the biological proof people kill because of genetics. You've killed, but no one called you evil."

"Sharing a strand of DNA doesn't prove anything."

"We'll see." He stood and came toward me, moving so that I

could see his face.

His eyes were exactly like my father's, a bland hazel color, wide set, deceivingly kind.

He extended a plastic cup to my lips. "Drink."

I turned away.

"Go on. I could have killed you a dozen times. I'm very good at killing. Ingenious, don't you think? I bet you were starting to think about different methods I might use next, weren't you? Checking out your microbiology texts, discussing it with your old lover from CDC." He forced the cup against my mouth and tilted the cup. "Very slutty, by the way, screwing a married man. You've certainly been making the rounds." He made a tisking sound. "Sounds like he's pretty good in bed, though. Almost as good as your other cop friend. I played the tapes for the deputy. You do know he's here, too, right?"

My heart fluttered like a small animal shivering inside my ribs.

How long had he been listening, watching me? I didn't want to know.

He held the cup up again, and I drank water.

"Not too much. You'll get sick." He removed the cup. "But you still don't know me, do you? Don't you remember ever seeing me?"

I shook my head.

"Maybe it's the pentothal. Leaves you hung over, I hear. It'll come to you later, I think." He pulled up a wooden ottoman where he sat and kept talking.

I pushed away his words, not wanting to hear, blinking, more able to assess my environment as my vision cleared.

The structure didn't look like a regular house. It was old and appeared to be made of rough-hewn logs.

"Julia? Are you listening to me?" he asked, touching my knee.

"Does it matter? Won't I die like the others?"

He laughed. "We all die sooner or later. But you're different – I'm going to save you." He stood and stepped toward me. "And you? You'll save me."

I flinched when he patted my shoulder, then he left the building through the same door that screeched when he pulled it closed behind him.

In the distance, I heard an engine start – not my Suburban. The sound faded away, leaving only my heartbeat crashing in my ears.

"Julie? Is he right? Is he really your brother?" Matt asked.

"Half-brother. Yes," I said, closing my eyes to those memories. "He looks like my dad." Thoughts raced through my mind. Why would the illegitimate son of a woman be angry enough to hunt down his biological father and kill him? I might understand that, given his story, but why so many others? Why not me? "He's Tucker's cousin," I said, "and Penny, J.P.'s sister. He killed her, too, and one of her kids."

"Are there other bodies on the property?" Matt's voice sounded dejected.

"Yeah, several." I said, waiting on him to be angry like I was, but there was no reaction. "He also has my mother held hostage, like you, according to his message yesterday. And he has Kim, somewhere."

"I'm sorry," he said. No fight at all in his words. "You mean Dr. Katz's daughter? How'd he get you both?"

"A setup," I said, not wanting to relive my biggest failure so far. "Are you hurt, Matt?"

Silence.

"Matt?"

"It doesn't matter," he muttered.

"What's that supposed to mean?"

"It means I'm too injured to escape or to fight. I'll die whenever he's ready for me to die." His voice sounded weaker, despondent.

"Damn you, Matthew Shannaker. I'm not going to let that happen. Don't you give up."

He was alive and talking. That was enough for me to think I'd be able to save him, wasn't it? Honestly though, I wondered in the next minutes of silence, whether I was going to be able to save anyone at all.

I fought panic and fear that swelled inside me, so great I had to remember to breathe, but if I didn't focus on the present, neither of us had a chance to escape, to beat Anthony.

"Where we are?" I asked, trying to change the subject to something helpful.

"On the Leelanau County coast, south of Peterson Park, a mile or a little more, up on a bluff," he said.

"Who owns the property?"

"Don't know. It's one of those places they rent out for summer parties and stuff." His voice degraded into a fit of weak wet-sounding coughing.

I waited until his breathing calmed. "What room are you in?"

"Part of the kitchen, I think. Are you facing the fireplace or the doors? Can you see the sun?"

"I'm facing the fireplace, but I can see out the west window. It's almost sunset."

"What's it look like?" he asked.

"A band of clouds, maybe a front coming in."

"What colors do you see?"

"What does it matter?" I asked crossly.

Silence.

"Matthew?"

"I can't see it."

"Which direction are you facing?"

"I can't see anything," he said softly. "He blinded me. Days ago, I think."

CHAPTER 69

Fear and anger surged through me like electricity when I remembered the note found at my house – *Matt won't be seeing you anymore.* I jerked my arms and legs in their cuffs, rattling them loudly but not producing anything except pain. Finally, there was nothing else I could do but vent the anguish in a shrill scream choked by tears.

"Stop it!" Matt yelled at me. "Get your shit together, Julie."

Sobbing until my cheeks were wet and my nose was runny, I sniffed so hard my ears popped. "Got any tissue?" I asked, hoping he got the joke. Instead, I wiped my nose on the shoulder of my shirt – the only thing within reach.

"Hanky in my back pocket," he said, and I knew he had smiled at least a little bit.

Darkness engulfed the house over the next hour. My watch was missing, as was my body armor. The house, nothing but a log cabin on a cement floor with no insulation, cooled quickly.

Over a few hours, my mind cleared out the drug-induced cobwebs. I worried about Kim – hoping her absence here meant she'd escaped.

My conversations with Matt were sparse as he quickly exhausted by the effort to speak. He coughed frequently, and I didn't dare imagine what else Anthony had done to him.

I told him about the case, step by step as it had unraveled in front of us. About the man found dead in Mrs. Shannaker's home, and how we'd initially thought it was him.

"I heard the gunshots," he said. "There was nothing I could do to help him."

Another lengthy silence.

"Did he kill Laser?" Matt asked.

"No, he didn't. The sheriff asked me to keep him at first. He got bored, but he's okay."

"He's coming back," Matt said as the sound of the vehicle approached again. "I'm not supposed to speak. And don't let him know I told you I couldn't see."

"Okay."

"And in case I don't get a chance to say it later, Julie, you mean the world to me. Thanks for everything, for being my friend. I wish things had been different."

"Please, Matt," I begged. "Don't give up."

"This is going to end ugly. Promise me you'll do whatever you have to do to get out of here and put him away."

"Matt!"

"Shut up, Julie. Just . . . shut up."

In a minute or so, the footsteps approached from behind as before. "Oh, Julia?" he called from the darkness.

Silence.

"I have a question for you," he said, suddenly very close to me.

"Fuck you."

"I don't think it would be appropriate since you're my sister, nor do I think you would care for it, despite your preference for men who like it rough." He snickered. "Your deputy friend seemed to like that, though. I have photos if you'd care to see them. Fair is fair."

Matt didn't respond.

"You are an evil, despicable excuse for a human being," I growled.

"We can discuss your definition of evil later," Bock said. "But somehow I think you've had time to reconsider whether evil is defined solely by killing, haven't you? There are worse things one can do than die."

I said nothing.

"Would you kill me if given the opportunity?" he asked.

"I'm not a monster like you are."

"We'll see about that," he taunted. "But you didn't answer my question. You killed your husband because you thought he had hurt you, didn't you? I don't think you'd let me go free if you had a chance to put a bullet in my head. Oh, I remember – you prefer the heart, don't you."

"Shooting David wasn't cold-blooded murder."

"Perhaps not. But you didn't feel guilty about it. I believe you have the same capacity and willingness to kill without, um, how did you put it? Without remorse, yes. I intend to prove it."

"You can't prove any such thing," I said, but I was suddenly terrified he might be able to do just that.

He got up and left through the door. Outside, I heard a vehicle door open and close. Then I heard the sounds of a struggle, a muffled moan.

"Do stop fussing. I don't *want* to have to hurt you," he giggled, "but I will."

Kim?

The sounds in the darkness came from behind me. The outside door opened again, and footsteps again came toward me. Finally in the shadows, I saw Anthony leading someone to another chair made of logs. I heard the clinking of handcuffs, then the familiar click. There was another whispering sound, followed by a gasp.

He came toward me and struck a wooden match to light a candle. Then he casually set about stacking wood in the fireplace.

As my eyes adjusted to the dim light of the candle, across the room from me, I twisted to see Kimberly Katz.

"Julie?" she shrieked, then began a howling chant of *Oh-my-God-oh-my-God-oh-my-God!*

"I thought she'd be happy to see you, Julia," he said over her hysterical voice.

"Kimberly, honey, stop!" I yelled at her.

She stopped abruptly and looked at me, wild-eyed, panting.

I wanted to tell her it was okay, but I couldn't lie. "Kimmie, are you hurt, Sweetie?"

"Just my foot," she whined. "I kicked something trying to get away. I can't walk on it."

"All right. Try to be calm, okay?"

She didn't answer but took a deep breath and nodded.

"Nice party list, so far, Anthony. Anyone else?" I asked sarcastically.

He grinned at me as the flame of another match caught a piece of dry kindling. "Nope, I thought this would be plenty, but I'd be happy to go fetch anybody else you'd like. Maybe your handsome Southern doctor? I'd certainly like to get a taste of him."

"If this is between you and me, why all of them?"

"I'm sure you know the answer to that." He leaned forward to poke at the fire with a long piece of wood.

"I have to go to the bathroom," Kim said.

"Have to wait." Content with the fledgling flames, he stretched out in a chair and propped up his legs on the coffee table to face me. "Did you figure out where you'd seen me before?"

"No. Didn't try." I lied.

While he was gone, it came to me how close he'd been. He was the man who rear-ended my truck when I first moved to Michigan. Maybe he was around me other times I never recognized him.

"I'm so disappointed," he mocked.

I shrugged.

"By the way, in general, I take great exception to being called evil." He smiled again. "But, based on your definition, I suppose you have it partially right. For example, I enjoyed making J.P. Tucker participate in the—" he looked toward Kim, "shall we say, in the games I played."

"You mean kidnapping and murder?"

"Oh, that and plenty more." He grinned like a hyena.

I felt nauseated by the way the fire increased his resemblance to my father.

"But I am a product of my environment and of my genetics, both screwed up by our father."

"What about conscience and choice?"

"Let me tell you a story about my childhood, then we can debate your nature or nurture theories," he said. "First, you know where half my genes came from. Listen to what your father left me to face from the other side of my DNA strand."

I nodded. I didn't want to hear another word, and yet, I knew this might be the only explanation anyone would ever hear.

Anthony told me. "Walking home from school was important to me, but when I got home, I could hear my father – the man I thought was my father – yelling at my mother. I knew better than to interrupt him when he was mad," he explained. "I snuck in and peeked through the vents of the wall furnace, watching him rubbing against my mother's back, his pants around his knees, making noises like he did at night sometimes.

"She begged him to stop hurting her. He reached into the drainer next to the sink and grabbed a knife and jerked it across her throat. Then he dropped it, and kept rubbing against her.

"I saw the blood spurting all over the counter and cabinets until she slumped. I listened to her last gurgling breath. When he finished, he tripped on his pants around his ankles, and the weight of her limp body knocked him off balance. He stumbled and struck his head on the cheap dinette table, then fell to the wooden floor unconscious.

"I snuck in. My mother was sprawled out, blood dripping on her otherwise spotless kitchen. Her dress was still pulled up. I wanted to look away but I couldn't. I was fascinated with the dark hair between her legs. And more blood.

"Years passed before I knew anything about sex, but I felt a tingle between my own legs. When I saw the knife, blood glistening, I was drawn to it. I didn't know why, but I knew not to touch the blood on the floor when I picked it up. I took it upstairs and hid it in the closet where no one would think to look, careful not to smear the blade. When my aunt came for me the next day, I made sure I packed it in my clothes with what few toys I took."

I said nothing. Words would do no justice to what I felt.

"So tell me, Julia, don't you think that contributes to making me do what I do?"

"No," I said.

Watching Bock rape and kill his mother surely had something to do with his behavior, but I refused to become his psychologist or confessor.

"Are you saying that your father's death didn't alter who you are and what you do?" he asked.

"I didn't start killing people because you murdered my father. Quite the opposite. I went into law enforcement instead."

“Oh, is that the reason? And were you able to solve his case?”

“No.”

“You didn’t even try. You still dream about his blood on your hands. You hate yourself because you couldn't save him, for running away. But you didn't get to see how I left him for you when I was done, did you? You never saw my final work. Pity. It might have made all the difference in how you turned out. I used that same knife on him, Julia. The same knife my so-called father used to killed my mother.”

I shrugged but breathing was an effort.

“The same knife I cut your throat with in Alamogordo.”

I suppressed a scream into a sound that only echoed in my head. He might as well have drawn that blade across my throat again for the pain it caused.

I wanted him to stop. I didn’t care if he killed me, if he would just quit talking.

“I’ve used it on your deputy,” he chided. “I'll cut your little friend over here with it,” he said, getting up and walking toward Kimberly. “I'll cut your mother up with it and feed her to the wild animals.”

“Stop it!” I bellowed, jerking my arms against the cuffs again. Rage tore through me, and it was all I could do to keep it from rising to panic.

“Oh, I’m sorry. I wanted that to be a surprise. Chances are they won’t find her body, or be able to identify it if they do,” he said and walked back to me.

I had to stop this mind-game. I was reacting exactly as he wanted.

I closed my eyes.

Whatever he has done is done. There is nothing I can do to change it. I have to focus on protecting Matthew and Kimberly now. I can’t let him control me, because he will kill them.

Anthony stood up across from me. He used the stick to poke at the fire again.

“I have a deal for you, Julia.”

I pretended not to listen.

“If you do not agree, however,” he said, moving around behind me to whisper in my ear, "then I will cut up the deputy into pieces in front of the girl, cutting off her eyelids if I have to in order to make her watch. Then I will fuck your beautiful little virgin friend there, and when I'm done, I'll cut her up in front of you and deliver pieces of her in boxes to her parents for a week. Then," he said, flashing a heavy kitchen knife in front of my eyes, "maybe after a little more fun with you, I will simply walk away a free man. Again. Regardless what happens, I want you to know that no one you care about will be safe for the rest of your life. Is that clear?"

Perfectly, I thought. I already believe that. I nodded. "What do you want?"

"I'll tell you my demand in the morning. You get one chance. When it's done, I drive away. Once I'm out of a range, the radio control for the bombs will no longer work, and you can free yourself."

I started to speak.

He moved to whisper in my other ear. "I know what you're thinking. If you screw up and try to kill me first, the bombs are set on a dead man's switch." He held up a small remote. "Try to escape tonight, and the entire house goes up." He walked around in front of me. "Fair enough?"

He stretched.

"It gets cold in here at night. Shall I pull the girl closer to the fire?"

I nodded.

"One warning. I also rigged alarms under the chairs. Don't get any heroic ideas about getting up to leave."

He scooted Kim's heavy chair close to mine, but not touching.

"I'm going to bed now. Don't stay up too late." He left us alone and went through a doorway where I thought Matt was.

The fire blazed, warming my side.

Kim was crying. I could hear her trying to do it quietly.

"Kimmie," I whispered. "Honey, I know you're scared. I am, too, but we're going to make it through this. You have to believe me and trust me, no matter what. Understand?"

"Umhmm," she whimpered.

She looked terrified.

Had it really been so easy for him to drug us both and drive away from there?

One tranquilizer dart each - I guess it had been pretty simple.

"I am so sorry, Kimberly. I didn't mean to . . . I mean, I didn't know he would . . . " I sighed, tears in my eyes again.

"Julie, it's okay. He didn't hurt me."

"And I don't think he will if I do what he wants."

"What's that?" she asked.

"I don't know," I lied. "But I'll find a way to get you out of here. I promise."

I meant that promise from the bottom of my heart because there was no way I could ever face Gerald or MaryAnne Katz again if anything happened to their daughter because of me.

"Try to sleep, Kim, okay?" I said softly. "Sleep while it's warm."

She finally fell asleep in a position I was sure would hurt her neck, based on how my own felt, but the sleep was more important for her.

I wanted to sleep, but could not get out of my mind the scenario Bock had painted.

Where was the closest help? How could I get Matthew out of the building? Was he otherwise physically injured besides being blinded?

For Kim's sake, I'd have to think of something. I did not want this pretty redheaded young woman to start her adulthood believing her life had been a bargain I made with the devil.

CHAPTER 70

I was still awake at the first light of dawn.

Anthony came in and saw me staring at the fireplace.

"What is it you want?" I whispered so as not to wake Kim.

"I want you," he said, looking over his shoulder toward where Matthew was, "to show me your face when you kill. I want to see you enjoy it as much as I do."

"You've watched me all this time. You saw what killing David did to me."

"Afterward, yes, but not the very moment you pulled the trigger. And the second shot? You actually smiled, did you know that? I think the blood we share from our father makes us alike in many ways, Julia. We share the blood of like souls. I intend to prove it."

"The best you can hope for is the joy of making me do something under duress. You can't make me like it."

"We'll see." He looked around. "Want to get it over with now or shall I have some fun with your little friend first?"

"I want you to drop dead."

He backhanded me across the face, leaving me stunned, tasting blood.

The sound woke Kimberly, who screamed.

"Now look what you've done," he said. He went to the kitchen and returned with a long section of duct tape, which he ran across her mouth and around her head. He clamped his hand over her nose, watching her struggle.

"Stop it!" I yelled.

"Ready to play, then?" he asked, letting her take a gasping

breath.

I'd had all night to decide whether I could do what I feared was ahead. My doubts always came back to the fact Anthony was most certainly lying about the way this was all going to end. When it came down to the decision, though, whatever the demand was, I knew there was no way I could walk away a sane woman if I didn't try to save Kimberly Katz from this monster.

"Whatever."

He pinched Kim's nose again, making a point to show how delicately he could control her.

"Okay, yes."

"Very well." He let go of her and stepped between the two of us, pulling out what I presumed was my stolen Smith & Wesson, which he leveled at Kim's chest. "I will shoot her if you challenge me." With the key, he undid the right cuff from the chair, then he stepped back and tossed the key in my lap where I could reach it. "Don't do anything stupid. Unlock the other side from the chair but leave them on your wrists. Then your shackles."

I complied.

"Stand up."

I did, waiting for the dizziness to subside. My legs and back ached.

"Okay, now go into the next room, where your deputy friend is. Unlock his cuffs from the chair as you did yours, and then move behind the chair."

Nausea rolled through me, and my head throbbed as my heart tried to catch up with the sudden demands on its body's exertion.

Matt's eyes were sunken and closed, with a thick greenish drainage that had leaked down his pale cheeks. His face was bruised and had several cuts and abrasions in various stages of healing. His lips were dry and cracked. Although he had a heavy blanket over his lap, his feet were bare and almost white from lack of blood flow. I could see scabbed wounds across the backs of both heels, where I'd guessed his Achilles' tendons had been cut, hobbling him permanently.

He was in worse shape than I'd imagined, hearing his voice.

I managed to do what Anthony told me, even though my hands

shook. It took several tries to put the tiny key into the lock on the handcuffs. I used the time making contact with Matt's arms, trying to be comforting.

He smiled a little.

I finally stood up and stepped behind the chair.

"From where you stand, cuff your right wrist to his right arm using both sets, then your left to his left."

I touched Matt's hands as I cuffed our arms together, feeling his cold skin.

I finished the task, confused at first as to the purpose of the exercise with the handcuffs. Until it made perfect awful sense.

"Now, hold your hands in the air," he said. "Higher."

He dragged Kimberly's chair so she could see us in the pale morning light.

"Don't make her watch," I pleaded.

"Shut up," he snapped again.

When her chair was set, I saw the tears in her eyes.

Anthony came into the kitchen area, and still holding the gun in Kim's direction, laid a knife on Matt's lap.

The knife.

"There you go," he said with a smile. "I think you know what to do now. If you don't do this right, you'll only make him suffer longer."

I had to reach to pick up the knife.

"Remember my father," Matt whispered.

My heart stuttered as I realized what he meant. I was about to commit the same sort of act that made me doubt Matthew – taking someone's life as a sacrifice for others.

"Shut up, deputy," Anthony demanded, moving away from us, keeping a clear aim at Kim.

I stood there, looking down at Matt's head. I felt my arms tremble.

"We're all waiting, Julia."

"I love you, Julie. Just do it," Matt begged.

CHAPTER 71

I had no idea how much time had passed before Kim's screams awakened me. Finally, I got loose and helped her as we stumbled away from the cabin. Not only were we both weak, but I'd been drugged again, and Kim was unable to bear weight on her injured foot.

We finally collapsed far enough from the building that I felt we were safe.

"Stay here," I told her, "I have to get Matthew."

She grabbed my arm. "No," she shrieked. "He said there was a bomb, Julie!"

"Kim, I can't just leave him." I tried to stand, hands on my knees, panting. I had blood all over my hands and arms. Four sets of handcuffs still dangled from my wrists. I didn't know what to say. I wasn't sure I'd ever know what to say. I had enough scars of my own to know this was bound to have a lasting effect on Kim's life.

"I won't tell," she promised. "I'll say he did it." She was looking at my bloody arms and clothes.

I dropped to my knees. "Oh, Kimmie, no. This isn't about me. What I did is all my responsibility. You tell the truth, okay? But I have to get Matt out –"

And then the explosion blasted us.

I fell over Kim to protect her from the flying debris. Then I stumbled to my feet and took a few steps toward the house, dazed, watching the flames and smoke blot out the morning sky. Close enough to feel the heat on my face. Tears stung my eyes, evaporated on my cheeks.

I could not turn away. I almost expected another blast. Might even have welcomed it at that moment.

Kim had saved my life by making me hesitate. I might have been inside the house when the bomb went off if she hadn't argued with me about going back.

I watched the fire engulf the cabin, what little of it was standing.

I had lost the fight – Anthony had proven I would kill again. Did it matter why?

I was still standing there when I heard sirens approaching.

Someone guided me away from the cabin.

Brandan unlocked the handcuffs from my arms. He tried to wipe away the blood, but I yanked my hands away from him and folded them, so he settled for a blanket to put around me.

Sitting on the rear steps of an ambulance, I watched the Northport Fire Department fogging the remains of the cabin from a safe distance.

Nothing seemed real when I looked down at my bloody hands, then back at the smoke.

"Julie," a voice said, trying to distract me from the images, though most of them were in my head. "Julie? Are you hurt?"

I had no answer for that.

Jeremy moved into my view, blocking the cabin from my eyes but not my memory.

"Julie!"

I finally looked up at his face.

"Dr. Katz called from the hospital," he said. "Kimberly is okay."

Hysterical insane laughter bubbled inside my chest, but I barely had energy to speak. "No, she isn't," I whispered. Another scene repeated in my head. "She watched me kill him."

"You killed Anthony?"

I shook my head again slowly, barely. "I killed Matthew." I looked back down at my hands.

"Oh, Julie. . . " he said, his gaze following mine. But he had no words, and he did not reach out to comfort me.

I closed my eyes, trying to squeeze out the world around me, the sounds, the smells, the man in front of me. When I opened them, he'd disappeared into the smoke.

Brandan came toward me, along with a firefighter in full turnout gear and white helmet.

"Julie," Brandan said. "This is Chief Adkins. He needs to ask you a few questions about other explosive devices."

He did, but I don't remember answering them.

The chief left, and while I could recite the words, I told Brandan what had happened, that Matt had been inside, bound to a chair. I told him what I had to do to get Kim out alive, both before and after Anthony Bock had left.

Saying them felt very much like bleeding to death, and I didn't want to have to say those words again.

Ever.

When the flames were extinguished, several firefighters entered the remains of the structure.

I wanted to watch when they brought Matthew out. I needed to sear that image into my memory for the day I'd find Anthony and kill him, too.

But I couldn't look.

It seemed like it took hours before they were done.

"Can I get a ride home now?" I asked, so exhausted that breathing was a conscious effort and hardly worthwhile.

"McNeeley left," Brandan said, taking my arm to stop me. "He asked me to give you this." He held out a blue velvet jewelry box and an envelope.

I shook my head and left him holding it as I walked away.

Nolan Forrester offered to take me back to Traverse City, and I wilted into his car.

He talked to me, though even his words didn't all register. "We think he'll leave the state as soon as possible. We have covered everything we can. Airlines, buses, trains. APB on single males traveling downstate and out. Trouble is, we don't have much to go on. No one has ever seen him."

"I have. Kim has." Anger began to displace the overwhelming emptiness inside me.

"And we'll do composites. We'll take everything you can tell us. We have voiceprints. We have fingerprints."

"You won't catch him with any of that. Take me to the office so

I can clean up."

"You need to go home."

"Damn you. You don't have a clue what I need! For all I know, he placed bombs there, too," I yelled. "I need to find my mother before he kills her. I have to go to New Mexico. You aren't going to catch him on public transportation. You won't pick him out at a roadblock. He doesn't look like a single male driver. He'll look like an old woman or a teenage gang-banger. The only way to catch him is to get to my mother first. You said so yourself, she's the ultimate way to manipulate me. So get me on a flight."

"I can't do that. There's an investigation into this fire. You killed a man. You can't just leave," he argued.

"Fine. Then stop the car and get the hell out of my sight."

"You're not thinking straight."

"No shit? You told me to do what I had to do and call it self-defense. He would have tortured Matthew and made Kim watch. Then he would have tortured her while I watched, and mailed pieces of her back to her parents!" I shrieked. "I don't know about your conscience, but despite being absolutely mortified about what I did to Matthew Shannaker, I bet I sleep tonight knowing what I did saved that girl. Matt knew what I had to do, that he was going to die regardless."

Nolan stopped at a red light behind several other cars, and I simply got out of the car and started walking. "You can't do this alone, Julie," he called through the door I left open.

"Then help me!"

He opened his door and stood up, screaming at me to stop, pounding on the roof of his car until drivers behind him started honking.

"Don't screw this up for me, Nolan!" I kept walking. "I have to go."

I had no keys, no identification on me, no money. I had to get to the house for that, but I was closer to the office, so I took off at a wobbly jog, hoping no one called me in as a drunken psycho running around with blood on her clothes.

I got to the Annex in time to catch Jordan Scott coming out the sallyport exit, and ran in past him, ignoring his questions.

A keycode for the elevator took me to the basement where I'd been sleeping, grabbed clean clothes from my stash and headed for the showers.

Scrubbing harder than necessary, I washed away Matt's blood, but the smell of it in the steam triggered flashes of memory. I began retching. Nothing came up.

I stood in a cold sweat, hot water almost scalding me. My hands trembled so badly I dropped the shampoo on my broken toes, and I burst into tears of desperation.

I cried until I was numb.

If I couldn't get my head together, I wouldn't be able to go on. I didn't know where to turn for help, but I knew I had to keep moving to save my mother.

I stepped out and dried off, wrapped my hair up in a towel. When I opened the door to the lockers, I came face to face with Nolan Forrester.

Holding a towel too small to cover up with, I didn't bother.

He took a step back, and his eyes fell for a moment, looking at what I couldn't hide.

"What? You want a look at all these scars, too? Fine," I said, and threw the towel at his feet. "Take a damned good look at why I have to go. I've paid for every one of these scars. One way or another, they all go back to Bock. Someone has to put an end to this."

"You can't do that –"

I took a step forward. "You know what the worst part about you stopping me would be, Nolan? He won't kill me. He'll screw up as much of my life as he can. He'll kill anyone I'm close to, and he'll back me into every corner possible to make me kill again. But he won't kill me."

"You don't know that."

"Yes, I do. I've known almost since the drugged candy, and certainly since yesterday. That bomb might have killed me today, but only because I would have gone back in. I don't know whether he was watching, but he let us get out of the cabin alive. It wouldn't be any fun if he killed me. I'm his perfect victim. He wants me to become what he is because he thinks I'm like him, because he thinks it will save me, whatever that means," I said. "I have to do this,

Nolan. I have to try to find my mother. With or without your help."

Nolan bent over and picked up the towel and tossed it into the dirty linen container.

"I know." He sighed and turned away from me. "There's a jet waiting for us."

CHAPTER 72

We were off the ground by one o'clock.

I slept on the jet, lulled by the engines into a dreamless rest I wouldn't have thought possible. My body must have shut down whatever was playing in my head. But when my brain kicked back into gear, my eyes snapped open like magnets repelling.

When I got up, I called Brandan, who confirmed Kimberly Katz was at least physically unharmed, save a sprained foot, and had been discharged home with her parents. He assured me they were all somewhere safe.

"Dr. McNeeley left for Atlanta. He asked me to give you a message with the box."

"Not right now," I said. "I can't. Please."

He seemed to weigh that and let it go. "Good luck then."

I disconnected.

Damn him. Jeremy had taken a good look at me, the real me covered in blood and tears, and he'd walked away. Again.

I couldn't do this by myself, and the man who had been making promises about wanting to try again had gone home to his wife and child.

I needed to turn all the emotions that were drowning me into energy I could use.

How do I find her, I thought? Where would the monster hide my mother?

She had said they would go into Ruidoso, and she would check her messages. Knowing the area like I did, there were hundreds of square miles where he could put her.

Thousands of barns and cabins, if he kept to his previous pattern.

What else had she said about it?

Renovations and workers. Would that really be true?

I passed the thought on to Nolan, who began to make calls.

Would Anthony tell her he was my half-brother before he left her alone?

A thought hit me.

I dialed again to Brandan's cell phone.

"Find my neighbor across the street in the gray brick house. She works in the lab at the hospital, so you might catch her there. Ask her about the man she thought was my brother." My heart was pounding. "Livvie. . ." I was trying to visualize her nametag. "Olivia Palmeri."

"Okay, but I don't follow."

"She asked me about someone she thought was my brother at my house recently, but I thought she meant Jeremy. I'm thinking maybe she saw Anthony there when I was at the hospital and he told her he's my brother. Maybe she remembers something else about him."

"I'll get right on it."

I asked Nolan how long before we touched down.

"About two more hours to Alamogordo."

"No, we have to go to Ruidoso. There's too much ground to cover by car. We don't know how long a jump we might have. I know the area, Nolan. I used to work there."

"I'll ask the pilot, but it's up to him where we land," he said, heading to the cockpit.

I picked up Nolan's laptop and scrolled over an aerial image with a roadmap overlay of the mountains and valleys of southeastern New Mexico until I found Ruidoso, then zoomed in until I could see an area 16 miles square.

The focus on the ground was incredible, and cars were even visible on the open highways when the image was taken.

I zoomed in another level and studied the area.

Nolan came back and sat down beside me, then chuckled. "I didn't think you'd have any problem with the software. You're pretty amazing. Want a job when all of this is done?"

"No." I said without hesitation and kept scrolling into smaller sections of the image and enlarging them. "Can we get a plot map and cross-reference owner names for land with construction permits? There may have been renovation begun lately." I explained my mother's message.

"That'll be a huge undertaking for the next two hours," he said, checking his watch. "Can't do it from here." He picked up a phone and relayed several orders to someone on the other end.

"You're only humoring me, right? You don't think we can find her, do you?" I asked when he was done.

"No, to both questions. I think if we have enough information, *you* will find her. But you need to change your approach. Quit looking for her like a cop. You won't like this, but think like he does. Do what you did when you told us about the room under the barn."

I looked at him skeptically.

"You're the only person who has enough pieces to do this. There are no profile clues that will help – so he's a white male over 40. You're the only one you can understand how he thinks. Tell me - what does he want? What does he need?"

I turned my attention to the satellite image in front of me. My mother could be anywhere in a hundred-mile radius of Ruidoso.

I stopped and took a deep breath to help me focus.

Okay, where would I hide a woman, based on where he had hidden bodies and held Matthew captive?

"Ten acres or more for privacy, with a horse barn. She talked about him riding with her group. He would need a place that would be convincing to her until she made that call. There would have to be a barn." I closed my eyes. "He's a compulsive neat freak. He wouldn't have patience for renovations to be done when he was there, so he must be living somewhere else, or maybe that was a lie. I bet he's owned this property for a long time, at least as long as when I moved from Albuquerque to Alamogordo. He's a veteran, and whoever's life he stole was also, so it would most likely be a VA loan." I looked up.

"Good, keep going." He was making notes on a legal pad.

I closed my eyes again.

"He has access to drugs," I ventured, thinking about how

Anthony had kept Matthew sedated, "and he knows enough about medicine to accomplish exactly what he wants. He blinded and crippled Matt without killing him. He used drug darts to capture Kim and me." I took a long breath. "He won't hurt my mother until I get there. He knows I'll be coming, somehow. That's why we got out of the cabin. He wants to make me do something else."

And for the next hour, I offered conjecture about the man who was my half-brother. Some of what I said made sense, but the rest was wild speculation. I talked my way through his career, his choices in travel, and his reasons for killing.

"He kills for sport. Like someone who fights dogs, he's thrilled by the game, but the victim is useless when he's done. He's a sexual sadist, organized, and he fits two of the three childhood characteristics of a serial killer – cruelty to animals, fire setting," I said.

"And I thought you didn't like FBI profiling," Nolan kidded. He asked a few questions as I went, more like a hypnotist would lead a subject's focus.

In the end, my head ached, and the ringing in my ears seemed as loud as the twin turbines outside the windows.

Forrester answered the phone when it chirped, then handed it to me.

"Hello?"

"It's Brandan. Your neighbor is a lady with quite a photographic memory. Not only did she give a description of this guy that matches yours, but she also remembered the Texas license plate. It's a corporate rate rental from Midland/Odessa. We got a name."

"What?" I asked, stunned with the information.

"Gregory Everett Lawson, New Mexico driver's license, address in Hobbs."

"That's it! Everett. That's his name." I scribbled down particulars on Nolan's pad and handed it to him. "See if we can match property to that." To Brandan, I said, "You may have broken this open."

"I didn't do it, Julie. It was your idea, remember?"

"Thanks for believing."

"Please be careful, okay?"

We landed in Ruidoso a little before 4 p.m. Mountain Time.

Was it soon enough, though? He couldn't drive that quickly, nor could he make his way on a commercial flight into anywhere but El Paso or Albuquerque in so little time, still leaving hours to drive. Beating him was my only hope.

Forrester had tracked down a property listing outside of Ruidoso, and had notified the local authorities of our impending arrival.

We hit the ground with all the squad cars and rescue vehicles the surrounding communities could muster.

Now it was a matter of looking in all the right places.

CHAPTER 73

In the mountains of southern New Mexico, two hours later, my cell phone rang.

"Hey, Blue Eyes."

"Zach? Are you okay?" I was astonished my phone had a signal here, and more flabbergasted that he'd call.

"Sure, I'm okay," he said with an uncharacteristic lilt to his voice. "Except Jeremy McNeeley and the monster both dropped by to visit me here in the hospital. Guess which one brought the gun."

"Tell her I came to kill one of her lovers," Anthony yelled at me in the background of the call. "I didn't expect them to be together."

Nolan looked up when he heard the string of profanity that exploded from me. We'd gathered to brainstorm other locations after the property belonging to Lawson had turned up nothing.

Anthony continued from across the room, "Here's your next choice: I kill your boys here and walk out of here unharmed, or your mother dies. If I'm not outside this hospital and in a cab in the next eight minutes so I can call and reset the timers, the bombs under the old lady's chair go off."

I heard Zach say to him, "Julie called you some very unflattering things that I don't think I can repeat." Then it sounded like he tossed the receiver down. "Talk to her yourself."

"Tell them how the deputy's warm blood poured over your hands, Julia. How much you enjoyed it."

I heard more voices I couldn't identify or understand.

"Hey Julia?" Anthony called to me. "It's your call. There are five people in this room with me. How many die today because of you?" He laughed. "Eeney meeney. . . "

Then I heard a shout and gunshots.

I bit my lip and listened instead of letting go of the primal scream locked in my lungs. I held my breath until my chest burned, straining to hear what was happening.

Several more shots. Breaking glass. Then shouting for the ER teams, chaos. More voices. Finally the phone crashed to the floor and the connection went dead in my ear.

I stood in the quiet peace of the Southern New Mexico mountains, feeling as alien as a star traveler – the outlander who brings death and destruction to strangers who have no immunity to evil.

Nolan came to find out what had happened. After the news, he went to coordinate a stand-down. Now that the bomb was possibly armed, the search was suspended rather than risking more lives. He and I, and more than thirty other officers from Lincoln County and other agencies had scouted a dozen possible locations outside Ruidoso, to no avail. There had to be dozens more.

I stood alone, leaning on the hood of his borrowed car. The crashing of my heartbeat echoed in my ears.

The sound of a helicopter overhead broke the stillness of the night.

Nolan Forrester had activated both the 571st Medical Company Evac helicopter from Fort Bliss in El Paso for standby, and the Joint Task Force Six Team to help with the search by air and ground. Even the U.S. Forest Service had sent up a helicopter with thermal cameras.

This was cooperation I could not have obtained on my own. It was welcomed, but too late.

I shoved the phone into my pocket.

The feeling in my stomach nearly doubled me over when Nolan's phone rang.

There could only more bad news ahead, I knew.

"Yeah. No kidding?" He shoved me toward the passenger's side. "They think they spotted her from the air!"

I took the phone to relay directions from a helicopter crewman as we drove.

Maybe the bomb is not on a timer. Maybe he wants a crowd again. Or maybe . . .

"Take the next left onto the dirt road," I repeated instructions. "Then a right at the next turn."

"There's a woman standing in the road about a tenth of a mile, waving frantically," the voice told me. "We have her in the lights."

Nolan made the turn, skidding on the gravel.

A tenth of a mile. The road was winding. I couldn't see more than a hundred feet at a time.

"Slow down!" the voice on the phone said. "Next curve to the right, she's there."

"Stop!" I yelled as the turn came into view.

Nolan brought the car to a sliding stop halfway through the turn.

I bolted from the car and raced toward the woman, who had turned away from the headlights careening toward her before disappearing in the dust that overtook us.

"Mother?" I screamed.

"Julie? Julie!" She turned toward me in the haze, arms open.

We were almost together when the bomb went off somewhere behind her.

She cowered to the ground, but I kept going the last few steps and embraced her as the pressure wave threw dirt and debris past us.

I could hear Nolan yelling on the radio somewhere near us.

Then a second explosion rocked us.

My mother was panting and crying and coughing.

"Are you okay?" I kept asking. "Are you hurt?"

"No, honey. I'm okay," she finally managed. She looked over her shoulder as the dirt began to settle, fire illuminating the dust an orange haze.

In the distance, illuminated by helicopter spotlights, was what appeared to have been a barn, now in flames.

"I remembered you telling me about the bomb, Julie," she said as Nolan helped us both to our feet. "I knew I had to get out of there somehow."

When she staggered a bit, Nolan didn't hesitate. He radioed that he wanted the Evac on the ground as close as possible for transport.

"It's only dehydration," she said, getting in the backseat with me. "I wouldn't drink the water because of the drugs. Wanted to keep my head clear."

"Doesn't matter," he said, whipping the car around to find the landing zone.

"Oh, Julie," she said, clinging to me. "Are you okay?"

"I'm fine, Mother," I lied. "Really, I'm just fine." I wouldn't be fine until I knew the aftermath of what had happened in St. Pete. Or maybe I wouldn't be fine then either.

The evac crew let me ride to William Beaumont Army Medical Center in El Paso.

My mother was treated for dehydration and exposure in the emergency department. Intravenous fluids, laboratory studies, electrocardiograms, chest x-ray. She kept fussing it was all very unnecessary, despite Nolan's insistence.

I was pacing the floor in a waiting area when my phone rang.

"Madigan," I said, almost regretting it.

"Julie," Dom Hurley said. "You got to your mother okay?"

"Yes," I said, tears beginning to choke me. Fear that the very worst could have come true. "What happened there?"

There was a long pause.

"Domino, damn you! Tell me what happened!"

"Here," he said. The phone changed hands.

"Julie? Bock is dead." The voice wavered – Zach's voice. "I'm so sorry. They couldn't do anything for Jeremy, but he saved our lives."

I collapsed to the floor, sobbing.

CHAPTER 74

Six weeks later. . .

I strolled in water up to my knees. Occasionally a wave tugged at the bottom of the gauzy red wrap I wore over my one-piece swimsuit.

I still couldn't peel away the clothes without thinking it over, even though I'd tanned enough in a few days to not look like I had spent years hiding in a cave or in snow-locked northern Michigan. But the beach was nearly empty, and I did consider removing the wrap.

I looked back and saw Zach, leaning back on his elbows on a mat, watching me.

He smiled.

The night before, with his arms around me like a child holding a teddy bear, we'd talked.

"Tell me what you dream," he'd asked softly, running his fingers through my hair. "You don't dream about monsters now, do you?"

I thought about it and squeezed his hand. "Not so much, no. I think I finally just sleep. I'm sure I dream, but I don't remember. The nightmares are fewer than before."

"I can tell." He kissed me. "I'm glad. I love to watch you sleep."

I still found it hard to believe he made me feel so completely safe when I hadn't felt that way in years.

"What made you fall in love with me so long ago?" I whispered.

"Tight blue jeans and long legs," he said, running his hand down my side to my hip.

I nudged him.

"How about your beautiful blue eyes? The way you laugh. The way you cry. The way you kissed me that first time," he said. "Tell me about your day."

"You've been with me. What's to tell?" I asked.

"I sent you off to the day spa today, didn't I? Tell me everything."

I could hear the sincerity of his words, but when he reached to caress my face, I felt his hand tremble. I kissed his fingers.

Thank you so much for reading one of
Val Conrad's *A Julie Madigan Thrillers*.
If you enjoyed the experience, please check out
the next book in the series!

Tears of Like Souls by Val Conrad

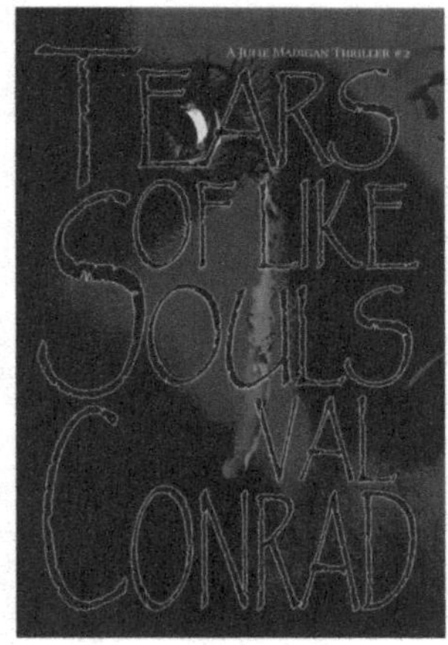